A Brighter
Coming Day

Frances E. W. Harper, from the frontispiece of an 1895 edition of *Iola Leroy*, Moorland-Spingarn Research Center, Howard University.

A Brighter Coming Day

A Frances Ellen Watkins Harper Reader

◆

Edited and with an Introduction by
Frances Smith Foster

The Feminist Press
at The City University of New York
New York

Published 1990 by The Feminist Press at The City University of New York,
311 East 94 Street, New York, N.Y. 10128
Distributed by The Talman Company, 150 Fifth Avenue, New York, N.Y. 10011
Printed in the United States of America on pH-neutral paper by
McNaughton & Gunn, Inc.

93 92 91 90 5 4 3 2 1

Library of Congress Cataloging-in-Publication Data

Harper, Frances Ellen Watkins, 1825–1911.
  A brighter coming day : a Frances Ellen Watkins Harper reader / edited and
with an introduction by Frances Smith Foster.
    p. cm.
  Includes bibliographical references (p.
  ISBN 1-55861-019-7 : $29.95. — ISBN 1-55861-020-0 (pbk.) : $14.95
  I. Foster, Frances Smith. II. Title.
PS1799.H7A8 1989
811'.3—dc20   89-26041
                                                                     CIP

Cover art: Sketch of Frances E. W. Harper, Moorland-Spingarn Research
Center, Howard University

Text design: Paula Martinac

This publication is made possible, in part, by funds from the New York
State Council on the Arts. The Feminist Press also gratefully acknowledges
the gift of Vivien Leone toward the publication of this book.

For those who work for brighter coming days
and especially for
Krishna, Crystal, Venette, and Tracy

Contents

◆

viii   ♦   **Contents**

Poetry

Essays and Speeches

x • **Contents**

Fiction

Part Three: 1876–1892

Poetry

Essays and Speeches

Fiction

Part Four: 1893–1911

Letters

Poetry

Acknowledgments

◆

Projects such as this have a way of growing larger and more complicated than expected. They are not completed without the assistance and support of many individuals. I thank, especially, Richard Yarborough for keeping me on track and following through on emergency requisitions; Jean Fagan Yellin for her extreme generosity in sharing her own bibliography of Harper material; Florence Howe, Nellie McKay, and Susannah Driver for believing that this project should be done and that I should do it; Cledith Johnson and the two students who participated in the mentor research programs, Kimberly Beasley and Bernadette Dobynes, for not only helping with the detail work but making me realize anew how important this all can be.

I thank San Diego State University and the University of California, San Diego for the released time and research grants that enabled me to visit the archives and libraries.

No institution owns copies of all the published works by Frances Harper and locating the material was in many instances quite challenging. I thank the interlibrary loan staffs of San Diego State University and the University of California, San Diego for their persistence. I am grateful to the following libraries and archives for their expertise and courtesy and for permission to view original editions of Harper's works and to use those works as sources for this book: the Henry P. Slaughter Collection, the Atlanta University Center Woodruff Library; the Library Company of Philadelphia; the Moorland-Spingarn Research Center, Howard University; the Philadelphia Historical Society; the Frances E. Watkins Harper Collection, Miscellaneous American Letters & Papers, Schomburg Center for Research in Black Culture, The New York Public Library Astor, Lenox, and Tilden Foundations; San Diego State University Love Library; the Charles P. Brockson Collection, Temple University; the Central University Library, University of California, San Diego; and the Rembert E. Stokes Library Resource Center, Wilberforce University.

Special acknowledgment goes to those staff members whose assistance exceeded professional courtesy: Esme Bahn, Charles R. Brockson, Jacqueline Brown, Paul Coates, Wilson N. Flemister, Sr., Diana Lachatanere, Philip Lapsansky, Jean Mulhern, and William Trott.

Permission to use the letters to Francis Grimké is by courtesy of the Moorland-Spingarn Research Center, Howard University, Washington, D.C.

Permission to include "Respectfully Dedicated to Dr. Alexander Crummell" is by courtesy of the Schomburg Center for Research in Black Culture, The New York Public Library.

A Brighter
Coming Day

Introduction

◆

Count life a dismal failure
    Unblessing and unblest,
That seeks in ceaseless ease
    For pleasure or for rest.
With courage, strength, and valor
    Your lives and actions brace;
Shrink not from pain and hardship,
    And dangers bravely face.

from "A Rallying Cry"

I

Frances Ellen Watkins Harper (1825–1911) was a member of the African-American intelligentsia and one of its most successful writers, but she did not have a room of her own when she created her most popular literature. And if the stress of being a sensitive and ambitious woman in nineteenth-century America was enough to send some women screaming into attics, one could certainly excuse a sensitive, ambitious black woman if she chose to barricade herself from the outside world. But Harper's work does not suggest any of the "anxiety of authorship" that Sandra M. Gilbert and Susan Gubar found in most women poets of that era and Harper's female characters are quite sane. Having been born into an articulate and well-respected free black family, Harper could have chosen to avoid many of the distressing realities that controlled the lives of the less fortunate members of her race. She chose not to do so. Harper decided that her personal survival and well-being were inextricably linked with the survival and well-being of the larger society and that confrontation, not silence, was the way to mental, if not physical, health. She gave up

3

her small but real claim to a life of relative leisure and privacy and became not only the most popular African-American writer of the nineteenth century but also one of the most important women in United States history.

Frances Harper was the best known and best loved African-American poet prior to Paul Laurence Dunbar. It was, in fact, her poetry and its experimentation with dialect as well as its original characterizations of ex-slaves, such as Aunt Chloe and Uncle Jacob, that paved the way for the younger Dunbar's success. Her extant prose includes essays, letters, short stories, and novels, but Harper's literary influence is far greater than the quantity of material might suggest. Her novel, *Iola Leroy*, while not the first by an African-American woman, did firmly establish the novel as a viable genre in African-American literature. And in modifying the depiction of the tragic mulatto and introducing heroic folk characters into the written African-American literary tradition, her work paved the way for the later, very popular fiction of Charles Chesnutt. Harper's contributions to the newspapers and magazines of her day were so influential that in his history of the African-American press, I. Garland Penn identifies her as "the journalistic mother, so to speak, of many brilliant young women who have entered upon her line of work so recently" (422).

Frances Harper's literary contributions, coupled with her active participation in political movements such as abolition, suffrage, temperance, and education, earned her a national reputation. She worked closely with such prominent African-American leaders as Frederick Douglass, Ida B. Wells-Barnett, and Charlotte Forten Grimké. She was cited by Fannie C. L. Bentley in the *African Methodist Episcopal Church Review* as a "Woman of Our Race Worthy of Imitation" and included in Lawson A. Scruggs' *Women of Distinction: Remarkable in Works and Invincible in Character*. At the same time, Harper commanded respect and admiration from many Anglo-Americans. In her *Daughters of America*, Phebe A. Hanaford wrote, "Frances E. W. Harper is one of the most eloquent women lecturers in the country. . . . She is one of the colored women of whom white women may be proud, and to whom the abolitionists can point and declare that a race which could show such women never ought to have been held in bondage" (326).

By the time she was thirty years old, Frances Watkins had already achieved such stature that her name was included in most compendiums of prominent black Americans. Details of her life and works were available throughout the rest of her life and after her death in textbooks such as William C. Nell's *Patriots of the American Revolution* (1855) and Edward

A. Johnson's *A School History of the Negro Race in America* (1911). She was cited in William Wells Brown's *The Black Man: His Antecedents and Genius* (1863), Monroe Major's *Noted Negro Women* (1893), and Charles F. White's *Who's Who in Philadelphia* (1912), and Hallie Q. Brown's *Homespun Heroines and Other Women of Distinction* (1926). Although she was not a member of that denomination, Harper is even included in Bishop Daniel Payne's *History of the African Methodist Episcopal Church* (1891). And even today, most modern reference works cite her name. Studies of African-American women's writings almost always begin with a consideration of Harper's work, and entries on her life are included in such texts as *Dictionary of American Biography, Dictionary of American Negro Biography, Dictionary of Literary Biography, Notable American Women,* and *Profiles of Negro Womanhood.*

Despite this extraordinary attention, most of the biographical data in twentieth-century references are derived from one source, a chapter in William Still's *The Underground Rail Road*, published in 1871.[1] A prominent abolitionist and Harper's long-time friend, Still devoted thirty pages of his history of the underground railroad to her biography because, as he noted, "There is not to be found in any written work portraying the Anti-slavery struggle, (except in the form of narratives) as we are aware of, a sketch of the labors of any eminent colored woman" (783). Since Still recognized that Harper was "the leading colored poet in the United States" and "one of the most liberal contributors, as well as one of the ablest advocates of the Underground Rail Road and of the slave" (783), he chose to reject the sexism that created essentially male histories, in which references to women were confined primarily to footnotes. In keeping with the purpose of his work, however, Still emphasizes Harper's abolitionist and reconstruction activities, and he recounts these experiences briefly, offering as he says, "No extravagant praise of any kind—only simple facts" (783). His account is liberally spliced with quotations from Harper's published writings and from her private correspondence during the period from 1853 until 1871. Although Still published a revised and updated version of his book in 1883, he did not change the chapter on Harper. Thus, despite the fact that Harper was a public figure for over a half century, details about her life are limited.

The information about her first twenty-five years is especially sparse. One of the more notable omissions concerns Harper's parents. Several sources note that Frances Ellen Watkins was born on September 24, 1825; however, none records the names of her parents. Most sources report that her mother died when Watkins was three years old and that she was cared for by an aunt. William Still also reports that Watkins attended the school founded by her uncle, the Reverend William Watkins, until she was thirteen years old. Given the invisibility of women in most public records, except those they themselves created, it is not surprising that her mother is not identified. However, given the prominence of the Watkins family in Baltimore at that time, it is intriguing that biographers do not identify or speculate about the identity of her father. This may be a conscious attempt to avoid any possibility that her status as a woman of distinction might be challenged by white bourgeois audiences, because it is quite possible that Frances Watkins, like many African-Americans, was fathered by a white man. Commentators often mentioned her color. One described her as "a red mulatto," and reporter Grace Greenwood volunteered that she was "about as colored as some of the Cuban belles I have met with at Saratoga" (Still, 812). Harper's own letters note that members of her audience often debated whether she was an African-American or "painted" to appear as one.

In *The Underground Rail Road*, William Still passes over the details of Harper's early life by declaring that "The want of space forbids more than a brief reference to her early life" (783). His only allusion to her parents is that Watkins was her maiden name and that she was "not of slave parentage" (784). Still quotes a letter from Harper which suggests that, despite having been taken in by relatives, she felt deprived of familial comforts. Wrote Harper, "Have I yearned for a mother's love? The grave was my robber. Before three years had scattered their blight around my path, death had won my mother from me. Would the strong arm of a brother have been welcome? I was my mother's only child" (784). Both William Still and another of Harper's mentors, William C. Nell, hint that her childhood was unusually problematic. Says Still, "She had many trials to endure which she would fain forget" (784). And according to Nell, she had "contended with a thousand disadvantages from early life" (211). But neither suggests what these problems were nor why, as the niece and protégée of one of Baltimore's most prominent educators, hers was such a difficult existence.

In describing her childhood, Still maintains that Watkins was a serious young woman, "noted for her industry, rarely trifling away time as most girls are wont to do in similar circumstances" (784). Undoubtedly, much of this had to do with her uncle's influence and the nature of her education at his academy.

The Reverend William Watkins was known as a man of great passion and dedication. As a young man, he helped found the Mental and Moral Improvement Society, which according to the Reverend William H. Morris, A.M., was a "a school of oratory, literature and debate" and "the only high school or college in which many intelligent Baltimoreans have been able to study" (6). In 1844, William Watkins became a Seventh-Day Adventist, but his evangelistic efforts extended beyond the confines of any particular denomination, and he was a frequent and effective speaker at five of the local Methodist churches. So well regarded was his lifetime of service to the African Methodist Episcopal Church (A.M.E.) that upon his death the *African Methodist Episcopal Church Review* published two articles and called for an endowed chair in his name at one of the A.M.E. colleges. William Watkins was a fervent abolitionist, a community leader, and a highly regarded teacher.

The William Watkins Academy for Negro Youth was well known for its emphasis upon biblical studies, the classics, and elocution. The Bible was read daily, Greek and Latin were a major part of the curriculum, and discipline was strict. As former student James H. A. Johnson, D.D., recalled, a favorite pedagogical tool was "that strap," which Johnson vows "was designed to make profound orthoepical, orthographical, geographical and mathematical impressions. And it made them" (11). Furthermore, Watkins held every student to high standards. "He was strict from the first letter in the alphabet down to the last paragraph in the highest reader," Johnson reports (12). Watkins' academy was so well regarded that slaveholders from neighboring states enrolled their favored children, and among its graduates were many of the most prominent and highly regarded public servants and speakers in the nation. In addition to high academic standards and Christian service, Watkins also stressed political leadership. The path that his niece, Frances, took was one selected by many of Watkins' protégés, including three of his own sons, who, like their cousin, frequented abolitionist circles and gained renown for their oratorical skills and social leadership.

Harper's intense commitment to abolitionist and other social welfare crusades, her familiarity with classical and Christian mythology, and her reputation for oratory and general deportment were obviously influenced by her education at the academy. Since William Watkins frequently contributed to papers such as the *Liberator*, it is also possible that he assisted her in her first efforts to publish.

Watkins' school days ended when she was about thirteen, but she continued to study informally. While still in adolescence, she acquired a reputation as an intelligent, talented young writer. At age fourteen she wrote an article that, Still says, "attracted the attention of the lady in whose family she was employed, and others" (784). Given the social norms of that time, it is not surprising, though nonetheless ironic, that her employment as a domestic worker had nothing to do with her scholastic preparation or her literary skills. Watkins was hired to sew and to care for children. But her employers, the Armstrongs, owned a bookstore, and with rare good fortune, in whatever free time she could find, Watkins was allowed to read from their stock. The intrepid young woman made good use of this opportunity.

Watkins continued to write and to publish her pieces in various periodicals. By 1845, Still reports that Watkins had composed enough poems and prose to compile a volume called *Forest Leaves*. Although several sources mention this volume, no known copies exist. Perhaps, *Forest Leaves* was similar to a volume published a few years earlier by another young African-American woman, Ann Plato. From the few known details of their lives, Watkins and Plato shared similar social status and attitudes. Judging from its title, and from the contents of Harper's earliest extant volume, *Poems on Miscellaneous Subjects* (1854), Harper's first book was probably, like Plato's *Essays*, a collection of poetry and prose on a variety of subjects including religious values, women's rights, social reform, Biblical history, and current events.

Life was not easy for nineteenth-century African-Americans, free or slave. It was particularly problematic for free blacks, such as the Watkinses, who lived in a slave state. As Frances Watkins grew to adulthood, the racial situation in the United States was becoming increasingly precarious. The abolitionist movement was but one of several transformative social and economic currents that were polarizing the young nation and that were affecting slaves and free blacks.

The Compromise of 1850 exacerbated their lives. This federal legislative package abolished the slave trade in the District of Columbia and admitted California as a free state, but it also decreed that "popular sovereignty," or the vote of the citizens of each new territory, would determine whether New Mexico, Utah, and subsequent areas would enter as free or slave states. This so-called compromise pleased no one and served instead to increase racial hostilities in the original states.

One part of it, the Fugitive Slave Act, was particularly destructive. This law removed authority over fugitive slaves from local jurisdiction and made such cases matters for the federal government. Regardless of whether a municipality was officially free or slave, the new law required citizens to cooperate with slave hunters, and it imposed severe fines for concealing or helping escaped slaves. It accepted as proof of ownership signed affidavits from the purported master, but it denied the alleged slave both the right to a jury trial and the right to testify on her or his own behalf. Moreover, the law compensated the federal commissioners $10 for every claim they ruled valid, but only $5 for every claim they denied.

About this time, and probably due to the increasingly hostile environment provoked by the Compromise of 1850, local officials forced William Watkins to sell his house and his school. At least one of his sons chose to remain in Baltimore, but William Watkins and others of his family joined the African-American exodus to Canada. Exactly what prompted his niece to go to Ohio rather than remain in Baltimore with her cousins or accompany her relatives to Canada is not known. But about 1850, Frances Watkins left the South to become the first female teacher at Union Seminary, a school near Columbus, Ohio, which had been founded a few years earlier by the A.M.E. Church. Although the details of her decision are unknown, such a choice was entirely consistent with the independence and courage demonstrated by many of the women in Watkins' published poems and prose.

Watkins' work at Union Seminary was satisfactory, but her tenure there was brief. In his report to the Ohio Conference of the A.M.E. Church, Principal John M. Brown praised her with these words: "Miss Watkins has taught a class in embroidery which numbers twelve; also a class in plain sewing . . . [she] has been faithful to her trust, and has manifested in every effort a commendable zeal for the cause of education; and a sacrificing spirit, so that it may be promoted. She has firmly braved the flood of opposition which has manifested itself from the beginning and I take great pleasure in commending her to the favorable notice of the brethren." Again, one must speculate on why her stay in Ohio was so short. Very likely her leaving was connected to problems the school was experiencing and not to any deficiencies on her part. According to the principal's report, Union Seminary was not receiving the support it had been led to expect, and its valiant faculty was struggling to educate 217 students despite the active opposition of the surrounding community.

About 1852, Watkins accepted a teaching position in Little York, Pennsylvania. If conditions at Union Seminary were bad, those in Little York were worse. There was little in her own experience as a student in an academy that catered to the black elite to prepare Watkins to contend with the group that Still describes as "fifty-three untrained little urchins" (786). Believing that "it is one of woman's most sacred rights to have the privilege of forming the symmetry and rightly adjusting the mental balance of an immortal mind," Watkins was distressed by her failure to motivate her students (Still, 786). She was frequently ill and despondent. In a letter to a friend, she asked, "What would you do if you were in my place? Would you give up and go back and work at your trade (dress-making)? . . . The condition of our people, the wants of our children, and the welfare of our race demand the aid of every helping hand, the God-speed of every Christian heart" (Still, 785). Though her teaching experiences were demanding and demoralizing, Harper found solace in her writing. She completed an essay on education and was, according to Still, writing "a small book" (786).

While Harper was trying to resolve the conflict between her philosophical resolve and her inability to carry it out with any pleasure, an incident occurred in her home state that answered her dilemma. About 1853, Maryland passed a law that forbid free blacks from the North to enter the state. The penalty was enslavement. Not long afterward, a man who had unsuspectingly violated that ordinance was arrested, enslaved, and sent to Georgia. The desperate man escaped, only to be recaptured. According to William Still, this unfortunate man died soon thereafter "from the effects of exposure and suffering" (786). While this situation illustrates the precariousness of freedom for any black person as long as slavery existed, for Frances Watkins, this case was particularly moving. She was a free black living in the North, and she knew that if she tried to visit any of her friends or relatives in Baltimore, she risked a similar fate. Her reaction to this incident was both personal and philosophical. Coming at a moment when she was searching for a way to contribute to the general welfare of her race, it became a major turning point in her life. "Upon that grave," Harper wrote, "I pledged myself to the Anti-Slavery cause" (Still, 786).

By 1854, she had moved to Philadelphia. There she lived at an Underground Railroad Station where she was able to experience first-hand the comings and goings of fugitive slaves. To prepare herself for an active abolitionist role, Watkins frequented the office of the local antislavery society, and read avidly on the subject. Although Still does not state this, Watkins may have been living in his own household, for his home was the most important Underground Railroad Station in Philadelphia and a favorite residence of many visiting abolitionists.

Her move to Philadelphia also stimulated Watkins' literary productivity by bringing her into contact with groups of educated black activists, many of whom were writers or editors, and by providing her with publishing contacts. Along with Mary Still (William's daughter), Sarah Douglass, and others, Watkins became a contributor to the Philadelphia-based *Christian Recorder*.

Her commitment to the antislavery cause and to writing found a happy convergence when she began to publish works in abolitionist papers. For example, Watkins was one of several African-American writers who were moved to poetic response by the 1852 publication of Harriet Beecher

Stowe's *Uncle Tom's Cabin*. Watkins wrote at least three such poems, "Eliza Harris," "To Harriet Beecher Stowe," and "Eva's Farewell." "Eliza Harris" was particularly well received. At least three papers, the *Aliened American*, *Frederick Douglass' Paper*, and the *Liberator*, published the poem within a few months of one another in 1853. Since these newspapers were nationally distributed, these publications assisted the growth of her reputation as a poet. The respect with which Watkin's writings were received is illustrated by the fact that Bishop Daniel Payne reprinted two of Watkins' poems, "The Soul" and "The Dying Christian," and cited her essays "Christianity" and "Women's Rights" in his summary of African-American literary achievements of 1852 and 1853 (302–305).

Overall, the move to Philadelphia was a positive one. Yet, Watkins failed to achieve her two dearest goals: to become an agent for the Underground Railroad and to publish a book. William Still explains it thus:

> Although anxious to enter the Anti-slavery field as a worker, her modesty prevented her from pressing her claims: consequently as she was but little known, being a young and homeless maiden (an exile by law), no especial encouragement was tendered her by Anti-slavery friends in Philadelphia. [786]

Frustrated, no doubt, but undaunted by her inability to achieve her goals in Philadelphia, this brave and determined young woman moved to Boston and then to the "hot-bed of the fugitives," New Bedford, Massachusetts. The New England abolitionists proved more hospitable to a "young and homeless maiden," and in August 1854, Watkins launched her public speaking career with a lecture entitled, "The Education and the Elevation of the Colored Race." Shortly thereafter, Watkins achieved what may have been another first for a black woman: She was employed as a traveling lecturer by the Maine Anti-Slavery Society.[2]

When Watkins began her professional lecturing career, she became part of what Lillian O'Connor characterizes as the "second generation" of women orators. As O'Connor reminds us in *Pioneer Women Orators*, during the mid-nineteenth century professional women speakers were rare and highly suspect. Women who spoke in public to mixed audiences were considered by most people to lack good sense and high moral character. To combat these negative assumptions, O'Connor explains that "The earliest speakers emphasized their own moral worth in terms acceptable to the audience of the day: they maintained that they were doing God's work and they displayed knowledge of the most respected book of the era, the Bible" (139). The price that the first generation, which included Amelia Bloomer, Elizabeth Cady Stanton, and Maria W. Stewart, paid for their speech making was not lost upon the women who followed them. Newcomers such as Watkins and her contemporaries, Emma Robinson Coe, Frances D. Gage, Jane Grey Swisshelm, and Martha Coffin Wright, were not surprised by the hostility their appearances often provoked. Nonetheless, female lecturers were well enough accepted that this generation of speakers could devote less energy to defending their own morals and could focus instead upon establishing the fact of women's intelligence and persuading the public that cultivation of this intelligence could benefit society as a whole. Representative of this group is Harriet Hunt's argument that "No one, who realizes how strong is the religious element in woman, will for a moment fear the use she will make of the highest educational advantages" (O'Connor, 140).

The high moral and religious tone of Frances Watkins' lectures is in part a standard rhetorical strategy for female lecturers. Her early training in the classics and the Bible and her close association with the A.M.E. Church were considerable assets. But Watkins' situation was far more tenuous than that of her colleagues. Not only was Watkins a woman in a profession of questionable propriety, but she was the youngest of the group, she was single, and she was black.

The handicap of youth was one of the factors that William Still cites as preventing Watkins' acceptance as an antislavery worker in Philadelphia. Not quite thirty years old, she was neither a matron nor a child. Too young to claim the wisdom conceded to women past the childbearing years, but well past the stage when being outspoken was attributed to girlish impulsiveness, Watkins was considered, as Still terms it, "a young and homeless maiden."

Her marital status was another barrier to being taken seriously. Being a single woman undermined her authority. The prevailing ideology of womanhood and woman's concerns declared that marriage was the only proper goal of a woman's life. As O'Connor summarizes it, "Failure to marry was synonymous with failure in life" (8). Moreover, proper ladies were discreet and demure. Rarely did they speak in public and never to a "promiscuous assemblage," as gatherings of men and women were then known. Thus, as a single woman who dared stand behind the lectern, Watkins risked censure as both a failed and a fallen woman.

And finally, as a woman who was black, Watkins faced other obstacles, for it is one of the ironies of the abolitionist movement that the shared dismay over slavery did not eliminate racism. Though they did form coalitions for specific causes and though integrated teams of lecturers sometimes spoke to integrated audiences, abolitionist groups tended to be segregated.[3] Several black women, including Josephine Brown, Mary Shadd Cary, and Sarah Parker Remond did occasionally write and speak to white antislavery groups and to integrated audiences, but only Sojourner Truth achieved a prominence comparable to that of Frances Watkins. And, of course, Truth's famous "Ain't I a Woman" speech testifies to the particular problems that black women faced. White women, even those audacious enough to speak in public, were accorded more respect.

Once launched into the circuit, however, Watkins lost no time in establishing herself as a popular and sought-after speaker. Her schedule was grueling. From September 5 until October 20, 1854, for example, Watkins gave at least thirty-three lectures in twenty-one New England cities and villages. To further complicate matters, her work did not end when she left the podium. Watkins' position as an employee of the Maine Anti-Slavery Society not only required that she lecture against slavery, but also forced her, and her white counterparts, to experiment with new social relationships. In a society that was segregated, sometimes by law and almost always by convention, Watkins quite often traveled, visited, worked, and rested in integrated situations.

The novelty of her position, as well as her own clear understanding of the social significance of her experiences, may be the reason why her published letters are more explicit about her activities among the white abolitionists than about the antislavery messages that she delivered. For example, the letters that describe her new job say little about the issues presented in her lectures or about the audiences' responses to those issues. Instead, they emphasize the social details. In August 1854, shortly after her "maiden lecture," Watkins wrote, "Last night I lectured in a white church in Providence. Mr. Gardener was present, and made the estimate of about six hundred persons. . . . My maiden lecture was Monday night in New Bedford on the Elevation and Education of our People. Perhaps as intellectual a place as any I was ever at of its size" (787). On September 28, she reported that "The agent of the State Anti-Slavery Society of Maine travels with me, and she is a pleasant, dear, sweet lady.[4] I do like her so. We travel together, eat together, and sleep together. (She is a white woman.) In fact I have not been in one colored person's house since I left Massachusetts; but I have a pleasant time" (787). Watkins' parenthetical identification of her partner's race and her reference to the absence of social contact with blacks suggest that these facts are noteworthy to her or to her correspondent or to both. Her remark, "*but* I have a pleasant time" [emphasis added], implies a measure of relief and self-satisfaction. Another time, she notes with pleasure that "A short while ago when I was down this way I took breakfast with the then Governor of Maine" (788).

Though her letters and her biographers are less specific about the blacks with whom she associated, Watkins was an integral part of the national black abolitionist network. Statements about not having "been in one colored person's house since I left Massachusetts" imply that she had established connections within black society when she left Philadelphia. The black press frequently published her writings and news of her appearances. Many of her lectures were held in black churches. Some of the acquaintances that she made became lifelong friends. For example, in 1854, Mary Shadd Cary, owner and publisher of the *Provincial Freedman*, printed two of Watkins' pieces, "Christianity" and "Died of Starvation." These two activists were still collaborating in 1898. Even when circumstances were not easy, Watkins apparently made it her business to seek out black communities. The often-published letter that she wrote from Niagara Falls in September 1856 came at the end of a trip that she took to the Upper Provinces of Canada in order to visit fugitive slaves. And it was apparently on the same trip that she spent time at the home of the Reverend J. W. Loguen, whose narrative, *The Rev. J. W. Loguen, as a Slave and as a Freeman*, was published three years later.

Sources are silent as to the circumstances that finally enabled Watkins to publish *Poems on Miscellaneous Subjects*. No doubt her experience on the lecture platform taught her how to press her claims more forcefully than she had been able to previously. In addition, the network of friends and acquaintances that grew from her frequent public appearances and extensive travels changed her status from a "little known ... young and homeless maiden" to a prominent black activist. Whatever the combination of factors and despite her many other obligations, Watkins' book was published in 1854 not only in Boston but also in Philadelphia. It was an immediate success. The Boston edition was reprinted that same year, and both the Boston and the Philadelphia volumes were reprinted in 1855. By 1857, the title page of the Philadelphia edition proclaimed 10,000 copies printed.

This volume included, but was not limited to, poems on abolitionist themes that Watkins sometimes incorporated into her antislavery speeches. Prominent among these were approximately ten poems about women and/or equal rights. In *Colored Patriots of the American Revolution*, published a year after *Poems on Miscellaneous Subjects* first appeared, William C. Nell described Watkins' volume as being "very creditable to her, both in a literary and moral point of view." Nell included two extracts from the book as proof of "a talent, which, if carefully cultivated, and properly encouraged, cannot fail to secure for herself a poetic reputation, and to deepen the interest already so extensively felt in the liberation and enfranchisement of the entire colored race" (212). William Wells Brown, another African-American writer and antislavery lecturer, declared that Watkins' writings were "characterized by chaste language, much thought, and a soul-stirring ring" (525).

As a writer and lecturer, Watkins was a complex and confounding figure. Her language was "chaste," her literature was "moral," and contemporary reporters rarely failed to note her "slender and graceful" form and her "soft musical voice." Watkins was by all accounts very ladylike in her public appearances. However, on the podium, as William Wells Brown says, "Her arguments are forcible, her appeals pathetic, her logic fervent, her imagination fervid, and her delivery original and easy" (525). And there was nothing demure or passive about her politics and her insistence upon her rights. Watkins' brand of abolitionism, firmly grounded in the philosophy of Christian morality, was of the same radical persuasion as that of Still, John Brown, and Henry Highland Garnet.

From the beginning, Watkins had aligned herself with those who advocated more than moral suasion. For example, she preached and practiced the politics of Free Produce: That is, she urged economic boycotts of slave-produced goods. Although this movement had begun as early as 1827, few areas outside Philadelphia were strongly influenced by the boycott movement, and among abolitionists themselves it definitely involved a minority. As historian Benjamin Quarles points out, "For every one [abolitionist] who abstained entirely from slave-labor goods or commodities, there were dozens who abstained only in part and then when not too inconvenient and hundreds who simply ignored the whole thing" (76).

Perhaps it was her radicalism that led to her separation from the Maine society. Again, the details of her departure are not known; however, by 1857, Watkins had returned to Philadelphia. This time, her reception was more cordial, for she returned as a prominent lecturer and the author of a book of poetry that had sold more than 10,000 copies. For the next four years, she lectured in the Great Lakes states and worked closely with other black abolitionists in Michigan, New Jersey, New York, Ohio, and Pennsylvania. From October 1857 until May 1858, she worked as a lecturer and agent for the Pennsylvania Anti-Slavery Society. In 1858, she was one of the signers of the constitution of the Ohio State Anti-Slavery Society and a member of its fund-raising committee.

It is quite possible that Watkins was personally involved in the transportation of fugitives along the Underground Railroad Route. Her letters and public lectures certainly reveal that she often traveled with agents of the railroad and that she regularly visited homes that were known stops along the way. Watkins inquired frequently about the disposition of individual cases, collected and forwarded donations, and usually included part of her earnings in her letters to William Still. However, it is doubtful that she ever became an independent agent. Her letters time and again allude to what seem to have been obdurate sexist attitudes of many underground railroad leaders who would limit or forbid women's involvement in such activities. Watkins chides in one letter, "This is a common cause; . . . I have a right to do my share of the work. The humblest and feeblest of us can do something; and though I may be deficient in many of the conventionalisms of city life, and be considered as a person of good impulses, but unfinished, yet if there is common rough work to be done, call on me" (Still, 790). And when Still apparently cautioned her about donating so much of her earnings to the antislavery effort, she brought him up short by saying, "Let me explain a few matters to you. In the first place, I am able to give something. In the second place, I am willing to do so" (792).

Although she was reportedly a woman of "delicate" form whose "manner is marked by dignity and composure," she has also been described by writers such as Benjamin Brawley as "a woman of strong personality" (386). Brawley did not elaborate upon this description, but something of what he meant may be seen in two incidents that occurred during 1858. In a letter reprinted in the April 23, 1858, issue of the *Liberator*, Watkins wrote:

> I have been insulted in several railroad cars. The other day, in attempting to ride in one of the city cars, after I had entered, the conductor came to me, and wanted me to go out on the platform. Now, was not that brave and noble? *As a matter of course*, I did not. Some one interfered, and asked or requested that I might be permitted to sit in a corner. I did not move, but kept the same seat. When I was about to leave, *he refused my money, and I threw it down on the car floor, and got out, after I had ridden as far as I wished.* Such impudence! [emphasis added]

In action and attitude, Watkins' tactics foreshadowed those employed by Daisy Bates, Coretta Scott King, Rosa Parks, Mary Church Terrell, and other black middle-class women who did not hesitate to lay aside their cloaks of decorum and social graces, flex the muscles of their displeasure, and then calmly wrap themselves again in dignity.

The second example comes in a letter from William C. Nell published in the September 11, 1858 edition of the *Liberator*. Nell reports that Watkins was in Detroit preparing to give a lecture when she heard of a case in Cincinnati in which a black man from Detroit had betrayed two fugitive slaves. She immediately arranged to have that meeting focus upon the incident and to have Henry Highland Garnet, who had recently arrived from Cincinnati and who had participated in the capture of the traitorous black man, discuss the incident. Watkins' meeting plans stirred such great interest that the Colored Methodist Conference deemed it wiser to adjourn its regular session and attend hers. Nell reports: "Miss Watkins, in the course of *one of her very best outbursts of eloquent indignation,* charged the treachery of this colored man upon the United States Government, which is the arch traitor to liberty, as shown by the Fugitive Slave Law and the Dred Scott decision" [emphasis added].

Watkins' work was dangerous and difficult, and the years of traveling, lecturing, and fighting racism and sexism among friends and foes alike did take their toll. Friends, fearing for her health and safety, advised her to become more cautious with her money and her personal security. To them she admitted she was considering retirement, not because she was afraid, but because she was losing her voice and her health was not "very strong" (Still, 792). However, it was not easy for a single woman to support herself, and given Watkins' particular circumstances, retirement was even more problematic. Not only was it difficult to withdraw from active involvement in the most important issue of the antebellum period, but until slavery was abolished, she was unable to return to her birthplace. She had pledged her life's energies to fighting the forces that had allowed a free person to be enslaved merely for entering a particular city. She had also been profoundly moved by the *Narrative of Solomon Northup,* a free black man who had been kidnapped in New York, and sold into slavery. During her travels, no doubt she learned of more such cases. Watkins knew that she was not particularly safe in the North, and though a free southerner by birth, she was not free to return home either. Watkins explained, "I might be so glad [to retire] if it was only so that I could go home among my own kindred and people, but slavery comes up like a dark shadow between me and the home of my childhood. Well, perhaps it is my lot to die from home and be buried among strangers; and yet I do not regret that I have espoused this cause" (Still, 792).

When John Brown and his men were apprehended at Harper's Ferry in October 1859, Watkins, like many African-Americans, considered them martyrs. In a letter to Brown, reprinted in James Redpath's *Echoes of Harper's Ferry,* Watkins wrote, "Although the hands of Slavery throw a barrier between you and me, . . . Virginia has no bolts or bars through which I dread to send you my sympathy" (418). She pledged to continue to assist his wife and asked for information about the families of any of his followers who might need her help. Watkins not only wrote and contributed financially on behalf of these men, but for two weeks she stayed with Mrs. Brown while she awaited the execution of her husband.

Watkins was generous with her time and her money, but as a single woman entirely dependent upon her own efforts for support, she was also well aware of the difficulties that women faced. As her health continued to fail, she did manage to save some of her earnings. Then, on November 22, 1860, she married Fenton Harper, a widower from Cincinnati whose name is conspicuously absent from those with whom Watkins was publicly associated. With her savings, she helped him purchase a farm near Columbus, Ohio, where they settled until his death on May 5, 1864.

Not much is known about the Harper marriage. A letter written by Harper some ten years later states that a guest would have found her in a "humble log house and seen me kneading bread and making butter" (Still, 806). In a speech delivered at the Eleventh Woman's Rights Convention in 1866, Harper mentions that she had become the mother of four, "one my own, and the others step-children," that she had been "a farmer's wife and made butter for the Columbus market," and that her husband "died in debt" (45). No doubt Frances Harper's marriage imposed new obligations, but her self-description as a "farmer's wife" may have been a bit of poetic license. As Mrs. F. E. W. Harper, she limited but did not curtail her public activities. She maintained her interest in politics, and she continued to publish and lecture, sometimes traveling as far as Rhode Island. According to Still, "Notwithstanding her family cares, consequent upon married life, she only ceased from her literary and Anti-slavery labors, when compelled to do so by other duties" (793). At best, Harper's marriage resulted in only a semi-retirement from public service. And it lasted only a few years. Within five months after her husband died, Frances Harper and her daughter, Mary, had moved to New England, and the papers were once again advertising her public lectures.

Unfortunately, we have no information about the effect that motherhood had upon her career or how Harper dealt with the problems of childcare. Perhaps, as her friend Ida B. Wells-Barnett did a few years later, Harper traveled with her child and hired someone to care for her while Harper was on the platform. Or like Jarena Lee, the A.M.E. minister earlier in the century, Harper may have left Mary with friends. Newspaper ads and notices of her lectures suggest that Harper restricted her travels to the Boston area. But it is clear that during the Civil War, Harper supported herself, her child, and the war effort through her lectures and the sale of her books.

After the war, Harper continued to work on a variety of social issues. With Susan B. Anthony, Frederick Douglass, and Elizabeth Cady Stanton, she was a leader in the campaign for suffrage, women's education, and other concerns of the American Equal Rights Association. However, her priorities were with the welfare of the newly freed slaves. Like Charlotte Forten, Harriet Jacobs, Maria W. Stewart, and others, Frances Harper devoted herself to the work of Reconstruction. Once again, she assumed a grueling and far-ranging schedule of lectures, but this time in the South. Harper traveled in every southern state except Arkansas and Texas. She visited cities and rural areas, meeting and working with members of every spectrum of southern society. Her message was one of reconciliation among fellow citizens. In a characteristic statement, Harper declared, "I hold that between the white people and the colored there is a community of interest, and the sooner they find it out, the better it will be for both parties; but that community of interests does not consist in increasing the privileges of one class and curtailing the rights of the other" (Still, 800).

Harper braved the suspicion of southern blacks who were wary of fast-talking Yankees of any hue and of southern whites whose methods of dealing with outside agitators were not softened if that agitator happened to be a woman. On another occasion, she said, "This part of the country reminds me of heathen ground, and though my work may not be recognized as part of it used to be in the North, yet never perhaps were my services more needed" (803). Notwithstanding the real danger of her situation, Harper did not confine her work to the lecture hall. She wrote:

> For my audiences I have both white and colored. On the cars, some find out that I am a lecturer, and then, again, I am drawn into conversation. "What are you lecturing about?" the question comes up, and if I say, among other topics politics, then I may look for an onset. There is a sensitiveness on this subject, a dread, it may be, that some one will "put the devil in the nigger's head," or exert some influence inimical to them; still, I get along somewhat pleasantly. Last week I had a small congregation of listeners in the cars, where I sat. I got in conversation with a former slave dealer, and we had rather an exciting time. I was traveling alone, but it is not worth while to show any signs of fear....
>
> Last Saturday I spoke in Sumter; a number of white persons were present, and I had been invited to speak there by the Mayor and editor of the paper. There had been some violence in the district, and some of my friends did not wish me to go, but I had promised, and, of course, I went. [Still, 797–98]

As a lecturer and teacher, Frances Harper never lacked for engagements and sometimes spoke twice a day. She was especially interested in working with women and frequently conducted private sessions with them "about their daughters, and about things connected with the welfare of the race." During this period she somehow found time to publish in such journals as the *Christian Recorder*, the *New National Era*, and the Philadelphia *Press* a number of new poems and seventeen installments of a short novel called "Minnie's Sacrifice." She was even able to arrange the publication of another volume of verse, *Moses: A Story of the Nile* (1869).

Harper returned to Philadelphia about 1871. There she organized Sunday schools and worked as Assistant Superintendent for the YMCA. Still's biography adds only that

> Mrs. Harper reads the best magazines and ablest weeklies, as well as more elaborate works, not excepting such authors as De Tocqueville, Mill, Ruskin, Buckle, Guizot, &c. In espousing the cause of the oppressed as a poet and lecturer, had she neglected to fortify her mind in the manner she did, she would have been weighed and found wanting long since. Before friends and foes, the learned and the unlearned, North and South, Mrs. Harper has pleaded the cause of her race in a manner that has commanded the greatest respect. [797–98]

Despite the absence of any significant biography that covers her life after 1871, the basic contours of Harper's later life can be sketched from public references. In 1871, Harper was forty-six years old. Her daughter, Mary, was somewhere between seven and ten years of age. Harper had settled in Philadelphia, where she eventually purchased a house at 1006 Bainbridge Street. She had ended her southern tour that same year, and had published *Poems*. Many of the selections in that volume had been published previously in newspapers and journals. However, the next year's volume, *Sketches of Southern Life*, was a substantially original work that rendered in poetic form many of the scenes and characters she had encountered during her travels in the Reconstruction South.

Conference programs and lecture announcements reveal that Harper continued to argue forcefully for the welfare of the newly freed slaves. In "The Great Problem to Be Solved" (reprinted here), Harper argued that their joy over emancipation must be tempered with the realization that the struggle was not over:

> It may not seem to be a gracious thing to mingle complaint in a season of general rejoicing.... And yet, with all the victories and triumphs which freedom and justice have won in this country, I do not believe there is another civilized nation under heaven where there are half so many people who have been brutally and shamefully murdered, with or without impunity, as in this republic within the last ten years. (220)

Harper argued for self-help and self-advancement, but she did not restrict her notion of "self." At given times, she quite pragmatically chose to emphasize one aspect of her identity over another. For example, during the crisis over the Fifteenth Amendment, Harper chose to support the vote for black men. Moreover, she refused to let the often subtle and sometimes blatant racism of her fellow feminists deter her from causes she knew to be right. Despite their racist remarks and threats not to support the enfranchisement of black men unless it accompanied their own, Harper tried to reason, and continued to work, with the women's suffrage leaders. Moreover, she was one of the very few African-American women able to gain some measure of acceptance in the American Women's Suffrage Association, the National Council of Women, and the Women's Christian Temperance Union. Her activities on behalf of women's rights brought her into frequent contact and conflict with women such as Susan B. Anthony and Frances E. Willard. While working with predominantly white organizations, she always campaigned for mutual recognition of their shared interests and for their cooperation with projects that would further those interests. Although she was often the only African-American woman in the group, Harper participated in their national conventions and served on their executive boards. In her presentations to predominantly white women's groups, Harper emphasized their obligation to create a society that was better for all involved. For example, her address at the 1891 meeting of the National Council of Women was entitled, "Our Duty to Dependent Races," and was included in the *Transactions of the National Council of Women of the United States* for 1891.

Her work with the Women's Christian Temperance Union was passionate. She served as the superintendent of the Philadelphia and the Pennsylvania "colored" chapters for at least seven years, and she remained active with the national organization until at least 1893. As part of her temperance work, Harper published regularly in the *African Methodist Episcopal Church Review* such articles as "The Woman's Christian Temperance Union and the Colored Woman." So important was her role that, in 1922, the World's Woman's Christian Temperance Union posthumously awarded her a position on their Red Letter Calendar. This "signal honor," Hallie Q. Brown declared, ensured that "wherever, around the world, the name of Frances E. Willard, the Lady Henry Somerset, with other staunch supporters of temperance are spoken, there too, will be heard the name of *Frances Ellen Watkins Harper*" [emphasis hers] (103).

Equally respected among her own race, Harper participated in the First Congress of Colored Women in the United States, and in 1896 she was a member of the historical meeting between the National Federation of Afro-American Women and the Colored Women's League that resulted in the formation of the National Council of Negro Women. At their second convention, Harper was elected vice-president. Despite her advanced years, Harper remained active in that organization. The 1899 conference program indicates that she presented a talk on "Racial Literature."

Little is known about her daughter, Mary, but presumably Harper also succeeded in her role as mother and nurturer. Her novel, *Iola Leroy,* is "lovingly dedicated" to Mary, and one volume of poetry, *Atlanta Offering,* includes Mary's picture on the page facing that of her mother. Mary obviously shared her mother's political views and her dedication to social activism. Mary Harper's name appears along with Frances Harper's on several political programs. When Frances Harper attended the American Association for the Education of Colored Youth conference in Atlantic City in 1897, Mary Harper was also on the program. The next year, the Harpers were in Wilmington, Delaware, where Mary also presented a paper and served on the nominating committee of that organization.

Even with this busy schedule, Harper continued to write and to publish her work. The title pages of her later works make it clear that she maintained control over the printing and the distribution of her material. Even with the time that this required, between 1892 and 1900 she published four volumes of poems and a novel.

The public record of Harper's activities after 1901 is virtually empty. We do know that Mary Harper died in 1909. Since the circumstances of her daughter's death are unrecorded, one can speculate that Frances Harper curtailed her public activities to care for her daughter, who apparently had never married and lived with her mother. Or maybe it was simply Frances Harper's own advancing age that slowed her down. Whatever the reason, less than three years after Mary's death, Frances Ellen Watkins Harper died of heart failure at the age of 85. Harper's funeral was held at the Unitarian Church on Chestnut Street, and she was buried in Eden Cemetery in Philadelphia.

Despite an extraordinary life of almost seventy years as a public person and a professional writer, Harper left few personal papers and, apparently, no diaries or journals. Nor did she publish an autobiography. Considering her prominence in social reform movements, the absence of an autobiography is especially noteworthy. As Estelle Jelinek has pointed out, it had become so commonplace by the late nineteenth century for "reform-minded and feminist women" such as Harper to publish their life histories that the output of these women alone constituted a "veritable renaissance in women's autobiographical history" (97). Although most of these writers were very circumspect about their professional lives and focused their narratives on their early personal lives, such a document likely would have provided more information about Harper's activities before and after her abolitionist period. And yet, as frustrating as it may be, the absence of a personal narrative from her canon is consistent with the values that Harper expressed both in her private letters and in her published literature. From her earliest writings, Harper advocated a life in which the personal and the public were merged in an effort to realize the moral, social, and economic development of society. Her literature was an essential tool to that end, and it is her literature that must, finally, serve as her presentation of self.

II

Evaluating Frances Ellen Watkins Harper's canon has not been easy. Until recently, her works were out of print and difficult to obtain. Although her novel, *Iola Leroy*, was for many years considered the earliest extant novel by an African-American woman, it was not available in paperback until 1987. The reasons for this reflect the general neglect and misreadings of literature by women. The ears of the American public are now, as they were then, more generally attuned to male voices. Even their supporters tend to undervalue women's words. Consider, for example, William Still's approach to Harper's work. He acknowledges that at the time of his writing, Harper was "the leading colored poet in the United States," and yet it is the "noble deeds of this faithful worker" that he wishes to record (783). To Still, Harper's poetry is useful only to document her continued interest in politics and to prove the "highly moral and elevating tone" that characterized Harper's mind.

But, to his credit, Still did not qualify Harper's success by proclaiming her the leading colored *woman* poet. His statement does not judge her against other women only, but suggests that she was considered the best of all African-American poets. Ironically, this attitude was more common among Harper's contemporaries than among the critics of the early twentieth century whose sexism was less mitigated. As the twentieth century advanced, Harper's literary contributions were relegated to footnotes or brief references. She became routinely identified as a minor writer, important to scholars only because she was a woman who did publish or because her work ensured the continuity of a written African-American literary tradition until the "major" (male) writers could evolve. Numerous feminist critics have established the fact that the so-called objective or aesthetic criteria that male critics have used to determine the canon are a construct of their own needs and desires and that as those needs and desires change, their literary expectations change also. It is relevant to our evaluation of Harper's literature to demonstrate briefly how this affected her literary reputation.

Black women writers have traditionally found their authority and authenticity challenged, but some, such as Harper, managed against the odds to achieve visibility and respect. Harper became prominent during a time when U.S. women were increasingly exercising their social and political strength, a time that culminated for black women in the 1890s with a period of intense literary production which they believed heralded the beginning of "the woman's era." But the reality was different. The twentieth-century United States was more interested in commercial and imperialistic issues. The nation had gone international, industrial, and martial. And though women also organized internationally, their campaigns for social welfare reform and moral integrity seemed less important than the international expansion and economic concerns that consumed most of the men.

By and large the black intellectual community was more concerned with the internal politics of the nation than with its foreign policy. Nonetheless, the increasing military expeditions and the rise in manufacturing offered black men opportunities not shared by black women. And, even more importantly, the trivialization of issues with which women were most often identified also encouraged a general trivialization of women. Mary Helen Washington's description of the founding of the American Negro Academy in 1897 provides a salient example. As Washington notes, ". . . the distinguished luminaries, among them Alexander Crummell, Francis Grimké, and W. E. B. Du Bois, proposed from the beginning that [this] . . . intellectual think tank . . . be open only to 'men of African descent.' " Washington argues that the exclusion of women was neither accidental nor justified:

> . . . when a number of leading black intellectuals decided to form "an organization of Colored authors, scholars, and artists," with the expressed intent of raising "the standard of intellectual endeavor among American Negroes," one of the invited members wrote to declare himself "decidedly opposed to the admission of women to membership" because "literary matters and social matters do not mix." . . . Imagine if you can, black women intellectuals and activists, who in the 1890s had taken on such issues as the moral integrity of black women, lynching, and the education of black youth being considered social decorations. [xviii]

With the twentieth century emerged new arbitrators who substituted indifference or paternalism for direct challenges. As Bert James Loewenberg and Ruth Bogin declared in *Black Women in Nineteenth-Century American Life,* "When black history was consciously written, it was the male, not the female, who recorded it. Women are conspicuous by their silence"

(4). In the case of literary history, it became as Washington states it remains today: "Women's writing is considered singular and anomalous, not universal and representative, and for some mysterious reason, writing about black women is not considered as racially significant as writing about black men.... Male critics go to great lengths to explain the political naiveté or racial ambivalence of male writers while they harshly criticize women writers for the same kinds of shortcomings" (xix).

Frances Harper's influence and her reputation were affected by these developments. When she began writing, literature was expected to be sincere and didactic. This was especially true of her poetry, most of which was composed during the antebellum and Reconstruction periods. Harper was quick to experiment with the various genres and to adopt those literary techniques that were compatible with her concept of literature's purpose and its audience. But Harper's literary aesthetics were formed during the first half of the nineteenth century, and her commitment to a literature of purpose and of wide appeal remained constant.

When Harper died in 1911, literary fashion had changed. In part, then, her longevity worked against her. W. E. B. Du Bois, one of the founders of the American Negro Academy, demonstrates the changing literary aesthetics in his eulogy for Harper. Du Bois maintains that she deserves to be remembered "for her attempts to forward literature among colored people." Du Bois intones, "She was not a great singer, but she had some sense of song; she was not a great writer, but she wrote much worth reading. She was, above all, sincere" (20). To Du Bois, Harper is "a worthy member of that dynasty, beginning with the dark Phyllis in 1773 and coming on down ... to Dunbar, Chesnutt and Braithwaite of our day" (21). Although the newest members on the line were all male, at least Du Bois places Harper within an African-American tradition of men and women. By 1937, when Saunders Redding published *To Make a Poet Black*, Harper had lost even more stature. Redding judges her "a trail blazer, hacking, however ineffectually, at the dense forest of propaganda" and trying to write in a more universal tone. However, Redding continues, "... the demands of her audience for the sentimental treatment of the old subjects sometimes overwhelmed her.... She was apt to gush with pathetic sentimentality," and her poetry was too much like all the poetry which "appeared with monotonous regularity in *Godey's Lady's Book* and other popular monthlies" (40).

Obvious here are both the sexism and the rejection of earlier literary criteria that esteemed sincerity, sentimentality, and popularity. Harper is but one of many writers, particularly women, whose literary reputations have suffered because of this shift in values, or perhaps more accurately, the ascendancy of a literary elite in partnership with the publishing industry.

Once again the critical tide is changing. A few scholars have begun to reexamine the literature, and the criteria by which it has been judged, and to offer new readings of the texts based upon questions and assumptions heretofore unacknowledged. Studies of Harper's works in the context of women's literature by critics such as Hazel Carby, Barbara Christian, Maryemma Graham, and Mary Helen Washington have been especially helpful in reevaluating Harper's achievement. As a result, Harper is beginning to be seen once again as the significant literary force she was.

Harper's position in literary history will be further enhanced if her writing is reexamined in terms of the expectations for popular literature. As Du Bois, Redding, and most critics have admitted, Harper was enormously popular with nineteenth-century readers. She was lauded as "a great and profound writer in both prose and poetry" (Scruggs, 13), and nineteenth-century writers, such as Monroe Majors, were proud that Harper's works enjoyed extensive readership among both white and black readers (23). The literary promise that attracted attention when she was but a teenager was realized in the publication of at least ten volumes of verse. Figures are not available for many of the later books, but during the antebellum period, her first two volumes reportedly sold over 50,000 copies (Wagner, 23). The earliest of her books, *Poems on Various Subjects*, merited at least twenty printings before her death. *Iola Leroy* was reprinted four times in four years.

To dismiss this popularity as a result of Harper's prominence as a lecturer and activist is a rather curious inversion of her own melding of life and works, but one which began with William Lloyd Garrison's prefatory remarks to *Poems on Miscellaneous Subjects*. Although Harper was a freeborn schoolteacher who had been writing poetry for sixteen years, Garrison devoted three of the four paragraphs in his preface to arguing his thesis that slavery and racial discrimination eradicated genius, buried the mind, and destroyed one's humanity. As he had done with Frederick Douglass's narrative some nine years earlier, Garrison subordinated the writer's literary achievements, stressing the volume as an artifact, as evidence that with freedom and education, blacks could produce a written literature. Garrison patronized Harper's poems by urging critics to remember that they are written by "one young in years, and identified in complexion and destiny with a depressed and outcast race" (4). He argued that "whatever is attempted [by blacks] in poetry or prose . . . should be viewed with a friendly eye, and criticized in a lenient spirit. To measure them by the same standard as we measure the productions of the favored white inhabitants of the land would be manifestly unjust" (4).

Among the several problematic elements in Garrison's statements and their underlying assumptions is his reference to "the same standard" by which white writers are judged and its clear implication of a critical homogeneity that did not exist. Ordinarily, one need not make much of Garrison's mistake. After all, he was a newspaper editor and a political activist, not a literary critic. But in this case, Garrison's comments are significant because literary critics have continued to behave as if there had been, and still is, one literary standard and that Harper, and in fact all nineteenth-century black writers, aspired to that standard, but being so culturally deprived, simply could not realize it.

This is a curious situation, for few critics assume that the same muse inspired the work of James Whitcomb Riley and Emily Dickinson or of Harriet Beecher Stowe and Herman Melville. And even though Nathaniel Hawthorne felt he and "the scribbling women" competed for the same audience, few scholars agree that he and Susan Warner, for example, were of the same ilk. In short, critics and other intellectuals have generally conceded the existence, if not the merit, of popular culture. Rather than treating its adherents as culturally deprived individuals who were incapable of writing aesthetically, they have evaluated their contributions according to the standards for popular literature. If this tolerance or recognition of diversity were to spill over into the tributary of African-American literature, it would become evident that Harper made a genuine contribution to popular literature in the United States.

But racist tones have a familiar sound, and it would serve little purpose to harp upon the cacophony they produce. More important to this discussion is the particular way in which racism and sexism have been combined with elitism. Twentieth-century scholars have favored the score over the performance and technical virtuosity over memorable lyrics. They have defined lyrical ballads as tunes of distinctly minor significance. To say that Harper's moving recitations of her poetry masked its technical flaws and to imply, then, that her mesmerized audience purchased her books as souvenirs is as much a trivialization of nineteenth-century popular aesthetics as it is of Harper's works. To appreciate her contributions properly, one must consider the audience, its literary criteria, and the ways in which Harper's poems met and sometimes exceeded those standards.

When Harper began her literary career, writing as a profession was thriving because literacy was increasing, the publishing industry was flourishing, and leisure time for reading was available as never before. Readers in the mid-nineteenth century were by and large, as Roy Harvey Pearce has stated, "literate but not literary, thinking but not thoughtful, caught up in the exhilarating busyness of day-to-day life" (194). These readers assumed that the aim of literature was education. They expected it to record, argue, or exhort, to point out the lessons in their everyday experiences, to be a weapon with which to defend good, expose hypocrisy, and abolish evil. As Pearce says: "The rule is this: that the poet who would reach the great audience had, willy-nilly, to cut himself down to its size. Such a cutting down does not imply only a falling below the standards of high art; it implies also the production of an art in some respects different in kind from high art, and to be judged and valued accordingly" (246).

When one recognizes this, then the fact that Harper's poetry often sounds better in recitation than in reading may be attributed to factors other than "errors of metrical construction" (Redding, 44). Harper knew that nineteenth-century popular audiences preferred poems with rhythms and rhymes that were easy to memorize and to recite. The aesthetics of popular poetry also required familiar verse forms such as the sonnet and the ballad, simple and didactic metaphors, and readily comprehensible and prosaic word order.

The poets most accomplished at this—and most popular when Harper published *Poems on Miscellaneous Subjects*—were the so-called Fireside poets: Oliver Wendell Holmes, Henry Wadsworth Longfellow, James Russell Lowell, and John Greenleaf Whittier. According to James D. Hart, "No one was willing to pay a dollar for Whitman's poems when for the same price they could have Longfellow's. . . . For the public, 1855 was the year of *Hiawatha*, not of *Leaves of Grass*. And so was 1856" (129). Whittier acknowledged that many of his poems "were written with no expectation that they would survive the occasions which called them forth: they were protests, alarm signals, trumpet-calls to actions, words wrung from the writer's heart, forged at white heat, and of course lacking the finish and careful word-selection which reflection and patient brooding over them might have given" (xxi–xxii).

In another time and another place, Harper might have chosen to brood and reflect patiently over her literary efforts, carefully choosing her words, perfecting her meters, perhaps even writing thoughtful prefaces to explain and justify her critical theory, for her biographers agree that she had an early thirst for knowledge, a love of beauty, and a talent for composition. Careful reading of Harper's writings proves them correct. Harper had an appreciation for aesthetics, and she was not reluctant to experiment with language, form, and technique. However, as "Christianity," one of her earliest works, reveals, her poetics dictated that the writer must first of all feel and say what is "right." In that piece she declared that literature is an elegance achieved by toil of pen and labor of pencil. Its purpose, she states, is to cultivate the intellect, enlighten the understanding, give scope to the imagination, and refine the sensibilities, but, she admonishes, these are all secondary, all "idle tales" unless infused with religious truths. Since "Christianity" was apparently published first in 1853, reprinted in the first edition of *Poems on Miscellaneous Subjects*, and included in all subsequent editions, it signals the standards that consistently informed her art.

In espousing this view, Harper places herself not only in the company of Whittier, but also within what William A. Rossetti called the "very modern phalanx of poets who persistently co-ordinate the impulse of sentiment with the guiding power of morals or religion" and who believe that "Everything must convey its 'lesson,' and is indeed set forth for the sake of its lesson.... The poet must not write because he has something of his own to say, but because he has something *right* to feel and say" (24).

Another early statement of Harper's literary philosophy can be seen in what is one of the earliest short stories by an African-American writer, "The Two Offers." Serialized in the *Anglo-African* in 1859, the story concerns two beautiful and cultivated young women who try to decide the best uses of their lives. Laura believes that being an old maid is unthinkable. Therefore, she ignores her conscience and marries a man whom she suspects is intellectually and morally inferior to her and whom she does not love. He becomes a gambler and a wastrel, and poor Laura, after much suffering, dies of a broken heart. Her cousin, Janette, would not compromise her standards, and when the death of her loved one shatters her dreams, she decides not to marry at all. Instead she becomes a writer who champions the causes of freedom and righteousness. At the end of the story, Janette is indeed "an old maid," but she is happy and successful as she strives to carry out her commitment "to make the world better by her example, gladder by her presence, and to kindle the fires of her genius on the altars of universal love and truth. She had a higher and better object in all her writings than the mere acquisition of gold, or acquirement of fame ... she had a high and holy mission on the battlefield of existence" (114). Janette's purpose is identical to that which Harper's letters indicate she laid out for herself. Like Janette, Harper "had a higher and better object" in all her writings. Rather than beautiful but "idle tales," Harper chose to use her words as weapons in the battle to save humanity. Harper believed that the progress of U.S. society was threatened by slavery and by religious and social hypocrisy. She believed that a corrective literature, one readily accessible to the emerging literate population, was crucial.

In evaluating Harper's writing, it is vital to recognize the literary tradition to which she wanted to belong, the expectations and limitations

of the audience that she sought, and the subtle ways in which she modi-
fied and corrected her popular images and attitudes. Writers such as Harper
recognized, as James D. Hart explains, "The dialectic of the popular mind
was by turns sentimental and homely, moral and humanitarian, religious
and patriotic, . . . a poem to be popular had to be pitched to one of them"
(125). Recognizing her audience's receptivity to guidelines for achieving
their ideals and their reluctance to view their present efforts negatively,
Harper carefully walked the fine line well known to black writers who
woo a white readership. Though she wrote to change minds and actions,
hers was not the poetry of confrontation, but of gentle persuasion. Har-
per played her audience, used her poetry to strike chords of sentiment,
to improvise upon familiar themes, and, thereby, to create songs more
in harmony with what she knew as the dictates of Christianity and
democracy. Esoteric displays of technical virtuosity were not only unneces-
sary but could be detrimental.

"The proof of poetry," said James Russell Lowell, is its ability to "reduce
to the essence of a single line the vague philosophy which is floating in
all men's minds" (Hart, 127). Sometimes, Harper had only to rearrange
the complex sentences of her prose into a series of simple concepts in
more quotable lines to satisfy the criteria of her audience and to achieve
her purposes. If we compare the language of her poem, "Free Labor" (on
page 81 of this book), with that of a letter which she wrote on the same
topic, her technique of reducing the "essence" to single lines is obvious.[5]
In a letter to William Still she says:

> I have reason to be thankful that I am able to give a little more for a Free
> Labor dress, if it is coarser. I can thank God that upon its warp and woof
> I see no stain of blood and tears; that to procure a little finer muslin for
> my limbs no crushed and broken heart went out in sighs, and that from
> the field where it was raised went up no wild and startling cry unto the throne
> of God to witness there in language deep and strong, that in demanding
> that cotton I was nerving oppression's hand for deeds of guilt and crime. [788]

She essentially rearranges those words in her poem, which begins:

> I wear an easy garment,
> O'er it no toiling slave
> Wept tears of hopeless anguish,
> In his passage to the grave.
>
> And from its ample folds
> Shall rise no cry to God,
> Upon its warp and woof shall be
> No stain of tears and blood.

It concludes five stanzas later:

And witness at the throne of God,
In language deep and strong,
That I have nerv'd Oppression's hand,
For deeds of guilt and wrong.

Harper's antislavery poems were typical of abolitionist poetry in that they confined their message to three basic facts: slaves were human; slavery violated inalienable human rights; slavery, therefore, trespassed the laws of God and country. During the antebellum period, legislators, scientists, and the general public were debating the basic humanity of the slaves. Harper's validation of the slaves' ability to experience love and to know truth, her documentation of their suffering and pain, and her exposition of slavery as a fundamentally flawed institution, rather than one which needed greater regulation, were all radical positions in that time. Like other abolitionist poets, Harper relied heavily upon narrative poems with well-known plots and familiar character types. She took advantage of the sentiments introduced or encouraged by other popular writers. For example, such poems as "Eliza Harris" and "Bible Defence of Slavery" echo the prose of Harriet Beecher Stowe and Lydia Maria Child, but offer subtly different interpretations. Like those created by most abolitionist writers, Harper's male slaves are heroic eunuchs, long-suffering, turn-the-other-cheek Christians. They do not march off to war, but steal away (usually to Jesus) when the burden becomes too great. Her slave women are "nerved by despair, and strengthened by woe" as they desperately strive to protect their children. Their most frequent emotions are despair, anguish, and grief. Within these stereotyped outlines, however, Harper paints more subtle shades.

Consider the ways in which she modified standard depictions of slave women. Many abolitionists portrayed slave women as victims of physical cruelty and especially of sexual violation, as persons so brutalized that even if proven to be human, they could hardly fit the prevalent notions of "True Womanhood."[6] The question in the opening stanza of John Greenleaf Whittier's "At Washington" is more than rhetorical. Along with Whittier, nineteenth-century readers could ask:

Pitying God! Is that a woman
On whose wrist the shackles clash?
Is that shriek she utters human,
Underneath the stinging lash? [295]

In Frances Harper's "The Slave Mother" (page 58), there is no such question:

> Heard you that shriek? It rose
> So wildly on the air,
> It seemed as if a burden'd heart
> Was breaking in despair.

After describing the physical manifestations of the mother's pain upon being separated from her son, Harper seems to address those underlying doubts directly:

> No marvel, then, these bitter shrieks
> Disturb the listening air:
> She is a mother, and her heart
> Is breaking in despair.

In assuring her readers not only that the voice belongs to a woman, but that she is a mother crying not for herself but from the agony of being separated from her clinging child, Harper moves past the popular mode of characterizing black women and addresses social preconceptions with authority.

Both Whittier and Harper used the common image of the brutalized slave woman to demonstrate the total depravity of the entire institution of slavery. Whittier's poem chastises a nation in whose capital city leaders indulge in parlor flirtations while outside slaves are beaten or sold. He includes the screaming woman to show the extent to which the country is not adhering to its ideals. Harper concentrates upon the feelings and sensibilities of those brutalized and shows how slavery denies some human beings the basic privileges of family and community.

The point and counterpoint of her poetry can be seen again when compared with another favorite scene in abolitionist literature, the slave auction. In "The Panorama," Whittier describes the "motley crowd" in attendance and "The shrewd-eyed salesman, garrulous and loud," "prompt to proclaim his honor" but never scrupling

> To sell the infant from its mother's breast,
> Break through all ties of wedlock, home, and kin,
> Yield shrinking girlhood up to graybeard sin; [325]

Whittier's concern is with the affront to Christian values and the hypocrisy of a democratic society that would allow such scenes.

In "The Slave Auction" (page 64), Harper chooses the same situation but again develops the slave's feelings and sufferings. In this poem one may also see how Harper manipulates the reader's own preconditioned attitudes to evoke not pity but sympathy. In stanza 1, Whittier's "shrinking girlhood" is still being yielded to "graybeard sin," but Harper emphasizes the girls' youth and innocence:

> The sale began—young girls were there,
> Defenceless in their wretchedness,
> Whose stifled sobs of deep despair
> Revealed their anguish and distress.

Harper's stanza 2 presents mothers "with streaming eyes" being separated from "dearest children." Stanza 3 identifies slave women as part of ideal womanhood:

> And woman, with her love and truth—
> For these in sable forms may dwell—
> Gaz'd on the husband of her youth,
> With anguish none may paint or tell.

Knowing that readers were aware of conventional auction block portrayals and could easily sketch its outlines, Harper directs their imaginative responses toward more specific identifications. "The Slave Auction" uses the reader's familiarity with standard abolitionist scenes and blatantly appeals to sentimentality, but does not encourage self-indulgence. Harper clearly informs her audience that love and truth are virtues possessed by blacks also, thereby establishing their common humanity. Stanza 5 builds upon this idea by directly addressing "Ye who have laid your love to rest," calling up their most anguished moments and linking their grief with that of slave families. Harper then goes on to declare that the slaves' grief is even worse, not because slaves are more sensitive, but because their sorrow is not mitigated by any sense of God's plan being fulfilled.

Although Harper considered literature a viable and significant way in which to contribute to social betterment and although to achieve this end she consciously adopted the traditions of popular literature, she was not reluctant to experiment with language, form, and technique. If this is obvious from her early work, it is increasingly clear later in her career. She was never simply an abolitionist poet. From the earliest extant work, one recognizes such important themes and subjects as gender equality, temperance, and Christian reform. However, after emancipation, when she was freer "to delve into the heart of the world," her poems and her prose reveal increasingly experimental techniques. For example, she created the character Aunt Chloe, an uneducated but decidedly informed and intelligent woman, modeled no doubt after many of the former slaves with whom Harper worked during Reconstruction. Chloe is a radical departure from the victimized slave woman and the tragic mulatto. African-American women writers such as Octavia Victoria Rogers Albert develop this character in later works.[7] Moreover, Harper's experimentation with dialect in the Aunt Chloe series and in parts of *Iola Leroy* has what Saunders Redding admits is "a fine racy, colloquial tang." Redding concedes, "In these poems she managed to hurdle a barrier by which Dunbar was later to feel himself tripped" (42–43).

In her novel, *Iola Leroy*, Harper candidly states that she has woven fact and fiction to awaken "in the hearts of our country men a stronger sense of justice and a more Christlike humanity" and to "inspire the children" to "embrace every opportunity, develop every faculty, and use every power God has given them to rise in the scale of character and condition." In 1895, Harper's literary objectives remained the same. In "Songs for the People" (page 371), she writes:

> Let me make the songs for the people,
>   Songs for the old and young;
> Songs to stir like a battle-cry
>   Wherever they are sung.
>
> Not for the clashing sabres,
>   For carnage nor for strife;
> But songs to thrill the hearts of men
>   With more abundant life.

As the black literary audience grew, Harper wrote more exclusively for them. Her songs for "more abundant life" continued to emphasize Christian values, but she adapted her calls for sobriety and sexual equality to demonstrate the value of temperance and democracy in increasing racial unity, racial pride, and racial progress. By 1892, Harper had decided that the time had come when black writers could and should choose subjects and treatments of those subjects from a broader range. She consciously integrated more humor and black folk life into her later works. She even implied that for other black writers, the pursuit of *belles lettres* could be worthwhile, as long as it was coupled with a commitment to the functional value of literature. In *Iola Leroy* she wrote:

> There are scattered among us materials for mournful tragedies and mirth-provoking comedies, which some hand may yet bring into the literature of the country, glowing with the fervor of the tropics and enriched by the luxuriance of the Orient, and thus add to the solution of our unsolved American problem. [212]

Her own life, however, was dedicated to the creation of an ideal practical literature, one that would influence the largest number for the greatest good. The writer must "grasp the pen and wield it as a power for good," she maintained. Neither her life nor her art was to be "frittered away in nonsense, or wasted away in trifling pursuits." Though born free and with opportunities, she, like her protagonist in "Moses: A Story of the Nile" (page 138), chose

> . . . to join
> The fortunes of my race, and to put aside
> All other bright advantages, save
> The approval of my conscience and the meed
> Of rightly doing.

To this end, Harper used the vehicle of popular literature, claiming it, developing it, and presenting it as a testimony to African-American participation in the American dream.

III

A Brighter Coming Day gathers all the poems from Harper's extant volumes, approximately forty poems published in various periodicals, and one which was discovered in manuscript form. Thus it is the most complete collection of Harper's poetry to date. This collection also contains every prose piece that Harper included in her separately published volumes as well as a selection of letters, short stories, and essays that were published elsewhere. Thus, *A Brighter Coming Day* brings together examples from every genre in which Frances Harper published and provides the first comprehensive survey of the works of this major figure in United States literary history.

The publishing history of Harper's works has made the creation of a comprehensive bibliography an unusually challenging task. Her books were published over a half century, in various parts of the country, for various audiences. Harper sometimes worked with established publishers such as James H. Earle; other times with printers popular with abolitionists such as J. B. Yerrinton and Son and Merrihew & Thompson. But, most often, she published her own works, hiring local printers to produce the works but apparently retaining absolute authority in the editing and distribution of her work. According to Maxwell Whiteman, the firm, Ferguson Brothers, with which Harper probably had the most extensive dealings was sold in the early 1950s and destroyed its Harper files then. And, so far, it appears that Harper left no other caches of unpublished correspondence or manuscripts.

The inconsistency of both Harper and her publishers in distinguishing between revised editions, printings, and new works further complicates efforts to establish a bibliography. For example, Harper published at least nine books with different titles. Most of these were collections of new and reprinted poetry, but a few included essays, letters, or short fiction. Some of these collections are different in title but identical in content, while others share the same title but have totally different contents. *Poems* of 1871 is not the same collection as *Poems* published in 1900, but *Idylls of the Bible*, which appeared in 1901, is the 1889 *Sketches of Southern Life*.

Finally, although a conservative estimate of ten to twelve separately published works is impressive enough, Frances Harper wrote many poems, essays, letters, and stories for the ephemeral media. As investigation of the popular press, especially those of particular audiences such as the African-American newspapers and the official journals of churches, reform organizations, and social clubs, continues, more Harper pieces will undoubtedly be discovered.

While distinctions among her editions and reprintings are often difficult to determine, Frances Harper did establish a fairly consistent pattern of organization. She sometimes revised a previously published poem before she included it in a collection, but she did not arrange the poems in her collections chronologically or group them by obvious themes. For example, all the antislavery poems do not appear in one section and all the equal rights ones in another. In subsequent enlarged editions, Harper usually appended new poems at the end of the earlier group. This volume, therefore, presents Harper's poems in the order they appear in her books and in the order that her books were published. In cases in which a particular poem or essay is known to have been published earlier, that information is included in a note to the work. The poems that were published separately and do not appear in any of Harper's books are included in order of publication between the groups from each volume. The contents of discrete volumes are listed in the Appendix.

Thus, *A Brighter Coming Day* offers the possibility of both autobiographical and comparative readings. Studying Harper's poetry in order of publication from *Poems on Miscellaneous Subjects* (1854) to *Idylls of the Bible* (1901) gives an overview of her poetic legacy and an indication of her artistic intentions. The works show, for example, both the evolution of social issues and Harper's own poetic development. One can recognize more readily the subtextual implications in much the same manner that her contemporaries would have, and one can contrast the subsequent differences in Harper's treatment of various themes and motifs. For example, her 1856 treatment of Moses in the poem "The Burial of Moses" contrasts significantly with the 1869 work, "Moses: A Story of the Nile." The former emphasizes heavenly reward, possibly a response to the fact that in 1856 the advent of emancipation was not certain. While African-

Americans could not be assured freedom in this world, they could believe their sufferings would be rewarded in the next. However, the ambiance of the Reconstruction Era during which the second work was created may have influenced Harper's increased emphasis upon individual sacrifice and personal commitment to a common human cause.

Harper's earliest extant volume, *Poems on Miscellaneous Subjects* (1854), concluded with a section of prose pieces that she collectively identified as "Miscellaneous Writings." Their subjects and themes were consistent with those in poems that preceded them. In later editions, Harper inserted additional poems before the prose selections. This suggests that while genre was less important than message and the title, "Poems on Miscellaneous Subjects," was intended to encompass both poetry and prose, Harper did try to maintain some formal distinctions. In keeping with the pattern of this and other books that Harper compiled, I have separated her work by genre.

The letters in this collection were selected to indicate the biographical context within which the other works were written as well as to illustrate Harper's own development of this genre. Most of these letters were published in her own lifetime either in William Still's *The Underground Rail Road* (1871) or in various periodicals. The letters are particularly important because they reveal the intimate connection between Harper's life and her literature.

The titles of her speeches and contemporary accounts indicate that Harper generally spoke on the same themes about which she wrote—abolition, equal rights, temperance, education, community service, morality, and personal integrity. She had a repertoire of speeches that she delivered extemporaneously and modified with references to recent or local events. Many of Harper's essays are the published versions of her speeches. The essays in this collection were selected to represent Harper's basic themes during each period.

In 1859, *The Anglo-African* published in two installments Harper's "The Two Offers," the work generally considered to be the first short story written by an African-American. Harper's experimentation with fiction culminated in 1892 with *Iola Leroy*, but between the two works she published at least four other serialized stories, two of which ran for several months and may well be considered novels. Unfortunately, some issues of the periodicals in which these stories were published may not have survived. The three selections included in this text come from an 1873–74 series published first under the title "Fancy Etchings" and then, after a few months, as "Fancy Sketches."

Unlike the poetry, most of the fiction that Harper included in her books apparently had not been published earlier. It encompasses a wide range of topics and literary techniques. In some cases, such as that of "Shalmanezer, Prince of Cosman" in *Sketches of Southern Life*, the theme is consistent with the other works in the collection, but the subject or tone is quite different.

Harper's earliest extant work was first published in 1853; therefore, this collection begins with that year. Harper's work is grouped in four sections: 1853–1864, 1865–1875, 1876–1892, and 1893–1911, since these periods correspond with identifiable historical movements that had a manifest influence upon Harper's work and since the publication dates of all her books, except her novel, cluster in the middle of each period.

Part One, covering 1853 to 1864, includes the decade generally known as the antebellum period and the Civil War itself. Not only were most of Harper's efforts devoted to the issue of slavery, but that period also saw her emergence as a writer of national reputation. The majority of her poetry from this period appears in the 1854 or the 1857 edition of *Poems on Miscellaneous Subjects*. Between 1857 and 1864, her writings appeared regularly in ephemeral sources, but Harper's energies were focused upon her career as an antislavery lecturer. Her letters, speeches, and much of her poetry during the antebellum and Civil War periods continue the themes in *Poems on Miscellaneous Subjects*, and examples of these writings are included in this section.

Part Two covers 1865 to 1875, the Reconstruction Era. The letters in this section describe her travels as a lecturer in the south. "The Great Problem Before Us" and "We Are All Bound up Together" are examples of the essays and speeches for this span. Harper's publications during this time include three of her most important books, *Moses: A Story of the Nile* (1869), *Poems* (1871), and *Sketches of Southern Life* (1872), as well as the less known but intriguing "Fancy Etchings" and "Fancy Sketches."

Part Three covers the period between 1876 and 1892, a time of the deconstruction of Reconstruction, when the civil rights gains of the postbellum period were reversed and African-Americans realized that emancipation had freed them from slavery but had not freed them into citizenship. During these years, Harper's literary interests took second place to her civic work as she struggled to protect and to develop organizations that allowed all Americans to exercise their rights and attempt to realize their dreams. Consequently, there are several essays in this section. Though many of Harper's activities were reported in the press, few of her letters, either public or private, have come to light.

Although Harper's works remained available and apparently sold well, most of the books published during this time were reprints. Harper's new poems were generally available only in newspapers and magazines. However, there was one important change. Between 1876 and 1892, Frances Harper shifted her publication focus from poetry and public letters to longer prose forms such as the essay and serialized fiction. In 1892, she published *Iola Leroy*, the most impressive novel by an African-American prior to the twentieth century.

Part Four, covering the period between 1893 and 1911, includes the Spanish-American War and is characterized by industrialization, expansion, and general optimism about the future of this country. Many African-American women believed that this was the time in history when their contributions would usher in the "Woman's Era," a time during which the country's rapid growth and prosperity would be infused with the moral and spiritual temper that would make the United States a kinder, gentler nation. From 1893 until her death, Frances Harper's publications were largely essays and occasional poems. Several volumes of poetry appeared under various titles, but they generally consisted of previously published material to which a few recent writings were appended.

At the beginning of her career, Harper wrote in "The Colored People of America" that she was part of a people "over whom weary ages of degradation have passed, whatever concerns them, as a race, concerns me" (38). But, she continued, "there is hope ... the day ... will dawn with unclouded splendor upon our downtrodden and benighted race" (40). Some forty years later, during the period many still consider the African-American nadir, Harper acknowledged the persecution but asserted, "There is light beyond the darkness," and she urged that intellect and faith would ensure the success of their continued struggle. Like Jenny in "Fancy Etchings," Frances Harper believed that her literature would help her "learn myself and be able to teach others to strive to make the highest ideal, the most truly real of our lives." As readers discover and consider the life and works of Frances Harper, her reputation, so long eclipsed, will once again shine with its faith and its power to effect a brighter coming day.

Notes

[1]Few sources offer additional information about Harper's life, and most directly reference Still as their source. Still's chapter also includes excerpts from Harper's poems, essays, and letters. The poems, essays, and a few of the letters were published in other sources as well, but most of the letters in Still's book appear to have been written to him and were not intended for publication. For these reasons, references to facts of Harper's life and to her letters, unless otherwise

indicated, are from the 1871 edition of *The Underground Rail Road* and are cited in the text.

[2]Watkins was not the first black woman to earn recognition as a public lecturer. Maria W. Stewart (1803–1879) is generally recognized as the first American-born woman, white or black, to lecture publicly before audiences of men and women. Stewart's first such lecture was in September 1832. Nor was Watkins the only other African-American woman abolitionist to lecture publicly. Sojourner Truth was her contemporary, and there were others. However, Watkins may have been the first one to be employed for that purpose.

[3]Antislavery groups were also separated by sex. The women's groups, both black and white, usually functioned as auxiliaries to the men's. Abolitionist papers are full of advertisements for the ladies' meetings and for various fund-raising bazaars by female antislavery groups, but the women who served as lecturers or spokespersons for the cause were few and far between.

[4]Although Harper uses the name "State Anti-Slavery Society of Maine" in this quotation, the official title of the society is the Maine Anti-Slavery Society.

[5]What Harper refers to as "Free Labor" was also known as the "Free Produce" movement. I refer to this earlier in discussing Harper's politics and her support of boycotts. For more discussion, see Quarles, 74–76.

[6]Several critics have delineated the concept of "True Womanhood." Perhaps the earliest to use this phrase was Barbara Welter in *Dimity Convictions* (Athens, Ohio: Ohio University Press, 1976).

[7]Albert's Aunt Charlotte in *The House of Bondage* is, like Chloe, an ex-slave who represents the rural folk who survived slavery with Christian strength, courage, and common sense.

Part One
1853–1864

◆

. . . I have a right to do my share of the work. The humblest and feeblest of us can do something; and though I may be deficient in many of the conventionalisms of city life, and be considered as a person of good impulses, but unfinished, yet if there is common rough work to be done, call on me.

from a letter to William Still, March 31, 1859(?)

Letters

◆

Frances Harper sometimes wrote short essays that she submitted to newspapers as letters to the editor. "An Appeal for the Philadelphia Rescuers" is one that addresses a particular issue and was published as an open letter from the author to the general public. However, during the nineteenth century, letter writing was generally considered to be a literary form, and private letters were often written with the understanding that portions of them would be shared among interested people. Correspondents commonly deleted personal information and published letters they received. Many of Harper's published letters were prefaced by remarks from "a friend," who had submitted them to the editors of each paper in which they were published. There was more than one such friend, but the primary conduit for Harper's letters was William Still, with whom she had a long-term correspondence and who included many of her letters in *The Underground Rail Road*. The "private" letters generally concern her travels, the public reception to her speeches, and other such information that would serve to advance the abolitionist cause.

◆

"Well, I Am out Lecturing"

[August 1854]

Well, I am out lecturing. I have lectured every night this week; besides

---

"Well, I Am out Lecturing": Still, 787.

addressed a Sunday-school, and I shall speak, if nothing prevent, to-night. My lectures have met with success. Last night I lectured in a white church in Providence. Mr. Gardener was present, and made the estimate of about six hundred persons. Never, perhaps, was a speaker, old or young, favored with a more attentive audience. . . . My voice is not wanting in strength, as I am aware of, to reach pretty well over the house. The church was the Roger Williams; the pastor, a Mr. Furnell, who appeared to be a kind and Christian man. . . . My maiden lecture was Monday night in New Bedford on the Elevation and Education of our People. Perhaps as intellectual a place as any I was ever at of its size.

"The Agent of the State Anti-Slavery Society of Maine Travels with Me"

[Buckstown Centre, Maine
September 28, 1854]

The agent of the State Anti-Slavery Society of Maine travels with me, and she is a pleasant, dear, sweet lady. I do like her so. We travel together, eat together, and sleep together. (She is a white woman.) In fact I have not been in one colored person's house since I left Massachusetts; but I have a pleasant time. My life reminds me of a beautiful dream. What a difference between this and York! . . . I have met with some of the kindest treatment up here that I have ever received. . . . I have lectured three times this week. After I went from Limerick, I went to Springvale; there I spoke on Sunday night at an Anti-Slavery meeting. Some of the people are Anti-Slavery, Anti-rum and Anti-Catholic; and if you could see our Maine ladies,—some of them among the noblest types of womanhood you have ever seen! They are for putting men of Anti-Slavery principles in office, . . . to cleanse the corrupt fountains of our government by sending men to Congress who will plead for our down-trodden and oppressed brethren, our crushed and helpless sisters, whose tears and blood bedew our soil, whose chains are clanking 'neath our proudest banners, whose cries and groans amid our loudest paeans rise.

On Free Produce

[Temple, Maine
October 20, 1854]

I spoke on Free Produce, and now by the way I believe in that kind of

"*The Agent* . . .": Still, 787.
On Free Produce: Still, 788.

Abolition. Oh, it does seem to strike at one of the principal roots of the matter. I have commenced since I read Solomon Northrup. Oh, if Mrs. Stowe has clothed American slavery in the graceful garb of fiction, Solomon Northrup comes up from the dark habitation of Southern cruelty where slavery fattens and feasts on human blood with such mournful revelations that one might almost wish for the sake of humanity that the tales of horror which he reveals were not so. Oh, how can we pamper our appetites upon luxuries drawn from reluctant fingers? Oh, could slavery exist long if it did not sit on a commercial throne? I have read somewhere, if I remember aright, of a Hindoo being loth to cut a tree because being a believer in the transmigration of souls, he thought the soul of his father had passed into it. . . . Oh, friend, beneath the most delicate preparations of the cane can you not see the stinging lash and clotted whip? I have reason to be thankful that I am able to give a little more for a Free Labor dress, if it is coarser. I can thank God that upon its warp and woof I see no stain of blood and tears; that to procure a little finer muslin for my limbs no crushed and broken heart went out in sighs; and that from the field where it was raised went up no wild and startling cry unto the throne of God to witness there in language deep and strong, that in demanding that cotton I was nerving oppression's hand for deeds of guilt and crime. If the liberation of the slave demanded it, I could consent to part with a portion of the blood from my own veins if that would do him any good.

Breathing the Air of Freedom

Niagara Falls [New York]
September 12, 1856

My Dear Friend:—I have just returned from Canada to-day. I gave one lecture at Toronto, which was well attended. . . . Well, I have gazed for the first time upon Free Land! And would you believe it, tears sprang to my eyes, and I wept. Oh! it was a glorious sight to gaze for the first time on a land where a poor slave, flying from our glorious land of liberty(!), would in a moment find his fetters broken, his shackles loosed, and whatever he was in the land of Washington, beneath the shadow of Bunker Hill Monument, or even Plymouth Rock, *here* he becomes "a man and a brother."

I had gazed on Harper's Ferry, or rather the Rock at the Ferry, tower-

---

Breathing the Air of Freedom: This letter was included in the 1857 edition of *Poems on Miscellaneous Subjects.* Excerpts were reprinted in several works including Still's *The Underground Rail Road,* Child's *Freedman's Book,* and the *National Anti-Slavery Standard,* October 4, 1856.

ing up in simple grandeur with the gentle Potomac gliding peacefully by its feet, and felt that that was God's Masonry; and my soul had expanded in gazing on its sublimity. I had seen the Ocean, singing its wild chorus of sounding waves, and ecstacy had thrilled upon the living chords of my heart. I have since then seen the rainbow-crowned Niagara, girdled with grandeur, and robed with glory, chanting the choral hymn of Omnipotence, but none of the sights have melted me as the first sight of Free Land.

Towering mountains, lifting their hoary summits to catch the first faint flush of day when the sunbeams kiss the shadows from morning's drowsy face, may expand and exalt your soul. The first view of the ocean may fill you with strange ecstacy and delight. Niagara, the great, the glorious Niagara, may hush your spirit with its ceaseless thunder; it may charm you with its robe of crested spray and rainbow crown; but the land of Freedom has a lesson of deeper significance than foaming waves or towering mountains.

It carries the heart back to that heroic struggle for emancipation, in Great Britain, in which the great heart of the people throbbed for liberty, and the mighty pulse of the nation beat for freedom till nearly 800,000 men, women and children arose redeemed from bondage and freed from chains.

"Oh, How I Miss New England"

[April 1858]

Oh, how I miss New England,—the sunshine of its homes and the freedom of its hills! When I return again, I shall perhaps love it more dearly than ever. Do you know that two of the brightest, most sunshiny (is not that tautology?) years of my life, since I have reached womanhood, were spent in New England? Dear old New England! It was there kindness encompassed my path; it was there kind voices made their music in my ear. The home of my childhood, the burial-place of my kindred, is not as dear to me as New England.

Now let me tell you about Pennsylvania. I have been travelling nearly four years, and have been in every New England State, in New York, Canada and Ohio: but of all these places, this is about the meanest of all, as far as the treatment of colored people is concerned. I have been insulted·in several railroad cars. The other day, in attempting to ride in one of

---

"Oh, How I Miss New England": Liberator, April 23, 1858.

the city cars, after I had entered, the conductor came to me, and wanted me to go out on the platform. Now, was not that brave and noble? As a matter of course, I did not. Some one interfered, and asked or requested that I might be permitted to sit in a corner. I did not move, but kept the same seat. When I was about to leave, he refused my money, and I threw it down on the car floor, and got out, after I had ridden as far as I wished. Such impudence!

On the Carlisle road, I was interrupted and insulted several times. Two men came after me in one day.

I have met, of course, with kindness among individuals and families; all is not dark in Pennsylvania; but the shadow of slavery, oh how drearily it hangs!

"I Have a Right to Do My Share"

[Tiffin, Ohio
March 31, 1859]

I see by the Cincinnati papers that you have had an attempted rescue and a failure. That is sad! Can you not give me the particulars? and if there is anything that I can do for them in money or words, call upon me. This is a common cause; and if there is any burden to be borne in the Anti-Slavery cause—anything to be done to weaken our hateful chains or assert our manhood and womanhood, I have a right to do my share of the work. The humblest and feeblest of us can do something; and though I may be deficient in many of the conventionalisms of city life, and be considered as a person of good impulses, but unfinished, yet if there is common rough work to be done, call on me.

Miss Watkins and the Constitution

[April 1859(?)]

I never saw so clearly the nature and intent of the Constitution before. Oh, was it not strangely inconsistent that men fresh, so fresh, from the baptism of the Revolution should make such concessions to the foul spirit

---

"I Have a Right . . .": Still, 790.

Miss Watkins . . .: National Anti-Slavery Standard, April 9, 1859. This letter was published under the title "Miss Watkins and the Constitution," but no date or place is given. The prefatory paragraph is signed by "j" and indicates that the letter refers to "having read Wendell Phillips's Extracts from the Madison Papers."

of Despotism! that, when fresh from gaining their own liberty, they could permit the African slave trade—could let their national flag hang a sign of death on Guinea's coast and Congo's shore! Twenty-one years the slave-ships of the new Republic could gorge the sea monsters with their prey; twenty-one years of mourning and desolation for the children of the tropics, to gratify the avarice and cupidity of men styling themselves free! And then the dark intent of the fugitive clause veiled under words so specious that a stranger unacquainted with our nefarious government would not know that such a thing was meant by it. Alas for these fatal concessions. They remind me of the fabulous teeth sown by Cadmus—they rise, armed men, to smite. Is it a great mystery to you why these things are permitted? Wait, my brother, awhile; the end is not yet. The Psalmist was rather puzzled when he saw the wicked in power and spreading like a Bay tree; but how soon their end! Rest assured that, as nations and individuals, God will do right by us, and we should not ask of either God or man to do less than that. In the freedom of man's will I read the philosophy of his crimes, and the impossibility of his actions having a responsible moral character without it; and hence the continuance of slavery does not strike me as being so very mysterious.

To Mary Brown

Farmer Centre, Ohio
November 14, [1859]

My Dear Madam:—In an hour like this the common words of sympathy may seem like idle words, and yet I want to say something to you, the noble wife of the hero of the nineteenth century. Belonging to the race your dear husband reached forth his hand to assist, I need not tell you that my sympathies are with you. I thank you for the brave words you have spoken. A republic that produces such a wife and mother may hope for better days. Our heart may grow more hopeful for humanity when it sees the sublime sacrifice it is about to receive from his hands. Not in vain has your dear husband periled all, if the martyrdom of one hero is worth more than the life of a million cowards. From the prison comes forth a shout of triumph over that power whose ethics are robbery of the feeble and oppression of the weak, the trophies of whose chivalry are

---

To Mary Brown: Still, 791. In a footnote to this letter, Still writes, "Mrs. Harper passed two weeks with Mrs. [John] Brown at the house of the writer while she was awaiting the execution of her husband, and sympathized with her most deeply."

a plundered cradle and a scourged and bleeding woman. Dear sister, I thank you for the brave and noble words that you have spoken. Enclosed I send you a few dollars as a token of my gratitude, reverence and love.

Yours respectfully,
Frances Ellen Watkins

Post Office address: care of William Still, 107 Fifth St., Philadelphia, Penn.

May God, our own God, sustain you in the hour of trial. If there is one thing on earth I can do for you or yours, let me be apprized. I am at your service.

To John Brown

Kendalville, Indiana
November 25, [1859]

Dear Friend: Although the hands of Slavery throw a barrier between you and me, and it may not be my privilege to see you in your prison-house, Virginia has no bolts or bars through which I dread to send you my sympathy. In the name of the young girl sold from the warm clasp of a mother's arms to the clutches of a libertine or a profligate,—in the name of the slave mother, her heart rocked to and fro by the agony of her mournful separations,—I thank you, that you have been brave enough to reach out your hands to the crushed and blighted of my race. You have rocked the bloody Bastile; and I hope that from your sad fate great good may arise to the cause of freedom. Already from your prison has come a shout of triumph against the giant sin of our country. The hemlock is distilled with victory when it is pressed to the lips of Socrates. The Cross becomes a glorious ensign when Calvary's page-browed sufferer yields up his life upon it. And, if Universal Freedom is ever to be the dominant power of the land, your bodies may be only her first stepping stones to dominion. I would prefer to see Slavery go down peaceably by men breaking off their sins by righteousness and their iniquities by showing justice and mercy to the poor; but we cannot tell what the future may bring forth. God writes national judgments upon national sins; and what may be slumbering in the storehouse of divine justice we do not know. We may earnestly hope that your fate will not be a vain lesson, that it will intensify our hatred of Slavery and love of freedom, and that your martyr grave

---

To John Brown: Redpath, 418–19.

will be a sacred altar upon which men will record their vows of undying hatred to that system which tramples on man and bids defiance to God. I have written to your dear wife, and sent her a few dollars, and I pledge myself to you that I will continue to assist her. May the ever-blessed God shield you and your fellow-prisoners in the darkest hour. Send my sympathy to your fellow-prisoners; tell them to be of good courage; to seek a refuge in the Eternal God, and lean upon His everlasting arms for a sure support. If any of them, like you, have a wife or children that I can help, let them send me word.

"My Lungs Are Weak ... I Need Rest"

[December 9, 1859]

I am in Ohio now, and speaking on the Fugitive bill. Is it not shocking, the boldness of the slave-hunters since the triumph of the Slave Power in Northern Ohio—that wretched swapping affair? Did you see the account of a late arrest of a man to whom about 15 minutes' trial was given? Fifteen minutes to bid adieu to freedom, and then to be cast into the gaping jaws of American despotism! Oh, my friend, do you not sometimes feel almost heart-sickened? But you, in your mountain home, only hear of these things; what must it be to dwell in the midst of them? Now, will you write to me as soon as possible? I shall not long make any demands on your friendship; the doctor thinks my lungs are weak, and that I need rest more than medicine. That rest may soon be the unbroken slumber of the grave. Well, I hope that the Everlasting Arms will shield me forever from the guilt, the power and pollution of sin. There the mortal woe and sorrow may never surge against me, and these cries of wrong and suffering never enter, to wake up my soul and disturb me. Should I not be permitted to labor much longer, will you not remember my poor blighted and crushed people, and do what you can for them? Virginia has sacrificed that dear old man who laid his hands upon the bloody citadel of American slavery and shook the guilty fabric to its base; shall not, my dear friend, his blood be a fresh baptism of freedom, his grave a new altar where men may record more earnest vows against slavery? Shall it not intensify your hatred of slavery and deepen your love of freedom, and give you fresh vigor to battle for justice and right?

"My Lungs Are Weak ...": National Anti-Slavery Standard, January 14, 1860.

"Poor Doomed and Fated Men!"

[Montpelier, Vermont
December 12, 1859]

I thank you for complying with my request. (She had previously ordered a box of things to be forwarded to them.) And also that you wrote to them. You see Brown towered up so bravely that these doomed and fated men may have been almost overlooked, and just think that I am able to send one ray through the night around them. And as their letters came too late to answer in time, I am better satisfied that you wrote. I hope the things will reach them. Poor doomed and fated men! Why did you not send them more things? Please send me the bill of expense. . . . Send me word what I can do for the fugitives. Do you need any money? Do I not owe you on the old bill (pledge)? Look carefully and see if I have paid all. Along with this letter I send you one for Mr. Stephens (one of Brown's men), and would ask you to send him a box of nice things every week till he dies or is acquitted. I understand the balls have not been extracted from him. Has not this suffering been overshadowed by the glory that gathered around the brave old man? . . . Spare no expense to make the last hours of his (Stephens') life as bright as possible with sympathy. . . . Now, my friend, fulfill this to the letter. Oh, is it not a privilege, if you are sisterless and lonely, to be a sister to the human race, and to place your heart where it may throb close to down-trodden humanity?

"I Am Able to Give Something"

[1859(?)]

How fared the girl who came robed in male attire? Do write me every time you write how many come to your house; and, my dear friend, if you have that much in hand of mine from my books, will you please pay the Vigilance Committee two or three dollars for me to help carry on the glorious enterprise. Now, please do not write back that you are not going to do any such thing. Let me explain a few matters to you. In the first place, I am able to give something. In the second place, I am willing to do so. . . . Oh, life is fading away, and we have but an hour of time!

"*Poor Doomed and Fated Men!*": Still, 791–2.
"*I Am Able. . .*": Still, 792.

Should we not, therefore, endeavor to let its history gladden the earth? The nearer we ally ourselves to the wants and woes of humanity in the spirit of Christ, the closer we get to the great heart of God; the nearer we stand by the beating of the pulse of universal love.

An Appeal for the Philadelphia Rescuers

[June 1860]

Mr. Editor:—I saw in a late number of your paper an appeal from one of the Philadelphia rescuers, and I would ask through the columns of your paper if this appeal does not find a ready and hearty response in the bosom of every hater of American despotism? Shall these men throw themselves across the track of the general government and be crushed by that mo[n]strous Juggernaut of organized villainy, the Fugitive Slave Law, and we sit silent, with our hands folded, in selfish inactivity? It is not enough to express our sympathy by words; we should be ready to crystalize it into actions. I am not content with simply offering them pecuniary assistance from my limited resources; I would call on others to aid these men in their hour of trial. Let the day-laborer bring his offering, and our men of wealth be ready with their contributions. Let the hands of toil release their hold upon their hard-won earnings, feeling that there is no poverty like the poverty of meanness, no bankruptcy like that of a heart bankrupt in just, kind, and generous feelings.

Brethren and sisters of the East and West, will you not rally around these men? Their's is a common cause; they bear a common standard. Do not stop to cavil and find fault by saying they were rash and imprudent, and engaged in a hopeless contest. Their ears were quicker than ours; they heard the death-knell of freedom sound in the ears of a doomed and fated brother, and to them they were clarion sounds, rousing their souls to deeds of noble daring—trumpet tones, inciting them to brave and lofty actions.

And now shall these men stand alone? Are we not all ready to contribute means and money to defray the expences of their trial—not as a matter of charity, but as a memorial of their services and a token of our gratitude? And let me, in conclusion, ask our young men and maidens, our pastors and people, to unite in giving a tangible expression to their

---

An Appeal...: Weekly Anglo-African, June 23, 1860. The incident to which this letter refers is probably the capture of Moses Horner, a fugitive slave. A group of Philadelphians failed in their rescue attempt, and ten of the rescuers, nine blacks and one white, were jailed.

sympathy by sustaining these men, with the consciousness that it is a privilege to do the humblest deed for freedom.

"Thank God That Thou Hast Spoken"

[July 1860]

Was there not something grand in that masterly exposition of "The Barbarism of Slavery"? No softening down of *slave* States into *capital* States; no unholy and craven pledges, if the bondmen should attempt to break their chains, on which the rust of centuries has gathered, that he and Massachusetts stand ready to quench their aspirations by bayonets and blood; no singing in the guilty ears of the slave master that Carolina, with half, or more than half, of her children in chains, is more developed than Great Britain, whose air has so little affinity with our intense despotism that it melts every fetter and dissolves every chain; no brutal flings at the alleged inferiority of the negro; no insults to our feebleness. Again we may say, Thank God that he has spoken!

Thank God that thou hast spoken
Words earnest, true, and brave;
The lightning of thy lips has smote
The fetters of the slave.

I thought the shadows darkened
Round the pathway of the slave,
As one by one his faithful friends
Were dropping in the grave.

When other hands had faltered
And loosed their hold on life,
Thy words rang like a clarion
For Freedom's noble strife.

Thy words were not soft echoes,
Thy tones no syren song;
They fell as battle-axes
Upon our giant wrong.

God grant thy words of power
May fall as precious seeds,
That yet shall bud and blossom
In high and holy deeds.

Thank God That Thou Hast Spoken: National Anti-Slavery Standard, July 17, 1860. The poem is printed in the 1871 edition of *Poems* with the title "Lines to Charles Sumner."

Poetry

◆

Frances Harper's literary reputation has been greatly influenced by the popularity of particular poems such as "The Slave Mother," "Eliza Harris," and "Bury Me in a Free Land"; by her indefatigable efforts as an abolitionist; and by a general tendency to associate blacks and their literature with slavery. Along with spirituals and slave narratives, Harper's poems have been recognized as providing the most authentic renditions of the slaves' points of view available to nineteenth-century readers.

Harper's poetry, however, was never exclusively devoted to topics of race or slavery. She wrote, as the title of her most popular book proclaims, *Poems on Miscellaneous Subjects* (1854). There are in that volume, for example, as many poems that address issues of equal rights and moral values as there are that deal explicitly with slavery and race. This is true not only of *Poems on Miscellaneous Subjects,* but of the previously uncollected poems from her earliest period. Neither "The Soul" or "The Burial of Moses" is directly concerned with race and slavery, and "To Mrs. Harriet Beecher Stowe" may be read as easily as a tribute to an advocate for righteousness as an abolitionist poem.

Generally, Harper's poetic innovations were in the particular interpretations that she gave to familiar subject matter. She was well within the popular currents of her time when she used Judeo-Christian and Greco-Roman mythology for subject matter. And her use of literature as a means of moving people to more socially responsible actions and more lofty spiritual pursuits was also in keeping with the literature of her times. Harper favored the lyrical ballad; that is, she generally wrote short narrative poems designed to evoke tender feelings. Many of her poems are in the familiar four-verse stanza with rhyme schemes of ABCB and ABAB.

Poems on Miscellaneous Subjects (1854)

In *The Underground Rail Road*, William Still said that Harper had put together a volume while she was teaching in York, Pennsylvania, and that her attempts to publish it when she moved to Philadelphia were frustrated because being "a young and homeless maiden" made it difficult for her to garner sufficient support. This was probably the work that was published in 1854 in both Boston and Philadelphia that we now know as *Poems on Miscellaneous Subjects*. The *National Union Catalog* describes the Boston edition as a forty-page volume of poetry and prose printed by J. B. Yerrinton & Son. The Philadelphia publication may have been a little later because it is a fifty-six page volume. The next year both versions were reprinted in Boston and in Philadelphia. The 1855 Philadelphia publication is labeled as "2nd series." By 1857 the title page bore the legend "tenth thousand." New printings of the 1857 version appeared regularly, with the 1871 printing designated as the twentieth edition.

Twenty-six of the thirty-six poems written by Harper between 1853 and 1864 that are extant were collected in the various editions of her one volume from this period, *Poems on Miscellaneous Subjects*. Antislavery poems comprise about a third of that book. Some, such as "The Slave Mother," "The Slave Auction," and "Eliza Harris," are subtle variations upon standard abolitionist topics. Others, such as "A Mother's Heroism" and "The Tennessee Hero," celebrate more radical acts of defiance. A common thread is the emphasis upon acts of ordinary individuals whose integrity and conviction give them the strength and courage they need to perform heroically in the face of evil.

Heroic women dominate the poems in this collection. Their faith and the urgency of their causes enable these women to demonstrate outstanding ability and strength. "The Syrophenician Woman" retells Mark 7:26–29 and Matthew 15:22–38; however, Watkins' version depicts a more complex woman than that portrayed in either of her sources. Moved to an articulate assertiveness by her determination to save her dying child, the character's cogent argument convinces an astonished Christ to grant her request. "Eliza Harris" is based upon the *Uncle Tom's Cabin* incident, but in this version Eliza is so emboldened by her determination that her child be free that she will not only cross a frozen river but brave "poverty, danger and death" to maintain that freedom.

◆

The Soul

Bring forth the balance, let the weight be gold!
We'd know the worth of a deathless soul;
Bring rubies and gems from every mine,
With the wealth of ocean, land and clime.

Bring the joys of the green, green earth,
Its playful smiles and careless mirth;
The dews of youth and flushes of health—
Bring! Oh, bring! the wide world's wealth.

Bring the rich, rare pearls of thought
From the depths of knowledge brought,
All that human ken may know,
Searching earth and heaven o'er.

Bring the fairest rolls of fame—
Rolls unwritten with a deed of shame;
Honor's guerdon, victory's crown,
Robes of pride, wreaths of renown.

We've brought the wealth of ev'ry mine,
We've ransacked ocean, land and clime,
And caught the joyous smiles away,
From the prattling babe to the sire gray.

We've wrought the names of the noble dead,
With those who in their footsteps tread,
Here are wreaths of pride and gems of thought,
From the battle-field and study brought.

Heap high the gems, pile up the gold,
For heavy's the weight of a deathless soul—
Make room for all the wealth of earth,
Its honors, joys, and careless mirth.

Leave me a niche for the rolls of fame—
Oh, precious, indeed, is a spotless name,

The Soul: Payne, 302. According to Payne, "The Soul" was published in the *Christian Recorder* in 1853.

For the robes, the wreaths, and gems of thought,
Let an empty space in the scales be sought.

With care we've adjusted balance and scale,
Futile our efforts we've seen them fail;
Lighter than dust is the wealth of earth,
Weighed in the scales with immortal worth.

Could we drag the sun from his golden car,
To lay in this balance with ev'ry star,
'Twould darken the day and obscure the night—
But the weight of the balance would still be light.

To Mrs. Harriet Beecher Stowe

I thank thee for thy pleading
  For the helpless of our race
Long as our hearts are beating
  In them thou hast a place.

I thank thee for thy pleading
  For the fetter'd and the dumb
The blessing of the perishing
  Around thy path shall come.

I thank thee for the kindly words
  That grac'd thy pen of fire,
And thrilled upon the living chords
  Of many a heart's deep lyre.

For the sisters of our race
  Thou'st nobly done thy part
Thou hast won thy self a place
  In every human heart.

The halo that surrounds thy name
  Hath reached from shore to shore
But thy best and brightest fame
  Is the blessing of the poor.

To Mrs. Harriet Beecher Stowe: Frederick Douglass' Paper, February 3, 1854. This is one of three extant poems written by Harper in response to *Uncle Tom's Cabin.*

The Syrophenician Woman

Joy to my bosom! rest to my fear!
Judea's prophet draweth near!
Joy to my bosom! peace to my heart!
Sickness and sorrow before him depart!

Rack'd with agony and pain,
Writhing, long my child has lain;
Now the prophet draweth near,
All our griefs shall disappear.

"Lord!" she cried with mournful breath,
"Save! Oh, save my child from death!"
But as though she was unheard,
Jesus answered not a word.

With a purpose nought could move,
And the zeal of woman's love,
Down she knelt in anguish wild—
"Master! save, Oh! save my child!"

" 'Tis not meet," the Saviour said,
"Thus to waste the children's bread;
I am only sent to seek
Israel's lost and scattered sheep."

"True," she said, "Oh gracious Lord!
True and faithful is thy word:
But the humblest, meanest, may
Eat the crumbs they cast away."

"Woman," said th' astonish'd Lord,
"Be it even as thy word!
By thy faith that knows no fail,
Thou hast ask'd, and shalt prevail."

The Slave Mother

Heard you that shriek? It rose
  So wildly on the air,

The Syrophenician Woman and the following eighteen poems (pages 58–76) represent
the entire poetry section of *Poems on Miscellaneous Subjects* (Boston: J. B. Yerrinton and
Son, 1854). They are reprinted here in the order in which they appear in that volume.

It seemed as if a burden'd heart
  Was breaking in despair.

Saw you those hands so sadly clasped—
  The bowed and feeble head—
The shuddering of that fragile form—
  That look of grief and dread?

Saw you the sad, imploring eye?
  Its every glance was pain,
As if a storm of agony
  Were sweeping through the brain.

She is a mother, pale with fear,
  Her boy clings to her side,
And in her kirtle vainly tries
  His trembling form to hide.

He is not hers, although she bore
  For him a mother's pains;
He is not hers, although her blood
  Is coursing through his veins!

He is not hers, for cruel hands
  May rudely tear apart
The only wreath of household love
  That binds her breaking heart.

His love has been a joyous light
  That o'er her pathway smiled,
A fountain gushing ever new,
  Amid life's desert wild.

His lightest word has been a tone
  Of music round her heart,
Their lives a streamlet blent in one—
  Oh, Father! must they part?

They tear him from her circling arms,
  Her last and fond embrace.
Oh! never more may her sad eyes
  Gaze on his mournful face.

No marvel, then, these bitter shrieks
  Disturb the listening air:
She is a mother, and her heart
  Is breaking in despair.

Bible Defence of Slavery

Take sackcloth of the darkest dye,
  And shroud the pulpits round!
Servants of Him that cannot lie,
  Sit mourning on the ground.

Let holy horror blanch each cheek,
  Pale every brow with fears:
And rocks and stones, if ye could speak,
  Ye well might melt to tears!

Let sorrow breathe in every tone,
  In every strain ye raise;
Insult not God's majestic throne
  With th' mockery of praise.

A "reverend" man, whose light should be
  The guide of age and youth,
Brings to the shrine of Slavery
  The sacrifice of truth!

For the direst wrong by man imposed,
  Since Sodom's fearful cry,
The word of life has been unclosed,
  To give your God the lie.

Oh! when ye pray for heathen lands,
  And plead for their dark shores,
Remember Slavery's cruel hands
  Make heathens at your doors!

Eliza Harris

Like a fawn from the arrow, startled and wild,
A woman swept by us, bearing a child;
In her eye was the night of a settled despair,
And her brow was o'ershaded with anguish and care.

Eliza Harris: Versions of this poem appeared in *The Liberator*, December 16, 1853; and in *Frederick Douglass' Paper*, December 23, 1853. There are references that cite an even earlier publication in the *Aliened American*. Stanzas 11 and 12, reprinted here from *The Liberator*, were included in the early versions but not in *Poems on Miscellaneous Subjects*. Both *The Liberator* and *Frederick Douglass' Paper* reprinted "Eliza Harris" in 1860.

She was nearing the river—in reaching the brink,
She heeded no danger, she paused not to think!
For she is a mother—her child is a slave—
And she'll give him his freedom, or find him a grave!

It was a vision to haunt us, that innocent face—
So pale in its aspect, so fair in its grace;
As the tramp of the horse and the bay of the hound,
With the fetters that gall, were trailing the ground!

She was nerv'd by despair, and strengthened by woe,
As she leap'd o'er the chasms that yawn'd from below;
Death howl'd in the tempest, and rav'd in the blast,
But she heard not the sound till the danger was past.

Oh! how shall I speak of my proud country's shame?
Of the stains on her glory, how give them their name?
How say that her banner in mockery waves—
Her "star spangled banner"—o'er millions of slaves?

How say that the lawless may torture and chase
A woman whose crime is the hue of her face?
How the depths of the forest may echo around
With the shrieks of despair, and the bay of the hound?

With her step on the ice, and her arm on her child,
The danger was fearful, the pathway was wild;
But, aided by Heaven, she gained a free shore,
Where the friends of humanity open'd their door.

So fragile and lovely, so fearfully pale,
Like a lily that bends to the breath of the gale,
Save the heave of her breast, and the sway of her hair,
You'd have thought her a statue of fear and despair.

In agony close to her bosom she press'd
The life of her heart, the child of her breast:—
Oh! love from its tenderness gathering might,
Had strengthen'd her soul for the dangers of flight.

But she's free—yes, free from the land where the slave
From the hand of oppression must rest in the grave;
Where bondage and torture, where scourges and chains,
Have plac'd on our banner indelible stains.

Did a fever e'er burning through bosom and brain,
Send a lava-like flood through every vein,

Till it suddenly cooled 'neath a healing spell,
And you knew, oh! the joy! you knew you were well?

So felt this young mother, as a sense of the rest
Stole gently and sweetly o'er *her* weary breast,
As her boy looked up, and, wondering, smiled
On the mother whose love had freed her child.

The bloodhounds have miss'd the scent of her way;
The hunter is rifled and foil'd of his prey;
Fierce jargon and cursing, with clanking of chains,
Make sounds of strange discord on Liberty's plains.

With the rapture love and fulness of bliss,
She plac'd on his brow a mother's fond kiss:—
Oh! poverty, danger and death she can brave,
For the child of her love is no longer a slave!

Ethiopia

Yes! Ethiopia yet shall stretch
    Her bleeding hands abroad;
Her cry of agony shall reach
    The burning throne of God.

The tyrant's yoke from off her neck,
    His fetters from her soul,
The mighty hand of God shall break,
    And spurn the base control.

Redeemed from dust and freed from chains,
    Her sons shall lift their eyes;
From cloud-capt hills and verdant plains
    Shall shouts of triumph rise.

Upon her dark, despairing brow,
    Shall play a smile of peace;
For God shall bend unto her wo,
    And bid her sorrows cease.

'Neath sheltering vines and stately palms
    Shall laughing children play,

Ethiopia: If Kletzing and Crogman are correct, "Ethiopia" was published before 1853 and is Harper's earliest extant poem. The poem appears also in *Frederick Douglass' Paper*, March 31, 1854.

And aged sires with joyous psalms
  Shall gladden every day.

Secure by night, and blest by day,
  Shall pass her happy hours;
Nor human tigers hunt for prey
  Within her peaceful bowers.

Then, Ethiopia! stretch, oh! stretch
  Thy bleeding hands abroad;
Thy cry of agony shall reach
  And find redress from God.

The Drunkard's Child

He stood beside his dying child,
  With a dim and bloodshot eye;
They'd won him from the haunts of vice
  To see his first-born die.
He came with a slow and staggering tread,
  A vague, unmeaning stare,
And, reeling, clasped the clammy hand,
  So deathly pale and fair.

In a dark and gloomy chamber,
  Life ebbing fast away,
On a coarse and wretched pallet,
  The dying sufferer lay:
A smile of recognition
  Lit up the glazing eye;
"I'm very glad," it seemed to say,
  "You've come to see me die."

That smile reached to his callous heart,
  Its sealéd fountains stirred;
He tried to speak, but on his lips
  Faltered and died each word.
And burning tears like rain
  Poured down his bloated face;
Where guilt, remorse and shame
  Had scathed, and left their trace.

"My father!" said the dying child,
  (His voice was faint and low,)

"Oh! clasp me closely to your heart,
  And kiss me ere I go.
Bright angels beckon me away,
  To the holy city fair—
Oh! tell me, father, ere I go,
  Say, will you meet me there?"

He clasped him to his throbbing heart,
  "I will! I will!" he said;
His pleading ceased—the father held
  His first-born and his dead!
The marble brow, with golden curls,
  Lay lifeless on his breast;
Like sunbeams on the distant clouds
  Which line the gorgeous west.

The Slave Auction

The sale began—young girls were there,
  Defenceless in their wretchedness,
Whose stifled sobs of deep despair
  Revealed their anguish and distress.

And mothers stood with streaming eyes,
  And saw their dearest children sold;
Unheeded rose their bitter cries,
  While tyrants bartered them for gold.

And woman, with her love and truth—
  For these in sable forms may dwell—
Gaz'd on the husband of her youth,
  With anguish none may paint or tell.

And men, whose sole crime was their hue,
  The impress of their Maker's hand,
And frail and shrinking children, too,
  Were gathered in that mournful band.

Ye who have laid your love to rest,
  And wept above their lifeless clay,
Know not the anguish of that breast,
  Whose lov'd are rudely torn away.

Ye may not know how desolate
  Are bosoms rudely forced to part,
And how a dull and heavy weight
  Will press the life-drops from the heart.

The Revel

"He knoweth not that the dead are there."

In yonder halls reclining
  Are forms surpassing fair,
And brilliant lights are shining,
  But, oh! the dead are there!

There's music, song and dance,
  There's banishment of care,
And mirth in every glance,
  But, oh! the dead are there!

The wine cup's sparkling glow
  Blends with the viands rare,
There's revelry and show,
  But still, the dead are there!

'Neath that flow of song and mirth
  Runs the current of despair,
But the simple sons of earth
  Know not the dead are there!

They'll shudder start and tremble,
  They'll weep in wild despair,
When the solemn truth breaks on them,
  That the dead, the dead are there!

That Blessed Hope

Oh! crush it not, that hope so blest,
  Which cheers the fainting heart,
And points it to the coming rest,
  Where sorrow has no part.

Tear from my heart each worldly prop,
  Unbind each earthly string,
But to this blest and glorious hope,
  Oh! let my spirit cling.

It cheer'd amid the days of old
  Each holy patriarch's breast;
It was an anchor to their souls,
  Upon it let me rest.

When wandering in dens and caves,
  In sheep and goat skins dress'd,
A peel'd and scatter'd people learned
  To know this hope was blest.

Help me, amidst this world of strife,
  To long for Christ to reign,
That when He brings the crown of life,
  I may that crown obtain!

The Dying Christian

The light was faintly streaming
  Within a darkened room,
Where a woman, faint and feeble,
  Was sinking to the tomb.

The silver cord was loosened,
  We knew that she must die;
We read the mournful token
  In the dimness of her eye.

We read it in the radiance
  That lit her pallid cheek,
And the quivering of the feeble lip,
  Too faint its joys to speak.

Like a child oppressed with slumber,
  She calmly sank to rest,
With her trust in her Redeemer,
  And her head upon His breast.

The Dying Christian: According to Payne, this poem also appeared in *The Christian Recorder* in 1853:

She faded from our vision,
   Like a thing of love and light;
But we feel she lives for ever,
   A spirit pure and bright.

Report

I heard, my young friend,
   You were seeking a wife,
A woman to make
   Your companion for life.

Now, if you are seeking
   A wife for your youth,
Let this be your aim, then—
   Seek a woman of truth.

She may not have talents,
   With greatness combined,
Her gifts may be humble,
   Of person and mind:

But if she be constant,
   And gentle, and true,
Believe me my friend,
   She's the woman for you!

Oh! wed not for beauty,
   Though fair is the prize;
It may pall when you grasp it,
   And fade in your eyes.

Let gold not allure you,
   Let wealth not attract;
With a house full of treasure,
   A woman may lack.

Let her habits be frugal,
   Her hands not afraid
To work in her household
   Or follow her trade.

Let her language be modest,
   Her actions discreet;

Her manners refined,
    And free from deceit.

Now if such you should find,
    In your journey through life,
Just open your mind,
    And make her your wife.

Advice to the Girls

Nay, do not blush! I only heard
    You had a mind to marry;
I thought I'd speak a friendly word,
    So just one moment tarry.

Wed not a man whose merit lies
    In things of outward show,
In raven hair or flashing eyes,
    That please your fancy so.

But marry one who's good and kind,
    And free from all pretence;
Who, if without a gifted mind,
    At least has common sense.

Saved by Faith

"She said, if I may but touch his clothes, I shall be
whole."

Life to her no brightness brought,
    Pale and striken was her brow,
Till a bright and joyous thought
    Lit the darkness of her woe.

Long had sickness on her preyed,
    Strength from every nerve had gone;
Skill and art could give no aid:
    Thus her weary life passed on.

Saved by Faith: Based on an incident described in Matthew 9:20–22 and Luke 8:43–48.

Like a sad and mournful dream,
   Daily felt she life depart,
Hourly knew the vital stream
   Left the fountain of her heart.

He who lull'd the storm to rest,
   Cleans'd the lepers, raised the dead,
Whilst a crowd around him press'd,
   Near that suffering one did tread.

Nerv'd by blended hope and fear,
   Reasoned thus her anxious heart;
"If to touch him I draw near,
   All my suffering shall depart.

"While the crowd around him stand,
   I will touch," the sufferer said;
Forth she reached her timid hand—
   As she touched her sickness fled.

"Who hath touched me?" Jesus cried;
   "Virtue from my body's gone."
From the crowd a voice replied,
   "Why inquire in such a throng?"

Faint with fear through every limb,
   Yet too grateful to deny,
Tremblingly she knelt to him,
   "Lord!" she answered, "it was I!"

Kindly, gently, Jesus said—
   Words like balm unto her soul—
"Peace upon thy life be shed!
   Child! thy faith has made thee whole!"

Died of Starvation

They forced him into prison,
   Because he begged for bread;
"My wife is starving—dying!"
   In vain the poor man plead.

Died of Starvation: Reprinted in the *Provincial Freeman*, March 7, 1857. When printed in *Poems on Miscellaneous Subjects* (1854), it bore the following footnote: "See this case, as touchingly related, in 'Oliver Twist,' by [Charles] Dickens."

They forced him into prison,
  Strong bars enclosed the walls,
While the rich and proud were feasting
  Within their sumptuous halls.

He'd striven long with anguish,
  Had wrestled with despair;
But his weary heart was breaking
  'Neath its crushing load of care.

And he prayed them in that prison,
  "Oh, let me seek my wife!"
For he knew that want was feeding
  On the remnant of her life.

That night his wife lay moaning
  Upon her bed in pain;
Hunger gnawing at her vitals,
  Fever scorching through her brain.

She wondered at his tarrying,
  He was not wont to stay;
'Mid hunger, pain and watching,
  The moments waned away.

Sadly crouching by the embers,
  Her famished children lay;
And she longed to gaze upon them,
  As her spirit passed away.

But the embers were too feeble,
  She could not see each face,
So she clasped her arms around them—
  'Twas their mother's last embrace.

They loosed him from his prison,
  As a felon from his chain;
Though his strength was hunger bitten,
  He sought his home again.

Just as her spirit linger'd
  On Time's receding shore,
She heard his welcome footstep
  On the threshold of the door.

He was faint and spirit-broken,
  But, rousing from despair,

He clasped her icy fingers,
　　As she breathed her dying prayer.

With a gentle smile and blessing,
　　Her spirit winged its flight,
As the morn, in all its glory,
　　Bathed the world in dazzling light.

There was weeping, bitter weeping,
　　In the chamber of the dead,
For well the striken husband knew
　　She had died for want of bread.

A Mother's Heroism

When the noble mother of Lovejoy heard of her son's death, she said, "It is well! I had rather he should die so than desert his principles."

The murmurs of a distant strife
　　Fell on a mother's ear;
Her son had yielded up his life,
　　Mid scenes of wrath and fear.

They told her how he'd spent his breath
　　In pleading for the dumb,
And how the glorious martyr wreath
　　Her child had nobly won.

They told her of his courage high,
　　Mid brutal force and might;
How he had nerved himself to die,
　　In battling for the right.

It seemed as if a fearful storm
　　Swept wildly round her soul;
A moment, and her fragile form
　　Bent 'neath its fierce control.

From lip and brow the color fled—
　　But light flashed to her eye:

A *Mother's Heroism*: Refers to Elizabeth Pattee Lovejoy, the mother of Elijah Parish Lovejoy, the abolitionist editor of the *Alton Observer*, whose refusal to modify his editorials led to his murder in 1837.

" 'T is well! 't is well!" the mother said,
 "That thus my child should die.

" 'T is well that, to his latest breath,
 He plead for liberty;
Truth nerved him for the hour of death,
 And taught him how to die.

"It taught him how to cast aside
 Earth's honors and renown;
To trample on her fame and pride,
 And win a martyr's crown."

The Fugitive's Wife

It was my sad and weary lot
 To toil in slavery;
But one thing cheered my lowly cot—
 My husband was with me.

One evening, as our children played
 Around our cabin door,
I noticed on his brow a shade
 I'd never seen before;

And in his eyes a gloomy night
 Of anguish and despair;—
I gazed upon their troubled light,
 To read the meaning there.

He strained me to his heaving heart—
 My own beat wild with fear;
I knew not, but I sadly felt
 There must be evil near.

He vainly strove to cast aside
 The tears that fell like rain:—
Too frail, indeed, is manly pride,
 To strive with grief and pain.

Again he clasped me to his breast,
 And said that we must part:
I tried to speak— but, oh! it seemed
 An arrow reached my heart.

"Bear not," I cried, "unto your grave,
  The yoke you've borne from birth;
No longer live a helpless slave,
  The meanest thing on earth!"

The Contrast

They scorned her for her sinning,
  Spoke harshly of her fall,
Nor lent the hand of mercy
  To break her hated thrall.

The dews of meek repentance
  Stood in her downcast eye:
Would no one heed her anguish?
  All pass her coldly by?

From the cold, averted glances
  Of each reproachful eye,
She turned aside, heart-broken,
  And laid her down to die.

And where was he, who sullied
  Her once unspotted name;
Who lured her from life's brightness
  To agony and shame?

Who left her on life's billows,
  A wrecked and ruined thing;
Who brought the winter of despair
  Upon Hope's blooming spring?

Through the halls of wealth and fashion,
  In gaiety and pride,
He was leading to the altar
  A fair and lovely bride!

None scorned him for his sinning,
  Few saw it through his gold;
His crimes were only foibles,
  And these were gently told.

* * *

Before him rose a vision,
  A maid of beauty rare;
Then a pale, heart-broken woman,
  The image of despair.

Next came a sad procession,
  With many a sob and tear;
A widow'd, childless mother
  Totter'd by an humble bier.

The vision quickly faded,
  The sad, unwelcome sight;
But his lip forgot its laughter,
  And his eye its careless light.

A moment, and the flood-gates
  Of memory opened wide;
And remorseful recollection
  Flowed like a lava tide.

That widow's wail of anguish
  Seemed strangely blending there,
And mid the soft lights floated
  That image of despair.

The Prodigal's Return

He came—a wanderer; years of sin
  Had blanched his blooming cheek,
Telling a tale of strife within,
  That words might vainly speak.

His feet were bare, his garments torn,
  His brow was deathly white;
His heart was bleeding, crushed and worn,
  His soul had felt a blight.

His father saw him; pity swept
  And yearn'd through every vein;
He ran and clasp'd his child, and wept,
  Murm'ring, "He lives again!"

The Prodigal's Return: Based upon Luke 15:20–24.

"Father, I've come, but not to claim
　　Aught from thy love or grace;
I come, a child of guilt and shame,
　　To beg a servant's place."

"Enough! enough!" the father said,
　　"Bring robes of princely cost!"—
The past with all its shadows fled,
　　For now was found the lost.

"Put shoes upon my poor child's feet,
　　With rings his hand adorn,
And bid my house his coming greet
　　With music, dance and song."

Oh! Saviour, mid this world of strife,
　　When wayward here we roam,
Conduct us to the paths of life,
　　And guide us safely home.

Then in thy holy courts above,
　　Thy praise our lips shall sound,
While angels join our song of love,
　　That we, the lost are found!

Eva's Farewell

Farewell, father! I am dying,
　　Going to the "glory land,"
Where the sun is ever shining,
　　And the zephyr's ever bland.

Where the living fountains flowing,
　　Quench the pining spirit's thirst;
Where the tree of life is growing,
　　Where the crystal fountains burst.

Father! hear that music holy
　　Floating from the spirit land!
At the pearly gates of glory,
　　Radiant angels waiting stand.

Eva's Farewell: Also appeared in *Frederick Douglass' Paper*, March 31, 1854.

Father! kiss your dearest Eva,
    Press her cold and clammy hand,
Ere the glittering hosts receive her,
    Welcome to their cherub band.

Be Active

Onward, onward, sons of freedom,
    In the great and glorious strife;
You've a high and holy mission
    On the battle field of life.

See oppression's feet of iron
    Grind a brother to the ground
And from bleeding heart and bosom,
    Gapeth many a fearful wound.

Sit not down with idle pity,
    Gazing on his mighty wrong;
Hurl the bloated tyrant from him—
    Say my brother, oh, be strong!

See that sad, despairing mother
    Clasp her burning brow in pain;
Lay your hand upon her fetters—
    Rend, oh! rend her galling chain!

Here's a pale and trembling maiden,
    Brutal arms around her thrown;
Christian father, save, oh! save her,
    By the love you bear your own!

Yearly lay a hundred thousand
    New-born babes on Moloch's shrine;
Crush these gory, reeking altars—
    Christians, let this work be thine.

Where the Southern roses blossom,
    Weary lives go out in pain;
Dragging to death's shadowy portals,
    Slavery's heavy galling chain,

Be Active: *Frederick Douglass' Paper*, January 11, 1856 and *Weekly Anglo-African*, July 30, 1859.

Men of every clime and nation,
    Every faith, and sect, and creed,
Lay aside your idle jangling,
    Come and staunch the wounds that bleed.

On my people's blighted bosom,
    Mountain weights of sorrow lay;
Stop not now to ask the question,
    Who shall roll the stone away?

Set to work the moral forces,
    That are yours of church and state;
Teach them how to war and battle
    'Gainst oppression, wrong, and hate.

Oh! be faithful! Oh! be valiant,
    Trusting not in human might;
Know that in the darkest conflict,
    God is on the side of right!

The Burial of Moses

And He buried him in a valley in the land of Moab,
over against Bethpeor; but no man knoweth of his
sepulchre unto this day."

                                        Deut. xxxiv.6.

By Nebo a lonely mountain,
    On this side Jordan's wave,
In a vale in the land of Moab
    There lies a lonely grave.
And no man dug that sepulchre,
    And no man saw it e'er;
For the angels of God upturned the sod,
    And laid the dead man there.

That was the grandest funeral
    That ever passed on earth,
But no man heard the trampling
    Or saw the train go forth.

The Burial of Moses: Provincial Freeman, May 24, 1856.

Noiselessly as the daylight
  Comes when the night is done,
And the crimson streak on ocean's cheek
  Grows into the great sun.

Noiselessly as the springtime
  Her crown of verdure weaves,
And all the trees on all the hills
  Open their thousand leaves:
So, without sound of music,
  Or voice of them that wept,
Silently down from the mountain's crown
  The great procession swept.

Perchance the bald old eagle,
  On grey Bethpeor's height,
Out of his rocky eirie
  Looked on the wondrous sight.
Perchance the lion stalking
  Still shuns that hallow'd spot:
For best [sic] and birds have seen and heard
  That which man knoweth not.

But when the warrior dieth,
  His comrades in the war,
With arms reversed and muffled drum,
  Follow the funeral car.
They show the banners taken,
  They tell his battles won,
And after him lead his masterless steed,
  While peals the minute gun.

Amid the noblest of the land
  Men lay the sage to rest,
And give the bard an honour'd place
  With costly marble drest
In the great minster transept,
  Where lights like glories fall,
And the sweet choir sings, and the organ rings
  Along the emblazoned wall.

This was the bravest warrior
  That ever buckled sword;
This the most gifted Poet
  That ever breath'd a word;

And never earth's philosopher
  Traced with his golden pen
On the deathless page truths half so sage
  As he wrote down for men.

And had he not high honour?
  The hill-side for his pall,
To lie in state while angels wait
  With stars for tapers tall,
And the dark rock pines like tossing plumes
  Over his bier to wave,
And God's own hand in that lonely land
  To lay him in the grave.

In that deep grave without a name,
  Whence his uncoffin'd clay
Shall break again, most wondrous thought
  Before the Judgment Day;
And stand with glory wrapped around
  On the hills he never trod,
And speak of the strife that won our life
  With th' Incarnate Son of God.

O lonely tomb in Moab's land,
  O dark Bethpeor' hill,
Speak to these curious hearts of ours,
  And teach them to be still.
God hath his mysteries of grace,
  Ways that we cannot tell;
He hides them deep like the secret sleep
  Of him He loved so well.

The Tennessee Hero

"He had heard his comrades plotting to obtain their
liberty, and rather than betray them he received 750
lashes and died."

He stood before the savage throng,
  The base and coward crew;

The Tennessee Hero: This and the following six poems were added to *Poems on Miscellaneous Subjects* in the 1857 edition (Philadelphia: Merrihew and Thompson).

A tameless light flashed from his eye,
  His heart beat firm and true.

He was the hero of his band,
  The noblest of them all;
Though fetters galled his weary limbs,
  His spirit spurned their thrall.

And towered, in its manly might,
  Above the murderous crew.
Oh! liberty had nerved his heart,
  And every pulse beat true.

"Now tell us," said the savage troop,
  "And life thy gain shall be!
Who are the men that plotting, say—
  'They must and will be free!' "

Oh, could you have seen the hero then,
  As his lofty soul arose,
And his dauntless eyes defiance flashed
  On his mean and craven foes!

"I know the men who would be free;
  They are the heroes of your land;
But death and torture I defy,
  Ere I betray that band.

And what! oh, what is life to me,
  Beneath your base control?
Nay! do your worst. Ye have no chains
  To bind my free-born soul."

They brought the hateful lash and scourge,
  With murder in each eye.
But a solemn vow was on his lips—
  He had resolved to die.

Yes, rather than betray his trust,
  He'd meet a death of pain;
'T was sweeter far to meet it thus
  Than wear a treason stain!

Like storms of wrath, of hate and pain,
  The blows rained thick and fast;

But the monarch soul kept true
  Till the gates of life were past.

And the martyr spirit fled
  To the throne of God on high,
And showed his gaping wounds
  Before the unslumbering eye.

Free Labor

I wear an easy garment,
  O'er it no toiling slave
Wept tears of hopeless anguish,
  In his passage to the grave.

And from its ample folds
  Shall rise no cry to God,
Upon its warp and woof shall be
  No stain of tears and blood.

Oh, lightly shall it press my form,
  Unladened with a sigh,
I shall not 'mid its rustling hear,
  Some sad despairing cry.

This fabric is too light to bear
  The weight of bondsmen's tears,
I shall not in its texture trace
  The agony of years.

Too light to bear a smother'd sigh,
  From some lorn woman's heart,
Whose only wreath of household love
  Is rudely torn apart.

Then lightly shall it press my form,
  Unburden'd by a sigh;
And from its seams and folds shall rise,
  No voice to pierce the sky,

And witness at the throne of God,
  In language deep and strong,
That I have nerv'd Oppression's hand,
  For deeds of guilt and wrong.

Lines

At the Portals of the Future,
  Full of madness, guilt and gloom,
Stood the hateful form of Slavery,
  Crying, Give, Oh! give me room—

Room to smite the earth with cursing,
  Room to scatter, rend and slay,
From the trembling mother's bosom
  Room to tear her child away;

Room to trample on the manhood
  Of the country far and wide;
Room to spread o'er every Eden
  Slavery's scorching lava-tide

Pale and trembling stood the Future,
  Quailing 'neath his frown of hate,
As he grasped with bloody clutches
  The great keys of Doom and Fate.

In his hand he held a banner
  All festooned with blood and tears:
'Twas a fearful ensign, woven
  With the grief and wrong of years.

On his brow he wore a helmet
  Decked with strange and cruel art;
Every jewel was a life-drop
  Wrung from some poor broken heart.

Though her cheek was pale and anxious,
  Yet, with look and brow sublime,
By the pale and trembling Future
  Stood the Crisis of our time.

And from many a throbbing bosom
  Came the words in fear and gloom,
Tell us, Oh! thou coming Crisis,
  What shall be our country's doom?

Shall the wings of dark destruction
  Brood and hover o'er our land,

Lines: Also appeared in *National Anti-Slavery Standard*, November 29, 1856.

Till we trace the steps of ruin
  By their blight, from strand to strand?

With a look and voice prophetic
  Spake the solemn Crisis then:
I have only mapped the future
  For the erring sons of men.

If ye strive for Truth and Justice,
  If ye battle for the Right,
Ye shall lay your hands all strengthened
  On God's robe of love and light;

But if ye trample on His children,
  To his ear will float each groan,
Jar the cords that bind them to Him,
  And they'll vibrate at his throne.

And the land that forges fetters,
  Binds the weak and poor in chains,
Must in blood or tears of sorrow
  Wash away her guilty stains.

The Dismissal of Tyng

"We have but three words to say, 'served him right.' "

Church Journal (Episcopa[l])]

Served him right! How could he dare
  To touch the idol of our day?
What if its shrine be red with blood?
  Why, let him turn his eyes away.

Who dares dispute our right to bind
  With galling chains the weak and poor?
To starve and crush the deathless mind,
  Or hunt the slave from door to door?

Who dares dispute our right to sell
  The mother from her weeping child?

The Dismissal of Tyng: Also appeared in *National Anti-Slavery Standard*, November 29, 1856, and *Frederick Douglass' Paper*, December 5, 1856.

To hush with ruthless stripes and blows
　Her shrieks and sobs of anguish wild?

'Tis right to plead for heathen lands,
　To send the Bible to their shores,
And then to make, for power and pelf,
　A race of heathens at our doors.

What holy horror filled our hearts—
　It shook our church from dome to nave—
Our cheeks grew pale with pious dread,
　To hear him breathe the name of slave.

Upon our Zion, fair and strong,
　His words fell like a fearful blight;
We turned him from our saintly fold;
　And this we did to "serve him right."

The Slave Mother

A Tale of the Ohio

I have but four, the treasures of my soul,
　They lay like doves around my heart;
I tremble lest some cruel hand
　Should tear my household wreaths apart.

My baby girl, with childish glance,
　Looks curious in my anxious eye,
She little knows that for her sake
　Deep shadows round my spirit lie.

My playful boys could I forget,
　My home might seem a joyous spot,
But with their sunshine mirth I blend
　The darkness of their future lot.

And thou my babe, my darling one,
　My last, my loved, my precious child,
Oh! when I think upon thy doom
　My heart grows faint and then throbs wild.

The Ohio's bridged and spanned with ice,
　The northern star is shining bright,

The Slave Mother (A Tale of the Ohio): Based upon the case of Margaret Garner that
occurred in 1856.

I'll take the nestlings of my heart
  And search for freedom by its light.

* * *

Winter and night were on the earth,
  And feebly moaned the shivering trees,
A sigh of winter seemed to run
  Through every murmur of the breeze.

She fled, and with her children all,
  She reached the stream and crossed it o'er,
Bright visions of deliverance came
  Like dreams of plenty to the poor.

Dreams! vain dreams, heroic mother,
  Give all thy hopes and struggles o'er,
The pursuer is on thy track,
  And the hunter at thy door.

Judea's refuge cities had power
  To shelter, shield and save,
E'en Rome had altars: 'neath whose shade
  Might crouch the wan and weary slave.

But Ohio had no sacred fane,
  To human rights so consecrate,
Where thou may'st shield thy hapless ones
  From their darkly gathering fate.

Then, said the mournful mother,
  If Ohio cannot save,
I will do a deed for freedom,
  She shall find each child a grave.

I will save my precious children
  From their darkly threatened doom,
I will hew their path to freedom
  Through the portals of the tomb.

A moment in the sunlight,
  She held a glimmering knife,
The next moment she had bathed it
  In the crimson fount of life.

They snatched away the fatal knife,
  Her boys shrieked wild with dread;
The baby girl was pale and cold,
  They raised it up, the child was dead.

Sends this deed of fearful daring
  Through my country's heart no thrill,
Do the icy hands of slavery
  Every pure emotion chill?

Oh! if there is any honor,
  Truth or justice in the land,
Will ye not, as men and Christians,
  On the side of freedom stand?

Rizpah, the Daughter of Ai

Tidings! sad tidings for the daughter of Ai,
They are bearing her prince and loved away,
Destruction falls like a mournful pall
On the fallen house of ill-fated Saul.

And Rizpah hears that her loved must die,
But she hears it all with a tearless eye;
And clasping her hand with grief and dread
She meekly bows her queenly head.

The blood has left her blanching cheek,
Her quivering lips refuse to speak,
Oh! grief like hers has learned no tone—
A world of grief is all its own.

But the deed is done, and the hand is stay'd
That havoc among the brethren made,
And Rizpah takes her lowly seat
To watch the princely dead at her feet.

The jackall crept out with a stealthy tread,
To batten and feast on the noble dead;
The vulture bore down with a heavy wing
To dip his beak in life's stagnant spring.

The hyena heard the jackall's howl,
And he bounded forth with a sullen growl,
When Rizpah's shriek rose on the air
Like a tone from the caverns of despair.

Rizpah . . .: Based on an incident described in 2 Samuel 21:8–14.

She sprang from her sad and lowly seat,
For a moment her heart forgot to beat,
And the blood rushed up to her marble cheek
And a flash to her eye so sad and meek.

The vulture paused in his downward flight,
As she raised her form to its queenly height,
The hyena's eye had a horrid glare
As he turned again to his desert lair.

The jackall slunk back with a quickened tread,
From his cowardly search of Rizpah's dead;
Unsated he turned from the noble prey,
Subdued by a glance of the daughter of Ai.

Oh grief! that a mother's heart should know,
Such a weary weight of consuming wo,
For seldom if ever earth has known
Such love as the daughter of Ai hath known.

Ruth and Naomi

Turn my daughters, full of wo,
  Is my heart so sad and lone?
Leave me children—I would go
  To my loved and distant home.

From my bosom death has torn
  Husband, children, all my stay,
Left me not a single one,
  For my life's declining day.

Want and wo surround my way,
  Grief and famine where I tread;
In my native land they say
  God is giving Jacob bread.

Naomi ceased, her daughters wept,
  Their yearning hearts were filled;
Falling upon her withered neck,
  Their grief in tears distill'd.

Ruth and Naomi: Based on an incident described in Ruth 1:8–17.

Like rain upon a blighted tree,
   The tears of Orpah fell;
Kissing the pale and quivering lip,
   She breathed her sad farewell.

But Ruth stood up, on her brow
   There lay a heavenly calm;
And from her lips came, soft and low,
   Words like a holy charm.

I will not leave thee, on thy brow
   Are lines of sorrow, age and care;
Thy form is bent, thy step is slow,
   Thy bosom stricken, lone and sear.

Oh! when thy heart and home were glad,
   I freely shared thy joyous lot;
And now that heart is lone and sad,
   Cease to entreat—I'll leave thee not.

Oh! if a lofty palace proud
   Thy future home shall be;
Where sycophants around thee crowd,
   I'll share that home with thee.

And if on earth the humblest spot,
   Thy future home shall prove;
I'll bring into thy lonely lot
   The wealth of woman's love.

Go where thou wilt, my steps are there,
   Our path in life is one;
Thou hast no lot I will not share,
   'Till life itself be done.

My country and my home for thee,
   I freely, willingly resign,
Thy people shall my people be,
   Thy God he shall be mine.

Then, mother dear, entreat me not
   To turn from following thee;
My heart is nerved to share thy lot;
   Whatever that may be.

Obituary for J. Edwards Barnes

Dead! when last we met his lips were fresh,
His eye was genial, kind and bright;
I came again, the lips had paled,
The eye was dimmed, and lost its light.

Dead! when last we met his words were kind,
They fell like music on my ear;
I came again, the soul had fled
That breathed those words of hope and cheer.

He is not dead! he only left
A precious robe of clay behind,
To draw a robe of love and light
Around his disembodied mind.

He is not dead! we only miss
His presence from the paths we roam;
Oh may his steps be tracks of light,
To guide us to our future home.

Lessons of the Street

Walking through life's dusty highways,
    Mid the tramp of hurrying feet,
We may gather much instruction
    From the 'lessons of the street.'

Now a beggar sues for succor—
    Nay, repress that look of pride!
'Neath that wrecked and shattered body
    Doth a human soul reside.

Here's a brow that seems to tell you,
    'I am prematurely old;
I have spent my youthful vigor
    In an eager search for gold.'

Obituary for J. Edwards Barnes: National Anti-Slavery Standard, March 6, 1858. This poem was untitled and prefaced by a letter indicating when Harper last saw Barnes.
Lessons of the Street: Liberator, May 14, 1858.

On the cheek of yon pale student
  Is a divorcement most unkind—
'Tis the cruel separation
  Of his body from his mind.

Here a painted child of shame
  Flaunts in costly robes of sin,
With a reckless mirth that cannot
  Hide the smouldering fires within.

And here's a face, so calm and mild,
  Mid the restless din and strife;
It seems to say, in every line,
  'I'm aiming for a higher life.'

Just then I caught a mournful glance,
  As on the human river rushed,
A harrowing look, which plainly said,
  'The music of my life is hushed.'

Look on that face, so deathly pale,
  Its bloom and flush forever fled:
I started, for it seemed to bear
  A message to the silent dead.

Thus hurries on the stream of life,
  To empty where Death's waters meet;
We pass along, we pass away—
  Thus end the lessons of the street.

The Careless Word

'Twas but a word, a careless word,
As thistle-down it seemed as light,
It paused a moment on the air,
Then onward winged its flight.

Another lip caught up the word,
And breathed it with a haughty sneer;
It gathered weight as on it sped,
That careless word, in its career.

The Careless Word: National Anti-Slavery Standard, July 3, 1858.

Then Rumor caught the flying word,
And busy Gossip gave it weight,
Until that little word became
A vehicle of angry hate.

And then that word was winged with fire,
Its mission was a thing of pain,
For soon it fell like lava-drops
Upon a wildly-tortured brain.

And then another page of life
With burning, scalding tears was blurr'd,
A load of care was heavier made,
Its added weight that careless word.

That careless word, O how it scorched
A fainting, bleeding, quivering heart!
'Twas like a hungry fire that searched
Through every tender, vital part.

How wildly throbbed that aching heart!
Deep agony its fountains stirred!
It calmed—but bitter ashes marked
The pathway of that careless word.

Gone to God

Finished now the weary throbbing,
  Of a bosom calmed to rest;
Laid aside the heavy sorrows,
  That for years upon it prest.

All the thirst for pure affection,
  All the hunger of the heart;
All the vain and tearful cryings,
  All forever now depart.

Clasp the pale and faded fingers,
  O'er the cold and lifeless form;
They shall never shrink and shiver,
  Homeless in the dark and storm.

Gone to God: Anglo-African Magazine 1 (1859):123.

Press the death-weights calmly, gently,
   O'er the eyelids in their sleep;
Tears shall never tremble from them,
   They shall never wake to weep.

Close the silent lips together,
   Lips once parted with a sigh;
Through their sealed, moveless portals,
   Ne'er shall float a bitter cry.

Bring no bright and blooming flowers,
   Let no mournful tears be shed,
Funeral flowers, tears of sorrow,
   They are for the cherished dead.

She has been a lonely wanderer,
   Drifting on the world's highway;
Grasping with her woman's nature,
   Feeble reeds to be her stay.

God is witness to the anguish,
   Of a heart that's all alone;
Floating blindly on life's current,
   Only bound unto His throne.

But o'er such, Death's solemn angel,
   Broodeth with a sheltering wing;
Till the hopeless hand's grown weary,
   Cease around earth's toys to cling.

Then kind hands will clasp them gently,
   On the still, unaching breast;
Softly treading by, they'll whisper,
   Of the lone one gone to rest.

"Days of My Childhood"

Days of my childhood I woo you not back,
With sunshine and shadow upon your track,
Far holier hopes in my soul have birth,
Than I learned in the days of my childish mirth.

"Days of My Childhood": Anti-Slavery Bugle, September 29, 1860. This poem was printed
without a title.

Childhood may boast of its path of flowers
Missing all the thistles and thorns of ours,
But who that has gazed on the true and right,
Should exchange them for childhood's laughing light.

Though the glittering dews of my early life,
Have been pressed in the cup of care and strife,
The silver of age mid my locks is spread,
And the lightsome step of my youth has fled.

To the future I lift my earnest gaze,
Nor sigh for the bloom of my vanished days;
Far clearer I see through life's mellowed light,
Than the rosy flush of its morning bright.

Oh! childhood had laughter, song and mirth,
The freshness of life, the sunshine of earth;
But instead of its gilded dreams and toys,
I have loftier hopes and calmer joys.

Help me spotless Christ by a life of truth,
To keep round my soul the dew of its youth;
That loving and pure I may yield it thee,
When the angel of death shall set me free.

To the Cleveland Union-Savers:
An Appeal from One of the Fugitive's Own Race

Men of Cleveland, had a vulture
    Clutched a timid dove for prey,
Would ye not, with human pity,
    Drive the gory bird away?

Had you seen a feeble lambkin
    Shrinking from a wolf so bold,
Would ye not, to shield the trembler,
    In your arms have made its fold?

But when she, a hunted sister,
    Stretched her hands that ye might save,
Colder far than Zembla's regions
    Was the answer that ye gave.

To the Cleveland Union-Savers: Liberator, March 8, 1861. Also published in the Anti-Slavery Bugle, February 23, 1861.

On your Union's bloody altar
  Was your helpless victim laid;
Mercy, truth, and justice shuddered,
  But your hands would give no aid.

And ye sent her back to torture,
  Stripped of freedom, robbed of right,—
Thrust the wretched, captive stranger
  Back to Slavery's gloomy night!

Sent her back where men may trample
  On her honor and her fame,
And upon her lips so dusky
  Press the cup of woe and shame.

There is blood upon your city,—
  Dark and dismal is the stain;
And your hands would fail to clea[n]se it,
  Though you should Lake Erie drain.

There's a curse upon your Union!
  Fearful sounds are in the air;
As if thunderbolts were forging
  Answers to the bondman's prayer.

Ye may bind your trembling victims,
  Like the heathen priests of old;
And may barter manly honor
  For the Union and for gold;—

But ye cannot stay the whirlwind,
  When the storm begins to break;
And our God doth rise in judgment
  For the poor and needy's sake.

And your guilty, sin-cursed Union
  Shall be shaken to its base,
Till ye learn that simple justice
  Is the right of every race.

Essays and Speeches

◆

According to Daniel Payne, "Christianity" was first published in 1853 in the *Christian Recorder*. This essay helped establish Frances Harper's national reputation. It was reprinted in both the *Provincial Freeman* and *Frederick Douglass' Paper*, and in 1855, William C. Nell quoted several parts in his *Colored Patriots of the American Revolution*. Harper included this essay in the 1854 editions of *Poems on Miscellaneous Subjects* (Boston and Philadelphia) and in all subsequent editions of that work. "Christianity" demonstrates the basic religious philosophy that permeates Harper's work, and it also reveals her fundamental aesthetic values. "Christianity," the essay begins, "is a system claiming God for its author, and the welfare of man for its object." Genius, philosophy, science, poetry, music, and learning all flourish and gain value in proportion to their adherence to its laws and precepts. This perspective is both unitarian and utilitarian. The various forms of literature like the various activities of life are parts of the same whole. Their ultimate purpose is to instill, to guide, and to encourage Christian living. As this essay reveals, Harper used rhetorical techniques in her writings from formal lectures, elocution, sermons, and stories.

"The Colored People in America" also appeared in *Poems on Miscellaneous Subjects*. This essay may be the text of one of Harper's earliest speeches, to which she referred in a letter as "Elevation and Education of Our People." Its structure is fairly typical of her essays and lectures. It begins with a statement of personal commitment to a common struggle. It presents a candid acknowledgment of weaknesses and needs but presents those elements within their historical and social contexts. The essay lists progress and achievements, declares that self-help should be supported by right thinking people, and optimistically asserts the eventual triumph of right.

The titles of Harper's lectures, which she presented several days in a row and sometimes twice a day, and their basic themes did not vary substantially. Yet, according to contemporary accounts, Harper did not give "cut and dried" speeches, but elaborated upon her basic ideas with references and examples from the areas where she spoke.

"Could We Trace the Record" was one of several addresses delivered during the Fourth Anniversary Meeting of the New York City Anti-Slavery Society, May 13, 1857. Harper's inclusion in the program and the subsequent publication of her remarks show that she was now considered a major abolitionist spokesperson. Although the full text of that speech was not recorded, the excerpt shows the basic religious and philosophical elements characteristic of Harper's work mentioned in the discussion of "Christianity." Because the reporter included parenthetical comments about the audience's response, this essay not only gives examples of some of Harper's rhetorical strategies to strengthen her antislavery message—irony, references to world history, and evocations of recent events—but also shows these strategies were successful with her listeners. The case to which Harper refers in this speech was probably that of Anthony Burns, who was captured in the spring of 1854 and returned from Boston to slavery. The capture of Anthony Burns set off a major riot, and federal troops were called in. Burns was the last fugitive officially remanded to slavery from Massachusetts, but at the time of this speech, the Fugitive Slave Bill remained a serious problem in most northern states.

In "Our Greatest Want," Harper contradicts two ideas that she perceived were being unduly privileged among the free black middle class. Harper reminds her readers that while economic independence and educational advancement were important for racial progress, the most important need was for women and men to be committed to the highest ideals of Christian service and sacrifice for the realization of "human brotherhood."

◆

Christianity

Christianity is a system claiming God for its author, and the welfare of man for its object. It is a system so uniform, exalted and pure, that the

---

Christianity: Poems on Miscellaneous Subjects (Philadelphia), 1857.

loftiest intellects have acknowledged its influence, and acquiesced in the justness of its claims. Genius has bent from his erratic course to gather fire from her altars, and pathos from the agony of Gethsemane and the sufferings of Calvary. Philosophy and science have paused amid their speculative researches and wondrous revelations, to gain wisdom from her teachings and knowledge from her precepts. Poetry has culled her fairest flowers and wreathed her softest, to bind her Author's "bleeding brow." Music has strung her sweetest lyres and breathed her noblest strains to celebrate His fame; whilst Learning has bent from her lofty heights to bow at the lowly cross. The constant friend of man, she has stood by him in his hour of greatest need. She has cheered the prisoner in his cell, and strengthened the martyr at the stake. She has nerved the frail and shrinking heart of woman for high and holy deeds. The worn and weary have rested their fainting heads upon her bosom, and gathered strength from her words and courage from her counsels. She has been the staff of decrepit age, and the joy of manhood in its strength. She has bent over the form of lovely childhood, and suffered it to a place in the Redeemer's arms. She has stood by the bed of the dying, and unveiled the glories of eternal life; gilding the darkness of the tomb with the glory of the resurrection.

Christianity has changed the moral aspect of nations. Idolatrous temples have crumbled at her touch, and guilt owned its deformity in her presence. The darkest habitations of earth have been irradiated with heavenly light, and the death-shriek of immolated victims changed for ascriptions of praise to God and the Lamb. Envy and Malice have been rebuked by her contented look, and fretful Impatience by her gentle and resigned manner.

At her approach, fetters have been broken, and men have risen redeemed from dust, and freed from chains. Manhood has learned its dignity and worth; its kindred with angels, and alliance to God.

To man, guilty, fallen and degraded man, she shows a fountain drawn from the Redeemer's veins; there she bids him wash and be clean. She points him to "Mount Zion, the city of the living God, to an innumerable company of angels, to the spirits of just men made perfect, and to Jesus, the Mediator of the New Covenant," and urges him to rise from the degradation of sin, renew his nature, and join with them. She shows a pattern so spotless and holy, so elevated and pure, that he might shrink from it discouraged, did she not bring with her a promise from the lips of Jehovah, that he would give power to the faint, and might to those who have no strength. Learning may bring her ample pages and her ponderous records, rich with the spoils of every age, gathered from every land,

and gleaned from every source. Philosophy and science may bring their abstruse researches and wondrous revelations—Literature her elegance, with the toils of the pen, and the labors of the pencil—but they are idle tales compared to the truths of Christianity. They may cultivate the intellect, enlighten the understanding, give scope to the imagination, and refine the sensibilities; but they open not, to our dim eyes and longing vision, the land of crystal founts and deathless flowers. Philosophy searches earth; Religion opens heaven. Philosophy doubts and trembles at the portals of eternity; Religion lifts the veil, and shows us golden streets, lit by the Redeemer's countenance, and irradiated by his smile. Philosophy strives to reconcile us to death; Religion triumphs over it. Philosophy treads amid the pathway of stars, and stands a delighted listener to the music of the spheres; but Religion gazes on the glorious palaces of God, while the harpings of the blood-washed, and the songs of the redeemed, fall upon her ravished ear. Philosophy has her place; Religion her important sphere; one is of importance here, the other of infinite and vital importance, both here and hereafter.

Amid ancient lore the Word of God stands unique and pre-eminent. Wonderful in its construction, admirable in its adaptation, it contains truths that a child may comprehend, and mysteries into which angels desire to look. It is in harmony with that adaptation of means to ends which pervades creation, from the polypus tribes, elaborating their coral homes, to man, the wondrous work of God. It forms the brightest link of that glorious chain which unites the humblest work of creation with the throne of the infinite and eternal Jehovah. As light, with its infinite particles and curiously-blended colors, is suited to an eye prepared for the alternations of day; as air, with its subtle and invisible essence, is fitted for the delicate organs of respiration; and, in a word, as this material world is adapted to man's physical nature; so the word of eternal truth is adapted to his moral nature and mental constitution. It finds him wounded, sick and suffering, and points him to the balm of Gilead and the Physician of souls. It finds him stained by transgression and defiled with guilt, and directs him to the "blood that cleanseth from all unrighteousness and sin." It finds him athirst and faint, pining amid the deserts of life, and shows him the wells of salvation and the rivers of life. It addresses itself to his moral and spiritual nature, makes provision for his wants and weaknesses, and meets his yearnings and aspirations. It is adapted to his mind in its earliest stages of progression, and its highest state of intellectuality. It provides light for his darkness, joy for his anguish, a solace for his woes, balm for his wounds, and heaven for his hopes. It unveils the unseen world, and reveals Him who is the light of creation, and the joy of the universe, reconciled through the death of His Son. It promises the faithful a blessed reünion in a land undimmed with tears, undarkened by sorrow. It affords a truth for the living and a refuge for the dying. Aided by the Holy Spirit, it guides us through life, points out the shoals, the quicksands and hidden rocks which endanger our path, and at last leaves us with the eternal God for our refuge, and his everlasting arms for our protection.

The Colored People in America

Having been placed by a dominant race in circumstances over which we have had no control, we have been the butt of ridicule and the mark of oppression. Identified with a people over whom weary ages of degradation have passed, whatever concerns them, as a race, concerns me. I have noticed among our people a disposition to censure and upbraid each other, a disposition which has its foundation rather, perhaps, in a want of common sympathy and consideration, than mutual hatred, or other unholy passions. Born to an inheritance of misery, nurtured in degradation, and cradled in oppression, with the scorn of the white man upon their souls, his fetters upon their limbs, his scourge upon their flesh, what can be expected from their offspring, but a mournful reaction of that cursed system which spreads its baneful influence over body and soul; which dwarfs the intellect, stunts its development, debases the spirit, and degrades the soul? Place any nation in the same condition which has been our hapless lot, fetter their limbs and degrade their souls, debase their sons and corrupt their daughters, and when the restless yearnings for liberty shall burn through heart and brain—when, tortured by wrong and goaded by oppression, the hearts that would madden with misery, or break in despair, resolve to break their thrall, and escape from bondage, then let the bay of the bloodhound and the scent of the human tiger be upon their track;—let them feel that, from the ceaseless murmur of the Atlantic to the sullen roar of the Pacific, from the thunders of the rainbow-crowned Niagara to the swollen waters of the Mexican gulf, they have no shelter for their bleeding feet, or resting-place for their defenceless heads;—let them, when nominally free, feel that they have only exchanged the iron yoke of oppression for the galling fetters of a vitiated public opinion;—let prejudice assign them the lowest places and the humblest positions, and make them "hewers of wood and drawers of water;"—let their

The Colored People in America: Poems on Miscellaneous Subjects (Philadelphia), 1857.

income be so small that they must from necessity bequeath to their children an inheritance of poverty and a limited education,—and tell me, reviler of our race! censurer of our people! if there is a nation in whose veins runs the purest Caucasian blood, upon whom the same causes would not produce the same effects; whose social condition, intellectual and moral character, would present a more favorable aspect than ours? But there is hope; yes, blessed be God! for our down-trodden and despised race. Public and private schools accommodate our children; and in my own southern home, I see women, whose lot is unremitted labor, saving a pittance from their scanty wages to defray the expense of learning to read. We have papers edited by colored editors, which we may consider it an honor to possess, and a credit to sustain. We have a church that is extending itself from east to west, from north to south, through poverty and reproach, persecution and pain. We have our faults, our want of union and concentration of purpose; but are there not extenuating circumstances around our darkest faults—palliating excuses for our most egregious errors? and shall we not hope, that the mental and moral aspect which we present is but the first step of a mighty advancement, the faintest corruscations of the day that will dawn with unclouded splendor upon our down-trodden and benighted race, and that ere long we may present to the admiring gaze of those who wish us well, a people to whom knowledge has given power, and righteousness exaltation?

"Could We Trace the Record of Every Human Heart"

Could we trace the record of every human heart, the aspirations of every immortal soul, perhaps we would find no man so imbruted and degraded that we could not trace the word liberty either written in living characters upon the soul or hidden away in some nook or corner of the heart. The law of liberty is the law of God, and is antecedent to all human legislation. It existed in the mind of Deity when He hung the first world upon its orbit and gave it liberty to gather light from the central sun.

Some people say, set the slaves free. Did you ever think, if the slaves were free, they would steal everything they could lay their hands on from now till the day of their death—that they would steal more than two thousand millions of dollars? (applause) Ask Maryland, with her tens of thousands of slaves, if she is not prepared for freedom and hear her answer: "I help supply the cofflegangs of the South." Ask Virginia, with her

---

Could We Trace . . .: National Anti-Slavery Standard, May 23, 1857.

hundreds of thousands of slaves, if she is not weary with her merchandise of blood and anxious to shake the gory traffic from her hands, and hear her reply: "Though fertility has covered my soil, though a genial sky bends over my hills and vales, though I hold in my hand a wealth of water-power enough to turn the spindles to clothe the world, yet, with all these advantages, one of my chief staples has been the sons and daughters I send to the human market and human shambles." (applause) Ask the farther South, and all the cotton growing states chime in, "We have need of fresh supplies to fill the ranks of those whose lives have gone out in unrequited toil on our distant plantations."

A hundred thousand new-born babes are annually added to the victims of slavery; twenty thousand lives are annually sacrificed on the plantations of the South. Such a sight should send a thrill of horror, through the nerves of civilization and impel the heart of humanity to lofty deeds. So it might, if men had not found a fearful alchemy by which this blood can be transformed into gold. Instead of listening to the cry of agony, they listen to the ring of dollars and stoop down to pick up the coin. (applause)

But a few months since a man escaped from bondage and found a temporary shelter almost beneath the shadow of Bunker Hill. Had that man stood upon the deck of an Austrian ship, beneath the shadow of the house of the Hapsburgs, he would have found protection. Had he been wrecked upon an island or colony of Great Britain, the waves of the tempest-lashed ocean would have washed him deliverance. Had he landed upon the territory of vine-encircled France and a Frenchman had reduced him to a thing and brought him here beneath the protection of our institutions and our laws, for such a nefarious deed that Frenchman would have lost his citizenship in France. Beneath the feebler light which glimmers from the Koran, the Bey of Tunis would have granted him freedom in his own dominions. Beside the ancient pyramids of Egypt he would have found liberty, for the soil laved by the glorious Nile is now consecrated to freedom. But from Boston harbour, made memorable by the infusion of three-penny taxed tea, Boston in its proximity to the plains of Lexington and Concord, Boston almost beneath the shadow of Bunker Hill and almost in sight in Plymouth Rock, he is thrust back from liberty and manhood and reconverted into a chattel. You have heard that, down South, they keep bloodhounds to hunt slaves. Ye bloodhounds, go back to your kennels! When you fail to catch the flying fugitive, when his stealthy tread is heard in the place where the bones of the revolutionary sires repose, the ready North is base enough to do your shameful service. (applause)

Slavery is mean because it tramples on the feeble and weak. A man comes with his affidavits from the South and hurries me before a commissioner; upon that evidence *ex parte* and alone he hitches me to the car of slavery and trails my womanhood in the dust. I stand at the threshold of the Supreme Court and ask for justice, simple justice. Upon my tortured heart is thrown the mocking words, "You are a negro; you have no rights which white men are bound to respect!" (long and loud applause) Had it been my lot to have lived beneath the Crescent instead of the Cross, had injustice and violence been heaped upon my head as a Mohammedan woman, as a member of a common faith, I might have demanded justice and been listened to by the Pasha, the Bey or the Vizier; but when I come here to ask justice, men tell me, "We have no higher law than the Constitution." (applause)

But I will not dwell on the dark side of the picture. God is on the side of freedom; and any cause that has God on its side, I care not how much it may be trampled upon, how much it may be trailed in the dust, is sure to triumph. The message of Jesus Christ is on the side of Freedom, "I come to preach deliverance to the captives, the opening of the prison doors to them that are bound." The truest and noblest hearts in the land are on the side of freedom. They may be hissed at by slavery's minions, their names cast out as evil, their characters branded with fanaticism, but O,

"To side with Truth is noble when we share her humble crust Ere the cause bring fame and profit and it's prosperous to be just."

May I not, in conclusion, ask every honest, noble heart, every seeker after truth and justice, if they will not also be on the side of freedom. Will you not resolve that you will abate neither heart nor hope till you hear the deathknell of human bondage sounded, and over the black ocean of slavery shall be heard a song more exulting than the song of Miriam when it floated o'er Egypt's dark sea, the requiem of Egypt's ruined hosts and the anthem of the deliverance of Israel's captive people? (great applause)

Our Greatest Want

Leading ideas impress themselves upon communities and countries. A thought is evolved and thrown out among the masses, they receive it and it becomes interwoven with their mental and moral life—if the thought be good the receivers are benefited, and helped onward to the truer life;

Our Greatest Want: Anglo-African Magazine 1 (1859):160.

if it is not, the reception of the idea is a detriment. A few earnest thinkers, and workers infuse into the mind of Great Britain, a sentiment of human brotherhood. The hue and cry of opposition is raised against it. Avarice and cupidity oppose it, but the great heart of the people throbs for it. A healthy public opinion dashes and surges against the British throne, the idea gains ground and progresses till hundreds of thousands of men, women and children arise, redeemed from bondage, and freed from chains, and the nation gains moral power by the act. Visions of dominion, proud dreams of conquest fill the soul of Napoleon Bonaparte, and he infuses them into the mind of France, and the peace of Europe is invaded. His bloodstained armies dazzled and misled, follow him through carnage and blood, to shake earth's proudest kingdoms to their base, and the march of a true progression is stayed by a river of blood. In America, where public opinion exerts such a sway, a leading is success. The politician who chooses for his candidate not the best man but the most available one.—The money getter, who virtually says let me make money, though I coin it from blood and extract it from tears—The minister, who stoops from his high position to the slave power, and in a word all who barter principle for expediency, the true and right for the available and convenient, are worshipers at the shrine of success. And we, or at least some of us, upon whose faculties the rust of centuries has lain, are beginning to awake and worship at the same altar, and bow to the idols. The idea if I understand it aright, that is interweaving itself with our thoughts, is that the greatest need of our people at present is money, and that as money is a symbol of power, the possession of it will gain for us the rights which power and prejudice now deny us.—And it may be true that the richer we are the nearer we are to social and political equality; but somehow, (and I may not fully comprehend the idea,) it does not seem to me that money, as little as we possess of it, is our greatest want. Neither do I think that the possession of intelligence and talent is our greatest want. If I understand our greatest wants aright they strike deeper than any want that gold or knowledge can supply. We want more soul, a higher cultivation of all our spiritual faculties. We need more unselfishness, earnestness and integrity. Our greatest need is not gold or silver, talent or genius, but true men and true women. We have millions of our race in the prison house of slavery, but have we yet a single Moses in freedom. And if we had who among us would be led by him?

I like the character of Moses. He is the first disunionist we read of in the Jewish Scriptures. The magnificence of Pharaoh's throne loomed up before his vision, its oriental splendors glittered before his eyes; but he turned from them all and chose rather to suffer with the enslaved, than rejoice with the free. He would have no union with the slave power of Egypt. When we have a race of men whom this blood stained government cannot tempt or flatter, who would sternly refuse every office in the nation's gift, from a president down to a tide-waiter, until she shook her hands from complicity in the guilt of cradle plundering and man stealing, then for us the foundations of an historic character will have been laid. We need men and women whose hearts are the homes of a high and lofty enthusiasm, and a noble devotion to the cause of emancipation, who are ready and willing to lay time, talent and money on the altar of universal freedom. We have money among us, but how much of it is spent to bring deliverance to our captive brethren? Are our wealthiest men the most liberal sustainers of the Anti-slavery enterprise? Or does the bare fact of their having money, really help mould public opinion and reverse its sentiments? We need what money cannot buy and what affluence is too beggarly to purchase. Earnest, self sacrificing souls that will stamp themselves not only on the present but the future. Let us not then defer all our noble opportunities till we get rich. And here I am not aiming to enlist a fanatical crusade against the desire for riches, but I do protest against chaining down the soul, with its Heaven endowed faculties and God given attributes to the one idea of getting money as stepping into power or even gaining our rights in common with others. The respect that is only bought by gold is not worth much. It is no honor to shake hands politically with men who whip women and steal babies. If this government has no call for our services, no aim for your children, we have the greater need of them to build up a true manhood and womanhood for ourselves. The important lesson we should learn and be able to teach, is how to make every gift, whether gold or talent, fortune or genius, subserve the cause of crushed humanity and carry out the greatest idea of the present age, the glorious idea of human brotherhood.

Fiction

◆

Most scholars consider "The Two Offers" to be the first short story published by an African-American. It appeared in 1859 in the *Anglo-African*, a magazine with a political philosophy congruent to that of the young Frances Watkins. Published by Thomas Hamilton in New York, the *Anglo-African* was designed to educate and to encourage, to speak for and to black Americans. All its articles "not otherwise designated" were "the products of the pens of colored men and women." Writings by Frances Ellen Watkins appeared regularly during 1859, its first year of publication. By 1860, Frances Watkins was listed as one of its editors.

"The Two Offers" and "The Triumph of Freedom—A Dream" (1860) mark the beginnings of Harper's published fiction. They echo the themes of their author's poetry, letters, and essays. They are stylistically similar to the popular romantic fiction by such writers as Charlotte Brontë and Edgar Allan Poe and especially Lydia Maria Child, "Sarah," Frederick Douglass, and Harriet Beecher Stowe whose fiction was featured in abolitionist periodicals.

◆

The Two Offers

"What is the matter with you, Laura, this morning? I have been watching you this hour, and in that time you have commenced a half dozen letters and torn them all up. What matter of such grave moment is puz-

---

The Two Offers: Anglo-African Magazine 1 (1859):288–91, 339–45.

zling your dear little head, that you do not know how to decide?"

"Well, it is an important matter: I have two offers for marriage, and I do not know which to choose."

"I should accept neither, or to say the least, not at present."

"Why not?"

"Because I think a woman who is undecided between two offers, has not love enough for either to make a choice; and in that very hesitation, indecision, she has a reason to pause and seriously reflect, lest her marriage, instead of being an affinity of souls or a union of hearts, should only be a mere matter of bargain and sale, or an affair of convenience and selfish interest."

"But I consider them both very good offers, just such as many a girl would gladly receive. But to tell you the truth, I do not think that I regard either as a woman should the man she chooses for her husband. But then if I refuse, there is the risk of being an old maid, and that is not to be thought of."

"Well, suppose there is, is that the most dreadful fate that can befall a woman? Is there not more intense wretchedness in an ill-assorted marriage—more utter loneliness in a loveless home, than in the lot of the old maid who accepts her earthly mission as a gift from God, and strives to walk the path of life with earnest and unfaltering steps?"

"Oh! what a little preacher you are. I really believe that you were cut out for an old maid; that when nature formed you, she put in a double portion of intellect to make up for a deficiency of love; and yet you are kind and affectionate. But I do not think that you know anything of the grand, over-mastering passion, or the deep necessity of woman's heart for loving."

"Do you think so?" resumed the first speaker; and bending over her work she quietly applied herself to the knitting that had lain neglected by her side, during this brief conversation; but as she did so, a shadow flitted over her pale and intellectual brow, a mist gathered in her eyes, and a slight quivering of the lips, revealed a depth of feeling to which her companion was a stranger.

But before I proceed with my story, let me give you a slight history of the speakers. They were cousins, who had met life under different auspices. Laura Lagrange, was the only daughter of rich and indulgent parents, who had spared no pains to make her an accomplished lady. Her cousin, Janette Alston, was the child of parents, rich only in goodness and affection. Her father had been unfortunate in business, and dying before he could retrieve his fortunes, left his business in an embarrassed state. His widow was unacquainted with his business affairs, and when the estate was settled, hungry creditors had brought their claims and the lawyers had received their fees, she found herself homeless and almost penniless, and she who had been sheltered in the warm clasp of loving arms, found them too powerless to shield her from the pitiless pelting storms of adversity. Year after year she struggled with poverty and wrestled with want, till her toil-worn hands became too feeble to hold the shattered chords of existence, and her tear-dimmed eyes grew heavy with the slumber of death. Her daughter had watched over her with untiring devotion, had closed her eyes in death, and gone out into the busy, restless world, missing a precious tone from the voices of earth, a beloved step from the paths of life. Too self reliant to depend on the charity of relations, she endeavored to support herself by her own exertions, and she had succeeded. Her path for a while was marked with struggle and trial, but instead of uselessly repining, she met them bravely, and her life became not a thing of ease and indulgence, but of conquest, victory, and accomplishments. At the time when this conversation took place, the deep trials of her life had passed away. The achievements of her genius had won her a position in the literary world, where she shone as one of its bright particular stars. And with her fame came a competence of worldly means, which gave her leisure for improvement, and the riper development of her rare talents. And she, that pale intellectual woman, whose genius gave life and vivacity to the social circle, and whose presence threw a halo of beauty and grace around the charmed atmosphere in which she moved, had at one period of her life, known the mystic and solemn strength of an all-absorbing love. Years faded into the misty past, had seen the kindling of her eye, the quick flushing of her cheek, and the wild throbbing of her heart, at tones of a voice long since hushed to the stillness of death. Deeply, wildly, passionately, she had loved. Her whole life seemed like the pouring out of rich, warm and gushing affections. This love quickened her talents, inspired her genius, and threw over her life a tender and spiritual earnestness. And then came a fearful shock, a mournful waking from that "dream of beauty and delight." A shadow fell around her path; it came between her and the object of her heart's worship; first a few cold words, estrangement, and then a painful separation; the old story of woman's pride—digging the sepulchre of her happiness, and then a new-made grave, and her path over it to the spirit world; and thus faded out from that young heart her bright, brief and saddened dream of life. Faint and spirit-broken, she turned from the scenes associated with the memory of the loved and lost. She tried to break the chain of sad associations that bound her to the mournful past; and so, pressing back the bitter sobs from her almost breaking heart, like the dying dolphin, whose beauty is born of its death anguish, her genius gathered strength from suffering and wonderous power and brilliancy from the agony she hid within the desolate chambers of her soul. Men hailed her as one of earth's strangely gifted children, and wreathed the garlands of fame for her brow, when it was throbbing with a wild and fearful unrest. They breathed her name with applause, when through the lonely halls of her stricken spirit, was an earnest cry for peace, a deep yearning for sympathy and heart-support.

But life, with its stern realities, met her; its solemn responsibilities confronted her, and turning, with an earnest and shattered spirit, to life's duties and trials, she found a calmness and strength that she had only imagined in her dreams of poetry and song. We will now pass over a period of ten years, and the cousins have met again. In that calm and lovely woman, in whose eyes is a depth of tenderness, tempering the flashes of her genius, whose looks and tones are full of sympathy and love, we recognize the once smitten and stricken Janette Alston. The bloom of her girlhood had given way to a higher type of spiritual beauty, as if some unseen hand had been polishing and refining the temple in which her lovely spirit found its habitation; and this had been the fact. Her inner life had grown beautiful, and it was this that was constantly developing the outer. Never, in the early flush of womanhood, when an absorbing love had lit up her eyes and glowed in her life, had she appeared so interesting as when, with a countenance which seemed overshadowed with a spiritual light, she bent over the death-bed of a young woman, just lingering at the shadowy gates of the unseen land.

"Has he come?" faintly but eagerly exclaimed the dying woman. "Oh! how I have longed for his coming, and even in death he forgets me."

"Oh, do not say so, dear Laura, some accident may have detained him," said Janette to her cousin; for on that bed, from whence she will never rise, lies the once-beautiful and light-hearted Laura Lagrange, the brightness of whose eyes has long since been dimmed with tears, and whose voice had become like a harp whose every chord is tuned to sadness—whose faintest thrill and loudest vibrations are but the variations of agony. A heavy hand was laid upon her once warm and bounding heart, and a voice came whispering through her soul, that she must die. But, to her, the tidings was a message of deliverance—a voice, hushing her wild sorrows to the calmness of resignation and hope. Life had grown so weary upon her head—the future looked so hopeless—she had no wish to tread again the track where thorns had pierced her feet, and clouds overcast her sky; and she hailed the coming of death's angel as the footsteps of a welcome friend. And yet, earth had one object so very dear to her weary heart. It was her absent and recreant husband; for, since that conversation, she had accepted one of her offers, and become a wife. But, before she married, she learned that great lesson of human experience and woman's life, to love the man who bowed at her shrine, a willing worshipper. He had a pleasing address, raven hair, flashing eyes, a voice of thrilling sweetness, and lips of persuasive eloquence; and being well versed in the ways of the world, he won his way to her heart, and she became his bride, and he was proud of his prize. Vain and superficial in his character, he looked upon marriage not as a divine sacrament for the soul's development and human progression, but as the title-deed that gave him possession of the woman he thought he loved. But alas for her, the laxity of his principles had rendered him unworthy of the deep and undying devotion of a pure-hearted woman; but, for awhile, he hid from her his true character, and she blindly loved him, and for a short period was happy in the consciousness of being beloved; though sometimes a vague unrest would fill her soul, when, overflowing with a sense of the good, the beautiful, and the true, she would turn to him, but find no response to the deep yearnings of her soul—no appreciation of life's highest realities—its solemn grandeur and significant importance. Their souls never met, and soon she found a void in her bosom, that his earth-born love could not fill. He did not satisfy the wants of her mental and moral nature—between him and her there was no affinity of minds, no intercommunion of souls.

Talk as you will of woman's deep capacity for loving, of the strength of her affectional nature. I do not deny it; but will the mere possession of any human love, fully satisfy all the demands of her whole being? You may paint her in poetry or fiction, as a frail vine, clinging to her brother man for support, and dying when deprived of it; and all this may sound well enough to please the imaginations of school-girls, or love-lorn maidens. But woman—the true woman—if you would render her happy, it needs more than the mere development of her affectional nature. Her conscience should be enlightened, her faith in the true and right established, and scope given to her Heaven-endowed and God-given faculties. The true aim of female education should be, not a development of one or two, but all the faculties of the human soul, because no perfect womanhood is developed by imperfect culture. Intense love is often akin to intense suffering, and to trust the whole wealth of a woman's nature on the frail bark of human love, may often be like trusting a cargo of gold and precious gems, to a bark that has never battled with the storm, or buffetted the waves. Is it any wonder, then, that so many life-barks go down, paving the ocean of time with precious hearts and wasted hopes? that so many float around us, shattered and dismasted wrecks? that so many are stranded on the shoals of existence, mournful beacons and solemn warnings for the thoughtless, to whom marriage is a careless and hasty rushing together of the affections? Alas that an institution so fraught with good for humanity should be so perverted, and that state of life, which should be filled with happiness, become so replete with misery. And this was the fate of Laura Lagrange. For a brief period after her marriage her life seemed like a bright and beautiful dream, full of hope and radiant with joy. And then there came a change—he found other attractions that lay beyond the pale of home influences. The gambling saloon had power to win him from her side, he had lived in an element of unhealthy and unhallowed excitements, and the society of a loving wife, the pleasures of a well-regulated home, were enjoyments too tame for one who had vitiated his tastes by the pleasures of sin. There were charmed houses of vice, built upon dead men's loves, where, amid a flow of song, laughter, wine, and careless mirth, he would spend hour after hour, forgetting the cheek that was paling through his neglect, heedless of the tear-dimmed eyes, peering anxiously into the darkness, waiting, or watching his return.

The influence of old associations was upon him. In early life, home had been to him a place of ceilings and walls, not a true home, built upon goodness, love and truth. It was a place where velvet carpets hushed his tread, where images of loveliness and beauty invoked into being by painter's art and sculptor's skill, pleased the eye and gratified the taste, where magnificence surrounded his way and costly clothing adorned his person; but it was not the place for the true culture and right development of his soul. His father had been too much engrossed in making money, and his mother in spending it, in striving to maintain a fashionable position in society, and shining in the eyes of the world, to give the proper direction to the character of their wayward and impulsive son. His mother put beautiful robes upon his body, but left ugly scars upon his soul; she pampered his appetite, but starved his spirit. Every mother should be a true artist, who knows how to weave into her child's life images of grace and beauty, the true poet capable of writing on the soul of childhood the harmony of love and truth, and teaching it how to produce the grandest of all poems—the poetry of a true and noble life. But in his home, a love for the good, the true and right, had been sacrificed at the shrine of frivolity and fashion. That parental authority which should have been preserved as a string of precious pearls, unbroken and unscattered, was simply the administration of chance. At one time obedience was enforced by authority, at another time by flattery and promises, and just as often it was not enforced at all. His early associations were formed as chance directed, and from his want of home-training, his character received a bias, his life a shade, which ran through every avenue of his existence, and darkened all his future hours. Oh, if we would trace the history of all the crimes that have o'ershadowed this sin-shrouded and sorrow-darkened world of ours, how many might be seen arising from the wrong home influences, or the weakening of the home ties. Home should always be the best school for the affections, the birthplace of high resolves, and the altar upon which lofty aspirations are kindled, from whence the soul may go forth strengthened, to act its part aright in the great drama of life, with conscience enlightened, affections cultivated, and reason and judgment dominant. But alas for the young wife. Her husband had not been blessed with such a home. When he entered the arena of life, the voices from home did not linger around his path as angels of guidance about his steps; they were not like so many messages to invite him to deeds of high and holy worth. The memory of no sainted mother arose between him and deeds of darkness; the earnest prayers of no father arrested him in his downward course; and before a year of his married life had waned, his young wife had learned to wait and mourn his frequent and uncalled-for absence. More than once had she seen him come home from his midnight haunts, the bright intelligence of his eye displaced by the drunkard's stare, and his manly gait changed to the inebriate's stagger; and she was beginning to know the bitter agony that is compressed in the mournful words, a drunkard's wife. And then there came a bright but brief episode in her experience; the angel of life gave to her existence a deeper meaning and loftier significance: she sheltered in the warm clasp of her loving arms, a dear babe, a precious child, whose love filled every chamber of her heart, and felt the fount of maternal love gushing so new within her soul. That child was hers. How overshadowing was the love with which she bent over its helplessness, how much it helped to fill the void and chasms in her soul. How many lonely hours were beguiled by its winsome ways, its answering smiles and fond caresses. How exquisite and solemn was the feeling that thrilled her heart when she clasped the tiny hands together and taught her dear child to call God "Our Father."

What a blessing was that child. The father paused in his headlong career, awed by the strange beauty and precocious intellect of his child; and the mother's life had a better expression through her ministrations of love. And then there came hours of bitter anguish, shading the sunlight of her home and hushing the music of her heart. The angel of death bent over the couch of her child and beaconed it away. Closer and closer the mother strained her child to her wildly heaving breast, and struggled with the heavy hand that lay upon its heart. Love and agony contended with death, and the language of the mother's heart was,

"Oh, Death, away! that innocent is mine;
   I cannot spare him from my arms
To lay him, Death, in thine.
   I am a mother, Death; I gave that darling birth
I could not bear his lifeless limbs
   Should moulder in the earth."

But death was stronger than love and mightier than agony and won the child for the land of crystal founts and deathless flowers, and the poor, stricken mother sat down beneath the shadow of her mighty grief, feeling as if a great light had gone out from her soul, and that the sunshine had suddenly faded around her path. She turned in her deep anguish to the father of her child, the loved and cherished dead. For awhile his words were kind and tender, his heart seemed subdued, and his tenderness fell upon her worn and weary heart like rain on perishing flowers, or cooling waters to lips all parched with thirst and scorched with fever; but the change was evanescent, the influence of unhallowed associations and evil habits had vitiated and poisoned the springs of his existence. They had bound him in their meshes, and he lacked the moral strength to break his fetters, and stand erect in all the strength and dignity of a true manhood, making life's highest excellence his ideal, and striving to gain it.

And yet moments of deep contrition would sweep over him, when he would resolve to abandon the wine-cup forever, when he was ready to forswear the handling of another card, and he would try to break away from the associations that he felt were working his ruin; but when the hour of temptation came his strength was weakness, his earnest purposes were cobwebs, his well-meant resolutions ropes of sand, and thus passed year after year of the married life of Laura Lagrange. She tried to hide her agony from the public gaze, to smile when her heart was almost breaking. But year after year her voice grew fainter and sadder, her once light and bounding step grew slower and faltering. Year after year she wrestled with agony, and strove with despair, till the quick eyes of her brother read, in the paling of her cheek and the dimning eye, the secret anguish of her worn and weary spirit. On that wan, sad face, he saw the death-tokens, and he knew the dark wing of the mystic angel swept coldly around her path. "Laura," said her brother to her one day, "you are not well, and I think you need our mother's tender care and nursing. You are daily losing strength, and if you will go I will accompany you." At first, she hesitated, she shrank almost instinctively from presenting that pale sad face to the loved ones at home. That face was such a tell-tale; it told of heart-sickness, of hope deferred, and the mournful story of unrequited love. But then a deep yearning for home sympathy woke within her a passionate longing for love's kind words, for tenderness and heart-support, and she resolved to seek the home of her childhood, and lay her weary head upon her mother's bosom, to be folded again in her loving arms, to lay that poor, bruised and aching heart where it might beat and throb closely to the loved ones at home. A kind welcome awaited her. All that love and tenderness could devise was done to bring the bloom to her cheek and the light to her eye; but it was all in vain; her's was a disease that no medicine could cure, no earthly balm would heal. It was a slow wasting of the vital forces, the sickness of the soul. The unkindness and neglect of her husband, lay like a leaden weight upon her heart, and slowly oozed away its life-drops. And where was he that had won her love, and then cast it aside as a useless thing, who rifled her heart of its wealth and spread bitter ashes upon its broken altars? He was lingering away from her when the death-damps were gathering on her brow, when his name was trembling on her lips! lingering away! when she was watching his coming, though the death films were gathering before her eyes, and earthly things were fading from her vision. "I think I hear him now," said the dying woman, "surely that is his step;" but the sound died away in the distance. Again she started from an uneasy slumber, "That is his voice! I am so glad he has come." Tears gathered in the eyes of the sad watchers by that dying bed, for they knew that she was deceived. He had not returned. For her sake they wished his coming. Slowly the hours waned away, and then came the sad, soul-sickening thought that she was forgotten, forgotten in the last hour of human need, forgotten when the spirit, about to be dissolved, paused for the last time on the threshold of existence, a weary watcher at the gates of death. "He has forgotten me," again she faintly murmured, and the last tears she would ever shed on earth sprung to her mournful eyes, and clasping her hands together in silent anguish, a few broken sentences issued from her pale and quivering lips. They were prayers for strength and earnest pleading for him who had desolated her young life, by turning its sunshine to shadows, its smiles to tears. "He has forgotten me," she murmured again, "but I can bear it, the bitterness of death is passed, and soon I hope to exchange the shadows of death for the brightness of eternity, the rugged paths of life for the golden streets of glory, and the care and turmoils of earth for the peace and rest of heaven." Her voice grew fainter and fainter, they saw the shadows that never deceive flit over her pale and faded face, and knew that the death angel waited to soothe their weary one to rest, to calm the throbbing of her bosom and cool the fever of her brain. And amid the silent hush of their grief the freed spirit, refined through suffering, and brought into divine harmony through the spirit of the living Christ, passed over the dark waters of death as on a bridge of light, over whose radiant arches hovering angels bent. They parted the dark locks from her marble brow, closed the waxen lids over the once bright and laughing eye, and left her to the dreamless slumber of the grave. Her cousin turned from that death-bed a sadder and wiser woman. She resolved more earnestly than ever to make the world better by her example, gladder by her presence, and to kindle the fires of her genius on the altars of universal love and truth. She had a higher and better object in all her writings than the mere ac-quisition of gold, or acquirement of fame. She felt that she had a high and holy mission on the battle-field of existence, that life was not given her to be frittered away in nonsense, or wasted away in trifling pursuits. She would willingly espouse an unpopular cause but not an unrighteous one. In her the down-trodden slave found an earnest advocate; the flying fugitive remembered her kindness as he stepped cautiously through our Republic, to gain his freedom in a monarchial land, having broken the chains on which the rust of centuries had gathered. Little children learned to name her with affection, the poor called her blessed, as she broke her bread to the pale lips of hunger. Her life was like a beautiful story, only it was clothed with the dignity of reality and invested with the sublimity of truth. True, she was an old maid, no husband brightened her life with his love, or shaded it with his neglect. No children nestling lovingly in her arms called her mother. No one appended Mrs. to her name; she was indeed an old maid, not vainly striving to keep up an appearance of girlishness, when departed was written on her youth. Not vainly pin-ing at her loneliness and isolation: the world was full of warm, loving hearts, and her own beat in unison with them. Neither was she always sentimentally sighing for something to love, objects of affection were all around her, and the world was not so wealthy in love that it had no use for her's; in blessing others she made a life and benediction, and as old age descended peacefully and gently upon her, she had learned one of life's most precious lessons, that true happiness consists not so much in the fruition of our wishes as in the regulation of desires and the full de-velopment and right culture of our whole natures.

The Triumph of Freedom—A Dream

It was a beautiful day in spring. The green sward stretched beneath my feet like a velvet carpet, fair flowers sprung up in my path, and peaceful

The Triumph of Freedom: Anglo-African Magazine 2 (1860):21–23.

streams swept laughingly by to gain their ocean home. Above me the heavens were eloquent with the praise of God, around me the earth was poetic with His ideas. It was one of those days when Nature, in the excess of her happiness, leans on the bosom of the balmy sunshine, listening to the gentle voices of the wooing winds. I had fallen into a state of dreamy, delicious languor, when I was roused to sudden con[s]ciousness by a startling shriek. I looked up, and, bending over me, I saw a spirit gazing upon me with a look of unmistakable sadness. "Come with me?" said she, laying her hand upon me and drawing me along with an irresistible impulse. Silently I followed, awed by her strange manner. "I wish," said she, after a few moments silence, "to show you the goddess of this place." Surely, thought I, that must be a welcome sight, for the loveliness of the place suggested to my mind a presiding genius of glorious beauty. "It is now her hour of worship, and I want to show you some of her rites and ceremonies, and also the priests of her shrine." Just then we came in sight of the goddess. She was seated on a glittering throne, all sparkling with precious gems and rubies; and, indeed, so bright was her throne, it threw a dazzling radiance over her sallow countenance. She wore a robe of flowing white, but it was not pure white, and I noticed that upon its hem and amid its seams and folds were great spots of blood. It was the hour of worship, and her priests were standing by, with their sacred books in their hands; it was one of their rites to search them for texts and passages to spread over the stains on her garment. When this was done, they bowed down their heads and worshipped, saying:—"Thou art the handmaid of Christianity; thy mission is heaven-appointed and divine." And all the people said "Amen." But during this worship I saw a young man arise, his face pale with emotion and horror, and he said, "It is false." That one word, so sublime in its brevity, sent a thrill of indignant fear through the hearts of the crowd. It lashed them into a tumultuous fury. Some of them dashed madly after the intruder, and hissed in his ears—"Fanatic, madman, traitor, and infidel." But the efforts they made to silence him only gained him a better hearing. They forced him into prison, but they had no chains strong enough to bind his freeborn spirit. A number of adherents gathered around the young man, and asked to know his meaning. "Come with me," said he, "and I will show you?" and while they still chanted the praises of the goddess, he drew them to the spot, where they might view the base and inside of the throne, and the foundation of her altar. I looked, (for I had joined them, led on by my guide,) and I saw a number of little hearts all filed together and quivering. "What," said I, "are these?" My guide answered, "They are the hearts of a hundred thousand new-born babes." I turned deathly sick, a fearful faintness swept over me, and I was about to fall, but she caught me in her arms, and said, "Look here," and beneath the throne were piles of hearts laid layer upon layer. I noticed that they seemed rocking to and fro, as if smitten with a great agony. "What are these?" said I, gazing horror-stricken upon them. "They are the hearts of desolate slave mothers, robbed of their little ones." I looked a little higher, and saw a row of poor, bruised and seared hearts. "What are these?" "These are the hearts out of which the manhood has been crushed; and these," said she, pointing to another pile of young, fresh hearts, from which the blood was constantly streaming, "are the hearts of young girls, sold from the warm clasp of their mothers' arms to the brutal clutches of a libertine or a profligate—from the temples of Christ to the altars of shame. And these," said she , looking sadly at a row of withered hearts, from which the blood still dropped, "are the hearts in which the manhood has never been developed." I turned away, heart-sickened, the blood almost freezing in my veins, and I saw the young man standing on an eminence, pointing to the throne and altar, his lips trembling with the burden of a heaven-sent message. He reminded me of the ancient seers, robed in the robes of prophecy, pronouncing the judgments of God against the oppressors of olden times. Some listened earnestly, and were roused by his words to deeds of noble daring. Others, within whose shrunken veins all noble blood was pale and thin, mocked him and breathed out their hatred against him; they set a price upon his head and tracked his steps with bitter malice, but he had awakened the spirit of Agitation, that would not slumber at their bidding.

The blood-stained goddess felt it shaking her throne, its earnest eye searching into the very depths of her guilty soul, and she said to her worshippers: "Hide me beneath your constitutions and laws—shield me beneath your parchments and opinions." And it was done; but the restless eye of Agitation pierced through all of them, as through the most transparent glass. "Hide me," she cried to the priests, "beneath the shadow of your pulpits; throw around me the robes of your religion; spread over me your altar clothes, and dye my lips with sacramental blood?" And yet, into the recesses of her guilty soul came the eye of this Agitation, and she trembled before its searching glance.

Then I saw an aged man standing before her altars; his gray hair floated in the air, a solemn radiance lit up his eye, and a lofty purpose sat enthroned upon his brow. He fixed his eye upon the goddess, and she cowered beneath his unfaltering gaze. He laid his aged hands upon her blood-cemented throne, and it shook and trembled to its base; her cheeks blanched with dread, her hands fell nerveless by her side. It seemed to me as if his very gaze would have almost annihilated her; but just then

I saw, bristling with bayonets, a blood-stained ruffian, named the General Government, and he caught the hands of the aged man and fettered them, and he was then led to prison. I know not whether the angels of the living God walked to and fro in his prison—that, amid the silent watches of the night, he heard the rustling of their garments—I only know that the old man was a host within himself. The goddess gathered courage when she knew that she could rely on the arm of her ruffian accomplice; the old man offered her freedom, but she answered him with a scaffold—the gallows bent beneath his aged form. Her minions drained the blood from his veins, and they thought they had conquered him, but it was a delusion. From the prison came forth a cry of victory; from the gallows a shout of triumph over that power whose ethics are robbery of the weak and oppression of the feeble; the trophies of whose chivalry are a plundered cradle and a scourged and bleeding woman. I saw the green sward stained with his blood, but every drop of it was like the terrible teeth sown by Cadmus; they woke up armed men to smite the terror-stricken power that had invaded his life. It seemed as if his blood had been instilled into the veins of freemen and given them fresh vigor to battle against the hoary forms of gigantic Error and collossal Theory, who stood as sentinels around the throne of the goddess. His blood was a new baptism of Liberty. I noticed that they fought against her till she tottered and fell, amid the shouts of men who had burst their chains, and the rejoicings of women newly freed, and Freedom, like a glorified angel, smiled over the glorious jubilee and stood triumphant on the very spot where the terrible goddess had reigned for centuries. I saw Truth and Justice crown her radiant brow, from joyful lips floated anthems of praise and songs of deliverance—just such songs as one might expect to hear if a thousand rainbows would melt into speech, or the music of the spheres would translate itself into words. Peace, like light dew, descended where Slavery had spread ruin and desolation, and the guilty goddess, cowering beneath the clear, open gaze of Freedom, and ashamed of her meanness and guilt, skulked from the habitations of men, and ceased to curse the land with her presence; but the first stepping-stones of Freedom to power, were the lifeless bodies of the old man and his brave companions.

Part Two
1865–1875

◆

. . . I go to join
The fortunes of my race, and to put aside
All other bright advantages, save
The approval of my conscience and the meed
Of rightly doing.

from "Moses: A Story of the Nile"

Letters

◆

During, and especially after, the Civil War, many agencies, both public and private, sent and supported teachers, nurses, and others to work with the Freedpeople in the South. Generally, those organizations were directed by men whose sexism proscribed the activities and authority of the hundreds of women who volunteered their time and talents. African-American women who wanted to be part of these organized groups had to endure the same gender restrictions that hindered other women. In addition, they had to confront racism that made it more difficult for them to be selected, that influenced their assignments, and that regularly allocated them less salary and their projects smaller budgets.

Some of the volunteers, such as Harriet Jacobs, Elizabeth Keckley, and Sojourner Truth, were former slaves who went to areas they knew or that were similar to those in which they had lived. Others, such as Charlotte Forten and Frances Harper, were freeborn women of middle-class background and urban experience. Once they arrived in the South, these women not only braved the hostility of the defeated rebels, but often discovered suspicion and cultural differences between themselves and their black sisters and brothers. Frequently, their interactions with southerners of both races were hampered by their extensive reliance on abolitionist theory and their ignorance of rural culture. Sometimes this resulted in tears and frustration. Other times it offered occasions for quiet contemplation, wry experiences, and even rather cruel jokes. However, the women persevered and in the process developed an even more profound respect for African-American culture. Of the two groups, the former slaves were less inclined

121

to publish personal accounts of their experiences during their tenure in the Reconstruction South, but letters from the field became a regular feature of the liberal press.

Frances Harper was one of the most prolific of these writers. Between excerpts from her letters, editors often inserted brief notes indicating what parts of the South Harper had then visited, reviewing her many lectures, and keeping readers informed of her whereabouts. Part of this was due to the fact that by then Harper was the leading African-American writer and a social activist of international stature. Harper's frequent letters chronicle not only her public appearances, but also her personal initiation into southern mores, her sometimes dangerous encounters, and her adjustments to the sometimes astonishing differences in race, sex, and class.

The letters here span the years 1867 to 1871, during which time Harper made several trips to the south, returning to Philadelphia and other northern cities for brief vacations or to attend important meetings of such organizations as the Pennsylvania Anti-Slavery Society and the Pennsylvania Peace Society. Letters such as those of May 13, 1867, from Darlington, South Carolina, and of February 1, 1870, from Athens, Georgia, reveal that Harper's postbellum southern tour was characterized by the same high enthusiasm and exhausting schedule as had been her abolitionist travels in the antebellum north. However, Harper's postbellum letters are more candid about her difficulties and setbacks. For example, she is more explicit about her own physical danger and discomfort. The letters from Georgia during the spring of 1870, in particular, show that Harper became increasingly frustrated and pessimistic about the changes that could be expected in the general society. And yet, the basic idea expressed earlier in the essay "Our Greatest Want," that the nation needed women and men to "lay time, talent and money on the altar of universal freedom," remained constant.

◆

"I Am in the Sunny South"

[Darlington, South Carolina
May 13, 1867]

You will see by this that I am in the sunny South. . . . I here read and see human nature under new lights and phases. I meet with a people eager to hear, ready to listen, as if they felt that the slumber of the ages had been broken, and that they were to sleep no more. . . . I am glad that

I Am in the Sunny South: Still, 797–98.

the colored man gets his freedom and suffrage together; that he is not forced to go through the same condition of things here, that has inclined him so much to apathy, isolation, and indifference, in the North. You, perhaps, wonder why I have been so slow in writing to you, but if you knew how busy I am, just working up to or past the limit of my strength. Traveling, conversing, addressing day and Sunday-schools (picking up scraps of information, takes up a large portion of my time), besides what I give to reading. For my audiences I have both white and colored. On the cars, some find out that I am a lecturer, and then, again, I am drawn into conversation. "What are you lecturing about?" the question comes up, and if I say, among other topics politics, then I may look for onset. There is a sensitiveness on this subject, a dread, it may be, that some one will "put the devil in the nigger's head," or exert some influence inimical to them; still, I get along somewhat pleasantly. Last week I had a small congregation of listeners in the cars, where I sat. I got in conversation with a former slave dealer, and we had rather an exciting time. I was traveling alone, but it is not worth while to show any signs of fear. . . . Last Saturday I spoke in Sumter; a number of white persons were present, and I had been invited to speak there by the Mayor and editor of the paper. There had been some violence in the district, and some of my friends did not wish me to go, but I had promised, and, of course, I went. . . . I am in Darlington, and spoke yesterday, but my congregation was so large, that I stood near the door of the church, so that I might be heard both inside and out, for a large portion, perhaps nearly half my congregation were on the outside; and this, in Darlington, where, about two years ago, a girl was hung for making a childish and indiscreet speech. Victory was perched on our banners. Our army had been through, and this poor, ill-fated girl, almost a child in years, about seventeen years of age, rejoicing over the event, and said that she was going to marry a Yankee and set up housekeeping. She was reported as having made an incendiary speech and arrested, cruelly scourged, and then brutally hung. Poor child! she had been a faithful servant—her master tried to save her, but the tide of fury swept away his efforts. . . . Oh, friend, perhaps, sometimes your heart would ache, if you were only here and heard of the wrongs and abuses to which these people have been subjected. . . . Things, I believe, are a little more hopeful; at least, I believe, some of the colored people are getting better contracts, and, I understand, that there's less murdering. While I am writing, a colored man stands here, with a tale of wrong—he has worked a whole year, year before last, and now he has been put off with fifteen bushels of corn and his food; yesterday he went to see about getting his money, and the person to whom he went, threatened to kick him off, and accused him of stealing. I don't know how the colored man will vote, but perhaps many of them will be intimidated at the polls.

Affairs in South Carolina

Wilmington [Delaware]
July 26, 1867

Col. Hinton: *Dear Sir*—I am about leaving the unreconstructed States. The South is a sad place, it is so rife with mournful memories and sad revelations of the past. Here you listen to heart-saddening stories of griev- ous old wrongs, for the shadows of the past have not been fully lifted from the minds of the former victims of slavery. We have had a mournful past in this country, enslaved in the South and proscribed in the North; still it is not best to dwell too mournfully upon "by-gones." If we have had no past, it is well for us to look hopefully to the future—for the shadows bear the promise of a brighter coming day; and in fact, so far as the colored man is concerned, I do not feel particularly uneasy about his future. With his breadth of physical organization, his fund of mental endurance, and his former discipline in the school of toil and privation, I think he will be able to force his way upward and win his recognition even in the South. To me one of the saddest features in the South is not even the old rebel class. It is said they are or have been dying "powerful fast." Perhaps the best thing for them and their country will be "short lives and happy deaths;" but the most puzzling feature of Southern social life is, what shall become of the poorer white classes? Freedom comes to the colored man with new hopes, advantages and opportunities. He stands on the threshold of a new era, with the tides of a new dispensation coursing through his veins; but this poor "cracken class," what is there for them? They were the dregs of society before the war, and their status is unchanged. I have seen them in my travels, and I do not remember ever to have noticed a face among a certain class of them that seemed lighted up with any ambition, hope or lofty aspirations. The victims and partisans of slavery, they have stood by and seen their brother outraged and wronged; have consented to the crime and received the curse into their souls.

I don't know what you all think of Gen. Sickles's letter about a more general amnesty; but I think the former ruling class in the South have proved that they are not fit to be trusted with the welfare of the whites nor the liberty of the blacks. Mr. Whittemore, of Darlington, who is perhaps as heartily disliked by the rebels as any man in eastern South

---

Affairs in South Carolina: National Anti-Slavery Standard, August 10, 1867.

Carolina, has been holding, in company with myself, some interesting meetings in the State. Our last meeting was in Marion. I spoke there on Monday evening, and then for North Carolina. You may judge of my work when I tell you that in two weeks I have spoken twelve times. Thank God! The work goes bravely on. Freedom of speech, which has been an outlaw in the South, has found a welcome and home among those whose lips were once sealed by the iron gags of slavery. But to return to Marion. While there I visited Jeff. Ghee. Do you know anything of Jeff. Ghee? He is a young man, under sentence of death, as an accomplice in a murder committed by two Union soldiers, escaping from that charnel house of death, Florence stockade. I have seen that place, where our men burrowed in the earth, and I have been a little further, where I have seen the thickened graves of the men whose lives went out in that modern Golgotha. This colored man hid these men several weeks. Was not that a deed to endear him to every Northern heart? to every woman, whose son's, husband's or brother's life was drained away by hunger, cold, want and miasma? He says that he is not guilty; that the man killed "would be living to-day, if he'd had his way." The soldiers escaped, and this man is under sentence of death, and was to have been executed the third Friday in July, and now the jailor tells me it is to be the second Friday in August. Shall this be? Shall Lee, with tens of thousands of murders clinging to his skirts, escape the full desert of his crimes, and this man, who aided his victims, die a felon's death? Shall Jefferson Davis, with his hands dripping with the blood of Andersonville, and Libby, and Florence, breathe the air of freedom, and this man, who probably risked his life in defence of our soldiers, be choked to death? Oh! friend, you are acquainted in Washington. For God's and humanity's sake lay this case before the men who have the power to change this decree of death, and try, for the honor of our country, to have his life saved.

"Here Is Ignorance to Be Instructed"

[Athens, Georgia
February 1, 1870]

. . . If those who can benefit our people will hang around places where they are not needed, they may expect to be discouraged. . . . Here is ignorance to be instructed; a race who needs to be helped up to higher planes of thought and action; and whether we are hindered or helped, we should try to be true to the commission God has written upon our

Here Is Ignorance . . .: Still, 801.

souls. As far as the colored people are concerned, they are beginning to get homes for themselves and depositing money in Bank. They have hundreds of homes in Kentucky. There is progress in Tennessee, and even in this State while a number have been leaving, some who stay seem to be getting along prosperously. In Augusta colored persons are in the Revenue Office and Post Office. I have just been having some good meetings there. Some of my meetings pay me poorly; but I have a chance to instruct and visit among the people and talk to their Sunday-schools and day-schools also. Of course I do not pretend that all are saving money or getting homes. I rather think from what I hear that the interest of the grown-up people in getting education has somewhat subsided, owing, perhaps, in a measure, to the novelty having worn off and the absorption or rather direction of the mind to other matters. Still I don't think that I have visited scarcely a place since last August where there was no desire for a teacher; and Mr. Fidler, who is a Captain or Colonel, thought some time since that there were more colored than white who were learning or had learned to read. There has been quite an amount of violence and trouble in the State; but we have the military here, and if they can keep Georgia out of the Union about a year or two longer, and the colored people continue to live as they have been doing, from what I hear, perhaps these rebels will learn a little more sense. I have been in Atlanta for some time, but did not stay until the Legislature was organized; but I was there when colored members returned and took their seats. It was rather a stormy time in the House; but no blood was shed. Since then there has been some "sticking;" but I don't think any of the colored ones were in it.

"Almost Constantly Either Traveling or Speaking

[Columbiana, Georgia (?)
February 20, 1870]

I am almost constantly either traveling or speaking. I do not think that I have missed more than one Sunday that I have addressed some Sunday-school, and I have not missed many day-schools either. And as I am giving all my lectures free the proceeds of the collections are not often very large; still as ignorant as part of the people are perhaps a number of them would not hear at all, and may be prejudice others if I charged even ten cents, and so perhaps in the long run, even if my work is wearing, I may be of some real benefit to my race. . . . I don't know but that you would

---

Almost Constantly . . . : Still, 802–3.

laugh if you were to hear some of the remarks which my lectures call forth: "She is a man," again "She is not colored, she is painted." Both white and colored come out to hear me, and I have very fine meetings; and then part of the time I am talking in between times, and how tired I am some of the time. Still I am standing with my race on the threshold of a new era, and though some be far past me in the learning of the schools, yet to-day, with my limited and fragmentary knowledge, I may help the race forward a little. Some of our people remind me of sheep without a shepherd.

"A Private Meeting with the Women"

[Greenville, Georgia
March 29, 1870(?)]

But really my hands are almost constantly full of work; sometimes I speak twice a day. Part of my lectures are given privately to women, and for them I never make any charge, or take any collection. But this part of the country reminds me of heathen ground, and though my work may not be recognized as part of it used to be in the North, yet never perhaps were my services more needed; and according to their intelligence and means perhaps never better appreciated than here among these lowly people. I am now going to have a private meeting with the women of this place if they will come out. I am going to talk with them about their daughters, and about things connected with the welfare of the race. Now is the time for our women to begin to try to lift up their heads and plant the roots of progress under the hearthstone. Last night I spoke in a school-house, where there was not, to my knowledge, a single window glass; to-day I write to you in a lowly cabin, where the windows in the room are formed by two apertures in the wall. There is a wide-spread and almost universal appearance of poverty in this State where I have been, but thus far I have seen no, or scarcely any, pauperism. I am not sure that I have seen any. The climate is so fine, so little cold that poor people can live off of less than they can in the North. Last night my table was adorned with roses, although I did not get one cent for my lecture. . . .

The political heavens are getting somewhat overcast. Some of this old rebel element, I think, are in favor of taking away the colored man's vote, and if he loses it now it may be generations before he gets it again. Well, after all perhaps the colored man generally is not really developed enough to value his vote and equality with other races, so he gets enough to eat

A Private Meeting . . . : Still, 803.

and drink, and be comfortable, perhaps the loss of his vote would not be a serious grievance to many; but his children differently educated and trained by circumstances might feel political inferiority rather a bitter cup.

After all whether they encourage or discourage me, I belong to this race, and when it is down I belong to a down race; when it is up I belong to a risen race.

"I Visited One of the Plantations"

[Eufaula, Alabama
December 9, 1870]

Last evening I visited one of the plantations, and had an interesting time. Oh, how warm was the welcome! I went out near dark, and between that time and attending my lecture, I was out to supper in two homes. The people are living in the old cabins of slavery; some of them have no windows, at all, that I see; in fact, I don't remember of having seen a pane of window-glass in the settlement. But, humble as their homes were, I was kindly treated, and well received; and what a chance one has for observation among these people, if one takes with her a manner that unlocks other hearts. I had quite a little gathering, after less, perhaps, than a day's notice; the minister did not know that I was coming, till he met me in the afternoon. There was no fire in the church, and so they lit fires outside, and we gathered, or at least a number of us, around the fire. To-night I am going over to Georgia to lecture. In consequence of the low price of cotton, the people may not be able to pay much, and I am giving all my lectures free. You speak of things looking dark in the South; there is no trouble here that I know of—cotton is low, but the people do not seem to be particularly depressed about it; this emigration question has been on the carpet, and I do not wonder if some of them, with their limited knowledge, lose hope in seeing full justice done to them, among their life-long oppressors; Congress has been agitating the St. Domingo question; a legitimate theme for discussion, and one that comes nearer home, is how they can give more security and strength to the government which we have established in the South—for there has been a miserable weakness in the security to human life. The man with whom I stopped, had a son who married a white woman, or girl, and was shot down, and there was, as I understand, no investigation by the jury; and a number of cases have occurred of murders, for which the punishment

---

I Visited . . . : Still, 801–2.

has been very lax, or not at all, and, it may be, never will be; however, I rather think things are somewhat quieter. A few days ago a shameful outrage occurred at this place—some men had been out fox hunting, and came to the door of a colored woman and demanded entrance, making out they wanted fire; she replied that she had none, and refused to open the door; the miserable cowards broke open the door, and shamefully beat her. I am going to see her this afternoon. It is remarkable, however, in spite of circumstances, how some of these people are getting along. Here is a woman who, with her husband, at the surrender, had a single dollar; and now they have a home of their own, and several acres attached—five altogether; but, as that was rather small, her husband has contracted for two hundred and forty acres more, and has now gone out and commenced operations.

"As Full as the Room Was"

[Montgomery, Alabama
December 29, 1870]

Did you ever read a little poem commencing, I think, with these words:

> A mother cried, Oh, give me joy,
> For I have born a darling boy!
> A darling boy! why the world is full
> Of the men who play at push and pull.

Well, as full as the room was of beds and tenants, on the morning of the twenty-second, there arose a wail upon the air, and this mundane sphere had another inhabitant, and my room another occupant. I left after that, and when I came back the house was fuller than it was before, and my hostess gave me to understand that she would rather I should be somewhere else, and I left again. How did I fare? Well, I had been stopping with one of our teachers and went back; but the room in which I stopped was one of those southern shells through which both light and cold enter at the same time; it had one window and perhaps more than half or one half the panes gone. I don't know that I was ever more conquered by the cold than I had been at that house, and I have lived parts of winter after winter amid the snows of New England; but if it was cold out of doors, there was warmth and light within doors; but here, if you opened the door for light, the cold would also enter, and so part of the time I sat by the fire, and that and the crevices in the house supplied me with light in one room, and we had the deficient window-sash, or

---

As Full as the Room Was: Still, 804–5.

perhaps it never had had any lights in it. You could put your finger through some of the apertures in the house; at least I could mine, and the water froze down to the bottom of the tumbler. From another such domicile may kind fate save me. And then the man asked me four dollars and half a week board.

One of the nights there was no fire in the stove, and the next time we had fires, one stove might have been a second-hand chamber stove. Now perhaps you think these people very poor, but the man with whom I stopped has no family that I saw, but himself and wife, and he would make two dollars and a half a day, and she worked out and kept a boarder. And yet, except the beds and bed clothing, I wouldn't have given fifteen dollars for all their house furniture. I should think that this has been one of the lowest down States in the South, as far as civilization has been concerned. In the future, until these people are educated, look out for Democratic victories, for here are two materials with which Democracy can work, ignorance and poverty. Men talk about missionary work among the heathen, but if any lover of Christ wants a field for civilizing work, here is a field. Part of the time I am preaching against men ill-treating their wives. I have heard though, that often during the war men hired out their wives and drew their pay. . . .

And then there is another trouble, some of our Northern men have been down this way and by some means they have not made the best impression on every mind here. One woman here has been expressing her mind very freely to me about some of our Northerners, and we are not all considered here as saints and angels, and of course in their minds I get associated with some or all the humbugs that have been before me. But I am not discouraged, my race needs me, if I will only be faithful, and in spite of suspicion and distrust, I will work on; the deeper our degradation, the louder our call for redemption. If they have little or no faith in goodness and earnestness, that is only one reason why we should be more faithful and earnest, and so I shall probably stay here in the South all winter. I am not making much money, and perhaps will hardly clear expenses this winter; but after all what matters it when I am in my grave whether I have been rich or poor, loved or hated, despised or respected, if Christ will only own me to His Father, and I be permitted a place in one of the mansions of rest.

"What a Field There Is Here"

[Demopolis, Alabama
March 1(?), 1871]

Oh, what a field there is here in this region! Let me give you a short account of this week's work. Sunday I addressed a Sunday-school in Taladega: on Monday afternoon a day-school. On Monday I rode several miles to a meeting; addressed it, and came back the same night. Got back about or after twelve o'clock. The next day I had a meeting of women and addressed them, and then lectured in the evening in the Court-House to both colored and white. Last night I spoke again, about ten miles from where I am now stopping, and returned the same night, and to-morrow evening probably I shall speak again. I grow quite tired part of the time. . . . And now let me give you an anecdote or two of some of our new citizens. While in Taladega I was entertained and well entertained, at the house of one of our new citizens. He is living in the house of his former master. He is a brick-maker by trade, and I rather think mason also. He was worth to his owner, it was reckoned, fifteen hundred or about that a year. He worked with him seven years; and in that seven years he remembers receiving from him fifty cents. Now mark the contrast! That man is now free, owns the home of his former master, has I think more than sixty acres of land, and his master is in the poor-house. I heard of another such case not long since: A woman was cruelly treated once, or more than once. She escaped and ran naked into town. The villain in whose clutch she found herself was trying to drag her downward to his own low level of impurity, and at last she fell. She was poorly fed, so that she was tempted to sell her person. Even scraps thrown to the dog she was hunger-bitten enough to aim for. Poor thing, was there anything in the future for her? Had not hunger and cruelty and prostitution done their work, and left her an entire wreck for life? It seems not. Freedom came, and with it dawned a new era upon that poor, overshadowed, and sin-darkened life. Freedom brought opportunity for work and wages combined. She went to work, and got ten dollars a month. She has contrived to get some education, and has since been teaching school. While her former mistress has been to her for help.

Do not the mills of God grind exceedingly fine? And she has helped that mistress, and so has the colored man given money, from what I heard, to his former master. After all, friend, do we not belong to one of the

---

What a Field There Is Here: Still, 808–9.

best branches of the human race? And yet, how have our people been murdered in the South, and their bones scattered at the grave's mouth! Oh, when will we have a government strong enough to make human life safe? Only yesterday I heard of a murder committed on a man for an old grudge of several years' standing. I had visited the place, but had just got away. Last summer a Mr. Luke was hung, and several other men also, I heard.

"Truth Is Stranger than Fiction"

Mobile, [Alabama]
July 5, 1871

My Dear Friend:—It is said that truth is stranger than fiction; and if ten years since some one had entered my humble log house and seen me kneading bread and making butter, and said that in less than ten years you will be in the lecture field, you will be a welcome guest under the roof of the President of the Confederacy, though not by special invitation from him, that you will see his brother's former slave a man of business and influence, that hundreds of colored men will congregate on the old baronial possessions, that a school will spring up there like a well in the desert dust, that this former slave will be a magistrate upon that plantation, that labor will be organized upon a new basis, and that under the sole auspices and moulding hands of this man and his sons will be developed a business whose transactions will be numbered in hundreds of thousands of dollars, would you not have smiled incredulously? And I have lived to see the day when the plantation has passed into new hands, and these hands once wore the fetters of slavery. Mr. Montgomery, the present proprietor by contract of between five and six thousand acres of land, has one of the most interesting families that I have ever seen in the South. They are building up a future which if exceptional now I hope will become more general hereafter. Every hand of his family is adding its quota to the success of this experiment of a colored man both trading and farming on an extensive scale. Last year his wife took on her hands about 130 acres of land, and with her force she raised about 107 bales of cotton. She has a number of orphan children employed, and not only does she supervise their labor, but she works herself. One daughter, an intelligent young lady, is postmistress and I believe assistant book-keeper. One son attends to the planting interest, and another daughter attends to one of the stores.

Truth Is Stranger than Fiction: Still, 806.

The business of this firm of Montgomery & Sons has amounted, I understand, to between three and four hundred thousand dollars in a year. I stayed on the place several days and was hospitably entertained and kindly treated. When I come, if nothing prevents, I will tell you more about them. Now for the next strange truth. Enclosed I send you a notice from one of the leading and representative papers of rebeldom. The editor has been, or is considered, one of the representative men of the South. I have given a lecture since this notice, which brought out some of the most noted rebels, among whom was Admiral Semmes. In my speech I referred to the Alabama sweeping away our commerce, and his son sat near him and seemed to receive it with much good humor. I don't know what the papers will say to-day; perhaps they will think that I dwelt upon the past too much. Oh, if you had seen the rebs I had out last night, perhaps you would have felt a little nervous for me. However, I lived through it, and gave them more gospel truth than perhaps some of them have heard for some time.

"A Room to Myself Is a Luxury"

[Rural Alabama
1871(?)]

I have been traveling the best part of the day. . . . Can you spare a little time from your book to just take a peep at some of our Alabama people? If you would see some instances of apparent poverty and ignorance that I have seen perhaps you would not wonder very much at the conservative voting in the State. A few days since I was about to pay a woman a dollar and a quarter for some washing in ten cent (currency) notes, when she informed me that she could not count it; she must trust to my honesty—she could count forty cents. Since I left Eufaula I have seen something of plantation life. The first plantation I visited was about five or six miles from Eufaula, and I should think that the improvement in some of the cabins was not very much in advance of what it was in Slavery. The cabins are made with doors, but not, to my recollection, a single window pane or speck of plastering; and yet even in some of those lowly homes I met with hospitality. A room to myself is a luxury that I do not always enjoy. Still I live through it, and find life rather interesting. The people have much to learn. The condition of the women is not very enviable in some cases. They have had some of them a terribly hard time

---

A Room to Myself . . .: Still, 809–10.

in Slavery, and their subjection has not ceased in freedom. . . . One man said of some women, that a man must leave them or whip them. . . . Let me introduce you to another scene: here is a gathering; a large fire is burning out of doors, and here are one or two boys with hats on. Here is a little girl with her bonnet on, and there a little boy moves off and commences to climb a tree. Do you know what the gathering means? It is a school, and the teacher, I believe, is paid from the school fund. He says he is from New Hampshire. That may be. But to look at him and to hear him teach, you would perhaps think him not very lately from the North; at least I do not think he is a model teacher. They have a church; but somehow they have burnt a hole, I understand, in the top, and so lectured inside, and they gathered around the fire outside. Here is another—what shall I call it?—meeting-place. It is a brush arbor. And what pray is that? Shall I call it an edifice or an improvised meeting-house? Well, it is called a brush arbor. It is a kind of brush house with seats, and a kind of covering made partly, I rather think, of branches of trees, and an humble place for pulpit. I lectured in a place where they seemed to have no other church; but I spoke at a house. In Glenville, a little out-of-the-way place, I spent part of a week. There they have two unfinished churches. One has not a single pane of glass, and the same aperture that admits the light also gives ingress to the air; and the other one, I rather think is less finished than that. I spoke in one, and then the white people gave me a hall, and quite a number attended. . . . I am now at Union Springs, where I shall probably room with three women. But amid all this roughing it in the bush, I find a field of work where kindness and hospitality have thrown their sunshine around my way. And Oh what a field of work is here! How much one needs the Spirit of our dear Master to make one's life a living, loving force to help men to higher planes of thought and action. I am giving all my lectures with free admission; but still I get along, and the way has been opening for me almost ever since I have been South. Oh, if some more of our young women would only consecrate their lives to the work of upbuilding the race! Oh, if I could only see our young men and women aiming to build up a future for themselves which would grandly contrast with the past—with its pain, ignorance and low social condition.

Poetry

◆

From the end of the Civil War until 1871, Frances Harper's primary occupation was lecturing in Southern cities, towns, and rural areas to black audiences as well as to white ones. *Poems on Miscellaneous Subjects* was reprinted in 1866, and a few new poems appeared in various publications, but her itinerant life and its consequent lack of time and solitude made it difficult to organize and negotiate the publication of original collections. Nonetheless, sometime during that period, probably about 1868, she published *Moses: A Story of the Nile*, a volume quite different from her earlier work. The earliest extant copy of *Moses* is the second edition, published in 1869.

Harper's lecture tours were less extensive after 1871. She devoted more time to writing, and she contributed many new poems to the media. Between 1865 and 1875, Frances Harper produced *Poems* (1871), her first new collection of poetry since 1854, and she published her two most innovative and important books of poetry, *Moses: A Story of the Nile* (1869) and *Sketches of Southern Life* (1872).

Moses: A Story of the Nile (1869)

Frances Harper had long been interested in the story of Moses. For Harper, as for most African-Americans, the name "Moses" was synonymous with "leader," and she, as they, compared the sufferings of African-Americans under slavery and their subsequent struggles with those of the Jews in bondage in Egypt. Moses was a key figure in Harper's personal mythology. As mentioned earlier, she had published a poem in 1856 called "The Burial of Moses," and in the 1859 essay, "Our Greatest Want," Harper had declared that she liked the character of Moses because he was a "disunionist," that is, he "would have no union with the slave power of Egypt." In that essay and in other writings, Harper continually called for more women and men to emulate Moses.

"Moses: A Story of the Nile" is a long narrative poem based on the Biblical story. It fuses Harper's Biblical scholarship with her desire to create works that would teach and inspire audiences to greater religious faith, respect for African-American contributions, and service to humankind. This poem is as close to an autobiographical statement as any that Harper wrote. Moses was an orphan who not only escaped the enslavement of his group but was adopted into a family of leaders and educated accordingly. Rather than enjoy his class privileges, Moses chose to identify with his enslaved race. With the courage born of religious faith, he helped free his people.

The poem is an ambitious attempt at dramatic narrative. Written in blank verse, it is one of Harper's most experimental poetic efforts. Abandoning for the first and only time her characteristic heavily metered and rhymed lyric form, she offers her longest and for many critics, such as Patricia Liggins Hill, her best work (11). Although "Moses" is highly symbolic and the characters are complex, the narrative is accessible and its characters are realistic and intriguing. Though its protagonist is male, "Moses," like most of Harper's poems, is especially sensitive to the feelings and actions of women.

The book *Moses* was first comprised of the poem and a prose piece, "The Mission of Flowers." This book was enlarged with additional poems and reissued in 1889 and again in 1893. In 1901, the 1889 edition was reissued as *Idylls of the Bible.*

Poems (1871)

The thirty-one poems that follow "Moses" comprise Harper's next published volume, *Poems.* In one way, *Poems* was Harper's return to the traditional poetic forms of her antebellum period. It included such poems as "President Lincoln's Proclamation of Freedom," "An Appeal to the American People," "Lines to Hon. Thaddeus Stevens," and "Words for the Hour," which refer to incidents or prominent people during and just after the Civil War. Most likely, these poems were published in newspapers or magazines years before being collected in this volume. Other poems, such as "Vashti" and "Fifteenth Amendment," had also been previously published but were more recent works.

On the other hand, the lyrics that make up *Poems* form a substantially new collection. There are still political poems, but antislavery subjects have been replaced by temperance topics. There are still poems that retell and reinterpret Biblical stories, but their tone is more defiant and their allusions more clearly related to Harper's postbellum and Reconstruction speeches. One of the more significant developments is the change in Harper's depiction of motherhood. From the antebellum emphasis upon slave mothers being separated from their children, she has shifted her focus to the joys of motherhood in the poems "Thank God for Little Children," "The Mother's Blessing," and "To a Babe Smiling in Her Sleep."

Sketches of Southern Life (1872)

In 1872, Harper published *Sketches of Southern Life*, which consists of the next nine poems in this section. Based upon her experiences during her Southern lecture tours, at the core of this volume are six poems: "Aunt Chloe," "The Deliverance," "Aunt Chloe's Politics," "Learning to Read," "Church Building," "The Reunion." These poems not only form a history of Reconstruction but also serve as the bases for her novel, *Iola Leroy*, written some twenty years later. Aunt Chloe is a significant contribution to African-American written literary expression. She is probably the first black female protagonist, outside the tragic mulatto tradition, to be presented as a model for life. Mrs. Chloe Fleet is not the young, talented, cultivated middle-class heroine of the sentimental novel, nor is she the weeping, shivering slave girl. She is "rising sixty," a mature ex-slave, one of the many who survived the auction block, separation from her children, and the toil and tribulations experienced by "ordinary" slave women. After slavery, Aunt Chloe went to work and learned to read "the hymns and Testament." Barely literate and unsophisticated, Aunt Chloe is a folk character, a no-nonsense woman of moral strength and great common sense.

With the Aunt Chloe sequence, Harper is again experimenting with poetic form. She has returned to the familiar four-verse stanza and the ABCB rhyme, but together the relatively short poems form a single 376-line historical narrative that retells the experiences of the Civil War and Reconstruction. Moreover, Harper's experimentation with the expanded possibilities of dialect place her in the forefront of the local color movement.

After the Aunt Chloe poems come two others: "I Thirst" and "The Dying Queen." While they seem a radical break with the folk sequence that preceded them, alluding as they do to historical and Biblical occasions, these poems do share the themes of perseverance and faith.

◆

To-Day Is a King in Disguise

To-day is a monarch in disguise,
  With no pageant nor dazzling train;
We pass him by with regardless eyes,
  He looks so common and plain.

Anointed he comes from the solemn bier
  Of yesterday, pale and dead.
He walks mid the crowded haunts of men,
  But they hear not his regal tread.

The minutes of time—a golden shower,
  Are scattered by his command;
Richer than pearls are the diamond hours
  That fall from his bountiful hand.

In the busy mart, where the restless feet
  Of eager trade run to and fro,
Men count their gains and clutch their gold,
  But the moments—unheeded they go.

The truly wise are they who know
  The unheralded step of this king;
Who count each hour with its weal or woe
  A sacred and solemn thing.

Who write on the desk of the passing hour
  Some record to be borne above;
Who endow the moments with living power,
  And transcribe them with deeds of love.

Moses: A Story of the Nile
The Parting—Chapter I

Moses

Kind and gracious princess, more than friend,
I've come to thank thee for thy goodness,
And to breathe into thy generous ears

To-Day Is a King in Disguise: *Christian Recorder*, June 23, 1866.

Moses: A Story of the Nile: The complete poetry section of the volume *Moses: A Story of the Nile* (1869). The 1869 edition is marked "2nd ed." Since no earlier copies are known to exist, the date of first publication is unknown; but it is unlikely that *Moses* was created before 1865.

My last and sad farewell. I go to join
The fortunes of my race, and to put aside
All other bright advantages, save
The approval of my conscience and the meed
Of rightly doing.

Princess

What means, my son, this strange election?
What wild chimera floats across thy mind?
What sudden impulse moves thy soul? Thou who
Hast only trod the court of kings, why seek
Instead the paths of labor? Thou, whose limbs
Have known no other garb than that which well
Befits our kingly state, why rather choose
The badge of servitude and toil?

Moses

Let me tell thee, gracious princess; 'tis no
Sudden freak nor impulse wild that moves my mind.
I feel an earnest purpose binding all
My soul unto a strong resolve, which bids
Me put aside all other ends and aims,
Until the hour shall come when God—the God
Our fathers loved and worshipped—shall break our chains,
And lead our willing feet to freedom.

Princess

Listen to me, Moses: thou art young,
And the warm blood of youth flushes thy veins
Like generous wine; thou wearest thy manhood
Like a crown; but what king e'er cast
His diadem in the dust, to be trampled
Down by every careless foot? Thou hast
Bright dreams and glowing hopes; could'st thou not live
Them out as well beneath the radiance
Of our throne as in the shadow of those
Bondage-darkened huts?

Moses

Within those darkened huts my mother plies her tasks,
My father bends to unrequited toil;

And bitter tears moisten the bread my brethren eat.
And when I gaze upon their cruel wrongs
The very purple on my limbs seems drenched
With blood, the warm blood of my own kindred race;
And then thy richest viands pall upon my taste,
And discord jars in every tone of song.
I cannot live in pleasure while they faint
In pain.

Princess

How like a dream the past floats back: it seems
But yesterday when I lay tossing upon
My couch of pain, a torpor creeping through
Each nerve, a fever coursing through my veins.
And there I lay, dreaming of lilies fair,
Of lotus flowers and past delights, and all
The bright, glad hopes, that give to early life
Its glow and flush; and thus day after day
Dragged its slow length along, until, one morn,
The breath of lilies, fainting on the air,
Floated into my room, and then I longed once more
To gaze upon the Nile, as on the face
Of a familiar friend, whose absence long
Had made a mournful void within the heart.
I summoned to my side my maids, and bade
Them place my sandals on my feet, and lead
Me to the Nile, where I might bathe my weary
Limbs within the cooling flood, and gather
Healing from the sacred stream.
I sought my favorite haunt, and, bathing, found
New tides of vigor coursing through my veins.
Refreshed, I sat me down to weave a crown of lotus leaves
And lilies fair, and while I sat in a sweet
Revery, dreaming of life and hope, I saw
A little wicker-basket hidden among
The flags and lilies of the Nile, and I called
My maidens and said, "Nillias and Osiria
Bring me that little ark which floats beside
The stream." They ran and brought me a precious burden.
'Twas an ark woven with rushes and daubed
With slime, and in it lay a sleeping child;

His little hand amid his clustering curls,
And a bright flush upon his glowing cheek.
He wakened with a smile, and reached out his hand
To meet the welcome of the mother's kiss,
When strange faces met his gaze, and he drew back
With a grieved, wondering look, while disappointment
Shook the quivering lip that missed the mother's
Wonted kiss, and the babe lifted his voice and wept.
Then my heart yearned towards him, and I resolved
That I would brave my father's wrath and save
The child; but while I stood gazing upon
His wondrous beauty, I saw beside me
A Hebrew girl, her eyes bent on me
With an eager, questioning look, and drawing
Near, she timidly said, "Shall I call a nurse?"
I bade her go; she soon returned, and with her
Came a woman of the Hebrew race, whose
Sad, sweet, serious eyes seemed overflowing
With a strange and sudden joy. I placed the babe
Within her arms and said, "Nurse this child for me;"
And the babe nestled there like one at home,
While o'er the dimples of his face rippled
The brightest, sweetest smiles, and I was well
Content to leave him in her care; and well
Did she perform her part. When many days had
Passed she brought the child unto the palace;
And one morning, while I sat toying with
His curls and listening to the prattle of his
Untrained lips, my father, proud and stately,
Saw me bending o'er the child and said,
"Charmian, whose child is this? who of my lords
Calls himself father to this goodly child?
He surely must be a happy man."

       Then I said, "Father, he is mine. He is a
Hebrew child that I have saved from death." He
Suddenly recoiled, as if an adder
Had stung him, and said, "Charmian, take that
Child hence. How darest thou bring a member
Of that mean and servile race within my doors?
Nay, rather let me send for Nechos, whose
Ready sword shall rid me of his hateful presence."

Then kneeling at his feet, and catching
Hold of his royal robes, I said, "Not so,
Oh! honored father, he is mine; I snatched
Him from the hungry jaws of death, and foiled
The greedy crocodile of his prey; he has
Eaten bread within thy palace walls, and thy
Salt lies upon his fresh young lips; he has
A claim upon thy mercy."

                              "Charmian," he said,
"I have decreed that every man child of that
Hated race shall die. The oracles have said
The pyramids shall wane before their shadow,
And from them a star shall rise whose light shall
Spread over earth a baleful glow; and this is why
I root them from the land; their strength is weakness
To my throne. I shut them from the light lest they
Bring darkness to my kingdom. Now, Charmian,
Give me up the child, and let him die."
Then clasping the child closer to my heart,
I said, "The pathway to his life is through my own;
Around that life I throw my heart, a wall
Of living, loving clay." Dark as the thunder
Clouds of distant lands became my father's brow,
And his eyes flashed with the fierce lightnings
Of his wrath; but while I plead, with eager
Eyes upturned, I saw a sudden change come
Over him; his eyes beamed with unwonted
Tenderness, and he said, "Charmian, arise,
Thy prayer is granted; just then thy dead mother
Came to thine eyes, and the light of Asenath
Broke over thy face. Asenath was the light
Of my home; the star that faded out too
Suddenly from my dwelling, and left my life
To darkness, grief and pain, and for her sake,
Not thine, I'll spare the child." And thus I saved
Thee twice—once from the angry sword and once
From the devouring flood. Moses, thou art
Doubly mine; as such I claimed thee then, as such
I claim thee now. I've nursed no other child
Upon my knee, and pressed upon no other
Lips the sweetest kisses of my love, and now,

With rash and careless hand, thou dost thrust aside that love.
There was a painful silence, a silence
So hushed and still that you might have almost
Heard the hurried breathing of one and the quick
Throbbing of the other's heart: for Moses,
He was slow of speech, but she was eloquent
With words of tenderness and love, and had breathed
Her full heart into her lips; but there was
Firmness in the young man's choice, and he beat back
The opposition of her lips with the calm
Grandeur of his will, and again he essayed to speak.

Moses

Gracious lady, thou remembrest well
The Hebrew nurse to whom thou gavest thy foundling.
That woman was my mother; from her lips I
Learned the grand traditions of our race that float,
With all their weird and solemn beauty, around
Our wrecked and blighted fortunes. How oft!
With kindling eye and glowing cheek, forgetful
Of the present pain, she would lead us through
The distant past: the past, hallowed by deeds
Of holy faith and lofty sacrifice.
How she would tell us of Abraham,
The father of our race, that he dwelt in Ur;
Of the Chaldees, and when the Chaldean king
Had called him to his sacrifice, that he
Had turned from his dumb idols to the living
God, and wandered out from kindred, home and race,
Led by his faith in God alone; and she would
Tell us—(we were three,) my brother Aaron,
The Hebrew girl thou sentest to call a nurse,
And I, her last, her loved and precious child;
She would tell us that one day our father
Abraham heard a voice, bidding him offer
Up in sacrifice the only son of his
Beautiful and beloved Sarah; that the father's
Heart shrank not before the bitter test of faith,
But he resolved to give his son to God
As a burnt offering upon Moriah's mount;
That the uplifted knife glittered in the morning

Sun, when, sweeter than the music of a thousand
Harps, he heard a voice bidding him stay his hand,
And spare the child; and how his faith, like gold
Tried in the fiercest fire, shone brighter through
Its fearful test. And then she would tell us
Of a promise, handed down from sire to son,
That God, the God our fathers loved and worshiped,
Would break our chains, and bring to us a great
Deliverance; that we should dwell in peace
Beneath our vines and palms, our flocks and herds
Increase, and joyful children crowd our streets;
And then she would lift her eyes unto the far
Off hills and tell us of the patriarchs
Of our line, who sleep in distant graves within
That promised land; and now I feel the hour
Draws near which brings deliverance to our race.

Princess

These are but the dreams of thy young fancy;
I cannot comprehend thy choice. I have heard
Of men who have waded through slaughter
To a throne; of proud ambitions, struggles
Fierce and wild for some imagined good; of men
Who have even cut in twain the crimson threads
That lay between them and a throne; but I
Never heard of men resigning ease for toil,
The splendor of a palace for the squalor
Of a hut, and casting down a diadem
To wear a servile badge.

                                        Sadly she gazed
Upon the fair young face lit with its lofty
Faith and high resolves—the dark prophetic eyes
Which seemed to look beyond the present pain
Unto the future greatness of his race.
As she stood before him in the warm
Loveliness of her ripened womanhood,
Her languid eyes glowed with unwonted fire,
And the bright tropical blood sent its quick
Flushes o'er the olive of her cheek, on which
Still lay the lingering roses of her girlhood.

Grief, wonder, and surprise flickered like shadows
O'er her face as she stood slowly crushing
With unconscious hand the golden tassels
Of her crimson robe. She had known life only
By its brightness, and could not comprehend
The grandeur of the young man's choice; but she
Felt her admiration glow before the earnest
Faith that tore their lives apart and led him
To another destiny. She had hoped to see
The crown of Egypt on his brow, the sacred
Leopard skin adorn his shoulders, and his seat
The throne of the proud Pharaoh's; but now her
Dream had faded out and left a bitter pang
Of anguish in its stead. And thus they parted,
She to brood in silence o'er her pain, and he
To take his mission from the hands of God
And lead his captive race to freedom.
With silent lips but aching heart she bowed
Her queenly head and let him pass, and he
Went forth to share the fortune of his race,
Esteeming that as better far than pleasures
Bought by sin and gilded o'er with vice.
And he had chosen well, for on his brow
God poured the chrism of a holy work.
And thus anointed he has stood a bright
Ensample through the changing centuries of time.

Chapter II

It was a great change from the splendor, light
And pleasure of a palace to the lowly huts
Of those who sighed because of cruel bondage.
                                    As he passed
Into the outer courts of that proud palace,
He paused a moment just to gaze upon
The scenes 'mid which his early life had passed—
The pleasant haunts amid the fairest flowers,—
The fountains tossing on the air their silver spray,—
The statues breathing music soft and low
To greet the first faint flushes of the morn,—
The obelisks that rose in lofty grandeur
From their stony beds—the sphynxes gaunt and grim,

With unsolved riddles on their lips—and all
The bright creation's painters art and sculptors
Skill had gathered in those regal halls, where mirth,
And dance, and revelry, and song had chased
With careless feet the bright and fleeting hours.
He was leavin[g] all; but no regrets came
Like a shadow o'er his mind, for he had felt
The quickening of a higher life, as if his
Soul had wings and he were conscious of their growth;
And yet there was a tender light in those
Dark eyes which looked their parting on the scenes
Of beauty, where his life had been a joyous
Dream enchanted with delight; but he trampled
On each vain regret as on a vanquished foe,
And went forth a strong man, girded with lofty
Purposes and earnest faith. He journeyed on
Till palaces and domes and lofty fanes,
And gorgeous temples faded from his sight,
And the lowly homes of Goshen came in view.
There he saw the women of his race kneading
Their tale of bricks; the sons of Abraham
Crouching beneath their heavy burdens. He saw
The increasing pallor on his sisters cheek,
The deepening shadows on his mother's brow,
The restless light that glowed in Aaron's eye,
As if a hidden fire were smoldering
In his brain; and bending o'er his mother
In a tender, loving way, he said, "Mother,
I've come to share the fortunes of my race,—
To dwell within these lowly huts,—to wear
The badge of servitude and toil, and eat
The bitter bread of penury and pain."
A sudden light beamed from his mother's eye,
And she said, "How's this, my son? but yesterday
Two Hebrews, journeying from On to Goshen,
Told us they had passed the temple of the Sun
But dared not enter, only they had heard
That it was a great day in On; that thou hadst
Forsworn thy kindred, tribe and race; hadst bowed
Thy knee to Egypt's vain and heathen worship;
Hadst denied the God of Abraham, of Isaac,

And of Jacob, and from henceforth wouldst
Be engrafted in Pharaoh's regal line,
And be called the son of Pharaoh's daughter.
When thy father Amram heard the cruel news
He bowed his head upon his staff and wept.
But I had stronger faith than that. By faith
I hid thee when the bloody hands of Pharaoh
Were searching 'mid our quivering heart strings,
Dooming our sons to death; by faith I wove
The rushes of thine ark and laid thee 'mid
The flags and lilies of the Nile, and saw
The answer to that faith when Pharaoh's daughter
Placed thee in my arms, and bade me nurse the child
For her; and by that faith sustained, I heard
As idle words the cruel news that stabbed
Thy father like a sword."
"The Hebrews did not hear aright; last week
There was a great day in On, from Esoan's gate
Unto the mighty sea; the princes, lords
And chamberlains of Egypt were assembled;
The temple of the sun was opened. Isis
And Osiris were unveiled before the people;
Apis and Orus were crowned with flowers;
Golden censers breathed their fragrance on the air;
The sacrifice was smoking on the altar;
The first fruits of the Nile lay on the tables
Of the sun: the music rose in lofty swells,
Then sank in cadences so soft and low
Till all the air grew tremulous with rapture.
The priests of On were there, with sacred palms
Within their hands and lotus leaves upon their
Brows; Pharaoh and his daughter sat waiting
In their regal chairs; all were ready to hear
Me bind my soul to Egypt, and to swear
Allegiance to her gods. The priests of On
Drew near to lay their hands upon my head
And bid me swear, 'Now, by Osiris, judge
Of all the dead, and Isis, mother of us
All,' that henceforth I'd forswear my kindred,
Tribe and race; would have no other gods
Than those of Egypt; would be engrafted

Into Pharaoh's royal line, and be called
The son of Pharaoh's daughter. Then, mother
Dear, I lived the past again. Again I sat
Beside thee, my lips apart with childish
Wonder, my eager eyes uplifted to thy
Glowing face, and my young soul gathering
Inspiration from thy words. Again I heard
Thee tell the grand traditions of our race,
The blessed hopes and glorious promises
That weave their golden threads among the sombre
Tissues of our lives, and shimmer still amid
The gloom and shadows of our lot. Again
I heard thee tell of Abraham, with his constant
Faith and earnest trust in God, unto whom
The promise came that in his seed should all
The nations of the earth be blessed. Of Isaac,
Blessing with disappointed lips his first born son,
From whom the birthright had departed. Of Jacob,
With his warm affections and his devious ways,
Flying before the wrath of Esau; how he
Slumbered in the wild, and saw amid his dreams
A ladder reaching to the sky, on which God's
Angels did descend, and waking, with a solemn
Awe o'ershadowing all, his soul exclaimed, 'How
Dreadful is this place. Lo! God is here, and I
Knew it not." Of Joseph, once a mighty prince
Within this land, who shrank in holy horror
From the soft white hand that beckoned him to sin;
Whose heart, amid the pleasures, pomp and pride
Of Egypt, was ever faithful to his race,
And when his life was trembling on its frailest chord
He turned his dying eyes to Canaan, and made
His brethren swear that they would make his grave
Among the patriarchs of his line, because
Machpelah's cave, where Abraham bowed before
The sons of Heth, and bought a place to lay
His loved and cherished dead, was dearer to his
Dying heart than the proudest tomb amid
The princely dead of Egypt.
        Then, like the angels, mother dear, who met
Our father Jacob on his way, thy words

Came back as messengers of light to guide
My steps, and I refused to be called the son
Of Pharaoh's daughter. I saw the priests of On
Grow pale with fear, an ashen terror creeping
O'er the princess' face, while Pharaoh's brow grew
Darker than the purple of his cloak. But I
Endured, as seeing him who hides his face
Behind the brightness of his glory.
And thus I left the pomp and pride of Egypt
To cast my lot among the people of my race."

Flight into Midian—Chapter III

The love of Moses for his race soon found
A stern expression. Pharaoh was building
A pyramid; ambitious, cold and proud,
He scrupled not at means to gain his ends.
When he feared the growing power of Israel
He stained his hands in children's blood, and held
A carnival of death in Goshen; but now
He wished to hand his name and memory
Down unto the distant ages, and instead
Of lading that memory with the precious
Fragrance of the kindest deeds and words, he
Essayed to write it out in stone, as cold
And hard, and heartless as himself.
                                    And Israel was
The fated race to whom the cruel tasks
Were given. Day after day a cry of wrong
And anguish, some dark deed of woe and crime,
Came to the ear of Moses, and he said,
"These reports are ever harrowing my soul;
I will go unto the fields where Pharaoh's
Officers exact their labors, and see
If these things be so—if they smite the feeble
At their tasks, and goad the aged on to toils
Beyond their strength—if neither age nor sex
Is spared the cruel smiting of their rods."
And Moses went to see his brethren.
                                    'Twas eventide,
And the laborers were wending their way
Unto their lowly huts. 'Twas a sad sight,—

The young girls walked without the bounding steps
Of youth, with faces prematurely old,
As if the rosy hopes and sunny promises
Of life had never flushed their cheeks with girlish
Joy; and there were men whose faces seemed to say,
We bear our lot in hopeless pain, we've bent unto
Our burdens until our shoulders fit them,
And as slaves we crouch beneath our servitude
And toil. But there were men whose souls were cast
In firmer moulds, men with dark secretive eyes,
Which seemed to say, to day we bide our time,
And hide our wrath in every nerve, and only
Wait a fitting hour to strike the hands that press
Us down. Then came the officers of Pharaoh;
They trod as lords, their faces flushed with pride
And insolence, watching the laborers
Sadly wending their way from toil to rest.
And Moses' heart swelled with a mighty pain; sadly
Musing, he sought a path that led him
From the busy haunts of men. But even there
The cruel wrong trod in his footsteps; he heard
A heavy groan, then harsh and bitter words,
And, looking back, he saw an officer
Of Pharaoh smiting with rough and cruel hand
An aged man. Then Moses' wrath o'erflowed
His lips, and every nerve did tremble
With a sense of wrong, and bounding forth he
Cried unto the smiter, "Stay thy hand; seest thou
That aged man? His head is whiter than our
Desert sands; his limbs refuse to do thy
Bidding because thy cruel tasks have drained
Away their strength." The Egyptian raised his eyes
With sudden wonder; who was this that dared dispute
His power? Only a Hebrew youth. His
Proud lip curved in scornful anger, and he
Waved a menace with his hand, saying, "Back
To thy task base slave, nor dare resist the will
Of Pharaoh." Then Moses' wrath o'erleaped the bounds
Of prudence, and with a heavy blow he felled
The smiter to the earth, and Israel had
One tyrant less. Moses saw the mortal paleness

Chase the flushes from the Egyptian's face,
The whitening lips that breathed no more defiance,
And the relaxing tension of the well knit limbs;
And when he knew that he was dead, he hid
Him in the sand and left him to rest.

        Another day Moses walked
Abroad, and saw two brethren striving
For mastery; and then his heart grew full
Of tender pity. They were brethren, sharers
Of a common wrong: should not their wrongs more
Closely bind their hearts, and union, not division,
Be their strength? And feeling thus, he said, "Ye
Are brethren, wherefore do ye strive together?"
But they threw back his words in angry tones
And asked if he had come to judge them, and would
Mete to them the fate of the Egyptian?
Then Moses knew the sand had failed to keep
His secret, that his life no more was safe
In Goshen, and he fled unto the deserts
Of Arabia and became a shepherd
For the priest of Midian.

Chapter IV

        Men grow strong in action, but in solitude
Their thoughts are ripened. Like one who cuts away
The bridge on which he has walked in safety
To the other side, so Moses cut off all retreat
To Pharaoh's throne, and did choose the calling
Most hateful to an Egyptian; he became
A shepherd, and led his flocks and herds amid
The solitudes and wilds of Midian, where he
Nursed in silent loneliness his earnest faith
In God and a constant love for kindred, tribe
And race. Years stole o'er him, but they took
No atom from his strength, nor laid one heavy weight
Upon his shoulders. The down upon his face
Had ripened to a heavy beard; the fire
That glowed within his youthful eye had deepened
To a calm and steady light, and yet his heart
Was just as faithful to his race as when he had
Stood in Pharaoh's courts and bade farewell

Unto his daughter.
There was a look of patient waiting on his face,
A calm, grand patience, like one who had lifted
Up his eyes to God and seen, with meekened face,
The wings of some great destiny o'ershadowing
All his life with strange and solemn glory.
But the hour came when he must pass from thought
To action,—when the hope of many years
Must reach its grand fruition, and Israel's
Great deliverance dawn. It happened thus:
One day, as Moses led his flocks, he saw
A fertile spot skirted by desert sands,—
A pleasant place for flocks and herds to nip
The tender grass and rest within its shady nooks;
And as he paused and turned, he saw a bush with fire
Aglow; from root to stem a lambent flame
Sent up its jets and sprays of purest light,
And yet the bush, with leaves uncrisped, uncurled,
Was just as green and fresh as if the breath
Of early spring were kissing every leaf.
Then Moses said I'll turn aside to see
This sight, and as he turned he heard a voice
Bidding him lay his sandals by, for Lo! he
Stood on holy ground. Then Moses bowed his head
Upon his staff and spread his mantle o'er
His face, lest he should see the dreadful majesty
Of God; and there, upon that lonely spot,
By Horeb's mount, his shrinking hands received
The burden of his God, which bade him go
To Egypt's guilty king, and bid him let
The oppressed go free.
                              Commissioned thus
He gathered up his flocks and herds and sought
The tents of Jethro, and said "I pray thee
Let me go and see if yet my kindred live;
And Jethro bade him go in peace, nor sought
To throw himself across the purpose of his soul.
Yet there was a tender parting in that home;
There were moistened eyes, and quivering lips,
And lingering claspings of the parting hand, as Jethro
And his daughters stood within the light of that

Clear morn, and gave to Moses and his wife
And sons their holy wishes and their sad farewells.
For he had been a son and brother in that home
Since first with manly courtesy he had filled
The empty pails of Reuel's daughters, and found
A shelter 'neath his tent when flying from
The wrath of Pharaoh.

                    They journeyed on,
Moses, Zipporah and sons, she looking back
With tender love upon the home she had left,
With all its precious memories crowding round
Her heart, and he with eager eyes tracking
His path across the desert, longing once more
To see the long-lost faces of his distant home,
The loving eyes so wont to sun him with their
Welcome, and the aged hands that laid upon
His youthful head their parting blessing. They
Journeyed on till morning's flush and noonday
Splendor glided into the softened, mellowed
Light of eve, and the purple mists were deep'ning
On the cliffs and hills, when Horeb, dual
Crowned, arose before him; and there he met
His brother Aaron, sent by God to be
His spokesman and to bear him company
To Pharaoh. Tender and joyous was their greeting.
They talked of home and friends until the lighter
Ripple of their thoughts in deeper channels flowed;
And then they talked of Israel's bondage,
And the great deliverance about to dawn
Upon the fortunes of their race; and Moses
Told him of the burning bush, and how the message
Of his God was trembling on his lips. And thus
They talked until the risen moon had veiled
The mount in soft and silvery light; and then
They rested until morn, and rising up, refreshed
From sleep, pursued their way until they reached
The land of Goshen, and gathered up the elders
Of their race, and told them of the message
Of their Father's God. Then eager lips caught up
The words of hope and passed the joyful "news
Around, and all the people bowed their heads

And lifted up their hearts in thankfulness
To God."
                                        That same day
Moses sought an audience with the king. He found
Him on his throne surrounded by the princes
Of his court, who bowed in lowly homage
At his feet. And Pharaoh heard with curving lip
And flushing cheek the message of the Hebrew's God,
Then asked in cold and scornful tones, "Has
Israel a God, and if so where has he dwelt
For ages? As the highest priest of Egypt
I have prayed to Isis, and the Nile has
Overflowed her banks and filled the land
With plenty, but these poor slaves have cried unto
Their God, then crept in want and sorrow
To their graves. Surely Mizraim's God is strong
And Israel's is weak; then wherefore should
I heed his voice, or at his bidding break
A single yoke?" Thus reasoned that proud king,
And turned a deafened ear unto the words
Of Moses and his brother, and yet he felt
Strangely awed before their presence, because
They stood as men who felt the grandeur
Of their mission, and thought not of themselves,
But of their message.

Chapter V

On the next day Pharaoh called a council
Of his mighty men, and before them laid
The message of the brethren: the Amorphel,
Keeper of the palace and nearest lord
Unto the king, arose, and bending low
Before the throne, craved leave to speak a word.
Amorphel was a crafty, treacherous man,
With oily lips well versed in flattery
And courtly speech, a supple reed ready
To bend before his royal master's lightest
Breath—Pharaoh's willing tool. He said
"Gracious king, thou has been too lenient
With these slaves; light as their burdens are, they
Fret and chafe beneath them. They are idle

And the blood runs riot in their veins. Now
If thou would'st have these people dwell in peace,
Increase, I pray thee, their tasks and add unto
Their burdens; if they faint beneath their added
Tasks, they will have less time to plot sedition
And revolt."

Then Rhadma, oldest lord in Pharaoh's court,
Arose. He was an aged man, whose white
And heavy beard hung low upon his breast,
Yet there was a hard cold glitter in his eye,
And on his face a proud and evil look.
He had been a servant to the former king,
And wore his signet ring upon his hand.
He said, "I know this Moses well. Fourscore
Years ago Princess Charmian found him
By the Nile and rescued him from death, and did
Choose him as her son, and had him versed in all
The mysteries and lore of Egypt. But blood
Will tell, and this base slave, with servile blood
Within his veins, would rather be a servant
Than a prince, and so, with rude and reckless hand,
He thrust aside the honors of our dear
Departed King. Pharaoh was justly wroth,
But for his daughter's sake he let the trespass
Pass. But one day this Moses slew an Egyptian
In his wrath, and then the king did seek his life;
But he fled, it is said, unto the deserts
Of Arabia, and became a shepherd for the priest
Of Midian. But now, instead of leading flocks
And herds, he aspires to lead his captive race
To freedom. These men mean mischief; sedition
And revolt are in their plans. Decree, I pray thee,
That these men shall gather their own straw
And yet their tale of bricks shall be the same."
And these words pleased Pharaoh well, and all his
Lords chimed in with one accord. And Pharaoh
Wrote the stern decree and sent it unto Goshen—
That the laborers should gather their own straw,
And yet they should not 'minish of their tale of bricks.
                    'Twas a sad day in Goshen;
The king's decree hung like a gloomy pall

Around their homes. The people fainted 'neath
Their added tasks, then cried unto the king,
That he would ease their burdens; but he hissed
A taunt into their ears and said, "Ye are
Idle, and your minds are filled with vain
And foolish thoughts; get you unto your tasks,
And ye shall not 'minish of your tale of bricks."
     And then they turned their eyes
Reproachfully on Moses and his brother,
And laid the cruel blame upon their shoulders.
'Tis an old story now, but then 'twas new
Unto the brethren,—how God's anointed ones
Must walk with bleeding feet the paths that turn
To lines of living light; how hands that bring
Salvation in their palms are pierced with cruel
Nails, and lips that quiver first with some great truth
Are steeped in bitterness and tears, and brows
Now bright beneath the aureola of God,
Have bent beneath the thorny crowns of earth.
      There was hope for Israel.
But they did not see the golden fringes
Of their coming morn; they only saw the cold,
Grey sky, and fainted 'neath the cheerless gloom.

Moses sought again the presence of the king;
And Pharaoh's brow grew dark with wrath,
And rising up in angry haste, he said,
Defiantly, "If thy God be great, show
Us some sign or token of his power."
Then Moses threw his rod upon the floor,
And it trembled with a sign of life;
The dark wood glowed, then changed into a thing
Of glistening scales and golden rings, and green,
And brown and purple stripes; a hissing, hateful
Thing, that glared its fiery eye, and darting forth
From Moses' side, lay coiled and panting
At the monarch's feet. With wonder open-eyed
The king gazed on the changed rod, then called
For his magicians—wily men, well versed
In sinful lore—and bade them do the same.
And they, leagued with powers of night, did
Also change their rods to serpents; then Moses'

Serpent darted forth, and with a startling his
And angry gulp, he swallowed the living things
That coiled along his path. And thus did Moses
Show that Israel's God had greater power
Than those dark sons of night.
                              But not by this alone
Did God his mighty power reveal: He changed
Their waters; every fountain, well and pool
Was red with blood, and lips, all parched with thirst,
Shrank back in horror from the crimson draughts.
And then the worshiped Nile grew full of life;
Millions of frogs swarmed from the stream—they clogged
The pathway of the priests and fill the sacred
Fanes, and crowded into Pharaoh's bed, and hopped
Into his trays of bread, and slumbered in his
Ovens and his pans.

Then came another plague, of loathsome vermin;
They were gray and creeping things, that made
Their very clothes alive with dark and sombre
Spots—things so loathsome in the land they did
Suspend the service of the temple; for no priest
Dared to lift his hand to any god with one
Of these upon him. And then the sky grew
Dark, as if a cloud were passing o'er its
Changeless blue; a buzzing sound broke o'er
The city, and the land was swarmed with flies.
The murrain laid their cattle low; the hail
Cut off the first fruits of the Nile; the locusts
With their hungry jaws, destroyed the later crops,
And left the ground as brown and bare as if a fire
Had scorched it through.
                              Then angry blains
And fiery boils did blur the flesh of man
And beast; and then for three long days, nor saffron
Tint, nor crimson flush, nor soft and silvery light
Divided day from morn, nor told the passage
Of the hours; men rose not from their seats, but sat
In silent awe. That lengthened night lay like a burden
On the air,—a darkness one might almost gather
In his hand, it was so gross and thick. Then came
The last dread plague—the death of the first born.

'Twas midnight,
And a startling shriek rose from each palace,
Home and hut of Egypt, save the blood-besprinkled homes
Of Goshen; the midnight seemed to shiver with a sense
Of dread, as if the mystic angels wing
Had chilled the very air with horror.
Death! Death! was everywhere—in every home
A corpse—in every heart a bitter woe.
There were anxious fingerings for the pulse
That ne'er would throb again, and eager listenings
For some sound of life—a hurrying to and fro—
Then burning kisses on the cold lips
Of the dead, bitter partings, sad farewells,
And mournful sobs and piercing shrieks,
And deep and heavy groans throughout the length
And breadth of Egypt. 'Twas the last dread plague,
But it had snapped in twain the chains on which
The rust of ages lay, and Israel was freed;
Not only freed, but thrust in eager haste
From out the land. Trembling men stood by and longed
To see them gather up their flocks and herds,
And household goods, and leave the land; because they felt
That death stood at their doors as long as Israel
Lingered there; and they went forth in haste,
To tread the paths of freedom.

Chapter VI

But Pharaoh was strangely blind, and turning
From his first-born and his dead, with Egypt's wail
Scarce still upon his ear, he asked which way had
Israel gone? They told him that they journeyed
Towards the mighty sea, and were encamped
Near Baalzephn.
Then Pharaoh said, "The wilderness will hem them in,
The mighty sea will roll its barriers in front,
And with my chariots and my warlike men
I'll bring them back, or mete them out their graves."
                    Then Pharaoh's officers arose
And gathered up the armies of the king,
And made his chariots ready for pursuit.
With proud escutcheons blazoned to the sun,

In his chariot of ivory, pearl and gold,
Pharaoh rolled out of Egypt; and with him
Rode his mighty men, their banners floating
On the breeze, their spears and armor glittering
In the morning light; and Israel saw,
With fainting hearts, their old oppressors on their
Track: then women wept in hopeless terror;
Children hid their faces in their mothers' robes,
And strong men bowed their heads in agony and dread;
And then a bitter, angry murmur rose,—
"Were there no graves in Egypt, that thou hast
Brought us here to die?"
Then Moses lifted up his face aglow
With earnest faith in God, and bade their fainting hearts
Be strong and they should his salvation see.
"Stand still," said Moses to the fearful throng
Whose hearts were fainting in the wild, "Stand still."
Ah, that was Moses' word, but higher and greater
Came God's watchword for the hour, and not for that
Alone, but all the coming hours of time.
"Speak ye unto the people and bid them
Forward go; stretch thy hand across the waters
And smite them with thy rod." And Moses smote
The restless sea; the waves stood up in heaps,
Then lay as calm and still as lips that just
Had tasted death. The secret-loving sea
Laid bare her coral caves and iris-tinted
Floor; that wall of flood which lined the people's
Way was God's own wondrous masonry;
The signal pillar sent to guide them through the wild
Moved its dark shadow till it fronted Egypt's
Camp, but hung in fiery splendor, a light
To Israel's path. Madly rushed the hosts
Of Pharaoh upon the people's track, when
The solemn truth broke on them—that God
For Israel fought. With cheeks in terror
Blenching, and eyes astart with fear, "Let
Us flee," they cried, "from Israel, for their God
Doth fight against us; he is battling on their side."
They had trusted in their chariots, but now
That hope was vain; God had loosened every

Axle and unfastened every wheel, and each
Face did gather blackness and each heart stood still
With fear, as the livid lightnings glittered
And the thunder roared and muttered on the air,
And they saw the dreadful ruin that shuddered
O'er their heads, for the waves began to tremble
And the wall of flood to bend. Then arose
A cry of terror, baffled hate and hopeless dread,
A gurgling sound of horror, as "the waves
Came madly dashing, wildly crashing, seeking
Out their place again," and the flower and pride
Of Egypt sank as lead within the sea
Till the waves threw back their corpses cold and stark
Upon the shore, and the song of Israel's
Triumph was the requiem of their foes.
Oh the grandeur of that triumph; up the cliffs
And down the valleys, o'er the dark and restless
Sea, rose the people's shout of triumph, going
Up in praise to God, and the very air
Seemed joyous, for the choral song of millions
Throbbed upon its viewless wings.
Then another song of triumph rose in accents
Soft and clear; " 'twas the voice of Moses' sister
Rising in the tide of song. The warm blood
Of her childhood seemed dancing in her veins;
The roses of her girlhood were flushing
On her cheek, and her eyes flashed out the splendor
Of long departed days, for time itself seemed
Pausing, and she lived the past again; again
The Nile flowed by her; she was watching by the stream,
A little ark of rushes where her baby brother lay;
The tender tide of rapture swept o'er her soul again
She had felt when Pharaoh's daughter had claimed
Him as her own, and her mother wept for joy
Above her rescued son. Then again she saw
Him choosing " 'twixt Israel's pain and sorrow
And Egypt's pomp and pride." But now he stood
Their leader triumphant on that shore, and loud
She struck the cymbals as she led the Hebrew women
In music, dance and song, as they shouted out
Triumphs in sweet and glad refrains.

Miriam's Song

A wail in the palace, a wail in the hut,
  The midnight is shivering with dread,
And Egypt wakes up with a shriek and a sob
  To mourn for her first-born and dead.

In the morning glad voices greeted the light,
  As the Nile with its splendor was flushed;
At midnight silence had melted their tones,
  And their music forever is hushed.

In the morning the princes of palace and court
  To the heir of the kingdom bowed down;
'Tis midnight, pallid and stark in his shroud
  He dreams not of kingdom or crown.

As a monument blasted and blighted by God,
  Through the ages proud Pharaoh shall stand,
All seamed with the vengeance and scarred with the wrath
  That leaped from God's terrible hand.

Chapter VII

They journeyed on from Zuphim's sea until
They reached the sacred mount and heard the solemn
Decalogue. The mount was robed in blackness,—
Heavy and deep the shadows lay; the thunder
Crashed and roared upon the air; the lightning
Leaped from crag to crag; God's fearful splendor
Flowed around, and Sinai quaked and shuddered
To its base, and there did God proclaim
Unto their listening ears, the great, the grand,
The central and the primal truth of all
The universe—the unity of God.
                  Only one God,—
This truth received into the world's great life,
Not as an idle dream nor speculative thing,
But as a living, vitalizing thought,
Should bind us closer to our God and link us
With our fellow man, the bothers and co-heirs
With Christ, the elder brother of our race.
Before this truth let every blade of war
Grow dull, and slavery, cowering at the light,
Skulk from the homes of men; instead
Of war bring peace and freedom, love and joy,

And light for man, instead of bondage, whips
And chains. Only one God! the strongest hands
Should help the weak who bend before the blasts
Of life, because if God is only one
Then we are the children of his mighty hand,
And when we best serve man, we also serve
Our God. Let haughty rulers learn that men
Of humblest birth and lowliest lot have
Rights as sacred and divine as theirs, and they
Who fence in leagues of earth by bonds and claims
And title deeds, forgetting land and water,
Air and light are God's own gifts and heritage
For man—who throw their selfish lives between
God's sunshine and the shivering poor—
Have never learned the wondrous depth, nor scaled
The glorious height of this great central truth,
Around which clusters all the holiest faiths
Of earth. The thunder died upon the air,
The lightning ceased its livid play, the smoke
And darkness died away in clouds, as soft
And fair as summer wreaths that lie around
The setting sun, and Sinai stood a bare
And rugged thing among the sacred scenes
Of earth.

Chapter VIII

It was a weary thing to bear the burden
Of that restless and rebellious race. With
Sinai's thunders almost crashing in their ears,
They made a golden calf, and in the desert
Spread an idol's feast, and sung the merry songs
They had heard when Mizraim's songs bowed down before
Their vain and heathen gods; and thus for many years
Did Moses bear the evil manners of his race—
Their angry murmurs, fierce regrets and strange
Forgetfulness of God. Born slaves, they did not love
The freedom of the wild more than their pots of flesh.
And pleasant savory things once gathered
From the gardens of the Nile.
If slavery only laid its weight of chains

Upon the weary, aching limbs, e'en then
It were a curse; but when it frets through nerve
And flesh and eats into the weary soul,
Oh then it is a thing for every human
Heart to loathe, and this was Israel's fate,
For when the chains were shaken from their limbs,
They failed to strike the impress from their souls.
While he who'd basked beneath the radiance
Of a throne, ne'er turned regretful eyes upon
The past, nor sighed to grasp again the pleasures
Once resigned; but the saddest trial was
To see the light and joy fade from their faces
When the faithless spies spread through their camp
Their ill report; and when the people wept
In hopeless unbelief and turned their faces
Egyptward, and asked a captain from their bands
To lead them back where they might bind anew
Their broken chains, when God arose and shut
The gates of promise on their lives, and left
Their bones to bleach beneath Arabia's desert sands.
But though they slumbered in the wild, they died
With broader freedom on their lips, and for their
Little ones did God reserve the heritage
So rudely thrust aside.

The Death of Moses—Chapter IX

His work was done; his blessing lay
Like precious ointment on his people's head,
And God's great peace was resting on his soul.
His life had been a lengthened sacrifice,
A thing of deep devotion to his race,
Since first he turned his eyes on Egypt's gild
And glow, and clasped their fortunes in his hand
And held them with a firm and constant grasp.
But now his work was done; his charge was laid
In Joshua's hand, and men of younger blood
Were destined to possess the land and pass
Through Jordan to the other side. He too
Had hoped to enter there—to tread the soil
Made sacred by the memories of his
Kindred dead, and rest till life's calm close beneath

The sheltering vines and stately palms of that
Fair land; that hope had colored all his life's
Young dreams and sent it mellowed flushes o'er
His later years; but God's decree was otherwise.
And so he bowed his meekened soul in calm
Submission to the word, which bade him climb
To Nebo's highest peak, and view the pleasant land
From Jordan's swells unto the calmer ripples
Of the tideless sea, then die with all its
Loveliness in sight.
As he passed from Moab's grassy vale to climb
The rugged mount, the people stood in mournful groups,
Some, with quivering lips and tearful eyes,
Reaching out unconscious hands, as if to stay
His steps and keep him ever at their side, while
Others gazed with reverent awe upon
The calm and solemn beauty on his aged brow,
The look of loving trust and lofty faith
Still beaming from an eye that neither care
Nor time had dimmed. As he passed upward, tender
Blessings, earnest prayers and sad farewells rose
On each wave of air, then died in one sweet
Murmur of regretful love; and Moses stood
Alone on Nebo's mount.
                         Alone! not one
Of all that mighty throng who had trod with him
In triumph through the parted flood was there.
Aaron had died in Hor, with son and brother
By his side; and Miriam too was gone.
But kindred hands had made her grave, and Kadesh
Held her dust. But he was all alone; nor wife
Nor child was there to clasp in death his hand,
And bind around their bleeding hearts the precious
Parting words. And yet he was not all alone,
For God's great presence flowed around his path
And stayed him in that solemn hour.

      He stood upon the highest peak of Nebo,
And saw the Jordan chafing through its gorges,
Its banks made bright by scarlet blooms
And purple blossoms. The placid lakes

And emerald meadows, the snowy crest
Of distant mountains, the ancient rocks
That dripped with honey, the hills all bathed
In light and beauty; the shady groves
And peaceful vistas, the vines opprest
With purple riches, the fig trees fruit-crowned
Green and golden, the pomegranates with crimson
Blushes, the olives with their darker clusters,
Rose before him like a vision, full of beauty
And delight. Gazed he on the lovely landscape
Till it faded from his view, and the wing
Of death's sweet angel hovered o'er the mountain's
Crest, and he heard his garments rustle through
The watches of the night.
                    Then another, fairer, vision
Broke upon his longing gaze; 'twas the land
Of crystal fountains, love and beauty, joy
And light, for the pearly gates flew open,
And his ransomed soul went in. And when morning
O'er the mountain fringed each crag and peak with light,
Cold and lifeless lay the leader. God had touched
His eyes with slumber, giving his beloved sleep.

Oh never on that mountain
Was seen a lovelier sight
Than the troupe of fair young angels
That gathered 'round the dead.
With gentle hands they bore him
That bright and shining train,
From Nebo's lonely mountain
To sleep in Moab's vale.
But they sung no mournful dirges,
No solemn requiems said,
And the soft wave of their pinions
Made music as they trod.
But no one heard them passing,
None saw their chosen grave;
It was the angels secret
Where Moses should be laid.
And when the grave was finished,
They trod with golden sandals
Above the sacred spot,

And the brightest, fairest flowers
Sprang up beneath their tread.
Nor broken turf, nor hillock
Did e'er reveal that grave,
And truthful lips have never said
We know where he is laid.

Lines to Hon. Thaddeus Stevens

Have the bright and glowing visions
  Faded from thy longing sight,
Like the gorgeous tints of ev'n
  Mingling with the shades of night?

Didst thou hope to see thy country
  Wearing Justice as a crown,
Standing foremost 'mid the nations
  Worthy of the world's renown?

Didst thou think the grand fruition
  Reached the fullness of its time,
When the crater of God's judgment
  Overflowed the nation's crime?

That thy people, purged by fire,
  Would have trod another path,
Careful, lest their feet should stumble
  On the cinders of God's wrath?

And again the injured negro
  Grind the dreadful mills of fate,
Pressing out the fearful vintage
  Of the nation's scorn and hate?

Sadder than the crimson shadows
  Hung for years around our skies,
Are the hopes so fondly cherished
  Fading now before thine eyes.

Lines to Hon. Thaddeus Stevens: This and the next thirty poems (pp. 167–195) represent the complete contents of *Poems* (1871). Unless otherwise noted they are reprinted from that volume.

  Congressman Thaddeus Stevens (1792–1868) focused his considerable political power upon antislavery and social justice issues. He was largely responsible for the passing of the Civil Rights Bill and for the continuation of the Freedmen's Bureau. This poem was probably written shortly after his death on August 11, 1868.

Not in vain has been thy hoping,
   Though thy fair ideals fade,
If, like one of God's tall aloes,
   Thou art rip'ning in the shade.

There is light beyond the darkness,
   Joy beyond the present pain;
There is hope in God's great justice,
   And the negro's rising brain.

Though before the timid counsels
   Truth and Right may seem to fail,
God hath bathed his sword in judgment,
   And his arm shall yet prevail.

An Appeal to the American People

When a dark and fearful strife
Raged around the nation's life,
And the traitor plunged his steel
Where your quivering hearts could feel,
When your cause did need a friend,
We were faithful to the end.

When we stood with bated breath,
Facing fiery storms of death,
And the war-cloud, red with wrath,
Fiercely swept around our path,
Did our hearts with terror quail?
Or our courage ever fail?

When the captive, wanting bread,
Sought our poor and lowly shed,
And the blood-hounds missed his way,
Did we e'er his path betray?
Filled we not his heart with trust
As we shared with him our crust?

With your soldiers, side by side,
Helped we turn the battle's tide,
Till o'er ocean, stream and shore,
Waved the rebel flag no more,
And above the rescued sod
Praises rose to freedom's God.

But to-day the traitor stands
With the crimson on his hands,
Scowling 'neath his brow of hate,
On our weak and desolate,
With the blood-rust on the knife
Aiméd at the nation's life.

Asking you to weakly yield
All we won upon the field,
To ignore, on land and flood,
All the offerings of our blood,
And to write above our slain
"They have fought and died in vain."

To your manhood we appeal,
Lest the traitor's iron heel
Grind and trample in the dust
All our new-born hope and trust,
And the name of freedom be
Linked with bitter mockery.

Truth

A rock, for ages, stern and high,
Stood frowning 'gainst the earth and sky,
And never bowed his haughty crest
When angry storms around him prest.

Morn springing from the arms of night
Had often bathed his brow with light,
And kissed the shadows from his face
With tender love and gentle grace.

Day, pausing at the gates of rest,
Smiled on him from the distant West,
And from her throne the dark-browed Night
Threw round his path her softest light.
And yet he stood unmoved and proud,
Nor love, nor wrath, his spirit bowed;

Truth: When Harper included "Truth" in *Atlanta Offering: Poems* (1895), the follow-
ing two lines were added at the end:

And o'er the fallen ruin weaves
The brightest blooms and fairest leaves.

He bared his brow to every blast
And scorned the tempest as it passed.

One day a tiny, humble seed—
The keenest eye would hardly heed—
Fell trembling at that stern rock's base,
And found a lowly hiding place.
A ray of light, and drop of dew,
Came with a message, kind and true;
They told her of the world so bright,
Its love, its joy, and rosy light,
And lured her from her hiding place,
To gaze upon earth's glorious face.

So, peeping timid from the ground,
She clasped the ancient rock around,
And climbing up with childish grace,
She held him with a close embrace.

Her clinging was a thing of dread;
Where'er she touched a fissure spread,
And he who'd breasted many a storm
Stood frowning there, a mangled form;
So Truth dropped in the silent earth,
May seem a thing of little worth,
Till, spreading round some mighty wrong,
It saps its pillars proud and strong.

Death of the Old Sea King

'Twas a fearful night—the tempest raved
  With loud and wrathful pride,
The storm-king harnessed his lightning steeds,
  And rode on the raging tide.

The sea-king lay on his bed of death.
  Pale mourners around him bent,
They knew the wild and fitful life
  Of their chief was almost spent.

His ear was growing dull in death
  When the angry storm he heard,
The sluggish blood in the old man's veins
  With sudden vigor stirred.

"I hear them call," cried the dying man,
  His eyes grew full of light,
"Now bring me here my warrior robes,
  My sword and armor bright.

"In the tempest's lull I heard a voice,
  I knew't was Odin's call.
The Valkyrs are gathering round my bed
  To lead me unto his hall.

"Bear me unto my noblest ship,
  Light up a funeral pyre;
I'll walk to the palace of the braves
  Through a path of flame and fire."

O! wild and bright was the stormy light
  That flashed from the old man's eye,
As they bore him from the couch of death
  To his battle-ship to die.

And lit with many a mournful torch
  The sea-king's dying bed,
And like a banner fair and bright
  The flames around him spread.

But they heard no cry of anguish
  Break through that fiery wall,
With rigid brow and silent lips
  He was seeking Odin's hall

Through a path of fearful splendor,
  While strong men held their breath,
The brave old man went boldly forth
  And calmly talked with death.

"Let the Light Enter!"
Dying Words of Goethe

Light! more light! the shadows deepen,
  And my life is ebbing low,
Throw the windows widely open!
  Light! more light! before I go.

Softly let the balmy sunshine
  Play around my dying bed,

E'er the dimly lighted valley
   I with lonely feet shall tread.

Light! more light! for death is weaving
   Shadows round my waning sight,
And I fain would gaze upon him
   Through a stream of earthly light.

Not for greater gifts of genius,
   Nor for thoughts more grandly bright,
All the dying poet whispers
   Is a prayer for light, more light.

Heeds he not the gathered laurels,
   Fading slowly from his sight;
All the poet's aspirations
   Centre in that prayer for light.

Blessed Jesus, when our day dreams
   Melt and vanish from the sight,
May our dim and longing vision
   Then be blessed with light, more light!

Youth in Heaven

"In heaven the angels are advancing continually to the spring-time of their youth, so that the oldest angel appears the youngest.

                             Swedenborg

Not for them the length'ning shadows
   Falling coldly round our lives,
Nearer, nearer through the ages
   Life's new spring for them arrives.

Not for them the doubt and anguish
   Of an old and loveless age,
Dropping sadly tears of sorrow
   On life's faded, blotted page.

Youth in Heaven: When this poem appeared in the *Anglo-African Magazine* in 1860, stanzas 3 and 4 were reversed.

Not for them the mournful dimming
 Of the weary, tear-stained eye,
That has seen the sad procession
 Of its dearest hopes go by.

Not for them the hopeless clinging
 To life's worn and feeble strands,
Till the last has ceased to tremble
 In our agéd, withered hands.

Never lines of light and darkness
 Thread the brows forever fair,
And the eldest of the angels
 Seems the youngest brother there.

There the stream of life doth never
 Cross the mournful plains of death,
And the pearly gates are ever
 Closed against his icy breath.

Death of Zombi

The Chief of a Negro Kingdom in South America

Cruel in vengeance, reckless in wrath,
The hunters of men bore down on our path;
Inhuman and fierce, the offer they gave
Was freedom in death or the life of a slave.
The cheek of the mother grew pallid with dread,
As the tidings of evil around us were spread,
And closer and closer she strained to her heart
The children she feared they would sever apart.
The brows of our maidens grew gloomy and sad;
Hot tears burst from eyes once sparkling and glad.
Our young men stood ready to join in the fray,
That hung as a pall 'round our people that day.
Our leaders gazed angry and stern on the strife,
For freedom to them was dearer than life.
There was mourning at home and death in the street,
For carnage and famine together did meet.
The pale lips of hunger were asking for bread,
While husbands and fathers lay bleeding and dead.
For days we withstood the tempests of wrath,
That scattered destruction and death in our path,

Till, broken and peeled, we yielded at last,
And the glory and strength of our kingdom were past.
But Zombi, our leader, and warlike old chief,
Gazed down on our woe with anger and grief;
The tyrant for him forged fetters in vain,
His freedom-girt limbs had worn their last chain.
Defiance and daring still flashed from his eye;
A freeman he'd lived and free he would die.
So he climbed to the verge of a dangerous steep,
Resolved from its margin to take a last leap;
For a fearful death and a bloody grave
Were dearer to him than the life of a slave.
Nor went he alone to the mystic land—
There were other warriors in his band,
Who rushed with him to Death's dark gate,
All wrapped in the shroud of a mournful fate.

Lines to Charles Sumner

Thank God that thou hast spoken
    Words earnest, true and brave,
The lightning of thy lips did smite
    The fetters of the slave.

I thought the shadows deepened,
    Round the pathway of the slave,
As one by one his faithful friends
    Were dropping in the grave.

When other hands grew feeble,
    And loosed their hold on life,
Thy words rang like a clarion
    For freedom's noble strife.

Thy words were not soft echoes,
    Thy tones no syren song;
They fell as battle-axes
    Upon our giant wrong.

Lines to Charles Sumner: Part of a letter published in the National Anti-Slavery Standard, July 17, 1860. It was published separately in the Liberator, as "To Charles Sumner" on July 20, 1860.

God grant thy words of power
   May fall as precious seeds,
That yet shall leaf and blossom
   In high and holy deeds.

"Sir, We Would See Jesus"

We would see Jesus; earth is grand,
Flowing out from her Creator's hand.
Like one who tracks his steps with light,
His footsteps ever greet our sight;
The earth below, the sky above,
Are full of tokens of his love;
But 'mid the fairest scenes we've sighed—
Our hearts are still unsatisfied.

We would see Jesus; proud and high
Temples and domes have met our eye.
We've gazed upon the glorious thought,
By earnest hands in marble wrought,
And listened where the flying feet
Beat time to music, soft and sweet;
But bow'rs of ease, and halls of pride,
Our yearning hearts ne'er satisfied.

We would see Jesus; we have heard
Tidings our inmost souls have stirred,
How, from their chambers full of night,
The darkened eyes receive the light;
How, at the music of his voice,
The lame do leap, the dumb rejoice.
Anxious we'll wait until we've seen
The good and gracious Nazarene.

The Bride of Death

They robed her for another groom,
For her bridal couch, prepared the tomb;
From the sunny love of her marriage day
A stronger rival had won her away;

The Bride of Death: Also appeared in the *National Anti-Slavery Standard* January 21, 1860.

His wooing was like a stern command,
And cold was the pressure of his hand.

Through her veins he sent an icy thrill,
With sudden fear her heart stood still;
To his dusty palace the bride he led,
Her guests were the pale and silent dead.
No eye flashed forth a loving light,
To greet the bride as she came in sight,
Not one reached out a joyous hand,
To welcome her home to the mystic land.

Silent she sat in the death still hall,
For her bridal robe she wore a pall;
Instead of orange-blossoms fair,
Willow and cypress wreathed her hair.
Though her mother's kiss lay on her cheek,
Her lips no answering love could speak,
No air of life stirred in her breath,
That fair young girl was the bride of death.

Thank God for Little Children

Thank God for little children,
  Bright flowers by earth's wayside,
The dancing, joyous lifeboats
  Upon life's stormy tide.

Thank God for little children;
  When our skies are cold and gray,
They come as sunshine to our hearts,
  And charm our cares away.

I almost think the angels,
  Who tend life's garden fair,
Drop down the sweet white blossoms
  That bloom around us here.

It seems a breath of heaven
  Round many a cradle lies,
And every little baby
  Brings a message from the skies.

The humblest home with children
  Is rich in precious gems,

That shame the wealth of monarchs,
  And pale their diadems.

Dear mothers, guard these jewels,
  As sacred offerings meet,
A wealth of household treasures
  To lay at Jesus' feet.

The Dying Fugitive

Slowly o'er his darkened features
  Stole the warning shades of death,
And we knew the mystic angel
  Waited for his parting breath.

He had started for his freedom,
  And his heart beat firm and high;
But before he won the guerdon
  Came the message—he must die.

He must die when just before him
  Lay the longed-for precious prize,
And the hopes that lit him onward
  Faded out before his eyes.

For awhile a fearful madness
  Rested on his weary brain,
And he thought the hateful tyrant
  Had rebound his galling chain.

Then he cried in bitter anguish,
  Take me where that good man dwells,
For a name to freedom precious
  Lingered 'mid life's shattered cells.

But as sunshine gently stealing
  On the storm-cloud's gloomy track,
Through the tempests of his bosom
  Came the light of reason back.

And, without a sigh or murmur
  For the friends he'd left behind,

The Dying Fugitive: A slightly different version was printed earlier in the *Anglo-African Magazine* 1 (1859):253; *Weekly Anglo-African*, August 8, 1859; and *National Anti-Slavery Standard*, February 18, 1860.

Calmly yielded he his spirit
   To the Father of mankind.

Thankful that so near to freedom
   He with eager feet had trod,
Ere his ransom'd spirit rested
   On the bosom of his God.

Bury Me in a Free Land

Make me a grave where'er you will,
In a lowly plain or a lofty hill;
Make it among earth's humblest graves,
But not in a land where men are slaves.

I could not rest, if around my grave
I heard the steps of a trembling slave;
His shadow above my silent tomb
Would make it a place of fearful gloom.

I could not sleep, if I heard the tread
Of a coffle-gang to the shambles led,
And the mother's shriek of wild despair
Rise, like a curse, on the trembling air.

I could not rest, if I saw the lash
Drinking her blood at each fearful gash;
And I saw her babes torn from her breast,
Like trembling doves from their parent nest.

I'd shudder and start, if I heard the bay
Of a bloodhound seizing his human prey;
And I heard the captive plead in vain,
As they bound, afresh, his galling chain.

If I saw young girls from their mother's arms
Bartered and sold for their youthful charms,
My eye would flash with a mournful flame,
My death-pale cheek grow red with shame.

I would sleep, dear friends, where bloated Might
Can rob no man of his dearest right;

Bury Me in a Free Land: Liberator, January 14, 1864. Harper included a copy of this poem in a letter that she wrote to one of John Brown's men who was awaiting execution for his part in the raid on Harper's Ferry.

My rest shall be calm in any grave
Where none can call his brother a slave.

I ask no monument, proud and high,
To arrest the gaze of the passers by;
All that my yearning spirit craves
Is—*Bury me not in a land of slaves!*

The Freedom Bell

Ring, aye, ring the freedom bell,
    And let its tones be loud and clear;
With glad hosannas let it swell
    Until it reach the Bondman's ear.

Through pain that wrings the life apart,
    And spasms full of deadly strife,
And throes that shake the nation's heart,
    The fainting land renews her life.

Where shrieks and groans distract the air,
    And sods grow red with crimson rain,
The ransom'd slave shall kneel in prayer
    And bury deep his rusty chain.

Where cheeks now pale with sickening dread,
    And brows grow dark with cruel wrath,
Shall Fre[e]dom's banner wide be spread
    And Hope and Peace attend her path.

White-robed and pure her feet shall move
    O'er rifts of ruin deep and wide;
Her hands shall span with lasting love
    The chasms rent by hate and pride.

Where waters, blush'd with human gore,
    Unsullied streams shall purl along;
Where crashed the battle's awful roar
    Shall rise the Freeman's joyful song.

Then ring, aye, ring the freedom bell,
    Proclaiming all the nation free;
Let earth with sweet thanksgiving swell
    And heaven catch up the melody.

Mary at the Feet of Christ

She stood at Jesus' feet,
  And bathed them with her tears,
While o'er her spirit surg'd
  The guilt and shame of years.

Though Simon saw the grief
  Upon the fair young face,
The stern man coldly thought
  For her this is no place.

Her feet have turned aside
  From paths of truth and right,
If Christ a prophet be
  He'll spurn her from his sight.

And silently he watched
  The child of sin and care,
Uncoil upon Christ's feet
  Her wealth of raven hair.

O Life! she sadly thought,
  I know thy bane and blight,
And yet I fain would find
  The path of peace and right.

I've seen the leper cleansed,
  I've seen the sick made whole,
But mine's a deeper wound—
  It eats into the soul.

And men have trampled down
  The beauty once their prize,
While women pass me by
  With cold, averted eyes.

But now a hope of peace
  Steals o'er my weary breast,
And from these lips of love
  There comes a sense of rest.

Mary at the Feet of Christ: Based on the incident described in Luke 7:36–50. Also published as "Mary at Christ's Feet" in the *Christian Recorder,* January 28, 1871.

The tender, loving Christ
    Gazed on her tearful eyes,
Then saw on Simon's face
    A look of cold surprise.

"Simon," the Saviour said,
    "Thou wast to me remiss,
I came thy guest, but thou
    Didst give no welcome kiss.

"Thou broughtest from thy fount
    No water cool and sweet,
But she, with many tears,
    Hath bent and kissed my feet.

"Thou pouredst on my head
    No oil with kindly care,
But she anoints my feet,
    And wipes them with her hair.

"I know her steps have strayed,
    Her sins they many be,
But she with love hath bound
    Her erring heart to me."

How sweetly fell his words
    Upon her bruiséd heart,
When, like a ghastly train,
    She felt her sins depart.

What music heard on earth,
    Or rapture moving heaven
Were like those precious words—
    "Thy sins are all forgiven!"

The Mother's Blessing

Oh, my soul had grown so weary
    With its many cares opprest,
All my heart's high aspirations
    Languish'd in a prayer for rest.

I was like a lonely stranger
    Pining in a distant land,

Bearing on her lips a language
  None around her understand.

Longing for a close communion
  With some kindred mind and heart,
But whose language is a jargon
  Past her skill, and past her art.

God in mercy looked upon me,
  Saw my fainting, pain, and strife,
Sent to me a blest evangel,
  Through the gates of light and life.

Then my desert leafed and blossom'd,
  Beauty decked its deepest wild,
Hope and joy, peace and blessing,
  Met me in my first-born child.

When the tiny hands, so feeble,
  Brought me smiles and joyful tears,
Lifted from my life the shadows,
  That had gathered there for years.

God, I thank thee for the blessing
  That at last has crown'd my life,
Soothed its weary, lonely anguish,
  Stay'd its fainting, calm'd its strife.

Gracious Parent! guard and shelter
  In thine arms my darling child
Till she treads the streets of jasper,
  Glorified and undefiled.

Vashti

She leaned her head upon her hand
  And heard the king's decree—
"My lords are feasting in my halls,
  Bid Vashti come to me.

"I've shown the treasures of my house,
  My costly jewels rare,

Vashti: Based on an incident described in Esther 1:13–22. Also published in *The New National Era*, September 22, 1870.

But with the glory of her eyes
   No rubies can compare.

"Adorn'd and crown'd I'd have her come,
   With all her queenly grace,
And, 'mid my lords and mighty men,
   Unveil her lovely face.

"Each gem that sparkles in my crown,
   Or glitters on my throne,
Grows poor and pale when she appears,
   My beautiful, my own!"

All waiting stood the chamberlains
   To hear the Queen's reply,
They saw her cheek grow deathly pale,
   But light flash'd to her eye:

"Go, tell the King," she proudly said,
   "That I am Persia's Queen,
And by his crowds of merry men
   I never will be seen.

"I'll take the crown from off my head
   And tread it 'neath my feet
Before their rude and careless gaze
   My shrinking eyes shall meet.

"A queen unveil'd before the crowd!—
   Upon each lip my name!—
Why, Persia's women all would blush
   And weep for Vashti's shame!

"Go back!" she cried, and waived her hand,
   And grief was in her eye:
"Go, tell the King," she sadly said,
   "That I would rather die."

They brought her message to the King,
   Dark flash'd his angry eye;
'Twas as the lightning ere the storm
   Hath swept in fury by.

Then bitterly outspoke the King,
   Through purple lips of wrath—
"What shall be done to her who dares
   To cross your monarch's path?"

Then spake his wily counsellors—
   "O King of this fair land!
From distant Ind to Ethiop,
   All bow to thy command.

"But if, before thy servants' eyes,
   This thing they plainly see,
That Vashti doth not heed thy will
   Nor yield herself to thee,

"The women, restive 'neath our rule,
   Would learn to scorn our name,
And from her deed to us would come
   Reproach and burning shame.

"Then, gracious King, sign with thy hand
   This stern but just decree,
That Vashti lay aside her crown,
   Thy Queen no more to be."

She heard again the King's command,
   And left her high estate,
Strong in her earnest womanhood,
   She calmly met her fate,

And left the palace of the King,
   Proud of her spotless name—
A woman who could bend to grief,
   But would not bow to shame.

The Change

The blue sky arching overhead,
The green turf 'neath my daily tread,
All glorified by freedom's light,
Grow fair and lovely to my sight.

The very winds that sweep along
Seemed burdened with a lovely song,
Nor shrieks nor groans of grief or fear,
Float on their wings and pain my ear.

No more with dull and aching breast,
Roused by the horn—I rise from rest
Content and cheerful with my lot,
I greet the sun and leave my cot.

For darling child and loving wife
I toil with newly waken'd life;
The light that lingers round her smile
The shadows from my soul beguile.

The prattle of my darling boy
Fills my old heart with untold joy;
Before his laughter, mirth and song
Fade out long scores of grief and wrong.

Oh, never did the world appear
So lovely to my eye and ear,
'Till Freedom came, with Joy and Peace,
And bade my hateful bondage cease!

The Dying Mother

Come nearer to me, husband,
  Now the aching leaves my breast,
But my eyes are dim and weary,
  And to-night I fain would rest.

Clasp me closer to your bosom
  Ere I calmly sleep in death;
With your arms enfolded round me
  I would yield my parting breath.

Bring me now my darling baby,
  God's own precious gift of love,
Tell her she must meet her mother
  In the brighter world above.

When her little feet grow stronger
  To walk life's paths untrod,
That earnest, true and hopeful,
  She must lay her hands on God.

Tell my other little children
  They must early seek His face;
That His love is a strong tower,
  And His arms a hiding place.

Tell them—but my voice grows fainter—
  Surely, husband, this is death—
Tell them that their dying mother
  Bless'd them with her latest breath.

Words for the Hour

Men of the North! it is no time
  To quit the battle-field;
When danger fronts your rear and van
  It is no time to yield.

No time to bend the battle's crest
  Before the wily foe,
And, ostrich-like, to hide your heads
  From the impending blow.

The minions of a baffled wrong
  Are marshalling their clan,
Rise up! rise up, enchanted North!
  And strike for God and man.

This is no time for careless ease;
  No time for idle sleep;
Go light the fires in every camp,
  And solemn sentries keep.

The foe ye foiled upon the field
  Has only changed his base;
New dangers crowd around you
  And stare you in the face.

O Northern men! within your hands
  Is held no common trust;
Secure the victories won by blood
  When treason bit the dust.

'Tis yours to banish from the land
  Oppression's iron rule;
And o'er the ruin'd auction-block
  Erect the common school.

To wipe from labor's branded brow
  The curse that shamed the land;
And teach the Freedman how to wield
  The ballot in his hand.

Words for the Hour: Appears in *Poems* (1871), but was obviously written during the Civil War.

This is the nation's golden hour,
  Nerve every heart and hand,
To build on Justice, as a rock,
  The future of the land.

True to your trust, oh, never yield
  One citadel of right!
With Truth and Justice clasping hands
  Ye yet shall win the fight!

President Lincoln's Proclamation of Freedom

It shall flash through coming ages;
  It shall light the distant years;
And eyes now dim with sorrow
  Shall be clearer through their tears.

It shall flush the mountain ranges;
  And the valleys shall grow bright;
It shall bathe the hills in radiance,
  And crown their brows with light.

It shall flood with golden splendor
  All the huts of Caroline,
And the sun-kissed brow of labor
  With lustre new shall shine.

It shall gild the gloomy prison,
  Darken'd by the nation's crime,
Where the dumb and patient millions
  Wait the better coming time.

By the light that gilds their prison,
  They shall seize its mould'ring key,
And the bolts and bars shall vibrate
  With the triumphs of the free.

Like the dim and ancient chaos,
  Shrinking from the dawn of light,
Oppression, grim and hoary,
  Shall cower at the light.

President Lincoln's Proclamation of Freedom: This poem was excerpted in Lydia Maria
Child's *Freedman's Book* (1865).

And her spawn of lies and malice
  Shall grovel in the dust,
While joy shall thrill the bosoms
  Of the merciful and just.

Though the morning seemed to linger
  O'er the hill-tops far away,
Now the shadows bear the promise
  Of the quickly coming day.

Soon the mists and murky shadows
  Shall be fringed with crimson light,
And the glorious dawn of freedom
  Break refulgent on the sight.

To a Babe Smiling in Her Sleep

Tell me, did the angels greet thee?
  Greet my darling when she smiled?
Did they whisper, softly, gently,
  Pleasant thoughts unto my child?

Did they whisper, 'mid thy dreaming,
  Thoughts that made thy spirit glad?
Of the joy-lighted city,
  Where the heart is never sad?

Did they tell thee of the fountains,
  Clear as crystal, fair as light,
And the glory-brightened country,
  Never shaded by a night?

Of life's pure, pellucid river,
  And the tree whose leaves do yield
Healing for the wounded nations—
  Nations smitten, bruised and peeled?

Of the city, ruby-founded,
  Built on gems of flashing light,
Paling all earth's lustrous jewels,
  And the gates of pearly white?

Darling, when life's shadows deepen
  Round thy prison-house of clay,

To a Babe . . .: Also published as "To My Daughter" in the *Weekly Anglo-African*, February 15, 1862.

May the footsteps of God's angels
  Ever linger round thy way.

The Artist

He stood before his finished work,
  His heart beat warm and high;
But they who gazed upon the youth
  Knew well that he must die.

For many days a fever fierce
  Had burned into his life;
But full of high impassioned art,
  He bore the fearful strife.

And wrought in extacy and hope
  The image of his brain;
He felt the death throes at his heart,
  But labored through the pain.

The statue seemed to glow with life—
  A costly work of art;
For it he paid the fervent blood
  From his own eager heart.

With kindling eye and flushing cheek
  But slowly laboring breath,
He gazed upon his finished work,
  Then sought his couch of death.

And when the plaudits of the crowd
  Came like the south wind's breath,
The dreamy, gifted child of art
  Had closed his eyes in death.

Jesus

Come speak to me of Jesus,
  I love that precious name,
Who built a throne of power
  Upon a cross of shame.

Unveil to me the beauty
  That glorifies his face—
The fullness of the Father—
  The image of his grace.

The Artist: Also published in the *Christian Recorder*, March 9, 1861.

My soul would run to meet Him;
  Restrain me not with creeds;
For Christ, the hope of glory,
  Is what my spirit needs.

I need the grand attraction,
  That centres 'round the cross,
To change the gilded things of earth,
  To emptiness and dross.

My feet are prone to wander,
  My eyes to turn aside,
And yet I fain would linger,
  With Christ the crucified.

I want a faith that's able
  To stand each storm and shock—
A faith forever rooted,
  In Christ the living Rock.

Fifteenth Amendment

Beneath the burden of our joy
  Tremble, O wires, from East to West!
Fashion with words your tongues of fire,
  To tell the nation's high behest.

Outstrip the winds, and leave behind
  The murmur of the restless waves;
Nor tarry with your glorious news,
  Amid the ocean's coral caves.

Ring out! ring out! your sweetest chimes,
  Ye bells, that call to prayer;
Let every heart with gladness thrill,
  And songs of joyful triumph raise.

Shake off the dust, O rising race!
  Crowned as a brother and a man;
Justice to-day asserts her claim,
  And from thy brow fades out the ban.

With freedom's chrism upon thy head,
  Her precious ensign in thy hand,

The Fifteenth Amendment: Also appeared in *The New National Era* on December 12, 1870.

Go place thy once despiséd name
  Amid the noblest of the land.

O ransomed race! give God the praise,
  Who led thee through a crimson sea,
And 'mid the storm of fire and blood,
  Turned out the war-cloud's light to thee.

Retribution

Judgment slumbered. God in mercy
  Stayed his strong avenging hand;
Sent them priests and sent them prophets,
  But they would not understand.

Judgment lingered; men, grown bolder,
  Gloried in their shame and guilt;
And the blood of God's poor children
  Was as water freely spilt.

Then arose a cry to heaven,
  Deep and startling, sad and wild,
Sadder than the wail of Egypt,
  Mourning for the first-born child.

For the sighing of the needy
  God at length did bare his hand,
And the footsteps of his judgments
  Echoed through the guilty land.

Oh! the terror, grief and anguish;
  Oh! the bitter, fearful, strife,
When the judgments of Jehovah
  Pressed upon the nation's life.

And the land did reel and tremble
  'Neath the terror of his frown,
For its guilt lay heavy on it,
  Pressing like an iron crown.

As a warning to the nations,
  Bathed in blood and swathed in fire,
Lay the once oppressing nation,
  Smitten by God's fearful ire.

The Sin of Achar

Night closed o'er the battl'ing army,
   But it brought them no success;
Victory perched not on their banners;
   Night was full of weariness.

Flushed and hopeful in the morning,
   Turned they from their leader's side:
Routed, smitten and defeated,
   Came they back at eventide.

Then in words of bitter mourning
   Joshua's voice soon arose:
"Tell us, O thou God of Jacob,
   Why this triumph of our foes?"

To his pleading came the answer
   Why the hosts in fear did yield:
" 'Twas because a fearful trespass
   'Mid their tents did lie concealed."

Clear and plain before His vision,
   With whom darkness is as light,
Lay the spoils that guilty Achar
   Covered from his brethren's sight.

From their tents they purged the evil
   That had ruin round them spread;
Then they won the field of battle,
   Whence they had in terror fled.

Through the track of many ages
   Comes this tale of woe and crime;
Let us read it as a lesson
   And a warning for our time.

Oh, for some strong-hearted Joshua!
   Faithful to his day and time,
Who will wholly rid the nation
   Of her clinging curse and crime.

The Sin of Achar: Refers to an incident in Joshua 7:4–26.

Till she writes on every banner
　All beneath these folds are free,
And the oppressed and groaning millions
　Shout the nation's Jubilee.

Lines to Miles O'Reiley

You've heard no doubt of Irish bulls,
　And how they blunder, thick and fast;
But of all the queer and foolish things,
　O'Reiley, you have said the last.

You say we brought the rebs supplies,
　And gave them aid amid the fight,
And if you must be ruled by rebs,
　Instead of black you want them white.

You blame us that we did not rise,
　And pluck from a fiery brand,
When Little Mac said if we did,
　He'd put us down with iron hand.

And when we sought to join your ranks,
　And battle with you, side by side,
Did men not curl their lips with scorn,
　And thrust us back with hateful pride?

And when at last we gained the field,
　Did we not firmly, bravely stand,
And help to turn the tide of death,
　That spread its ruin o'er the land?

We hardly think we're worse than those
　Who kindled up this fearful strife,
Because we did not seize the chance
　To murder helpless babes and wife.

And had we struck, with vengeful hand,
　The rebel where he most could feel,

Lines to Miles O'Reiley: Charles Halpine, an Irish immigrant and former Union officer, wrote a series of articles under the pen name of "Miles O'Reilly." O'Reilly was supposedly a private in the 47th New York Volunteers among whose "works" was the poem "Sambo's Right to Be Kilt." "Lines to Miles O'Reiley" [sic] was published in the October 16, 1867 edition of the Philadelphia Press as "The Other Side."

Were you not ready to impale
   Our hearts upon your Northern steel?

O'Reiley, men like you should wear
   The gift of song like some bright crown,
Nor worse than ruffians at the ring,
   Strike at a man because he's down.

The Little Builders

Ye are builders little builders,
   Not with mortar, brick and stone,
But your work is far more glorious—
   Ye are building freedom's throne.

Where the ocean never slumbers
   Works the coral 'neath the spray,
By and by a reef or island
   Rears its head to greet the day

Then the balmy rains and sunshine
   Scatter treasures o'er the soil,
'Till a place for human footprints,
   Crown the little builder's toil.

When the stately ships sweep o'er them.
   Cresting all the sea with foam,
Little think these patient toilers,
   They are building man a home.

Do you ask me, precious children,
   How your little hands can build,
That you love the name of freedom,
   But your fingers are unskilled?

Not on thrones or in proud temples,
   Does fair freedom seek her rest;
No, her chosen habitations,
   Are the hearts that love her best.

Would you gain the highest freedom?
   Live for God and man alone,
Then each heart in freedom's temple,
   Will be like a living stone.

Fill your minds with useful knowledge,
   Learn to love the true and right;
Thus you'll build the throne of freedom,
   On a pedestal of light.

The Dying Child to Her Blind Father

Dear father, I hear a whisper,
   It tells me that I must go,
And my heart returns her answer
   In throbbings so faint and low.

I'm sorry to leave you, father,
   I know you will miss me so,
And the world for you will gather
   A gloomier shade of woe.

You will miss me, dearest father,
   When the violets wake from sleep,
And timidly from their hedges
   The early snow-drops peep,

I shall not be here to gather
   The flowers by stream and dell,
The bright and beautiful flowers,
   Dear Father, you love so well.

You will miss my voice, dear father,
   From every earthly tone,
All the songs that cheered your darkness,
   And you'll be so sad and lone.

I can scarcely rejoice, dear father,
   In hope of the brighter land,
When I know you'll pine in sadness,
   And miss my guiding hand.

You are weeping, dearest father,
   Your sobs are shaking my soul,
But we'll meet again where the shadow
   And night from your eyes shall roll.

And then you will see me, father,
   With visions undimmed and clear,

Your eyes will sparkle with rapture—
You know there's no blindness there.

Light in Darkness

We've room to build holy altars
Where our crumbling idols lay;
We've room for heavenly visions,
When our earth dreams fade away.

Through rifts and rents in our fortune
We gazed with blinding tears,
Till glimpses of light and beauty
Gilded our gloomy fears.

An angel stood at our threshold,
We thought him a child of night,
Till we saw the print of his steps
Made lines of living light.

We had much the world calls precious;
We had heaps of shining dust;
He laid his hand on our treasures,
And wrote on them moth and rust.

But still we had other treasures,
That gold was too poor to buy,
We clasped them closer and closer,
But saw them fade and die.

Our spirit grew faint and heavy,
Deep shadows lay on our years,
Till light from the holy city,
Streamed through our mist of tears.

And we thanked the chastening angel
Who shaded our earthly light,
For the light and beautiful visions
That broke on our clearer sight.

Our first view of the Holy City
Came through our darken'd years,
The songs that lightened our sorrows,
We heard 'mid our night of tears.

Our English Friends

Your land is crowned with regal men,
Whose brows ne'er wore a diadem,—
The men who, in our hour of need,
Reached out their hands and bade God speed.

Who watched across the distant strand
The anguish of our fainting land,
And grandly made our cause their own,
Till Slavery tottered on her throne.

When Slavery, full of wrath and strife,
Was clutching at the Nation's life,
How precious were your words of cheer
That fell upon the listening ear.

And when did Fame, with glowing pen,
Record the deeds of nobler men,—
The men who, facing want and pain,
Loved freedom more than paltry gain.

O noble men! ye bravely stood
True to our country's highest good;
May God, who saw your aims and ends,
Forever bless our English friends!

Aunt Chloe

I remember, well remember,
  That dark and dreadful day,
When they whispered to me, "Chloe,
  Your children's sold away!"

It seemed as if a bullet
  Had shot me through and through,
And I felt as if my heart-strings
  Was breaking right in two.

And I says to cousin Milly,
  "There must be some mistake;
Where's Mistus?" "In the great house crying—
  Crying like her heart would break.

Our English Friends: This poem and the ones on pages 196–209 represent the complete text of the 1872 edition of *Sketches of Southern Life.*

"And the lawyer's there with Mistus;
    Says he's come to 'ministrate,
'Cause when master died he just left
    Heap of debt on the estate.

"And I thought 'twould do you good
    To bid your boys goodbye—
To kiss them both and shake their hands
    And have a hearty cry.

"Oh! Chloe, I knows how you feel,
    'Cause I'se been through it all;
I thought my poor old heart would break
    When master sold my Saul."

Just then I heard the footsteps
    Of my children at the door,
And I rose right up to meet them.
    But I fell upon the floor.

And I heard poor Jakey saying,
    "Oh, mammy, don't you cry!"
And I felt my children kiss me
    And bid me, both, good-bye.

Then I had a mighty sorrow,
    Though I nursed it all alone;
But I wasted to a shadow,
    And turned to skin and bone.

But one day dear uncle Jacob
    (In heaven he's now a saint)
Said, "Your poor heart is in the fire,
    But child you must not faint."

Then I said to uncle Jacob,
    If I was good like you,
When the heavy trouble dashed me
    I'd know just what to do.

Then he said to me, "Poor Chloe,
    The way is open wide:"
And he told me of the Saviour,
    And the fountain in His side.

Then he said, "Just take your burden
    To the blessed Master's feet;

I takes all my troubles, Chloe,
  Right unto the mercy-seat."

His words waked up my courage,
  And I began to pray,
And I felt my heavy burden
  Rolling like a stone away.

And a something seemed to tell me,
  You will see your boys again—
And that hope was like a poultice
  Spread upon a dreadful pain.

And it often seemed to whisper,
  Chloe, trust and never fear;
You'll get justice in the kingdom,
  If you do not get it here.

The Deliverance

Master only left old Mistus
  One bright and handsome boy;
But she fairly doted on him,
  He was her pride and joy.

We all liked Mister Thomas,
  He was so kind at heart;
And when the young folkes got in scrapes,
  He always took their part.

He kept right on that very way
  Till he got big and tall,
And old Mistus used to chide him,
  And say he'd spile us all.

But somehow the farm did prosper
  When he took things in hand;
And though all the servants liked him,
  He made them understand.

One evening Mister Thomas said,
  "Just bring my easy shoes:
I am going to sit by mother,
  And read her up the news."

Soon I heard him tell old Mistus
  "We're bound to have a fight;

But we'll whip the Yankees, mother,
  We'll whip them sure as night!"

Then I saw old Mistus tremble;
  She gasped and held her breath;
And she looked on Mister Thomas
  With a face as pale as death.

"They are firing on Fort Sumpter;
  Oh! I wish that I was there!—
Why, dear mother! what's the matter?
  You're the picture of despair."

"I was thinking, dearest Thomas,
  'Twould break my very heart
If a fierce and dreadful battle
  Should tear our lives apart."

"None but cowards, dearest mother,
  Would skulk unto the rear,
When the tyrant's hand is shaking
  All the heart is holding dear."

I felt sorry for old Mistus;
  She got too full to speak;
But I saw the great big tear-drops
  A running down her cheek.

Mister Thomas too was troubled
  With choosing on that night,
Betwixt staying with his mother
  And joining in the fight.

Soon down into the village came
  A call for volunteers;
Mistus gave up Mister Thomas,
  With many sighs and tears.

His uniform was real handsome;
  He looked so brave and strong;
But somehow I couldn't help thinking
  His fighting must be wrong.

Though the house was very lonesome,
  I thought 'twould all come right,
For I felt somehow or other
  We was mixed up in that fight.

And I said to Uncle Jacob,
  "Now old Mistus feels the sting,
For this parting with your children
  Is a mighty dreadful thing."

"Never mind," said Uncle Jacob,
  "Just wait and watch and pray,
For I feel right sure and certain,
  Slavery's bound to pass away;

"Because I asked the Spirit,
  If God is good and just,
How it happened that the masters
  Did grind us to the dust.

"And something reasoned right inside,
  Such should not always be;
And you could not beat it out my head,
  The Spirit spoke to me."

And his dear old eyes would brighten,
  And his lips put on a smile,
Saying, "Pick up faith and courage,
  And just wait a little while."

Mistus prayed up in the parlor
  That the Secesh all might win;
We were praying in the cabins,
  Wanting freedom to begin.

Mister Thomas wrote to Mistus,
  Telling 'bout the Bull's Run fight,
That his troops had whipped the Yankees,
  And put them all to flight.

Mistus' eyes did fairly glisten;
  She laughed and praised the South,
But I thought some day she'd laugh
  On tother side her mouth.

I used to watch old Mistus' face,
  And when it looked quite long
I would say to Cousin Milly,
  The battle's going wrong;

Not for us, but for the Rebels.—
  My heart 'would fairly skip,

When Uncle Jacob used to say,
  "The North is bound to whip."

And let the fight go as it would—
  Let North or South prevail—
He always kept his courage up,
  And never let it fail.

And he often used to tell us,
  "Children, don't forget to pray;
For the darkest time of morning
  Is just 'fore the break of day."

Well, one morning bright and early
  We heard the fife and drum,
And the booming of the cannon—
  The Yankee troops had come.

When the word ran through the village,
  The colored folks are free—
In the kitchens and the cabins
  We held a jubilee.

When they told us Mister Lincoln
  Said that slavery was dead,
We just poured our prayers and blessings
  Upon his precious head.

We just laughed, and danced, and shouted,
  And prayed, and sang, and cried,
And we thought dear Uncle Jacob
  Would fairly crack his side.

But when old Mistus heard it,
  She groaned and hardly spoke;
When she had to lose her servants,
  Her heart was almost broke.

'Twas a sight to see our people
  Going out, the troops to meet,
Almost dancing to the music,
  And marching down the street.

After years of pain and parting,
  Our chains was broke in two,
And we was so mighty happy,
  We did'nt know what to do.

But we soon got used to freedom,
　　Though the way at first was rough;
But we weathered through the tempest,
　　For slavery made us tough.

But we had one awful sorrow,
　　It almost turned my head,
When a mean and wicked cretur
　　Shot Mister Lincoln dead.

'Twas a dreadful solemn morning,
I just staggered on my feet;
And the women they were crying
　　And screaming in the street.

But if many prayers and blessings
　　Could bear him to the throne,
I should think when Mister Lincoln died,
　　That heaven just got its own.

Then we had another President,—
　　What do you call his name?
Well, if the colored folks forget him
　　They would'nt be much to blame.

We thought he'd be the Moses
　　Of all the colored race;
But when the Rebels pressed us hard
　　He never showed his face.

But something must have happened him,
　　Right curi's I'll be bound,
'Cause I heard 'em talking 'bout a circle
　　That he was swinging round.

But everything will pass away—
　　He went like time and tide—
And when the next election came
　　They let poor Andy slide.

But now we have a President,
　　And if I was a man
I'd vote for him for breaking up
　　The wicked Ku-Klux Klan.

And if any man should ask me
　　If I would sell my vote,

I'd tell him I was not the one
    To change and turn my coat;

If freedom seem'd a little rough
    I'd weather through the gale;
And as to buying up my vote,
    I hadn't it for sale.

I do not think I'd ever be
    As slack as Jonas Handy;
Because I heard he sold his vote
    For just three sticks of candy.

But when John Thomas Reeder brought
    His wife some flour and meat,
And told her he had sold his vote
    For something good to eat,

You ought to seen Aunt Kitty raise,
    And heard her blaze away;
She gave the meat and flour a toss,
    And said they should not stay.

And I should think he felt quite cheap
    For voting the wrong side;
And when Aunt Kitty scolded him,
    He just stood up and cried.

But the worst fooled man I ever saw
    Was when poor David Rand
Sold out for flour and sugar;
    The sugar was mixed with sand.

I'll tell you how the thing got out;
    His wife had company,
And she thought the sand was sugar,
    And served it up for tea.

When David sipped and sipped the tea,
    Somehow it did'nt taste right;
I guess when he found he was sipping sand,
    He was mad enough to fight.

The sugar looked so nice and white—
    It was spread some inches deep—
But underneath was a lot of sand;
    Such sugar is mighty cheap.

You'd laughed to seen Lucinda Grange
  Upon her husband's track;
When he sold his vote for rations
  She made him take 'em back.

Day after day did Milly Green
  Just follow after Joe,
And told him if he voted wrong
  To take his rags and go.

I think that Curnel Johnson said
  His side had won the day,
Had not we women radicals
  Just got right in the way.

And yet I would not have you think
  That all our men are shabby;
But 'tis said in every flock of sheep
  There will be one that's scabby.

I've heard, before election came
  They tried to buy John Slade;
But he gave them all to understand
  That he wasn't in that trade.

And we've got lots of other men
  Who rally round the cause,
And go for holding up the hands
  That gave us equal laws.

Who know their freedom cost too much
  Of blood and pain and treasure,
For them to fool away their votes
  For profit or for pleasure.

Aunt Chloe's Politics

Of course, I don't know very much
  About these politics,
But I think that some who run 'em
  Do mighty ugly tricks.

I've seen 'em honey-fugle round,
  And talk so awful sweet,
That you'd think them full of kindness,
  As an egg is full of meat.

Now I don't believe in looking
  Honest people in the face,
And saying when you're doing wrong,
  That "I haven't sold my race."

When we want to school our children,
  If the money isn't there,
Whether black or white have took it,
  The loss we all must share.

And this buying up each other
  Is something worse than mean,
Though I thinks a heap of voting,
  I go for voting clean.

Learning to Read

Very soon the Yankee teachers
  Came down and set up school;
But, oh! how the Rebs did hate it,—
  It was agin' their rule.

Our masters always tried to hide
  Book learning from our eyes;
Knowledge did'nt agree with slavery—
  'Twould make us all too wise.

But some of us would try to steal
  A little from the book,
And put the words together,
  And learn by hook or crook.

I remember Uncle Caldwell,
  Who took pot-liquor fat
And greased the pages of his book,
  And hid it in his hat.

And had his master ever seen
  The leaves upon his head,
He'd have thought them greasy papers,
  But nothing to be read.

And there was Mr. Turner's Ben,
  Who heard the children spell,
And picked the words right up by heart,
  And learned to read 'em well.

Well, the Northern folks kept sending
  The Yankee teachers down;
And they stood right up and helped us,
  Though Rebs did sneer and frown.

And, I longed to read my Bible,
  For precious words it said;
But when I begun to learn it,
  Folks just shook their heads,

And said there is no use trying,
  Oh! Chloe, you're too late;
But as I was rising sixty,
  I had no time to wait.

So I got a pair of glasses,
  And straight to work I went,
And never stopped till I could read
  The hymns and Testament.

Then I got a little cabin—
  A place to call my own—
And I felt as independent
  As the queen upon her throne.

Church Building

Uncle Jacob often told us,
  Since freedom blessed our race
We ought all to come together
  And build a meeting place.

So we pinched, and scraped, and spared,
  A little here and there;
Though our wages was but scanty,
  The church did get a share.

And, when the house was finished,
  Uncle Jacob came to pray;
He was looking mighty feeble,
  And his head was awful grey

But his voice rang like a trumpet;
  His eyes looked bright and young;
And it seemed a mighty power
  Was resting on his tongue.

And he gave us all his blessing—
   'Twas parting words he said,
For soon we got the message
   The dear old man was dead.

But I believe he's in the kingdom,
   For when we shook his hand
He said, "Children, you must meet me
   Right in the promised land;

"For when I'm done a moiling
   And toiling here below,
Through the gate into the city
   Straightway I hope to go."

The Reunion

Well, one morning real early
   I was going down the street,
And I heard a stranger asking
   For Missis Chloe Fleet.

There was a something in his voice
   That made me feel quite shaky,
And when I looked right in his face,
   Who should it be but Jakey!

I grasped him tight, and took him home—
   What gladness filled my cup!
And I laughed, and just rolled over,
   And laughed, and just give up.

"Where have you been? O Jakey, dear!
   Why did'nt you come before?
Oh! when you children went away
   My heart was awful sore."

"Why, mammy, I've been on your hunt
   Since ever I've been free,
And I have heard from brother Ben,—
   He's down in Tennessee.

"He wrote me that he had a wife."
   "And children?" "Yes, he's three."
"You married, too?" "Oh no, indeed,
   I thought I'd first get free."

"Then, Jakey, you will stay with me,
   And comfort my poor heart;
Old Mistus got no power now
   To tear us both apart.

"I'm richer now than Mistus,
   Because I have got my son;
And Mister Thomas he is dead,
   And she's got 'nary one.

"You must write to brother Benny
   That he must come this fall,
And we'll make the cabin bigger,
   And that will hold us all.

"Tell him I want to see 'em all
   Before my life do cease:
And then, like good old Simeon,
   I hope to die in peace."

"I Thirst"

First Voice

I thirst, but earth cannot allay
   The fever coursing through my veins;
The healing stream is far away—
   It flows through Salem's lovely plains.

The murmurs of its crystal flow
   Break ever o'er this world of strife;
My heart is weary, let me go,
   To bathe it in the stream of life;

For many worn and weary hearts
   Have bathed in this pure healing stream
And felt their griefs and cares depart,
   E'en like some sad forgotten dream.

Second Voice

"The Word is nigh thee, even in thy heart."

Say not, within thy weary heart,
   Who shall ascend above,

To bring unto thy fever'd lips
　The fount of joy and love.

Nor do thou seek to vainly delve
　Where death's pale angels tread,
To hear the murmur of its flow
　Around the silent dead.

Within, in thee is the living fount,
　Fed from the springs above;
There quench thy thirst till thou shalt bathe
　In God's own sea of love.

The Dying Queen

"I would meet death awake."

The strength that bore her on for years
　Was ebbing fast away,
And o'er the pale and life-worn face,
　Death's solemn shadows lay.

With tender love and gentle care,
　Friends gathered round her bed,
And for her sake each footfall hushed
　The echoes of its tread.

They knew the restlessness of death
　Through every nerve did creep,
And carefully they tried to lull
　The dying Queen to sleep.

In vain she felt Death's icy hand
　Her failing heart-strings shake;
And, rousing up, she firmly said,
　"I'd meet my God awake."

Awake, I've met the battle's shock,
　And born the cares of state;
Nor shall I take your lethean cup,
　And slumber at death's gate.

Did I not watch with eyes alert,
　The paths where foes did tend;
And shall I veil my eyes with sleep,
　To meet my God and friend?

Nay, rather from my weary lids,
    This heavy slumber shake,
That I may pass the mystic vale,
    And meet my God awake.

Something to Do

Life is made for earnest action,
    With our shoulders to the wheel;
We at least may share the burden,
    That so many hearts do feel.

We may wipe the tear of sorrow,
    From the hapless orphan child;
And may plant the fairest roses,
    Mid life's deserts, drear and wild.

We may scatter rays of sunshine,
    Over many paths of gloom;
And may smooth the sloping pathway,
    Of the aged to the tomb.

We may point the child of errors,
    When her wandering feet do stray;
From the mazes full of sorrow,
    To the better and brighter way.

To the sin crushed and despondent,
    Who the depths of grief have stirred;
We at least may give the solace,
    Of a kind and loving word.

And if others climb the mountain,
    Where our feet are sure to fail;
If we linger at the bottom,
    We may cheer them from the vale.

If we sow amid life's furrows,
    Holy thoughts and deeds of love,
We shall gladly reap the harvest;
    In the fields of light above.

Something to Do: Christian Recorder, April 6, 1872.

Lines to M.A.H.

'Tis well for thee my daughter
   To choose the narrow road,
To lay thy life's fresh fragrance
   On the altar of thy God.

'Tis said a young disciple,
   Was the one whom Christ loved best,
Who at the mournful supper,
   Did lean upon his breast.

Would'st thou have my darling daughter,
   A safe and sure retreat?
Like the Mary of the Gospel,
   Find a place at Jesus' feet.

Lay thy fair young head my daughter,
   On the dear Redeemer's breast,
May his gracious arms enclose thee,
   And his bosom be thy rest.

A Christmas Carol

The Child is born, the Child is born,
   So sang the angels on that morn;
When all the jasper streets above,
   O'er flowed with joy, with peace and love.

Throughout the bright and vast domain,
   In joyous tones outgushed the strain
And fragrance fainted on the air
   From every golden vial there.

The burden of this heavenly strain,
   Was joy for grief, was ease for pain;
Instead of darkness, death and strife,
   It sang of light, of love, and life.

Oh, holy child, by thy dear love,
   Draw our poor hearts to things above;

Lines to M.A.H.: Printed in the *Christian Recorder*, April 13, 1872. It bore the following footnote: "Said to be the younger or youngest disciple." M.A.H. is Harper's daughter, Mary, who would have been about 11 years old at this time.

A *Christmas Carol*: *Christian Recorder*, December 28, 1872. A slightly revised revision was reprinted in the *Christian Recorder*, January 3, 1889.

Unto our feet that go astray,
  Oh, be the new and living way.

Oh, fill our souls with thy great peace,
  A stream whose flow shall never cease;
To our dim eyes and longing sight,
  Reveal the true and only light.

Peace

Welcome Peace! thou blest evangel—
  Welcome to this war-cursed land;
O'er the weary waiting millions
  Let thy banner be unfurled.
On the burning brow of anger
  Lay thy gentle, soothing hand;
Say to Carnage and Destruction,
  Ye shall cease to blight the land.

Plead in tones of love and mercy,
  'Mid the battle's crash and roar;
'Till the nations new created
  Learn the art of war no more.
On the brow of martial Glory
  Bid the people place their ban;
Nothing in the world is sacred
  Like the sacredness of man.

Heroes grasping fame and laurels
  On the bloody fields of crime;
'Tis a fearful path to glory,
  Over human hearts to climb.
God for man did light each planet,
  Warmed the sun, and bade it shine;
And upon each human spirit
  Left his finger prints divine.

Bury deep your proud ambitions.
  Cease your struggles, fierce and wild;
Oh, 'tis higher bliss to rescue,
  Than to trample down God's child.
Better far to aid the feeble,

Peace: Christian Recorder, June 26, 1873.

Raise the groveller from the clod;
Lives are only great and noble
   When they clasp both man and God.

A Dialogue

Inquirer

Oh, who hath a balm that will impart,
   Strength to the fevered heart and brain?
I've looked upon earth and seen many a heart,
   Weary and fainting with pain.

Wealth

I've heaps, rich heaps of shining dust,
   I've gems from every mine;
Bid the weary spirit learn to trust,
   In gold that glitters and gems that shine.

Inquirer

Oh, vain were the hopes of that heart,
   Sighing its sorrows should cease;
That would search 'mid gold and gems,
   For the priceless pearl of peace.

Fame

I've wreaths, fair wreaths for the fainting brow;
   They are bright and my name is, Fame;
Will not the heart forget its woe
   When I write it a deathless name?

Inquirer

No, your wreaths and your laurels rare
   Would blanche and fade on a brow unblest;
And the heart still mindful of its care
   Would ache and throb with the same unrest.

A Dialogue: *Christian Recorder*, July 3, 1873.

Pleasure

Oh, I am a queen of a numerous train,
  Whose hearts are ever glad;
I've a nectar cup for every pain,
  We drink and forget to be sad.

Inquirer

But I have seen the cheek all pale,
  When life was fading from the heart:
'Twas then I saw thy nectar fail,
  I watched and saw thy smiles depart.

Religion

Oh, I am from the land of light,
  My home is the world on high;
But I dwell mid the weary sons of night,
  And bid their darkness fly.

I have no wreaths of fading fame,
  No records of decaying worth;
But God's remembrance and a name
  That can't be written in the earth.

I have no heaps of shining dust,
  No gems from every mine;
But gifts to beautify the just,
  On the brow of the pure they'll shine.

When pleasure's smile shall all depart,
  Her nectar but increase the thirst;
I'll point the fevered brow and heart
  To crystal founts that freshly burst.

Inquirer

Thy words do better hope impart
  Than Pleasure, Wealth or Fame;
Thou hast the balm for the wounded heart,
  Tell me kind stranger, thy name.

Religion

My name and my nature is love;
  'Twas God only wise formed the plan;
That missioned me down from above,

As the guide and the solace of man.

Inquirer

Then I'll tell the weary brain and heart,
  Thou hast balm for its wounds, peace for its strife;
And the guerdons which thou dost impart
  Are the pearl of peace and crown of life.

Saved at Last

Time with its narrow shores receded,
  And fainter grew life's din;
Behind me lay earth's sorrows,
  Its suffering, want and sin.

Behind me were life's fetters,
  Its conflict and unrest;
Before me were the pearly gates,
  And mansions of the blest.

Behind me were earth's pleasant scenes,
  Its grandeur, gild and glow;
But oh, how faded were the things
  I valued once below.

Honor and fame were fleeting breaths,
  And gold was dust and dross;
The only glory that I saw
  Was streaming round the cross.

Behind me dreadful incense rose,
  From censers filled with vice;
Before me were the pleasant airs
  That breathed through Paradise.

Behind me were the storms of life,
  Its rooks and shoals were past;
My bark was anchored by the throne,
  And I was saved at last.

Through misty doubts and chilling fears,
  Through storms of wild discord;
The port is gained and I shall be
  Forever with the Lord.

Saved at Last: Christian Recorder, August 7, 1873.

Speeches

◆

"We Are All Bound up Together" was delivered to the Eleventh National Woman's Rights Convention held in New York in May 1866. Among Harper's fellow speakers at the conference were Susan B. Anthony, Frances D. Gage, Lucretia Mott, and Elizabeth Cady Stanton. This speech marked the beginning of Harper's prominence in national feminist organizations. Though she would continue to work with many of these women, Harper often experienced frustration caused by racism in general in the country and in particular among her feminist colleagues. This speech indicates that she was aware of cultural differences and many of the potential problems. She understood, for example, that many feminists were racists and that many people who urged the empowerment of blacks did not include black women in their visions. Throughout her southern tour, Harper spoke on behalf of equal rights for all people. She interpreted equal rights to apply to race, gender, and class. As she says in this speech, she does not object to President Johnson because he was "a poor white man." It was his behavior that condemned him in her eyes.

"The Great Problem to Be Solved" was delivered at the Centennial Anniversary of the Pennsylvania Society for Promoting the Abolition of Slavery on April 14, 1875. Harper's references to history, science, and contemporary events reveal a wide range of reading and interests. In this lecture as in others, Harper emphasizes the responsibilities of both races for creating a society that is more harmonious with what she understands as the intentions of God. Thus, while both of these speeches were deliv-

216

ered in the north, they fairly represent the ideas that Harper espoused in both the south and the north during this era.

♦

We Are All Bound up Together

I feel I am something of a novice upon this platform. Born of a race whose inheritance has been outrage and wrong, most of my life had been spent in battling against those wrongs. But I did not feel as keenly as others, that I had these rights, in common with other women, which are now demanded. About two years ago, I stood within the shadows of my home. A great sorrow had fallen upon my life. My husband had died suddenly, leaving me a widow, with four children, one my own, and the others step-children. I tried to keep my children together. But my husband died in debt; and before he had been in his grave three months, the administrator had swept the very milk-crocks and wash tubs from my hands. I was a farmer's wife and made butter for the Columbus market; but what could I do, when they had swept all away? They left me one thing—and that was a looking-glass! Had I died instead of my husband, how different would have been the result! By this time he would have had another wife, it is likely; and no administrator would have gone into his house, broken up his home, and sold his bed, and taken away his means of support.

I took my children in my arms, and went out to seek my living. While I was gone; a neighbor to whom I had once lent five dollars, went before a magistrate and swore that he believed I was a non-resident, and laid an attachment on my very bed. And I went back to Ohio with my orphan children in my arms, without a single feather bed in this wide world, that was not in the custody of the law. I say, then, that justice is not fulfilled so long as woman is unequal before the law.

We are all bound up together in one great bundle of humanity, and society cannot trample on the weakest and feeblest of its members without receiving the curse in its own soul. You tried that in the case of the negro. You pressed him down for two centuries; and in so doing you crippled the moral strength and paralyzed the spiritual energies of the white men of the country. When the hands of the black were fettered, white men were deprived of the liberty of speech and the freedom of the press. Society cannot afford to neglect the enlightenment of any class of its members. At the South, the legislation of the country was in behalf of the rich slaveholders, while the poor white man was neglected. What is the consequence to-day? From that very class of neglected poor white men,

---

We Are All Bound up Together: Proceedings of the Eleventh Woman's Rights Convention, May 1866, 45–48.

comes the man who stands to-day with his hand upon the helm of the nation. He fails to catch the watchword of the hour, and throws himself, the incarnation of meanness, across the pathway of the nation. My objection to Andrew Johnson is not that he has been a poor white man; my objection is that he keeps "poor whits" all the way through. (Applause.) That is the trouble with him.

This grand and glorious revolution which has commenced, will fail to reach its climax of success, until throughout the length and brea[d]th of the American Republic, the nation shall be so color-blind, as to know no man by the color of his skin or the curl of his hair. It will then have no privileged class, trampling upon and outraging the unprivileged classes, but will be then one great privileged nation, whose privilege will be to produce the loftiest manhood and womanhood that humanity can attain.

I do not believe that giving the woman the ballot is immediately going to cure all the ills of life. I do not believe that white women are dew-drops just exhaled from the skies. I think that like men they may be divided into three classes, the good, the bad, and the indifferent. The good would vote according to their convictions and principles; the bad, as dictated by preju[d]ice or malice; and the indifferent will vote on the strongest side of the question, with the winning party.

You white women speak here of rights. I speak of wrongs. I, as a colored woman, have had in this country an education which has made me feel as if I were in the situation of Ishmael, my hand against every man, and every man's hand against me. Let me go to-morrow morning and take my seat in one of your street cars—I do not know that they will do it in New York, but they will in Philadelphia—and the conductor will put up his hand and stop the car rather than let me ride.

A Lady—They will not do that here.

Mrs. Harper—They do in Philadelphia. Going from Washington to Baltimore this Spring, they put me in the smoking car. (Loud Voices—"Shame.") Aye, in the capital of the nation, where the black man consecrated himself to the nation's defence, faithful when the white man was faithless, they put me in the smoking car! They did it once; but the next time they tried it, they failed; for I would not go in. I felt the fight in me; but I don't want to have to fight all the time. To-day I am puzzled where to make my home. I would like to make it in Philadelphia, near my own friends and relations. But if I want to ride in the streets of Philadelphia, they send me to ride on the platform with the driver. (Cries of "Shame.") Have women nothing to do with this? Not long since, a colored woman took her seat in an Eleventh Street car in Philadelphia, and the conductor stopped the car, and told the rest of the passengers to get out, and left the car with her in it alone, when they took it back to the station. One day I took my seat in a car, and the conductor came to me and told me to take another seat. I just screamed "murder." The man said if I was black I ought to behave myself. I knew that if he was white he was not behaving himself. Are there not wrongs to be righted?

The Great Problem to Be Solved

Ladies and Gentlemen:

The great problem to be solved by the American people, if I understand it, is this—whether or not there is strength enough in democracy, virtue enough in our civilization, and power enough in our religion to have mercy and deal justly with four millions of people but lately translated from the old oligarchy of slavery to the new commonwealth of freedom: and upon the right solution of this question depends in a large measure the future strength, progress, and durability of our nation. The most important question before us colored people is not simply what the Democratic party may do against us or the Republican party do for us; but what are we going to do for ourselves? What shall we do towards developing our character, adding our quota to the civilization and strength of the country, diversifying our industry, and practising those lordly virtues that conquer success, and turn the world's dread laugh into admiring recognition? The white race has yet work to do in making practical the political axiom of equal rights, and the Christian idea of human brotherhood; but while I lift mine eyes to the future I would not ungratefully ignore the past. One hundred years ago and Africa was the privileged hunting-ground of Europe and America, and the flag of different nations hung a sign of death on the coast of Congo and Guinea, and for years unbroken silence had hung around the horrors of the African slave trade. Since then Great Britain and other nations have wiped the bloody traffic from their hands, and shaken the gory merchandise from their fingers, and the brand of piracy has been placed upon the African slave trade. Less than fifty years ago mob violence belched out its wrath against the men who dared to arraign the slaveholder before the bar of conscience and Christendom. Instead of golden showers upon his head, he who garrisoned the front had a halter around his neck. Since, if I may borrow the idea, the nation has caught the old inspiration from his lips and written it in the new organic world. Less than twenty-five years ago slavery

---

The Great Problem . . .: This lecture was delivered during the Centennial Anniversary of the Pennsylvania Society for Promoting the Abolition of Slavery held at Philadelphia on April 14, 1875.

clasped hands with King Cotton, and said slavery fights and cotton conquers for American slavery. Since then slavery is dead, the colored man has exchanged the fetters on his wrist for the ballot in his hand. Freedom is king and Cotton a subject.

It may not seem to be a gracious thing to mingle complaint in a season of general rejoicing. It may appear like the ancient Egyptians seating a corpse at their festal board to avenge the Americans for their shortcomings when so much has been accomplished. And yet with all the victories and triumphs which freedom and justice have won in this country, I do not believe there is another civilized nation under Heaven where there are half so many people who have been brutally and shamefully murdered, with or without impunity, as in this republic within the last ten years. And who cares? Where is the public opinion that has scorched with red-hot indignation the cowardly murderers of Vicksburg and Louisiana? Sheridan lifts up the vail from Southern society, and behind it is the smell of blood, and our bones scattered at the grave's mouth; murdered people; a White League with its "covenant of death and agreement with hell." And who cares? What city pauses one hour to drop a pitying tear over these mangled corpses, or has forged against the perpetrator one thunderbolt of furious protest? But let there be a supposed or real invasion of Southern rights by our soldiers, and our great commercial emporium will rally its forces from the old man in his classic shades, to clasp hands with "Dead Rabbits" and "Plug-uglies" in protesting against military interference. What we need to-day in the onward march of humanity is a public sentiment in favor of common justice and simple mercy. We have a civilization which has produced grand and magnificent results, diffused knowledge, overthrown slavery, made constant conquests over nature, and built up a wonderful material prosperity. But two things are wanting in American civilization—a keener and deeper, broader and tenderer sense of justice—a sense of humanity, which shall crystallize into the life of a nation the sentiment that justice, simple justice, is the right, not simply of the strong and powerful, but of the weakest and feeblest of all God's children; a deeper and broader humanity, which will teach men to look upon their feeble breth[r]en not as vermin to be crushed out, or beasts of burden to be bridled and bitted, but as the children of the living God; of that God whom we may earnestly hope is in perfect wisdom and in perfect love working for the best good of all. Ethnologists may differ about the origin of the human race. Huxley may search for it in protoplasms, and Darwin send for the missing links, but there is one thing of which we may rest assured—that we all come from the living God and that He is the common Father. The nation that has no reverence for man is also lacking in reverence for God and needs to be instructed. As fellow–citizens, leaving out all humanitarian views—as a matter of political economy it is better to have the colored race a living force animated and strengthened by self-reliance and self-respect, than a stagnant mass, degraded and self-condemned. Instead of the North relaxing its efforts to diffuse education in the South, it behooves us for our national life, to throw into the South all the healthful reconstructing influences we can command. Our work in this country is grandly constructive. Some races have come into this world and overthrown and destroyed. But if it is glory to destroy, it is happiness to save; and Oh! what a noble work there is before our nation! Where is there a young man who would consent to lead an aimless life when there are such glorious opportunities before him? Before young men is another battle—not a battle of flashing swords and clashing steel—but a moral warfare, a battle against ignorance, poverty, and low social condition. In physical warfare the keenest swords may be blunted and the loudest batteries hushed; but in that great conflict [f]or moral and spiritual progress your weapons shall be brighter for their service and better for their use. In fighting truly and nobly for others you win the victory for yourselves.

Give power and significance to your own life, and in the great work of upbuilding there is room for woman's work and woman's heart. Oh, that our hearts were alive and our vision quickened, to see the grandeur of the work that lies before. We have some culture among us, but I think our culture lacks enthusiasm. We need a deep earnestness and a lofty unselfishness to round out our lives. It is the inner life that develops the outer, and if we are in earnest the precious things lie all around our feet, and we need not waste our strength in striving after the dim and unattainable. Woman in your golden youth; mother, binding around your heart all the precious ties of life—let no magnificence of culture, or amplitude of fortune, or refinement of sensibilities, repel you from helping the weaker and less favored. If you have ampler gifts, hold them as larger opportunities with which you can benefit others. Oh, it is better to feel that the weaker and feebler our race the closer we will cling to them than it is to isolate ourselves from them in selfish, or careless unconcern, saying there is a lion without. Inviting you to this work I do not promise you fair sailing and unclouded skies. You may meet with coolness where you expect sympathy; disappointment where you feel sure of success; isolation and loneliness instead of heart-support and cooperation. But if your lives are based and built upon these divine certitudes, which are the only enduring strength of humanity, then whatever defeat and discomfiture may overshadow your plans or frustrate your schemes, for a life that is in harmony with God and sympathy for man there is no such word as fail. And in conclusion, permit me to say, let no misfortunes crush you;

no hostility of enemies or failure of friends discourage you. Apparent failure may hold in its rough shell the germs of a success that will blossom in time, and bear fruit throughout eternity. What seemed to be a failure around the Cross of Calvary and in the garden, has been the grandest recorded success.

Fiction

◆

As "The Two Offers" proves, Frances Harper began experimenting with fiction relatively early in her career. "The Mission of the Flowers" was included with the dramatic narrative, "Moses: A Story of the Nile," in 1869. As a companion to the celebration of a great emancipator, this piece prevents misinterpretations which might suggest that Harper believed the Moses model the more important to emulate. As the rose discovers, each of God's creations has "her own earth-mission," and one must seek neither to remake others in her own image nor to remake oneself in the image of others.

Harper also published in the *Christian Recorder,* an official publication of the African Methodist Episcopal Church, at least three other works that are not collected in her books. "Minnie's Sacrifice" (1869) is a serialized novel with many episodes in which Harper employed cliffhangers to maintain reader expectations. "Opening the Gates" (1871) is a brief short story. And "Fancy Etchings"/"Fancy Sketches" (1873–74) are discrete narratives involving the same characters. Unfortunately, many issues of this journal have been damaged or lost, and only fragments of some of these works are available.

"Fancy Etchings"/"Fancy Sketches" are the same series, but sometime during the run, the title was changed from "Fancy Etchings" to "Fancy Sketches." Missing issues make it difficult to determine exactly when "Fancy Etchings" was first published and when or why its title was changed to "Fancy Sketches." However, there are at least five in the series. The selec-

223

tions included here appear to be autobiographical. Jenny is in action and attitude a version of the young Harper. Uncle Glumby could be William Watkins. And the issues discussed are those of Harper's poetry and essays.

◆

Fancy Etchings [April 24, 1873]

"Why! aunt Jane this is delightful. I was saying that I hoped you would come this morning, and lo! you are here; a pleasant exemplification of the beautiful adage, talk of the angels and they will show their wings."

"Well, darling, I am glad that you have leisure to sit awhile with me; I feared that you would be engaged in house cleaning, and that I would find you too busy to have a pleasant little chat."

"Oh no, I shall not commence that job till next week, and were I in the midst of it, I do not think I should be too busy to give you hearty welcome; so just let me take your things and give you this easy chair, and I do hope that we will have an uninterrupted morning."

"Well, Jenny, I am at your disposal; hand me my knitting, darling, if you please. Do you remember this satchel?"

"I should think I did, when some of the pleasantest memories of my childhood are connected with it. Don't you remember how we children used to ransack it for gum-drops and pepper mints, and how you used to shake your head and say you feared the little rogues loved your satchel better than they loved you."

"Do I remember it? Ah, you and your sister Anna lifted too many shadows from my lonely widowed life, and scattered too much sunshine around my path for me to forget those pleasant days of yore."

"And these pleasant interviews which we now have, only seem to me like a lengthening out of those warm bright days of childhood, days gilded with love and flecked with gladness."

"Yes, Jenny, I feel that the love I bear you, strengthens with my years, and you are far dearer to me than when tired of play you used to nestle in my arms and fall to sleep! and one reason is that you have so pleasantly surprised me."

"How so, Aunty?"

"Why, Jenny, when you returned from college having graduated with such high honors, I feared that you might think Aunty is too old fashioned for companionship, and that I should lose my loving, little girl in the accomplished woman; but instead of that I retained them both."

Fancy Etchings: Christian Recorder.

"Ah, Aunty, you don't know how much your love was a stimulous to my exertions; and one of my first thoughts after graduating was, how this will please Aunty. Aunty I want to be a poet, to earn and take my place among the poets of the nineteenth century; but with all the glowing enthusiasms that light up my life I cannot help thinking, that more valuable than the soarings of genius are the tender nestlings of love. Genius may charm the intellect, but love will refresh the spirit."

"I am glad, Jenny, that you feel so, for I think the intellect that will best help our race must be heart supplied: but do you think by being a poet you can best serve our people?"

"I think, Aunty, the best way to serve humanity, is by looking within ourselves, and becoming acquainted with our powers and capacities. The fact is we should all go to work and make the most of ourselves, and we cannot do that without helping others."

"And so having sounded the depths of your inner life, you have come to the conclusion that you have a talent or genius for poetry."

"Aunty, do you remember that poem I wrote some months since which you and others admired so? To me that poem was a revelation, I learned from it that I had power to create, and it gave me faith in myself, and I think faith in one's self is an element, of success. Perhaps you think this is egotism."

"Oh no, I do not think that consciousness of one's ability to perform certain things, is egotism. If a woman is beautiful it is not vanity for her to know what the looking glass constantly reveals. A knowledge of powers and capacities should be an incentive to growth and not a stimulus for vain glory; but, Jenny, what do you expect to accomplish among our people by being a poet?"

"Aunty I want to learn myself and be able to teach others to strive to make the highest ideal, the most truly real of our lives[.]"

"But, Jenny, will not such an endeavor be love's labor lost? what time will our people have in their weary working every day life to listen to your songs?"

"It is just because our lives are apt to be so hard and dry, that I would scatter the flowers of poetry around our paths; and would if I could amid life's sad discords introduce the most entrancing strains of melody. I would teach men and women to love noble deeds by setting them to the music, of fitly spoken words. The first throb of interest that a person feels in the recital of a noble deed, a deed of high and holy worth, the first glow of admiration for suffering virtue, or thrill of joy in the triumph of goodness, forms a dividing line between the sensuous and material and the spiritual and progressive. I think poetry is one of the great agents of culture, civilization and refinement. What grander poetry can you find than among the ancient Hebrews; and to-day the Aryan race with all the splendor of its attainments and the magnificence of its culture; still lights the lamp of its devotion at Semitic altars. Ages have passed since the blind beggar of Chios was denied a pension, in his native place, but his poetry is still green in the world's memory."

Fancy Etchings [May 1, 1873]

"What does uncle Glumby think about your being a poet?"

"He says, it is all moonshine, that poetry is like the measles, it generally breaks out in the young; and that in a few years I will be over, what he calls, my new fancy."

"Have you ever read him any of your poems."

"Yes, Aunty, and that to my sorrow."

"How so, Jenny."

"Oh! he is so unappreciative. I don't believe he hardly knows one piece of poetry from the other. Aunty, you do not know how provoking it is, after you have racked your brain, for thoughts, to have some one listen to you with an indifferent air, and when you have finished, to say with a yawn—that sounds well; but I think that I have seen something like it before. Do you remember that poem I wrote on the "Shadows of Morning?"

"Yes, and I thought it was very fine. What did uncle Glumby think?"

"Why, Aunty, I don't believe you'd find out if you guessed for an hour. I was so provoked, I could have cried and I thought, I would never read any of my verses to him again as long as I lived. When I had finished and sat waiting for his opinion he peered at me through his spectacles and asked, "Can you cook a beef steak?"

"Ha! ha! ha! that is just like my dear, prosy, matter of fact, brother; my niece, builds her beautiful air castles and he stands at the threshold and cries, "beef! beef! beef!!!"

"Aunty, that's just what he does. I never saw two people more unlike than you both are. I wonder if he is not changing. You are lovely, imaginative and sympathetic, he is obtuse, sober and prosaic."

"I think, Jenny, that brother and I represent two entirely different phases in our parents lives. John was their first child. Father and mother were both poor and young when they married, but they were very anxious to get along in the world, and were so engrossed in bettering their condition, that I think their mental state impressed itself on the mind of our brother who was born during those days of early struggle, and that his intense soberness and matter of fact cast of mind, may be easily traced to his antenatal history. Is it not, sometimes the case that parents stamp certain mental traits upon their children's character, and afterwards impatiently punish them for the reproduction of their own faults?"

"But, Aunty, how happened it that you are so different, when you are both the children of the same parents?"

"I, Jenny, was born under pleasanter auspices; our parents had succeeded in acquiring wealth. The early struggle was over, and my mother who was a gifted and superior woman had found both leisure and means to gratify her intellectual and esthetic taste. I have heard my mother say, that, for years her tastes were held in obeyance while she helped father in building up his fortune; and that when the opportunity came that she just reveled in a world of literature, song and art; and so if my tastes differ from brother's, I was born under a pleasanter condition of things."

"Well, Aunty, I think the laws of transmission and hereditary descent are very little understood; and in dealing with the dangerous and the perishing classes, these laws should be largely taken into consideration."

"Hark! I thought I heard carriage wheels; now there's a ring."

"I wonder who it is. Why, Aunty, I am just delighted, it is sister Anna."

"Why, Anna my dear sister, where did you came from? Oh I am so glad to see you."

"I am just from Moontown, my husband and I are going to teach school in New Paradose."

"Well, that is one of the last places I would go to teach school. I know of no salary that would tempt me to place myself in the power of those who control the affairs of New Paradose. It seems to me that matters are constantly getting into some kind of snarl. I should think the efficiency of the schools would be impaired by their dissensions."

"Well Jenny, I think Stuart Mill's speaks of a state of society where all equals are enemies, and I am afraid that some of us are not far past that state. I fear that part of our intellectual people stand too much alone and unrelated."

"Of course, Anna, the possession of power is something of a novelty to some of the New Paradosians; but I hope that they will speedily realize that union and not divisions should be their strength. But how do you like Moontown?"

"Oh very well, it is a fine city, well laid out and possesses many advantages although at present it is cursed with an abundance of grog shops."

"Well, Anna I have been to Moontown a number of times, and the place has very little attraction for me. I think the people are very hard to get acquainted with. They mostly impress you with this idea, they neither like nor dislike you, we don't care any thing about you—we are going one way, and you are going another."

"Now, Jenny, don't be too hard on the Moontowners, if you knew them better perhaps you would like them more; if they seem repellant to you, it may be that you seem shy, cold and distant to them[.]"

"Perhaps I do. I generally feel very careful about intruding on them."

"Jenny, I sometimes think the physical objects of a place impress themselves on a people's character, and help to mould it. Now, in Moontown the land is level, and the river I believe somewhat sluggish, and if our people lack warmth of feeling and enthusiasm of spirit—they have industry, staidness, and respectability."

"Well, Anna, I don't pretend to say that the Moontowners haven't all the lordly virtues that conquer success; but I do think they lack that fine social culture which assures you of a generous welcome and makes you feel at home with them. When I am there I miss the warm clasp of friendly hands, and the light sunshine of welcoming eyes, and I must prefer the courtesy of the country that recognizes the stranger by bowing to his humanity, to the coldness of the city which keeps you a stranger to your next door neighbors."

"Well, Jenny, I have very little social ambition. I am no gifted child of song and art, I am only a simple one, who believes in love and home, and who hopes to deserve written on her tombstone:

> I pray thee, then,
> Write me as one who loves her fellow men."

"My dear precious little sister, I hope that you will richly deserve such an epitaph; but I am in no hurry to see it, and I am glad that your heart did not get starved and chilled in Moontown."

"I had too much love at home for that; and then, I think that every heart ought to learn to feed itself and to rest for strength and happiness on the Arm that never fails; and the Love that never wanes."

"That's true, Anna and if we did that always, what an amount of restlessness, pain and disquietude we might save ourselves."

Fancy Sketches [January 15, 1874]

"Why Aunty, what makes you look so serious this morning. You look

---

as sober as if some dear old widower had made you an offer to take care of him and his six motherless children. Let me inquire in poetic parlance— 'Why that shadow on thy brow?' "

"I am a little puzzled, Jenny, to know how to answer a letter from a dear young friend of mine. She is a girl who has surmounted difficulties, and borne quite an amount of privation in obtaining an education, but owing to the bill which has lately passed in her state she has lost her school."

"What does she say and what does she intend doing?"

"She writes to me saying, 'My dear friend, the tidal wave of progress has reached us here and I feel that the ground has suddenly slidden from under my feet. The authorities have closed my school, and like Othello 'my occupation is gone.' Some of my friends say, 'Go South,' but I am the mainstay of my widowed mother, and so necessary am I to her comfort that I can not think of leaving her. The wide field of domestic duty is before me, but perhaps you will call it false pride, but I do not feel that I have either inclination or aptitude for that mode of life; and to learn any trade or business now would consume months which I feel I can not well [a]fford to give. Now what am I to do?' This is the question, Jenny; which has been ringing in my mind all this morning. What am I to do?"

"Well, Aunty, while I can not help rejoicing at the passage of this bill, I can not fail to sympathise with those young girls who have fitted themselves for the position of teachers and who feel as she does that the ground is about to slip from under their feet. Aunty, I do wish we women could vote. It seems to me that the men who vote, find in that vote increased advantage, and I do wish that at the late National civil rights meeting, some wom[e]n had been sent as delegates."

"What for? to have kept better order?"

"No, but to have given them an opportunity to present unto that convention some views of vital importune to the future of our woman."

"Would you have opposed the civil rights, on the plea that mixed schools would close up a [nu]mber of avenues against many of our girls?"

"No Aunty, I would not have done that, for I look upon such measures, as mixing the children as one of those reformatory or revolutionary schemes, which, while it causes present pain eventuates in permanent good."

"I think, Jenny, that just such a closing up of the gates should make us more earnest to open up avenues in other directions."

"Aunty I was just thinking, (though the thought may seem Utopian): That it would be an excellent plan if some of our colored men who possessed money could only unite upon some plan by which we could build up some thriving industries of our own. Suppose we had a large number of persons personally interested in building up a cotton factory, could not this thing be effected among us by the power of combination? We can combine together for pleasure, could we not do the same for business?"

"We could, Jenny, provided we had firm faith in each other's honesty, and ability to carry on business."

"Well, Aunty I am not surpri[s]ed if colored men are a little slow to combine in civil associations. That men who acquire slowly and painfully will be somewhat timid in risking what it has cost them so much to attain is quite natural. I don't know what can be done for our young women, but I do wish some of the most thoughtful men and women of our race would take into consideration some plan for opening the fields of occupation for us. If white women feel that they are limited by their sex, how must it be with us who have the shadows of the past still projected into our lives? What they call limitation would be to us broad liberty. The most that I dread, is that some of our girls will be discouraged, and missing the stimulus of hope will not struggle as earnestly as they might to get a thorough education."

"I hope that instead of abating heart and hope, that they will strive to reach the highest point of efficiency as teachers; believing as Daniel Webster once said, "There is always room in the upper story.""

"And though prejudice has not died out of the American mind, and you can not legislate hatred and contempt out of people's hearts, you may so change the condition of things, as to create a new class of associations; and as patience, industry and skill can change the "Mulberry leaf into satin" so united, earnest and faithful endeavor may yet change the world's dread into admiring recognition."

"I think Aunty that after the civil rights bill is passed that 'the cap sheaf will have been placed on the temple of our liberties, and that the most important thing then for us to consider, is not simply what this party will do for us, or the other one against us; but what are we going to do as for ourselves, to diversify our industry, build up our character, better our condition, and intensify our spiritual life. Congress may make its statute books black with laws for our defence, but all the help that comes from without is not like the help that comes from within and this is the force we must generate if we take our place fairly and squarely alongside the other branches of the human race in this Western Hemisphere.[' "]

The Mission of the Flowers

In a lovely garden, filled with fair and blooming flowers, stood a beautiful rose tree. It was the centre of attraction, and won the admiration of

---

The Mission of the Flowers: Moses: A Story of the Nile (1869) 44–47.

every eye; its beauteous flowers were sought to adorn the bridal wreath and deck the funeral bier. It was a thing of joy and beauty, and its earth mission was a blessing. Kind hands plucked its flowers to gladden the chamber of sickness and adorn the prisoner's lonely cell. Young girls wore them 'mid their clustering curls, and grave brows relaxed when they gazed upon their wondrous beauty. Now the rose was very kind and generous hearted, and, seeing how much joy she dispensed, wished that every flower could only be a rose, and like herself have the privilege of giving joy to the children of men; and while she thus mused, a bright and lovely spirit approached her and said, "I know thy wishes and will grant thy desires. Thou shalt have power to change every flower in the garden to thine own likeness. When the soft winds come wooing thy fairest buds and flowers, thou shalt breathe gently on thy sister plants, and beneath thy influence they shall change to beautiful roses." The rose tree bowed her head in silent gratitude to the gentle being who had granted her this wondrous power. All night the stars bent over her from their holy homes above, but she scarcely heeded their vigils. The gentle dews nestled in her arms and kissed the cheeks of her daughters; but she hardly noticed them;— she was waiting for the soft airs to awaken and seek her charming abode. At length the gentle airs greeted her, and she hailed them with a joyous welcome, and then commenced her work of change. The first object that met her vision was a tulip superbly arrayed in scarlet and gold. When she was aware of the intention of her neighbor, her cheeks flamed with anger, her eyes flashed indignantly, and she haughtily refused to change her proud robes for the garb the rose tree had prepared for her; but she could not resist the spell that was upon her, and she passively permitted the garments of the rose to enfold her yielding limbs. The verbenas saw the change that had fallen upon the tulip and dreading that a similar fate awaited them, crept closely to the ground, and, while tears gathered in their eyes, they felt a change pass through their sensitive frames, and instead of gentle verbenas they were blushing roses. She breathed upon the sleepy poppies; a deeper slumber fell upon their senses, and when they awoke, they too had changed to bright and beautiful roses. The heliotrope read her fate in the lot of her sisters, and, bowing her fair head in silent sorrow, gracefully submitted to her unwelcome destiny. The violets, whose mission was to herald the approach of spring, were averse to losing their identity. "Surely," said they, "we have a mission as well as the rose;" but with heavy hearts they saw themselves changed like their sister plants. The snow drop drew around her robes of virgin white; she would not willingly exchange them for the most brilliant attire that ever decked a flower's form; to her they were the emblems of purity and innocence; but the rose tree breathed upon her, and with a bitter sob she reluctantly consented to the change. The dahlias lifted their heads proudly and defiantly; they dreaded the change, but scorned submission; they loved the fading year, and wished to spread around his dying couch their brightest, fairest flowers; but vainly they struggled, the doom was upon them, and they could not escape. A modest lily that grew near the rose tree shrank instinctively from her; but it was in vain, and with tearful eyes and trembling limbs she yielded, while a quiver of agony convulsed her frame. The marygolds sighed submissively and made no remonstrance. The garden pinks grew careless, and submitted without a murmur, while other flowers, less fragrant or less fair, paled with sorrow or reddened with anger; but the spell of the rose tree was upon them, and every flower was changed by her power, and that once beautiful garden was overrun with roses; it had become a perfect wilderness of roses; the garden had changed, but that variety which had lent it so much beauty was gone, and men grew tired of roses, for they were everywhere. The smallest violet peeping faintly from its bed would have been welcome, the humblest primrose would have been hailed with delight,—even a dandelion would have been a harbinger of joy; and when the rose saw that the children of men were dissatisfied with the change she had made, her heart grew sad within her, and she wished the power had never been given her to change her sister plants to roses, and tears came into her eyes as she mused, when suddenly a rough wind shook her drooping form, and she opened her eyes and found that she had only been dreaming. But an important lesson had been taught; she had learned to respect the individuality of her sister flowers, and began to see that they, as well as herself, had their own missions,—some to gladden the eye with their loveliness and thrill the soul with delight; some to transmit fragrance to the air; others to breathe a refining influence upon the world; some had power to lull the aching brow and soothe the weary heart and brain into forgetfulness; and of those whose mission she did not understand, she wisely concluded there must be some object in their creation, and resolved to be true to her own earth-mission, and lay her fairest buds and flowers upon the altars of love and truth.

Part Three
1876–1892

◆

"Doctor," said Iola, ". . . I wish I could do something more for our people than I am doing. . . ."

"Why not," asked Dr. Latimer, "write a good strong book which would be helpful to them?"

from Iola Leroy

Poetry

◆

Between 1876 and 1892, Frances Harper continued to write new poems that emphasized the need for individuals to use their time and talents for "high and lofty" deeds and especially for the relief of "crushed humanity." However, the volumes of poetry that Harper published during this time were reprints and revised or enlarged editions of earlier works. *Poems* (1871) was reissued without change in 1880. In 1886, Harper enlarged *Sketches of Southern Life* (1872) from twenty-four to fifty-eight pages by deleting "Our English Friends" and appending seven new poems to the original collection. This revised *Sketches* was then reissued in 1888, 1890, and 1891.* In 1889, Harper revised *Moses: A Story of the Nile* by adding two poems.

If she had not been solely responsible for the selection, publication, and distribution of her writings already, it is clear that Harper took an increasingly active role in the promulgation of her literature from this period on. By 1889, her books were being marked as published for the author

---

*There may have been two or three different publications of this work. Some extant copies indicate publication in Philadelphia by Ferguson Brothers in 1888 and also in 1888 in Philadelphia by Merrihew and Son. The cover of one identifies the publisher as Ferguson Brothers with a date of 1887, while its title page says Merrihew and Son, 1888. Determining the number of editions, the publication sequence, and the size of each run is nearly impossible. When Merrihew & Thompson went out of business, Ferguson and Company acquired the stereotype plates. When Ferguson and Company was sold in the mid-1950s, much of the Harper material was discarded.

or with her home address in place of a publishing firm's name. In some ways, this ameliorates the lack of extant letters from this era, for knowing that Harper had authority over the content and structure of these texts allows the reader to surmise that her interests and concerns had not substantially changed. Her new poems consisted primarily of retellings of biblical stories and paeans to temperance. These topics correspond with the newspaper reports of her lectures. "John and Jacob—A Dialogue on Women's Rights" is remarkable for its resemblance to the Aunt Chloe poems, especially in its use of humor. And Harper's emphasis upon historical narrative poems presages her entry into what was for her an entirely new genre, the novel.

Sketches of Southern Life (1886)

The major addition to the 1886 edition of Sketches of Southern Life is a long, narrative poem, "The Jewish Grandfather's Story." Harper again returns to the Old Testament for an allegorical tale. She uses the example of the Jewish people's struggle to live true to their heritage and their goals and frames the poem as a story told to young ones as a means of teaching and inspiring, of continuing a legacy. This poem chronicles the Old Testament history, emphasizing the series of obstacles overcome, the many leaders who guided and motivated, but most of all, the struggles of an entire people. Harper's poem emphasizes their perseverance, unity, and faith, a combination that ultimately results in their triumph and peace.

Harper's other poems of this period focus on those lost or abandoned, those reunited, or those committed to rescuing and reuniting, but all continue the theme of "The Jewish Grandfather" and the Aunt Chloe series,—that freedom requires unified, continuous struggle.

Moses: A Story of the Nile (1889)

In 1889, Harper expanded the 1869 volume of Moses: A Story of the Nile by appending two temperance poems, "The Ragged Stocking" and "The Fatal Pledge." Though different in subject matter, these poems share similarities with "Moses." Each tells a story about a decisive moment and the results of that decision in an individual's life. Each is in that sense a lesson in living for the reader. While "Moses" approaches epic proportions, chronicling a momentous decision of a historical figure who changed the fortunes of an entire race, "The Ragged Stocking" and "The Fatal Pledge" are more in the tradition of Charles Dickens in describing lives and fortunes on the smaller scale of domestic sentimental fiction. Yet, all three poems feature individuals who must come to terms with their responsibility to themselves and to their society.

Each poem uses dialogue and suggests a theatrical awareness of au-
dience. In the early part of "Moses," the sections are labeled by character
to emphasize the dramatic aspects of the work. In "The Ragged Stock-
ing," the narrator responds to the reactions of the imaginary listener, there-
by creating a story told within a dynamic and immediate context, with
the reader becoming a character within the tale of a tale. Both "Moses"
and "The Ragged Stocking" include female characters who verify the pro-
tagonists' decisions and serve supportive roles. In "The Fatal Pledge," Harper
presents one of her few negative portrayals of a woman. A young man
loses himself to drink because of the "thoughtless words" of his fiancée.
Her punishment for this is a lifetime of remorse.

Occasional Poems

From the beginning of her career, Harper sometimes wrote poems to com-
memorate particular situations. The poems written to Harriet Beecher
Stowe in 1854 and after the death of J. Edwards Barnes in 1858 are exam-
ples. In writing occasional poems such as these, Harper was participating
in a United States literary tradition that was practiced even before this
territory had been conceived as a new nation. Occasional poems appear
regularly in the literature of Puritan settlers, for example, and in African-
American literature this tradition extends as far as the earliest extant poem,
"Bar's Fight," by Lucy Terry (1746). From 1876 on, such poems appear
more frequently because, by this time, Frances Harper was performing
as an unofficial African-American poet laureate and was often called upon
to memorialize important events. Poems such as "For the Twenty-Fifth
Anniversary of the 'Old Folks' Home' " and "To Mr. and Mrs. W. F. John-
son . . ." were both written for specific occasions honoring the life and
works of people whom Harper knew and with whom she had worked.

◆

We Are Rising

We are rising, as a people,
　We are rising, to the light;
For our God has changed the shadows
　Of our dark and dreary night.
In the prison house of bondage,
　When we bent beneath the rod,

We Are Rising: Christian Recorder, November 9, 1876. A prefatory note explains that
this poem was written "for the unveiling of the Allen Monument." The poem was reprinted
in Arnett, Benjamin. *Centennial Thanksgiving Sermon at St. Paul A.M.E. Church.* Urbana,
Ohio: n.p., 1876.

And our hearts were faint and weary,
  We first learned to trust in God.

We are marching along, we are marching along,
The hand that broke our fetters was powerful strong.
We are marching along, we are marching along,
We are rising as a people, and we're marching along.

For the sighing of the needy,
  God, himself did bare his hand,
And the footsteps of his judgments,
  Echoed through the guilty land:
When the rust of many ages,
  On our galling fetters lay,
He turned our grief to gladness,
  And our darkness into day.
        We are marching along, etc.

Unto God, be *all* the glory,
  That our eyes behold the sight,
Of a people, peeled and scattered
  Rising into freedom's light.
Though the morning seemed to linger,
  O'er the hill tops far away
And the night was long and gloomy,
  Yet he was our shield and stay.
        We are marching along, etc.

Help us, Oh! great Deliverer,
  To be faithful to thy Word,
Till the nation's former bondmen,
  Be the freemen of the Lord.
Teach, Oh, Lord, our hands to battle
  'Gainst the hosts of vice, and sin,
And with Jesus, for our Captain,
  The victory we shall win.
        We are marching along, etc.

The Widow's Mites

Only two mites, the widow said,
  And meekly gazed upon her store

The Widow's Mites: Christian Recorder, December 27, 1877. The incident referred to

While by her passed the Pharisee,
  His garb inscribed with sacred lore.

Besides the gifts of wealthy men,
  Her offering seemed so scant and small
This temple service claimed her heart,
  And willingly she gave her all.

Little thought she, when her two mites
  Fell with a simple, humble chime,
That they would float as music sweet
  Through all the corridors of time.

Nor dreamed that [o'er] an ocean's bed,
  Should lay a gem whose lucent light,
Would be as lovely, fair and pure,
  As that which gathered round her mite.

That when her hands were pale and cold
  And folded from the cares of earth,
Her gift of love would glow and shine,
  Mid deeds of high and holy worth.

It Shall Not Come Nigh Thee

The wild winds flowed from out God's hand,
A fearful tempest swept the land;
But 'mid the hours of gloom and dread
His hand upheld my drooping head.

'Tis a solemn thing, with bated breath
To clasp your hands and look on death;
But sweet, in the arms of death to be,
And feel the evil shall not come nigh [thee]—

To feel, when the storm is raging wild,
That God remembers his feeblest child,
That his love and power are everywhere,
And we have not "drifted beyond His care"—

To feel assured, though war should spread
His blood stained banner o'er our head,

---

is cited in Mark 12:42 and Luke 21:2. The A.M.E. Church about this time instituted a missionary program for children called "The Mite Society."

  It Shall Not Come Nigh Thee: Christian Recorder, November 14, 1878.

And famine stalk with meagre face,
His love shall be our resting place—

When pestilence in robes of pain
On midnight dews distills her bane
And scatters death at light noontide
Wither His arms to safely hide—

To feel that Death's destroying arm
Can bring us neither ill nor harm,
That souls on God's sure mercies cast
Are safe until life's storms are past.

John and Jacob—A Dialogue on Woman's Rights

Jacob

I don't believe a single bit
    In those new-fangled ways
Of women running to the polls
    And voting now adays.
I like the good old-fashioned times
    When women used to spin,
And when you came from work you knew
    Your wife was always in.
Now there's my Betsy, just as good
    As any wife need be,
Who sits and tells me day by day
    That women are not free;
And when I smile and say to her,
    "You surely make me laff;
This talk about your rights and wrongs
    Is nothing else but chaff."

John

Now, Jacob, I don't think like you;
    I think that Betsy Ann
Has just as good a right to vote
    As you or any man.

John and Jacob . . . : New York *Freeman*, November 28, 1885.

Jacob

Now, John, do you believe for true
   In women running round,
And when you come to look for them
   They are not to be found?
Pray, who would stay at home to nurse,
   To cook, to wash, and sew,
While women marched unto the polls?
   That's what I want to know.

John

Who stays at home when Betsy Ann
   Goes out day after day
To wash and iron, cook and sew,
   Because she gets her pay?
I'm sure she wouldn't take quite so long
   To vote and go her way,
As when she leaves her little ones
   And works out day by day.

Jacob

Well, I declare, that is the truth!
   To vote, it don't take long;
But, then, I kind of think somehow
   That women's voting's wrong.

John

The masters thought before the war
   That slavery was right:
But we who felt the heavy yoke
   Didn't see it in that light.
Some thought that it would never do
   For us in Southern lands,
To change the fetters on our wrists
   For the ballot in our hands.
Now if you don't believe 'twas right
   To crowd us from the track,
How can you push your wife aside
   And try to hold her back?

Jacob

But, John, I think for women's feet
  The polls a dreadful place;
To vote with rough and brutal men
  Seems like a deep disgrace.

John

But, Jacob, if the polls are vile,
  Where women shouldn't be seen,
Why not invite them in to help
  Us men to make them clean?

Jacob

Well, wrong is wrong, and right is right,
  For woman as for man;
I almost think that I will go
  And vote with Betsy Ann.

John

I hope you will, and show the world
  You can be brave and strong—
A noble man, who scorns to do
  The feeblest woman wrong.

To Mr. and Mrs. W. F. Johnson on Their Twenty-Fifth Wedding Anniversary

God curtained from thy vision
  His great and glorious light,
But made for thee a pathway
  Which still was fair and bright.

Where death invades with sorrow
  And orphan children come,
Thou hast wrought within the shadow
  The Howard Orphan Home.

To Mr. and Mrs. W. F. Johnson ...: New York *Freeman*, January 9, 1886.

To-day I send my greeting
   To thee and thy dear wife,
Who has been in light and darkness
   True companion of thy life;

Always loving, true and truthful,
   To thy spirit more than sight;
May her heart be full of gladness—
   Her soul of love and light.

May the peace of God surround you,
   And his love with you abide
Till life's shadows all are faded
   And there's light at eventide.

When the storms of life are sweeping
   And the wolves of hunger bark,
May you leave upon the sands of time
   An ever shining mark.

May the children you have sheltered
   Within your earthly home,
Meet you mid the many mansions
   Where darkness cannot come.

In Commemoration of the Centennial of the A.M.E. Church

A little seed, in weakness sown,
   Fell in the desert dust—
In Allen's hand that seed became
   A sacred, precious trust.

Around it swept the arid airs
   Of prejudice and hate,
But heaven's bright dew upon it fell
   And God watched o'er its fate.

And Faith and Sacrifice, like rain,
   Fell softly at its base
Until, amid the elder trees,
   A scion took its place.

In Commemoration . . .: Benjamin W. Arnett, ed., *The Centennial Budget, Containing an Account of the Celebration* (November 1887): 549–50. Also published in: *Christian Recorder,* November 10, 1887, and in *African Methodist Episcopal Church Review,* 7 (1892): 292.

Now, where the broad Atlantic breaks
  In sprays of crested foam,
Or, sobbing near our sunset mounts,
  Is heard Pacific's moan—

From shore to shore its branches spread,
  From snow-clad hills of Maine
To where, against our coral reefs,
  The wild waves dash in vain.

Its roots have run beyond the sea
  To Hayti's sunny strand
And spread its branches far away
  In Africa's distant land.

May ev'ry fruit of God's rich grace,
  This tree for men afford,
And flourish 'mid the vales of life,
  A planting of the Lord.

Beneath its shade may weary hearts
  Find shelter, love and rest,
And with a glad surrender make
  Our earth more bright and blest.

May He who prunes and bears away
  The branch he cannot own
Help this to be a fruitful tree
  To plant around His throne.

The Jewish Grandfather's Story

Come, gather around me, children,
  And a story I will tell.
How we builded the beautiful temple—
  The temple we love so well.

I must date my story backward
  To a distant age and land,

The Jewish Grandfather's Story: This and the following six poems (pages 244–256) are the poems added to Sketches of Southern Life for its 1886 publication, in the order in which they appear in that volume.

When God did break our fathers' chains
   By his mighty outstretched hand

Our fathers were strangers and captives,
   Where the ancient Nile doth flow;
Smitten by cruel taskmasters,
   And burdened by toil and woe.

As a shepherd, to pastures green
   Doth lead with care his sheep,
So God divided the great Red Sea,
   And led them through the deep.

You've seen me plant a tender vine,
   And guard it with patient care,
Till its roots struck in the mellow earth,
   And it drank the light and air.

So God did plant our chosen race,
   As a vine in this fair land;
And we grew and spread a fruitful tree,
   The planting of his right hand.

The time would fail strove I to tell,
   All the story of our race—
Of our grand old leader, Moses,
   And Joshua in his place,

Of all our rulers and judges,
   From Joshua unto Saul,
Over whose doomed and guilty head
   Fell ruin and death's dark pall.

Of valiant Jepthath, whose brave heart
   With sudden grief did bow,
When his daughter came with dance and song
   Unconscious of his vow.

Of Gideon, lifting up his voice
   To him who rules the sky,
And wringing out his well drenched fleece,
   When all around was dry.

How Deborah, neath her spreading palms,
   A judge in Israel rose,
And wrested victory from the hands
   Of Jacob's heathen foes.

Of Samuel, an upright judge,
  The last who ruled our tribes,
Whose noble life and cleanly hands,
  Were pure and free from bribes.

Of David, with his checkered life
  Our tuneful minstrel king,
Who breathed in sadness and delight,
  The psalms we love to sing.

Of Solomon, whose wandering heart,
  From Jacob's God did stray,
And cast the richest gifts of life,
  In pleasure's cup away.

How aged men advised his son,
  But found him weak and vain,
Until the kingdom from his hands
  Was rudely rent in twain.

Oh! sin and strife are fearful things,
  They widen as they go,
And leave behind them shades of death,
  And open gates of woe.

A trail of guilt, a gloomy line,
  Ran through our nation's life,
And wicked kings provoked our God,
  And sin and woe were rife.

At length, there came a day of doom—
  A day of grief and dread;
When judgment like a fearful storm
  Swept o'er our country's head.

And we were captives many years,
  Where Babel's stream doth flow;
With harps unstrung, on willows hung,
  We wept in silent woe.

We could not sing the old, sweet songs,
  Our captors asked to hear;
Our hearts were full, how could we sing
  The songs to us so dear?

As one who dreams a mournful dream,
  Which fades, as wanes the night,

So God did change our gloomy lot
  From darkness into light.

Belshazzar in his regal halls,
  A sumptuous feast did hold;
He praised his gods and drank his wine
  From sacred cups of gold

When dance and song and revelry
  Had filled with mirth each hall,
Belshazzar raised his eyes and saw
  A writing on the wall.

He saw, and horror blanched his cheek,
  His lips were white with fear;
To read the words he quickly called
  For wise men, far and near.

But baffled seers, with anxious doubt
  Stood silent in the room,
When Daniel came, a captive youth,
  And read the words of doom.

That night, within his regal hall,
  Belshazzar lifeless lay;
The Persians grasped his fallen crown,
  And with the Mede held sway.

Darius came, and Daniel rose
  A man of high renown;
But wicked courtiers schemed and planned
  To drag the prophet down.

They came as men who wished to place
  Great honors on their king—
With flattering lips and oily words,
  Desired a certain thing.

They knew that Daniel, day by day
  Towards Salem turned his face,
And asked the king to sign a law
  His hands might not erase.

That till one moon had waned away,
  No cherished wish or thing
Should any ask of men or Gods,
  Unless it were the king.

But Daniel, full of holy trust,
  His windows opened wide,
Regardless of the king's command,
  Unto his God he cried.

They brought him forth that he might be
  The hungry lion's meat,
Awe struck, the lions turned away
  And crouched anear his feet.

The God he served was strong to save
  His servant in the den;
The fate devised for Daniel's life
  O'er took those scheming men.

And Cyrus came, a gracious king,
  And gave the blest command,
That we, the scattered Jews, should build
  Anew our fallen land.

The men who hated Juda's weal
  Were filled with bitter rage,
And 'gainst the progress of our work
  Did evil men engage.

Sanballat tried to hinder us,
  And Gashmu uttered lies,
But like a thing of joy and light,
  We saw our temple rise.

And from the tower of Hananeel
  Unto the corner gate,
We built the wall and did restore
  The places desolate.

Some mocked us as we labored on
  And scoffingly did say
"If but a fox climb on the wall,
  Their work will give away."

But Nehemiah wrought in hope,
  Though heathen foes did frown
"My work is great," he firmly said,
  "And I cannot come down."

And when Shemai counselled him
  The temple door to close,

To hide, lest he should fall a prey
  Unto his cruel foes.

Strong in his faith, he answered, "No,
  He would oppose the tide,
Should such as he from danger flee,
  And in the temple hide?"

We wrought in earnest faith and hope
  Until we built the wall,
And then, unto a joyful feast
  Did priest and people call.

We came to dedicate the wall
  With sacrifice and joy—
A happy throng, from aged sire
  Unto the fair-haired boy.

Our lips so used to mournful songs,
  Did joyous laughter fill,
And strong men wept with sacred joy
  To stand on Zion's hill.

Mid scoffing foes and evil men,
  We built our city blest,
And 'neath our sheltering vines and palms
  To-day in peace we rest.

Out in the Cold

Out in the cold mid the dreary night,
Under the eaves of homes so bright;
Snowflakes falling o'er mother's grave
Will no one rescue, no one save?

A child left out in the dark and cold,
A lamb not sheltered in any fold,
Hearing the wolves of hunger bark,
Out in the cold! and out in the dark.

Missing to-night the charming bliss,
That lies in the mother's good-night kiss;
And hearing no loving father's prayer,
For blessings his children all may share.

Creeping away to some wretched den,
To sleep mid the curses of drunken men

And women, not as God has made,
Wrecked and ruined, wronged and betrayed.

Church of the Lord reach out thy arm,
And shield the hapless one from harm;
Where the waves of sin are dashing wild;
Rescue and save the drifting child.

Wash from her life guilt's turbid foam,
In the fair haven of a home;
Tenderly lead the motherless girl
Up to the gates of purest pearl.

The wandering feet which else had strayed,
From thorny paths may yet be stayed;
And a crimson track through the cold dark night
May exchange to a line of loving light.

Save the Boys

Like Dives in the deeps of Hell
I cannot break this fearful spell,
Nor quench the fires I've madly nursed,
Nor cool this dreadful raging thirst.
Take back your pledge—ye come too late!
Ye cannot save me from my fate,
Nor bring me back departed joys;
But ye can try to save the boys.

Ye bid me break my fiery chain,
Arise and be a man again,
When every street with snares is spread,
And nets of sin where'er I tread.
No; I must reap as I did sow.
The seeds of sin bring crops of woe;
But with my latest breath I'll crave
That ye will try the boys to save.

These bloodshot eyes were once so bright;
This sin-crushed heart was glad and light;
But by the wine-cup's ruddy glow
I traced a path to shame and woe.
A captive to my galling chain,
I've tried to rise, but tried in vain—

The cup allures and then destroys.
Oh! from its thraldom save the boys.

Take from your streets those traps of hell
Into whose gilded snares I fell.
Oh! freemen, from these foul decoys
Arise, and vote to save the boys.
Oh ye who license men to trade
In draughts that charm and then degrade,
Before ye hear the cry, Too late,
Oh, save the boys from my sad fate.

Nothing and Something

It is nothing to me, the beauty said,
With a careless toss of her pretty head;
The man is weak if he can't refrain
From the cup you say is fraught with pain.
It was something to her in after years,
When her eyes were drenched with burning tears,
And she watched in lonely grief and dread,
And startled to hear a staggering tread.

It is nothing to me, the mother said;
I have no fear that my boy will tread
In the downward path of sin and shame,
And crush my heart and darken his name.
It was something to her when that only son
From the path of right was early won,
And madly cast in the flowing bowl
A ruined body and sin-wrecked soul.

It is nothing to me, the young man cried:
In his eye was a flash of scorn and pride;
I heed not the dreadful things ye tell:
I can rule myself I know full well.
It was something to him when in prison he lay
The victim of drink, life ebbing away;
And thought of his wretched child and wife,
And the mournful wreck of his wasted life.

It is nothing to me, the merchant said,
As over his ledger he bent his head;

I'm busy to-day with tare and tret,
And I have no time to fume and fret.
It was something to him when over the wire
A message came from a funeral pyre—
A drunken conductor had wrecked a train,
And his wife and child were among the slain.

It is nothing to me, the voter said,
The party's loss is my greatest dread;
Then gave his vote for the liquor trade,
Though hearts were crushed and drunkards made.
It was something to him in after life,
When his daughter became a drunkard's wife
And her hungry children cried for bread,
And trembled to hear their father's tread.

Is it nothing for us to idly sleep
While the cohorts of death their vigils keep?
To gather the young and thoughtless in
And grind in our midst a grist of sin?

It is something, yes, all, for us to stand
Clasping by faith our Saviour's hand;
To learn to labor, live and fight
On the side of God and changeless light.

Wanderer's Return

My home is so glad, my heart is so light,
My wandering boy has returned to-night.
He is blighted and bruised, I know, by sin,
But I am so glad to welcome him in.

The child of my tenderest love and care
Has broken away from the tempter's snare;
To-night my heart is o'erflowing with joy,
I have found again my wandering boy.

My heart has been wrung with a thousand fears,
Mine eyes been drenched with the bitterest tears;
Like shadows that fade are my past alarms,
My boy is enclasped in his mother's arms.

The streets were not safe for my darling child;
Where sin with its evil attractions smiled.

But his wandering feet have ceased to roam,
And to-night my wayward boy is at home—

At home with the mother that loves him best,
With the hearts that have ached with sad unrest,
With the hearts that are thrilling with untold joy
Because we have found our wandering boy.

In that wretched man so haggard and wild
I only behold my returning child,
And the blissful tears from my eyes that start
Are the overflow of a happy heart.

I have trodden the streets in lonely grief,
I have sought in prayer for my sole relief;
But the depths of my heart to-night are stirred,
I know that the mother's prayer has been heard.

If the mother-love be so strong and great
For her child, sin-weary and desolate,
Oh what must the love of the Father be
For souls who have wandered like you and me!

"Fishers of Men"

I had a dream, a varied dream:
  Before my ravished sight
The city of my Lord arose,
  With all its love and light.

The music of a myriad harps
  Flowed out with sweet accord;
And saints were casting down their crowns
  In homage to our Lord.

My heart leaped up with untold joy;
  Life's toil and pain were o'er;
My weary feet at last had found
  The bright and restful shore.

Just as I reached the gates of light,
  Ready to enter in,
From earth arose a fearful cry
  Of sorrow and of sin.

I turned, and saw behind me surge
  A wild and stormy sea;

And drowning men were reaching out
  Imploring hands to me.

And ev'ry lip was blanched with dread
  And moaning for relief;
The music of the golden harps
  Grew fainter for their grief.

Let me return, I quickly said,
  Close to the pearly gate;
My work is with these wretched ones,
  So wrecked and desolate.

An angel smiled and gently said:
  This is the gate of life,
Wilt thou return to earth's sad scenes,
  Its weariness and strife,

To comfort hearts that sigh and break,
  To dry the falling tear,
Wilt thou forego the music sweet
  Entrancing now thy ear?

I must return, I firmly said,
  The strugglers in that sea
Shall not reach out beseeching hands
  In vain for help to me.

I turned to go; but as I turned
  The gloomy sea grew bright,
And from my heart there seemed to flow
  Ten thousand cords of light.

And sin-wrecked men, with eager hands,
  Did grasp each golden cord;
And with my heart I drew them on
  To see my gracious Lord.

Again I stood beside the gate.
  My heart was glad and free;
For with me stood a rescued throng
  The Lord had given me.

Signing the Pledge

Do you see this cup—this tempting cup—
  Its sparkle and its glow?

I tell you this cup has brought to me
  A world of shame and woe.

Do you see that woman sad and wan?
  One day with joy and pride,
With orange blossoms in her hair,
  I claimed her as my bride.

And vowed that I would faithful prove
  Till death our lives should part;
I've drenched her soul with floods of grief,
  And almost crushed her heart.

Do you see that gray-haired mother bend
  Beneath her weight of years?
I've filled that aged mother's eyes
  With many bitter tears.

Year after year for me she prays,
  And tries her child to save;
I've almost brought her gray hairs down
  In sorrow to the grave.

Do you see that boy whose wistful eyes
  Are gazing on my face?
I've overshadowed his young life
  With sorrow and disgrace.

He used to greet me with a smile,
  His heart was light and glad;
I've seen him tremble at my voice,
  I've made that heart so sad.

Do you see this pledge I've signed to-night?
  My mother, wife, and boy
Shall read my purpose on that pledge
  And smile through tears of joy.

To know this night, this very night,
  I cast the wine-cup down,
And from the dust of a sinful life
  Lift up my manhood's crown.

The faded face of my young wife
  With roses yet shall bloom,
And joy shall light my mother's eyes
  On the margin of the tomb.

I have vowed to-night my only boy,
  With brow so fair and mild,
Shall not be taunted on the streets,
  And called a drunkard's child.

Never again shall that young face
  Whiten with grief and dread,
Because I've madly staggered home
  And sold for drink his bread.

This strong right arm unnerved by rum
  Shall battle with my fate;
And peace and comfort crown the home
  By drink made desolate.

Like a drowning man, tempest-tossed,
  Clings to a rocky ledge,
With trembling hands I've learned to grasp
  The gospel and the pledge.

A captive bounding from my chain,
  I've rent each hateful band,
And by the help of grace divine
  A victor hope to stand.

His Name

From regions ever fair and bright,
  On angel lips it came;
'T was uttered in a lowly home,
  A precious, sacred name.

It came to men bowed down beneath
  Great weights of sin and shame;
They lifted up their weary heads
  And trusted in His name.

The martyr, by the dreadful rack,
  Walled in by fire and flame,
Stood victor by the side of death,
  Triumphant in His name.

From halls of pleasure, pride and ease
  Fair maids and matrons came

His Name: Christian Recorder, March 31, 1887.

To staunch the wounds that sin had made,
  And labor in His name.

Men, cold and cruel, heard the word;
  Their savage breasts grew tame.
Tender and loving, strong and true
  They worshiped in His name.

Along the dusty paths of life
  The halt, the blind, the lame
Heard sweetly stealing o'er their way
  The music of His name.

Down from the cross, an ensign once
  Of horrors and of shame,
Still streams the light that gathers 'round
  The glory of His name.

Oh, never victor, wreathed and crowned
  By honor or by fame,
Gave to the world the wonderous power
  That lies within His name.

His love has laid upon our hearts
  An everlasting claim;
Our strength in life, our hope in death
  Is refuge in His name.

The Ragged Stocking

Do you see this ragged stocking,
  Here a rent and there a hole?
Each thread of this little stocking
  Is woven around my soul.

Do you wish to hear my story?
  Excuse me, the tears will start,
For the sight of this ragged stocking
  Stirs the fountains of my heart.

You say that my home is happy;
  To me 'tis earth's fairest place,
But its sunshine, peace and gladness
  Back to this stocking I trace.

The Ragged Stocking: Moses: A Story of the Nile (1889).

I was once a wretched drunkard;
　　Ah! you start and say not so;
But the dreadful depths I've sounded,
　　And I speak of what I know.

I was wild and very reckless
　　When I stood on manhood's brink,
And, joining with pleasure-seekers
　　Learned to revel and drink.

Strong drink is a raging demon,
　　In his hands are shame and woe;
He mocketh the strength of the mighty
　　And bringeth the strong man low.

The light of my home was darkened
　　By the shadow of my sin;
And want and woe unbarr'd the door,
　　And suffering entered in.

　　　　　　*　*　*

The streets were full one Christmas eve,
　　And alive with girls and boys,
Merrily looking through window-panes
　　At bright and beautiful toys.

And throngs of parents came to buy
　　The gifts that children prize,
And homeward trudged with happy hearts
　　The love-light in their eyes.

I thought of my little Charley
　　At home in his lowly bed,
With the shadows around his life,
　　And in shame I bowed my head.

I entered my home a sober man,
　　My heart by remorse was wrung,
And there in the chimney corner,
　　This little stocking was hung.

Faded and worn as you see it;
　　To me 'tis a precious thing,
And I never gaze upon it
　　But unbidden tears will spring.

I began to search my pockets,
  But scarcely a dime was there;
But scanty as was the pittance,
  This stocking received its share.

For a longing seized upon me
  To gladden the heart of my boy,
And I bought him some cakes and candy,
  And added a simple toy.

Then I knelt by this little stocking
  And sobbed out an earnest prayer,
And arose with strength to wrestle
  And break from the tempter's snare.

And this faded, worn-out stocking,
  So pitiful once to see,
Became the wedge that broke my chain,
  And a blessing brought to me.

Do you marvel then I prize it?
  When each darn and seam and hole
Is linked with my soul's deliverance
  From the bondage of the bowl?

And to-night my wife will tell you,
  Though I've houses, gold and land,
He holds no treasure more precious
  Than this stocking in my hand.

The Fatal Pledge

"Pledge me with wine," the maiden cried,
  Her tones were gay and light;
"From others you have turned aside,
  I claim your pledge to-night."

The blood rushed to the young man's cheek
  Then left it deadly pale;
Beneath the witchery of her smile
  He felt his courage fail.

For many years he'd been a slave
  To the enchanting bowl,

The Fatal Pledge: Moses: A Story of the Nile (1889).

Until he grasped with eager hands
  The reins of self-control;

And struggled with his hated thrall,
  Until he rent his chain,
And strove to stand erect and free,
  And be a man again.

When others came with tempting words
  He coldly turned aside,
But she who held the sparkling cup
  Was his affianced bride;

And like a vision of delight,
  Bright, beautiful and fair,
With thoughtless words she wove for him
  The meshes of despair.

From jeweled hands he took the cup,
  Nor heard the serpent's hiss;
Nor saw beneath its ruby glow
  The deadly adder's hiss.

Like waves that madly, wildly dash,
  When dykes are overthrown,
The barriers of his soul gave way,
  Each life with wrecks was strewn.

And she who might have reached her hand
  To succor and to save,
Soon wept in hopeless agony
  Above a drunkard's grave.

And bore through life with bleeding heart
  Remembrance of that night,
When she had urged the tempted man
  With wine to make his plight.

Woman's Work

God gave the word, and woman heard,
Unto its depths her heart was stirred,
An ancient foe evil and strong,
Had wrung her heart with cruel wrong.

Woman's Work: Christian Recorder, February 7, 1889.

O'er many homes once fair and bright
Had come a dark and withering blight,
High hearts were crushed, strong men brought low,
And poverty clasped hands with woe.

And still the curse from strand to strand,
With wreck and ruin strewed the land;
Men learned the tempting cup to crave,
And maddened sank into the grave.

Baptised in prayer, she rose at length,
Strong only in the Master's strength;
With weapons by her heart throbs made,
She organized the grand crusade.

With mission from the hand of God,
Her willing feet then onward trod;
She saw and met the hour's demand,
For God, and home, and native land.

She saw the drunkard's pain and grief,
And reached her hand to bring relief;
The foul fiend saw her work with dread,
As like a sacred fire it spread.

Amid earth's sorrow, pain and wrong,
God's love could only make her strong;
To strive to succor, and to bless
The children's homes of wretchedness.

On statue books she laid her hand,
To save the children of the land;
Unarmed she would not let them go,
To meet their mocking cruel foe.

Where drink had been a lava tide,
She scattered knowledge far and wide;
Against the hosts of Sin and Shame
Her hands have wrought in Jesus' name.

Fair maidens learned to clasp her hand,
And lead the loyal legion band;
And point a better brighter way
For youthful feet so apt to stray.

Since on that frosty morning air
Arose the first Crusader's prayer,

What wond'rous changes have been wrought,
What fruits of tender, loving thought!

The fight may yet be fierce and long,
The foe is old, and base, and strong,
And men for power, pelf and gain,
May hesitate to break his chain.

Although the breastplate that we wear,
Is but a ribbon white and fair,
We know that in the fiercest fight,
Our God is on the side of right.

Firmer and closer may we stand
Against this foe of every land;
We have reached the place where we must take
New courage for the Master's sake.

O may our hearts and hands be strong
To work with God against this wrong,
Until with our white ribbon bound,
The world is belted all around.

For the Twenty-Fifth Anniversary of the "Old Folks' Home"

We come, but not to celebrate,
Amid the flight and whirl of years,
The deeds of heroes, on whose brows
Are laurels, drenched with blood and tears.

Nor yet to tell of wondrous deeds
Performed on fields of bloodless strife;
But of the lonely precious things,
That bless and beautify our life.

And from the annals of the poor
We would unfold a shining page;
And tell of kindly hands that smoothed
The rugged path of faltering age.

To shelter those who long have borne
Life's chilling storms and searching heat,

For the Twenty-Fifth Anniversary . . .: Twenty-fifth Annual Report of the Home for the Aged
and Infirm Colored People, 1889, 13–14.

In restful homes, with love alight
What charity more pure and sweet?

But not beneath this spacious Home
Was laid the first foundation stone,
But in the hearts that learned to feel
For woman stricken, old and lone.

To Hall and Truman, Still and Laing
Was given power to aid and bless;
And, faithful to her sacred charge,
Constant, and helping, stood Ann Jess.

May Sarah Pennock, whose kind hand
Has often brought the "Home" relief
Feel life replete with God's great peace;
Find light in darkness, joy in grief.

Custodian of the Generous purse
May Israel Johnson long remain—
And reach at last the happy land,
Where faithful service meets its gain.

And join again departed forms
Of wife and sister passed before;
Who gave their treasure to the Lord,
By generous gifts unto His poor.

And some who met with us erewhile,
Have passed unto the other side;
Like precious fragrance, may their deeds
Within our heart of hearts abide.

Year after year, within these walls,
Did Dillwyn Parrish faithful stand;
Til He "Who gives his loved ones sleep"
Released, in death, his helpful hand

Of those who scattered flowers fair
Around the verge of parting life,
We would record with grateful words,
The names of Stephen Smith and wife

Whose hands, enriched with golden store,
Gave of their wealth to build this "Home,"
And changed a narrow domicile
Into a grand and stately dome.

Oh! When our earthly homes shall fail
And vanish from our fading sight
May friends and patrons meet again
In God's fair halls of love and light

Where homeless ones shall never weep,
Nor weary aged wanderers roam;
But walk amid the golden streets
Secure within our Father's home.

To White Ribbons of Maine Who Gave to Me Their Blessed Gifts

Oh sisters, kind and loving,
    When your gifts to me shall tell
Of the hours swiftly passing,
    May I learn to use them well.

And write upon them records
    For the brighter world above,
Of a life endowed with power,
    And transcribed with deeds of love.

How thoughtful was the kindness
    Which bestowed the fleecy fold,
To shield a stranger sister
    'Mid your virgin snows and cold.

I will say to other women,
    Labor, struggle and achieve,
In our land are noble women,
    Who in God and man believe.

Who say not to a comrade,
    With sun caressed and darker brow
"Stand by thyself, come not thou near;
    I am holier than thou."

May all white-ribboned sisters
    Learn from gifts so kind and rare,

To White Ribbons of Maine . . .: *Christian Recorder*, December 15, 1890. Preceding this poem a note explained that "A committee of Maine ladies presented our distinguished townswoman with a beautiful gold watch and shawl." The white ribbon was a symbol of the temperance movement.

To give the poor and hated
  Tender, loving, Christly care.

May God's great peace surround you,
  'Till life's toil and pain are o'er;
And grant us all a greeting,
  On the bright and restful shore;

Where the least of all his brethren
  Shall behold their Saviour's face,
Who will gather all his people,
  From each kindred, tribe and race.

The Rallying Cry

O children of the tropics,
  Amid our pain and wrong,
Have you no other mission
  Than music, dance and song?

While through the weary ages
  Our dripping tears still fall;
Is this a time to dally
  With pleasure's silken thrall?

Go muffle all your viols,
  As heroes learn to stand
With faith in God's great justice;
  Nerve every heart and hand.

Dream not of ease nor pleasure,
  Nor honor, wealth nor fame,
Till from the dust you've lifted
  Our long dishonored name.

And crown that name with glory
  By deeds of holy worth;
To shine in light emblazoned
  The noblest name on earth.

Engrave upon your banners,
  In words of golden light;
That mercy, truth and justice
  Are more than godless might.

The Rallying Cry: Christian Recorder, January 15, 1891.

Count life a dismal failure
  Unblessing and unblest,
That seeks in ceaseless ease
  For pleasure or for rest.

With courage, strength and valor
  Your lives and actions brace;
Shrink not from pain and hardship
  And dangers bravely face.

Above earth's pain and sorrow
  Christ's dying face I see
I hear the cry of anguish
  Why'st Thou forsaken me?

The pallor of that anguish
  Reveals the only light
To flood with joy and gladness
  Earth's sorrow, pain and night.

Arrayed in Christly armor,
  'Gainst error, crime and sin;
The victory can't be doubtful
  For God is sure to win.

Thine Eyes Shall See the King in His Beauty

I know that it must be pleasant
  To walk with the saints in white;
To dwell in the radiant city,
  With the glory of God its light.

I know that it must be blissful
  To cool life's fever and thirst
In the streams that flow from the throne of God,
  Where the living fountains burst.

It must be a deep refreshment,
  After our hunger and grief,
To rest 'neath the shadow of that tree
  With healing in every leaf.

It must be exquisite rapture,
  After earth's discord and din,

Thine Eyes Shall See . . .: *Christian Recorder*, August 27, 1891.

To hear the songs of the angels
  As they gladly welcome us in.

But oh, for the joy extatic!
  Can earth ever coin a word
To tell the soul's exultation
  When gazing first on the Lord?

To Bishop Payne

Written for the special celebration of the fortieth an-
niversary of Daniel A. Payne as bishop of the A.M.E.
Church, 1892.

The prison house in which you dwell,
  Is falling to decay.
May God renew thy spirit's youth,
  Within those walls of clay.

And while a dimness slowly creeps
  Around Earth's fairest light,
May heaven grow clearer to your view,
  And fairer to thy sight.

And when Earth's sweetest harmonies
  Grow duller to your ear,
May music from your father's house
  Begin to float more near.

Then let the pillars of your home
  Crumble and fall away.
So God's dear love within thy soul
  Renews it day by day.

Until life's toil and pain are o'er,
  Its sorrow and its night.
And on thy raptured gaze shall burst
  The beatific sight.

With saints redeemed and martyrs crowned,
  And loved ones mayest thou meet;
And rest with them thy crown of life,
  At our Redeemer's feet.

To Bishop Payne: *Journal of the 20th Session and 19th Quadrennial Session of the Central Conference of the African Methodist Episcopal Church* (May 2, 1892):61.

A Poem

Composed for the reception tendered the Reverend
Henry L. Phillips and wife in celebration of their return
from West Indies in 1902 and of his twenty-five years of
service as rector of the Church of the Crucifixion,
Philadelphia.

Over the foaming ocean,
  Over the restless sea;
Back to thy field of labor,
  We are waiting to welcome thee.

Back from the land of flowers,
  Kissed by the ardent sun;
With thy brightest, gladdest welcome,
  Thy people here are come.

In the long, long Lenten season,
  Ere thy journeyings were o'er;
We will not forget the lessons,
  Taught us by our Brother More.

In the work thou placed before,
  He has laid his earnest heart;
So tonight within thy welcome
  He must surely take a part.

Youth and maiden here will greet thee,
  Who were not confirmed before;
Greet thee here tonight as pastor,
  By the work of Brother More.

With the consort of thy bosom,
  As down the stream of life ye glide;
May the love of God surround you
  With His light at eventide.

In the years of early manhood,
  On thy brow the dews of youth,
Thou gaves't to a needed people
  Many words of love and truth.

A Poem: From Graham, 210–12. Originally appeared in George F. Bragg, *Golden Jubilee of Henry Laird Phillips*, c. 1929.

Now we welcome thee, dear Father,
  As one who points the way
Amid earth's pomps and vanities
  To Heaven's brighter day.

May rich and copious blessing
  Upon thy life descend,
As we greet thee with a welcome,
  Our Father and our friend.

Where sin clasps hand with sorrow,
  May we thy flock be found;
As followers of the Master,
  Who in his love abound.

To strive by high endeavor
  To make the world more bright;
To change life's dull and rugged paths,
  To lines of living light.

With hearts of glad surrender,
  Not seeking wealth or fame;
O Guide and Shepherd teach us
  To live in Jesus' name.

With peace and joy and comfort,
  May all thy life be blessed;
And angels welcome thee at last
  Within the gates of rest.

With all the saints and martyrs,
  Who tried with pain and might;
With bleeding feet the thorny paths,
  Now luminous with light.

Like a holy Benediction,
  Thy presence may it be;
Till in the Holy City
  Thy flock shall welcome thee.

Essays and Speeches

◆

"Coloured Women of America" is excerpted from Harper's speech to the Women's Congress. It was reprinted in the January 1878 issue of the *English Woman's Review*. Many of the examples of progress by African-American women that Harper cites are taken from those she discovered during her southern travels and of which she wrote in her letters to Still.

"A Factor in Human Progress" was printed in the *African Methodist Episcopal Church Review* of July 1885. Here Harper reminds readers that education is not an end in itself but a means of arming oneself in the battle for human dignity. Harper demonstrates this with her references to the poetry of the popular British writer George Eliot. In making the analogy between "The Spanish Gypsy" and the situation of the postbellum generation of African-Americans, she also suggests a comparison between her own work and that of her British sister. Moses again is one of her examples of the historical precedents for "self-surrender for the sake of others." The examples of the courageous slave who endured a fatal beating rather than betray his fellow slaves and of the colored man who sacrificed his life to save the boatload of soldiers reappear seven years later in *Iola Leroy*.

"The Woman's Christian Temperance Union and the Colored Woman" was published in the *African Methodist Episcopal Church Review* of July 1888. At this time, Frances Harper had been working with the Woman's Christian Temperance Union (WCTU) for almost a decade and for the last five years had been serving as its national superintendent of the

270

African-American division. In this essay, Harper directly addresses the issue of racial separation, declaring that this organization, too, had its bigots, but that the "leaven of more liberal sentiments has been at work" and that progress was being made. While she notes that Christianity requires "the union of Christians to do Christly work," Frances Harper, in fact, distinguishes "Christian affiliation" from "social equality." Her emphasis upon the talent and achievements of the black sections within the WCTU and upon the equal rights of those groups within the national organization suggests that integration may be not only unnecessary but undesirable.

"Enlightened Motherhood" was an address to the Brooklyn [N.Y.] Literary Society on November 15, 1892. This essay illustrates the consistency of Frances Harper's campaign against sexism. In her warning that marriage must be for love, but that women must not trust their futures to men who drift where they ought to steer, Harper repeats the themes of antebellum poems such as "Advice to Girls" and of her short story, "The Two Offers." In her disparagement of women who would guard the purity of their daughters but allow their sons to philander, and of women who shun fallen women but entertain the men who caused those women to fall, Harper echoes such poems as "The Contrast" that she published nearly forty years earlier.

♦

Coloured Women of America

The women as a class are quite equal to the men in energy and executive ability. In fact I find by close observation, that the mothers are the levers which move in education. The men talk about it, especially about election time, if they want an office for self or their candidate, but the women work most for it. They labour in many ways to support the family, while the children attend school. They make great sacrifices to spare their own children during school hours. I know of girls from sixteen to twenty-two who iron till midnight that they may come to school in the day. Some of our scholars, aged about nineteen, living about thirty miles off, rented land, ploughed, planted, and then sold their cotton, in order to come to us. A woman near me, urged her husband to go in debt 500 dollars for a home, as the titles to the land they built on were insecure, and she said to me, "We have five years to pay it in, and I shall begin to-day to do it, if life is spared. I will make a hundred dollars at washing, for I have done it." Yet they have seven little children to feed, clothe, and educate.

Coloured Women of America: Englishwoman's Review, January 15, 1878. First presented as a speech to the Women's Congress.

In the field the women receive the same wages as the men, and are often preferred, clearing land, hoeing, or picking cotton, with equal ability.

In different departments of business, coloured women have not only been enabled to keep the wolf from the door, but also to acquire property, and in some cases the coloured woman is the mainstay of the family, and when work fails the men in large cities, the money which the wife can obtain by washing, ironing, and other services, often keeps pauperism at bay. I do not suppose, considering the state of her industrial lore and her limited advantages, that there is among the poorer classes a more helpful woman than the coloured woman as a labourer. When I was in Mississippi, I stopped with Mr. Montgomery, a former slave of Jefferson Davis's brother. His wife was a woman capable of taking on her hands 130 acres of land, and raising one hundred and seven bales of cotton by the force which she could organise. Since then I have received a very interesting letter from her daughter, who for years has held the position of Assistant Post-mistress. In her letter she says: "There are many women around me who would serve as models of executiveness anywhere. They do double duty, a man's share in the field, and a woman's part at home. They do any kind of field work, even ploughing, and at home the cooking, washing, milking, and gardening. But these have husbands; let me tell you of some widows and unaided women:—

"1st. Mrs. Hill, a widow, has rented, cultivated, and solely managed a farm of five acres for five years. She makes her garden, raises poultry, and cultivates enough corn and cotton to live comfortably, and keep a surplus in the bank. She saves something every year, and this is much, considering the low price of cotton and unfavourable seasons.

"2nd. Another woman, whose husband died in the service during the war, cultivated one acre, making vegetables for sale, besides a little cotton. She raises poultry, spins thread, and knits hose for a living. She supports herself comfortably, never having to ask credit or to borrow.

"[3rd.] Mrs. Jane Brown and Mrs. Halsey formed a partnership about ten years ago, leased nine acres and a horse, and have cultivated the land all that time, just the same as men would have done. They have saved considerable money from year to year, and are living independently. They have never had any expenses for labour, making and gathering the crops themselves.

"4th. Mrs. Henry, by farming and peddling cakes, has the last seven years laid up seven hundred dollars. She is an invalid, and unable to work at all times. Since then she has been engaged in planting sweet potatoes and raising poultry and hogs. Last year she succeeded in raising 250 hogs, but lost two-thirds by disease. She furnished eggs and chickens enough for family use, and sold a surplus of chickens, say fifty dozen chickens. On nine acres she made 600 bushels of sweet potatoes. The present year she has planted ten acres of potatoes. She has 100 hogs, thirty dozen chickens, a small lot of ducks and turkeys, and also a few sheep and goats. She has also a large garden under her supervision, which is planted in cabbages. She has two women and a boy to assist. Miss Montgomery, a coloured lady, says: 'I have constantly been engaged in bookkeeping for eight years, and for ten years as assistant post-mistress, doing all the work of the office. Now, instead of bookkeeping, I manage a school of 133 pupils, and I have an assistant, and I am still attending to the post-office." Of her sister she says, she is a better and swifter worker than herself; that she generally sews, but that last year she made 100 dozen jars of preserved fruit for sale. An acquaintance of mine, who lives in South Carolina, and has been engaged in mission work, reports that, in supporting the family, women are the mainstay; that two-thirds of the truck gardening is done by them in South Carolina; that in the city they are more industrious than the men; that when the men lose their work through their political affiliations, the women stand by them, and say, 'stand by your principles.' And I have been informed by the same person that a number of women have homes of their own, bought by their hard earnings since freedom. Mr. Stewart, who was employed in the Freedmen's bank, says he has seen scores of coloured women in the South working and managing plantations of from twenty to 100 acres. They and their boys and girls doing all the labour, and marketing in the fall from ten to fifty bales of cotton. He speaks of a mulatto woman who rented land, which she and her children worked until they had made enough to purchase a farm of 130 acres. She then lived alone upon it, hiring help and working it herself, making a comfortable living, and assisting her sons in the purchase of land. The best sugar maker, he observes, he ever saw was a stupid looking coloured woman, apparently twenty-five years old. With a score or more of labourers, she was the 'boss,' and it was her eye which detected the exact consistency to which the syrup had boiled, and, while tossing it in the air, she told with certainty the point of granulation."

In higher walks of life too, the coloured women have made progress. The principal of the Coloured High School in Philadelphia was born a slave in the District of Columbia; but in early life she was taken North, and she resolved to get knowledge. When about fifteen years old, she obtained a situation as a house servant, with the privilege of going every other day to receive instruction. Poverty was in her way, but instead of making it a stumbling block, she converted it into a stepping stone. She lived in one place about six years, and received seven dollars a month.

A coloured lady presented her a scholarship, and she entered Oberlin as a pupil. When she was sufficiently advanced, Oberlin was brave enough to accord her a place as a teacher in the preparatory department of the college, a position she has held for several years, graduating almost every year a number of pupils, a part of whom are scattered abroad as teachers in different parts of the country. Nearly all the coloured teachers in Washington are girls and women, a large percentage of whom were educated in the district of Columbia. Nor is it only in the ranks of teachers that coloured women are content to remain. Some years since, two coloured women were studying in the Law School of Howard University. One of them, Miss Charlotte Ray, a member of this body, has since graduated, being, I believe, the first coloured woman in the country who has ever gained the distinction of being a graduated lawyer. Others have gone into medicine and have been practising in different States of the Union. In the Woman's Medical College of Pennsylvania, two coloured women were last year pursuing their studies as Matriculants, while a young woman, the daughter of a former fugitive slave, has held the position of an assistant resident physician in one of the hospitals. Miss Cole, of Philadelphia, held for some time the position of physician in the State Orphan Asylum in South Carolina.

In literature and art we have not accomplished much, although we have a few among us who have tried literature. Miss Foster has written for the *Atlantic Monthly*, and Mrs. Mary Shadd Cary for years edited a paper called the *Provincial Freeman*, and another coloured woman has written several stories, poems, and sketches, which have appeared in different periodicals. In art, we have Miss Edmonia Lewis, who is, I believe, allied on one side to the negro race. She exhibited several pieces of statuary, among which is Cleopatra, at the Centennial.

The coloured women have not been backward in promoting charities for their own sex and race. One of the most efficient helpers is Mrs. Madison, who although living in a humble and unpretending home, had succeeded in getting up a home for aged coloured women. By organized effort, coloured women have been enabled to help each other in sickness, and provide respectable funerals for the dead. They have institutions under different names; one of the oldest, perhaps the oldest in the country, has been in existence, as I have been informed, about fifty years, and has been officered and managed almost solely by women for about half a century. There are also, in several States, homes for aged coloured women: the largest I know of being in Philadelphia. This home was in a measure built by Stephen and Harriet Smith, coloured citizens of the State of Pennsylvania. Into this home men are also admitted. The city of Philadelphia has also another home for the homeless, which, besides giving them a temporary shelter, provides a permanent home for a number of aged coloured women. In looking over the statistics of miscellaneous charities, out of a list of fifty-seven charitable institutions, I see only nine in which there is any record of coloured inmates. Out of twenty-six Industrial Schools, I counted four. Out of a list of one hundred and fifty-seven orphan asylums, miscellaneous charities, and industrial schools, I find fifteen asylums in which there is some mention of coloured inmates. More than half the reform schools in 1874, had admitted coloured girls. The coloured women of Philadelphia have formed a Christian Relief Association, which has opened sewing schools for coloured girls, and which has been enabled, year after year, to lend a hand to some of the more needy of their race, and it also has, I understand, sustained an employment office for some time.

A Factor in Human Progress

In the last number of the A.M.E. Review was a thoughtful paper entitled, "We must educate." The first question asked was: How shall we educate? and a line of action was finely mapped. Alongside the suggestions of that paper arises the query, How can we best utilize this education? The culture of the moral and spiritual faculties is destined to play the most important part in our future development. Knowledge is power, the great mental lever which has lifted up man in the scale of social and racial life; but a towering intellect, grand in its achievements, and glorious in its possibilities, may, with the moral and spiritual faculties held in abeyance, be one of the most dangerous and mischievous forces in the world. There is force in the tempest's wrath when gallant ships are sinking beneath its fury, power in the earthquake's throbbing when it lays cities and towns in ruins; but when the storm has spent its fury and the earthquake has done its work of desolation, sunlight and sapphire skies will bend over the desolate city, and the ocean will keep no track of the wrecks that slumber in her hold. Physical forces have their limitations, but who can fix the boundary line of the ideal and impalpable forces that bring their bane or blessing to mankind? A wicked man, intellectual and gifted, may send his influence for evil across the track of unborn ages, and hurl with mortmain hand a legacy of maledictions to future generations; while, on the other hand, from some bulrush ark and lowly manager or humble habitation, has come the teacher with the chrism of a new era upon his brow, and left upon the centuries the fragrance of his memory.

*A Factor in Human Progress: African Methodist Episcopal Church Review 2 (1885):14–18.

We are living in the midst of a people who have in their veins the blood of some of the strongest nations on earth—nations who have been pioneers of civilization, macadamizers of paths untrod, masters of achievement, and we have need of the best educational influences of the home, school and church to prepare us to fill our places nobly and grandly in the arena of life; for this we need more than the training of the intellectual faculties. I have heard of a scientist, who, in trying an experiment in hatching chickens, made an unequal distribution of temperature, applying cold where heat should have been more uniform, and the result was deformity and malformation. The education of the intellect and the training of the morals should go hand-in-hand. The devising brain and the feeling heart should never be divorced, and the question worth asking is not simply, What will education do for us? but, What will it help us to do for others? Do you point me with pride to your son, and tell me the best college in the country is his *alma mater*; that he has passed triumphantly through its curriculum; that he is well versed in ancient lore and modern learning, and that his mind is an arsenal of well-stored facts, fully equipping him for the battle of life? I ask, in reply, Is he noble and upright? Does he prefer integrity to gold, principle to ease, true manhood to self-indulgence? Is he chaste in his conversation, and pure in his life? If not, I answer, his education is unfinished. He may be brilliant and witty; eager, keen and alert for the main chance; but he is not prepared to be a moral athlete, armed for glorious strife, ready to win on hotly-contested fields new battles for humanity. George Eliot in her poem, "The Spanish Gypsy," has for one of her characters a Gypsy chieftain, a captain of the Spaniards, who discovers in the affianced bride of the Duke of Alva his long-lost daughter, who years before was stolen from him and reared by the duke's mother. Before her the vista of the future is opening with all the light and joy of young wedded love in a ducal palace, when suddenly her father appears upon the scene and discloses her origin, and with words of peculiar power he urges her to join the Zincalas, and clasp with him their fortunes in her hand. In revealing himself to her, he says:

"I lost you as a man may lose a diamond
Wherein he has compressed his total wealth,
On the right hand whose cunning makes him great:
I lost you by a trivial accident.
Marauding Spaniards, sweeping like a storm
Over a spot within the Spanish bounds,
Near where our camp lay, doubtless snatched you up,
When Zind, your nurse, as she confessed, was urged
By burning thirst to wander towards the stream,

And leave you on the sand some paces off,
Playing with pebbles, while she, dog-like, lapped.
It was so I lost you . . ."

But now, in finding her, he tells her that she is a Zincala—

"Of a blood,
Unmixed as virgin wine-juice."

Fedalma asks,—

"Of a race
More outcast and despised than Moor or Jew?"

To which Zarca replies—

"Yes: wanderers whom no God took knowledge of
To give them laws, or fight for them, or blight
Another race to make them ample room;
A people with no home even in memory;
No dimmest lore of giant ancestors
To make a common hearth for piety."

Fedalma, his daughter, answers:

"A race that lives on prey, as foxes do
With stealthy, petty rapine; so despised,
It is not persecuted, only spurned,
Crushed under foot, warred on by chance, like rats,
Or swarming flies, or reptiles of the sea
Dragged in the net unsought, and flung far off
To perish as they may?"

Zarca:—

"You paint us well.
So abject are the men whose blood we share;
Untutored, unbefriended, unendowed;
No favorites of heaven or of men,
Therefore I cling to them! Therefore no lure
Shall draw me to disown them or forsake
The meagre, wandering herd that lows for help
And needs me for its guide, to seek my pasture
Among the well-fed beeves that graze at will.
Because our race have no great memories
I will so live they shall remember me
For deeds of such divine beneficence
As rivers have, that teach men what is good
By blessing them. I have been schooled,—have caught

> Lore from the Hebrew, deftness from the Moor,—
> Know the rich heritage, the milder life,
> Of nations fathered by a mighty Past;
> But were our race accursed (as they who make
> Good luck a god count all unlucky men)
> I would espouse their cause, sooner than take
> My gifts from brethren naked of all good,
> And lend them to the rich for usury."

Where, in the wide realms of poet[r]y and song, will we find nobler sentiments expressed with more tenderness, strength and beauty? However low down a people may be in the scale of character and condition, absorbed in providing for their physical wants, or steeped in sensuous gratifications, the moment their admiration is awakened and their aspirations kindled by the recital, or the example of deeds of high and holy worth, and the spirit of self-sacrifice and self-surrender for some good cause is awakened and developed, there comes in that race a dividing line between the sensuous and material, and the spiritual and progressive. On this subject of self-surrender for the sake of others, there has been a fine symphony of thought under different forms of religion and various phases of civilization. In the Hebrew Scriptures we have the picture of Moses entreating God to forgive the sin of his people, or blot his name out of the book he had written. Was ever human love more tender and devoted than that which could forego God's remembrance for the sake of a people who could smite his ears with cruel murmurs, and be almost ready to stone him in their disappointed wrath? We see a manifestation of the same sentiment in the story of Bhooda, whose young soul, oppressed with a sense of the ills of life that threw their shadows around his path, exchanges his princely station for a mendicant's position in his search for knowledge. "Let me see," he said, "the absolute, eternal law of things, and I can give peace to mankind." Turning a deaf ear to the entreaties of kindred love, he resolved, "I will never return to the palace till I have attained the sight of the divine law." And feeling that he had attained what he sought, he decided to become a teacher, although conscious that his teaching would bring opposition, neglect and scorn. The same idea is seen in the legend which tells of the chasm which yawned in ancient Rome, where issued pestilential vapors, and that the sooth-sayers said, whoever should bring the most costly offering should have power to close that chasm; that "man and maiden" brought their precious offerings, but still the chasm yawned. Then Curtius remembered that Rome had something more valuable than her treasures—it was her manhood, with its valor and patriotism; and mounting his horse, he leaped into the chasm to close it by the surrender of his life. The same thought occurs in the Greek myth of Theseus, who confronts peril and death in delivering Greece from the dreadful Minotaur, who annually demanded his tribute of maidens and youths. This same idea, ennobled and glorified, gathers around the cross of Calvary, and deepens around the garden grave, till it changes a symbol of horror and shame into a throne of power and an ensign of victory. In the poem to which I have referred, the Gypsy tells his daughter, "No curse has fallen upon us till we have ceased to help each other." Men cannot help each other in the right spirit without helping themselves. The reflex of good deeds is in their own lives. Do you wish to know anything of the moral and spiritual status of a people, find out, not simply how they use their working hours, but how they spend their leisure moments. If these moments are only devoted to amusements and entertainments; if their religion largely consists of emotional fervors, without corresponding practice; if, in the midst of grog-shops and debauchery, they can shout and sing, and be unwilling to make any effort, or practice any self-denial to stay those tides of death whose dreadful breakers dash around the church and home, submerging youth and manhood beneath the waves of intemperance, such a people may produce gifted and brilliant talkers and thinkers, and religious enthusiasts, but it is only as the spirit of self-surrender enters into their lives that its true strength is developed. Self-sacrifice and self-surrender have been the golden cords that have lifted men nearer to God, and brought heaven closer to earth. Had Moses preferred the luxury of an Egyptian palace to the endurance of hardships with his people, would the Jews have been the race to whom we owe the most, not perhaps for science and art, but for the grandest of all sciences, the science of a true life of joy and trust in God, of God-like forgiveness and divine self-surrender? Had the noble army of martyrs cared for no one but themselves, would they have ever trodden with bleeding feet the paths that have since turned to lines of living light? Had the fathers of this republic stood apart, lacking confidence in each other, would American independence have been achieved, and our nation started upon its wonderful career of prosperity and power? In the world of thought and action, self-sacrifice and self-surrender have been the great factors of development, and as they pervade the life of a people, they lift them up. Nor has this spirit of self-devotion been only confined to the strongest races of the earth. During the days of slavery we read of a man who knew the plan of some of his fellow slaves to obtain their freedom, but rather than betray them, he received seven hundred and fifty lashes, and died. Among the annals of the civil war is the story of a colored man who was in a boat which became stranded, and there was a lack of strength to shove her from the sand, unless some one would expose himself to the fire of rebel bullets, and this man, comprehending the situation, exclaimed, "Some one must die to get us out of this. I mought's well be him as any. You are soldiers and can fight. If they kill me it is nothing." And facing danger and death, he shoved the boat from the treacherous sands, received a number of bullets, and died. Who shall say that the race out of which such men could spring from under the dark shadow of slavery has not within it the elements out of which a great people may yet be produced? What a field of usefulness lies before the educated young men and women of our race! What possibilities are in their hands! As "sculptors of life, they stand with their work before them." What shall the carving be? Images of beauty, love and truth? or weakness, vanity and selfishness? I remember once talking with a school teacher in a Southern State, who, speaking of her lack of society, said of those by whom she was surrounded: "They all talk gossip, and wouldn't improve me." Suppose she had viewed the social condition of her neighbors from another standpoint, and said, These women cannot improve me, but I will try to improve them. If they talk nothing but gossip, I will try to raise the tone of conversation, and show them a more excellent way. I will study to teach these mothers how to take care of their little ones; I will learn something of the sophistries of strong drink, of the effect of stimulants and narcotics on the human system, and teach them how intemperance adds to the burdens, waste and miseries of society; because I have had advantages that were denied them; as a friend and sister, I will gladly share with them my richer heritage. Would not such a resolution have given a new significance to her life, and added power which no wealth of intellectual attainments could have given without it? for the best test of a good education is not simply what we know, but what we do, and what we are. When the last lay of the minstrel shall die upon his ashy lips and the sweetest numbers of the poet shall cease to charm the death-dulled ear, when we are ready to lay aside much that we learned as a garment we have outworn and outgrown, then we hope that the science of well-spent hours will go with us through the valley and shadow of death, only to grow brighter and brighter through the eternities.

Philadelphia, Pa.

The Woman's Christian Temperance Union and the Colored Woman

A Woman sat beneath the shadow of her home, while the dark waves of intemperance dashed against human hearts and hearthstones, but there came an hour when she found that she could do something else besides wring her hands and weep over the ravages of the liquor traffic, which had darkened so many lives and desolated so many homes. Where the enemy spreads his snares for the feet of the unwary, inexperienced and tempted, she, too, could go and strive to stay the tide of ruin which was sending its floods of sorrow, shame and death to the habitations of men, and 1873 witnessed the strange and wondrous sight of the Woman's Crusade, when the mother-heart was roused up in defense of the home and all that the home held dearest. A Divine impulse seemed to fan into sudden flame and touch with living fire earnest hearts, which rose up to meet the great occasion. Lips that had been silent in the prayer meeting were loosened to take part in the wonderful uprising. Saloons were visited, hardships encountered, insults, violence, and even imprisonment endured by women, brave to suffer and strong to endure. Thousands of saloon visits were made, many were closed. Grand enthusiasms were aroused, moral earnestness awakened, and a fire kindled whose beacon lights still stream o'er the gloomy track of our monster evil. Victor Hugo has spoken of the nineteenth century as being woman's era, and among the most noticeable epochs in this era is the uprising of women against the twin evils of slavery and intemperance, which had foisted themselves like leeches upon the civilization of the present age. In the great anti-slavery conflict women had borne a part, but after the storm cloud of battle had rolled away, it was found that an enemy, old and strong and deceptive, was warring against the best interests of society; not simply an enemy to one race, but an enemy to all races—an enemy that had entrenched itself in the strongholds of appetite and avarice, and was upheld by fashion, custom and legislation. To dislodge this enemy, to put prohibition not simply on the statute book, but in the heart and conscience of a nation, embracing within itself such heterogeneous masses, is no child's play, nor the work of a few short moons. Men who were subjects in their own country and legislated for by others, become citizens here, with the power to help legislate for native born Americans. Hundreds of thousands of new citizens have been translated from the old oligarchy of slavery into the new commonwealth of freedom, and are numerically strong enough to hold the

The Woman's Christian Temperance Union: African Methodist Episcopal Church Review 4 (1888):313–16.

balance of power in a number of the States, and sway its legislators for good or evil. With all these conditions, something more is needed than grand enthusiasms lighting up a few consecrated lives with hallowed brightness. We need patient, persevering, Christly endeavor, a consecration of the moral earnestness, spiritual power and numerical strength of the nation to grapple with this evil and accomplish its overthrow.

After the knowledge and experience gained by the crusade, women, instead of letting all their pure enthusiasms become dissipated by expending in feeling what they should utilize in action, came together and formed the Woman's Christian Temperance Union. From Miss Willard we learn that women who had been crusading all winter called conventions for consultation in respective States, and that several organizations, called Temperance Leagues, were formed. Another step was the confederation of the States into the National Christian Temperance Union. A circular, aided by an extensive circulation through the press, was sent out to women, in different parts of the country, and a convention was called, which met in Cleveland in November, 1874, to which sixteen States responded. A plan of work was adopted, financial arrangements made, and the publishing of an organ resolved upon. Mrs. Whittemyer, of Philadelphia, was elected President, and Miss Willard, of Illinois, Corresponding Secretary. This Union has increased in numbers and territory until at its last convention it embraced thirty-seven States and Territories. For years I knew very little of its proceedings, and was not sure that colored comradeship was very desirable, but having attended a local Union in Philadelphia, I was asked to join and acceded to the request, and was made city and afterwards State Superintendent of work among colored people. Since then, for several years I have held the position of National Superintendent of work among the colored people of the North. When I became National Superintendent there were no colored women on the Executive Committee or Board of Superintendents. Now there are two colored women on the Executive Committee and two on the Board of Superintendents. As a matter of course the colored question has come into this work as it has into the Sons of Temperance, Good Templars and elsewhere. Some of the members of different Unions have met the question in a liberal and Christian manner; others have not seemed to have so fully outgrown the old shards and shells of the past as to make the distinction between Christian affiliation and social equality, but still the leaven of more liberal sentiments has been at work in the Union and produced some hopeful results.

One of the pleasantest remembrances of my connection with the Woman's Christian Temperance Union was the kind and hospitable reception

I met in the Missouri State Convention, and the memorable words of their President, Mrs. Hoffman, who declared that the color-line was eliminated. A Superintendent was chosen at that meeting for colored work in the State, at whose home in St. Louis the National Superintendent was for some time a guest. The State Superintendent said in one of the meetings to the colored sisters, "You can come with us, or you can go by yourselves." There was self-reliance and ability enough among them to form a Union of their own, which was named after the National Superintendent. Our work is divided into about forty departments, and among them they chose several lines of work, and had departments for parlor meetings, juvenile and evangelistic work, all of which have been in working order. The Union held meetings in Methodist and Baptist churches, and opened in the African Methodist Episcopal Church an industrial school for children, which increased in size until from about a dozen children at the beginning, it closed with about one hundred and fifty, as I understand. Some of the Unions, in their outlook upon society, found that there was no orphan asylum for colored children, except among the Catholics, and took the initiative for founding an asylum for colored children, and in a short time were successful in raising several hundred dollars for that purpose. This Union has, I have been informed, gathered into its association seventeen school teachers, and I think comprises some of the best brain and heart of the race in the city. From West Virginia a lady informs the National Superintendent that her Union has invited the colored sisters to join with them, and adds, "Praise God, from whom all blessings flow." In a number of places where there are local Unions in the North the doors have been opened to colored women, but in the farther South separate State Unions have been formed. Southern white women, it may be, fail to make in their minds the discrimination between social equality and Christian affiliation. Social equality, if I rightly understand the term, is the outgrowth of social affinities and social conditions, and may be based on talent, ability or wealth, on either or all of these conditions. Christian affiliation is the union of Christians to do Christly work, and to help build up the kingdom of Christ amid the sin and misery of the world, under the spiritual leadership of the Lord Jesus Christ. At our last National Convention two States were represented by colored representatives. The colored President of an Alabama Union represented a Union composed of white and colored people, and is called No. 2, instead of Colored Union, as it was not composed entirely of colored people, and in making its advent into the National Union brought, as I was informed, more than twice the amount of State dues which was paid by the white Alabama Union, No 1. The question of admission into the White Ribbon Army was brought before the National President, through a card sent from Atlanta. Twenty-three women had formed a Union, and had written to the National Superintendent of colored work in the North asking in reference to their admission, and if black sheep must climb up some other way to tell them how. I showed the card to Miss Willard, who gave it as her opinion "That the National could not make laws for a State. If the colored women of Georgia will meet and form a Woman's Christian Temperance Union for the State, it is my opinion that their officers and delegates will have the same representation in the National." The President of the Second Alabama was received and recognized in the National as a member of the Executive Committee, and had a place, as I was informed, on the Committee of Resolutions. Believing, as I do, in human solidarity, I hold that the Woman's Christian Temperance Union has in its hands one of the grandest opportunities that God ever pressed into the hands of the womanhood of any country. Its conflict is not the contest of a social club, but a moral warfare for an imperiled civilization. Whether or not the members of the farther South will subordinate the spirit of caste to the spirit of Christ, time will show. Once between them and the Negro were vast disparities, which have been melting and disappearing. The war obliterated the disparity between freedom and slavery. The civil law blotted out the difference between disfranchisement and manhood suffrage. Schools have sprung up like wells in the desert dust, bringing the races nearer together on the intellectual plane, while as a participant in the wealth of society the colored man has, I believe, in some instances, left his former master behind in the race for wealth. With these old landmarks going and gone, one relic remains from the dead past, "Our social customs." In clinging to them let them remember that the most ignorant, vicious and degraded voter outranks, politically, the purest, best and most cultured woman in the South, and learn to look at the question of Christian affiliation on this subject, not in the shadow of the fashion of this world that fadeth away, but in the light of the face of Jesus Christ. And can any one despise the least of Christ's brethren without despising Him? Is there any path that the slave once trod that Jesus did not tread before him, and leave luminous with the light of His steps? Was the Negro bought and sold? Christ was sold for thirty pieces of silver. Has he been poor? "The birds had nests, the foxes had holes, but the Son of man had not where to lay His head." Were they beaten in the house of bondage? They took Jesus and scourged Him. Have they occupied a low social position? "He made himself of no reputation, and was numbered with the transgressors." Despised and trodden under foot? He was despised and rejected of men; spit upon by the rabble, crucified between thieves, and died as died Rome's meanest criminal slave. Oh, my brothers and sisters, if God chastens every son whom He receiveth, let your past history be a stimulus for the future. Join with the great army who are on the side of our God and His Christ. Let your homes be the best places where you may plant your batteries against the rum traffic. Teach your children to hate intoxicating drinks with a deadly hatred. Though scorn may curl her haughty lip, and fashion gather up her dainty robes from social contact, if your lives are in harmony with God and Christly sympathy with man, you belong to the highest nobility in God's universe. Learn to fight the battle for God and man as athletes armed for a glorious strife, encompassed about with a cloud of witnesses who are in sympathy with the highest and holiest endeavors.

Enlightened Motherhood

It is nearly thirty years since an emancipated people stood on the threshold of a new era, facing an uncertain future—a legally unmarried race, to be taught the sacredness of the marriage relation; an ignorant people, to be taught to read the book of the Christian law and to learn to comprehend more fully the claims of the gospel of the Christ of Calvary. A homeless race, to be gathered into homes of peaceful security and to be instructed how to plant around their firesides the strongest batteries against the sins that degrade and the race vices that demoralize. A race unversed in the science of government and unskilled in the just administration of law, to be translated from the old oligarchy of slavery into the new commonwealth of freedom, and to whose men came the right to exchange the fetters on their wrists for the ballots in their right hands—a ballot which, if not vitiated by fraud or restrained by intimidation, counts just as much as that of the most talented and influential man in the land.

While politicians may stumble on the barren mountain of fretful controversy, and men, lacking faith in God and the invisible forces which make for righteousness, may shrink from the unsolved problems of the hour, into the hands of Christian women comes the opportunity of serving the ever blessed Christ, by ministering to His little ones and striving to make their homes the brightest spots on earth and the fairest types of heaven. The school may instruct and the church may teach, but the home is an institution older than the church and antedates school, and

---

Enlightened Motherhood: Pamphlet, *Enlightened Motherhood: An Address by Mrs. Frances E. W. Harper Before the Brooklyn Literary Society, November 15, 1892.*

that is the place where children should be trained for useful citizenship on earth and a hope of holy companionship in heaven.

Every mother should endeavor to be a true artist. I do not mean by this that every woman should be a painter, sculptor, musician, poet, or writer, but the artist who will write on the tablet of childish innocence thoughts she will not blush to see read in the light of eternity and printed amid the archives of heaven, that the young may learn to wear them as amulets around their hearts and throw them as bulwarks around their lives, and that in the hour of temptation and trial the voices from home may linger around their paths as angels of guidance, around their steps, and be incentives to deeds of high and holy worth.

The home may be a humble spot, where there are no velvet carpets to hush your tread, no magnificence to surround your way, nor costly creations of painter's art or sculptor's skill to please your conceptions or gratify your tastes; but what are the costliest gifts of fortune when placed in the balance with the confiding love of dear children or the true devotion of a noble and manly husband whose heart can safely trust in his wife? You may place upon the brow of a true wife and mother the greenest laurels; you may crowd her hands with civic honors; but, after all, to her there will be no place like home, and the crown of her motherhood will be more precious than the diadem of a queen.

As marriage is the mother of homes, it is important that the duties and responsibilities of this relation should be understood before it is entered on. A mistake made here may run through every avenue of the future, cast its shadow over all our coming years, and enter the lives of those whom we should shield with our love and defend with our care. We may be versed in ancient lore and modern learning, may be able to trace the path of worlds that roll in light and power on high, and to tell when comets shall cast their trail over our evening skies. We may understand the laws of stratification well enough to judge where lies the vein of silver and where nature has hidden her virgin gold. We may be able to tell the story of departed nations and conquering chieftains who have added pages of tears and blood to the world's history; but our education is deficient if we are perfectly ignorant how to guide the little feet that are springing up so gladly in our path, and to see in undeveloped possibilities gold more fine than the pavements of heaven and gems more precious than the foundations of the holy city. Marriage should not be a blind rushing together of tastes and fancies, a mere union of fortunes or an affair of convenience. It should be "a tie that only love and truth should weave and nothing but death should part."

Marriage between two youthful and loving hearts means the laying the foundation stones of a new home, and the woman who helps erect that home should be careful not to build it above the reeling brain of a drunkard or the weakened fibre of a debauchee. If it be folly for a merchant to send an argosy, laden with the richest treasures, at midnight on a moonless sea, without a rudder, compass, or guide, is it not madness for a woman to trust her future happiness, and the welfare of the dear children who may yet nestle in her arms and make music and sunshine around her fireside, in the unsteady hands of a characterless man, too lacking in self-respect and self-control to hold the helm and rudder of his own life; who drifts where he ought to steer, and only lasts when he ought to live?

The moment the crown of motherhood falls on the brow of a young wife, God gives her a new interest in the welfare of the home and the good of society. If hitherto she had been content to trip through life a lighthearted girl, or to tread amid the halls of wealth and fashion the gayest of the gay, life holds for her now a high and noble service. She must be more than the child of pleasure or the devotee of fashion. Her work is grandly constructive. A helpless and ignorant babe lies smiling in her arms. God has trusted her with a child, and it is her privilege to help that child develop the most precious thing a man or woman can possess on earth, and that is a good character. Moth may devour our finest garments, fire may consume and floods destroy our fairest homes, rust may gather on our silver and tarnish our gold, but there is an asbestos that no fire can destroy, a treasure which shall be richer for its service and better for its use, and that is a good character.

But the question arises, What constitutes an enlightened motherhood? I do not pretend that I will give you an exhaustive analysis of all that a mother should learn and of all she should teach. In the Christian scriptures the story is told of a mother of whom it was said: "From henceforth all nations shall call her blessed." While, in these days of religious unrest, criticism, and investigation, numbers are ready to relegate this story to the limbo of myth and fiction; whether that story be regarded as fact or fiction, there are lessons in it which we could not take into our lives without its making life higher, better, and more grandly significant. It is the teaching of a divine overshadowing and a touching self-surrender which still floats down the ages, fragrant with the aroma of a sweet submission. "The handmaid of the Lord, be it done unto me according to Thy word."

We read that Christ left us an example that we should tread in His footsteps; but does not the majority of the Christian world hold it as a sacred creed that the first print of His feet in the flesh began in the days of His antenatal life; and is not the same spirit in the world now which was there when our Lord made His advent among us, bone of our bone and flesh of our flesh; and do we not need the incarnation of God's love and light in our hearts as much now as it was ever needed in any preceding generation? Do we not need to hold it as a sacred thing, amid sorrow, pain, and wrong, that only through the love of God are human hearts made strong? And has not every prospective mother the right to ask for the overshadowing of the same spirit, that her child may be one of whom it may be truly said, "Of such is the kingdom of heaven," and all his life he shall be lent to the Lord? Had all the mothers of this present generation dwelt beneath the shadow of the Almighty, would it have been possible for slavery to have cursed us with its crimes, or intemperance degraded us with its vices? Would the social evil still have power to send to our streets women whose laughter is sadder than their tears, and over whose wasted lives death draws the curtains of the grave and silently hides their sin and shame? Are there not women, respectable women, who feel that it would wring their hearts with untold anguish, and bring their gray hairs in sorrow to the grave, if their daughters should trail the robes of their womanhood in the dust, yet who would say of their sons, if they were trampling their manhood down and fettering their souls with cords of vice, "O, well, boys will be boys, and young men will sow their wild oats."

I hold that no woman loves social purity as it deserves to be loved and valued, if she cares for the purity of her daughters and not her sons; who would gather her dainty robes from contact with the fallen woman and yet greet with smiling lips and clasp with warm and welcoming hands the author of her wrong and ruin. How many mothers to-day shrink from a double standard for society which can ostracise the woman and condone the offense of the man? How many mothers say within their hearts, "I intend to teach my boy to be as pure in his life, as chaste in his conversation, as the young girl who sits at my side encircled in the warm clasp of loving arms?" How many mothers strive to have their boys shun the gilded saloon as they would the den of a deadly serpent? Not the mother who thoughtlessly sends her child to the saloon for a beverage to make merry with her friends. How many mothers teach their boys to shrink in horror from the fascinations of women, not as God made them, but as sin has degraded them?

To-night, if you and I could walk through the wards of various hospitals at home and abroad, perhaps we would find hundreds, it may be thousands, of young men awaiting death as physical wrecks, having burned the candle of their lives at both ends. Were we to bend over their dying couches with pitying glances, and question them of their lives, perhaps numbers of them could tell you sad stories of careless words from thoughtless lips, that tainted their imaginations and sent their virus through their lives; of young eyes, above which God has made the heavens so eloquent with His praise, and the earth around so poetic with His ideas, turning from the splendor of the magnificent sunsets or glorious early dawns, and finding allurement in the dreadful fascinations of sin, or learning to gloat over impure pictures and vile literature. Then, later on, perhaps many of them could say, "The first time I went to a house where there were revelry and song, and the dead were there and I knew it not, I went with men who were older than myself; men, who should have showed me how to avoid the pitfalls which lie in the path of the young, the tempted, and inexperienced, taught me to gather the flowers of sin that blossom around the borders of hell."

Suppose we dared to question a little further, not from idle curiosity, but for the sake of getting, from the dying, object lessons for the living, and say, "God gave you, an ignorant child, into the hands of a mother. Did she never warn you of your dangers and teach you how to avoid them?" How many could truthfully say, "My mother was wise enough to teach me and faithful enough to warn me." If the cholera or yellow-fever were raging in any part of this city, and to enter that section meant peril to health and life, what mother would permit her child to walk care-lessly through a district where pestilence was breathing its bane upon the morning air and distilling its poison upon the midnight dews? And yet, when boys go from the fireside into the arena of life, how many ever go there forewarned and forearmed against the soft seductions of vice, against moral conditions which are worse than "fever, plague and palsy, and mad-ness *all* combined?"

Among the things I would present for the enlightenment of mothers are attention to the laws of heredity and environment. Mrs. Winslow, in a paper on social purity, speaks of a package of letters she had received from a young man of talent, good education, and a strong desire to live a pure and useful life. In boyhood he ignorantly ruined his health, and, when he resolved to rise above his depressed condition, his own folly, his heredity and environment, weighed him down like an incubus. His appeals, she says, are most touching. He says: "If you cannot help me, what can I do? My mother cursed me with illegitimacy and hereditary insanity. I have left only the alternative of suicide or madness." A fearful legacy! For stolen money and slandered character we may make repara-tion, but the opportunity of putting the right stamp on an antenatal life, if once gone, is gone forever; and there never was an angel of God, however bright, terrible, or strong he may be, who was ever strong enough to roll away the stone from the grave of a dead opportunity.

In the annals of this State may be found a record of six generations of debased manhood and womanhood, and prominent among them stands the name of Margaret, the mother of criminals. She is reported as having five sisters, the greater number of whom trailed the robes of their womanhood in the dust, and became fallen women. Some time since, their posterity was traced out, and five hundred and forty persons are represented as sharing the blood of these unfortunate women; and it is remarkable, as well as very sad, to see the lines of debasement and weakness, vice and crime, which are displayed in their record. In the generation of Margaret, fifty per cent. of the women were placed among the fallen, and in all the generations succeeding, including only those of twelve years of age and over, to the extent of fifty per cent.; and of this trail of weakness there were three families in the sixth generation who had six children sent to the house of refuge. Out of seven hundred and nine members of this family, nearly one-ninth have been criminals, and nearly one-tenth paupers; twenty-two had acquired property, and eight had lost property; nearly one-seventh were illegitimate, and one sister was the mother of distinctively pauperized lines.

Or, take another line of thought. Would it not be well for us women to introduce into all of our literary circles, for the purpose of gaining knowledge, topics on this subject of heredity and the influence of good and bad conditions upon the home life of the race, and study this subject in the light of science for our own and the benefit of others? For instance, may we not seriously ask the question, Can a mother or father be an habitual tippler, or break God's law of social purity, and yet impart to their children, at the same time, abundant physical vitality and strong moral fibre? Can a father dash away the reins of moral restraint, and, at the same time, impart strong will-power to his offspring?

A generation since, there lived in a Western city a wealthy English gentleman who was what is called a high liver. He drank his toddy in the morning, washed down his lunch with champagne, and finished a bottle of port for dinner, though he complained that the heavy wines here did not agree with him, owing to the climate. He died of gout at fifty years, leaving four sons. One of them became an epileptic, two died from drinking. Called good fellows, generous, witty, honorable young men, but before middle age miserable sots. The oldest of the brothers was a man of fixed habits, occupying a leading place in the community, from his keen intelligence, integrity, and irreproachable morals. He watched over his brothers, laid them in their graves, and never ceased to denounce the vice which had ruined them ; and when he was long past middle-age, financial trouble threw him into a low, nervous condition, for which wine was prescribed. He drank but one bottle. Shortly after, his affairs were righted and his health and spirits returned, but it was observed that once or twice a year he mysteriously disappeared for a month or six weeks. Nor wife, nor children, nor even his partner, knew where he went; but at last, when he was old and gray headed, his wife was telegraphed from an obscure neighboring village, where she found him dying of *mania a potu.* He had been in the habit of hiding there when the desire for liquor became maddening, and when there he drank like a brute.

May Wright Sewall, president of the Woman's National Council, writing of disinherited children, tells of a country school where health and joyousness and purity were the rule, vulgarity and coarseness the exception, and morbid and mysterious manners quite unknown. There came one morning, in her childhood, two little girls, sisters, of ten and twelve years. They were comfortably dressed. At the noon day meal their baskets opened to an abundant and appetizing lunch. But they were not like other children. They had thin, pinched faces, with vulgar mouths, and a sidelong look from their always downcast eyes which made her shudder; and skin, so wrinkled and yellow, that her childish fears fancied them to be witches' children. They held themselves aloof from all the rest. For two or three years they sat in the same places in that quiet school doing very little work, but, not being disorderly, they were allowed to stay. One day, when my father had visited the school, as we walked home together, I questioned him as to what made Annie and Minnie so different from all the other little girls at the school, and the grave man answered: Before they were born their father sold their birthright, and they must feed on pottage all their lives. She felt that an undefined mystery hovered around their blighted lives. She knew, she says, that they were blighted, as the simplest child knows the withered leaf of November from the glowing green of May, and she questioned no more, half conscious that the mystery was sin and that knowledge of it would be sinful too.

But we turn from these sad pictures to brighter pages in the great books of human life. To Benjamin West saying: "My mother's kiss made me a painter." To John Randolph saying: "I should have been an atheist, if it had not been for one recollection, and that was the memory of the time when my departed mother used to take my little hands in hers and sank me on my knees to say: 'Our Father, who art in heaven.' " Amid the cold of an Arctic expedition, Adam Isles found sickness had settled on part of his comrades, and the request came to him, I think from one of the officers of the ship, "Isles, for God's sake, take some spirits, or we will be lost." Then the memory of the dear mother came back, and looking the entreaty in the face, he said, "I promised my mother I would not do it, and I wouldn't do it if I die in the ice."

I would ask, in conclusion, is there a branch of the human race in the Western Hemisphere which has greater need of the inspiring and up-lifting influences that can flow out of the lives and examples of the truly enlightened than ourselves? Mothers who can teach their sons not to love pleasure or fear death; mothers who can teach their children to embrace every opportunity, employ every power, and use every means to build up a future to contrast with the old sad past. Men may boast of the aristocracy of blood; they may glory in the aristocracy of talent, and be proud of the aristocracy of wealth, but there is an aristocracy which must ever out-rank them all, and that is the aristocracy of character.

The work of the mothers of our race is grandly constructive. It is for us to build above the wreck and ruin of the past more stately temples of thought and action. Some races have been overthrown, dashed in pieces, and destroyed; but to-day the world is needing, fainting, for something better than the results of arrogance, aggressiveness, and indomitable power. We need mothers who are capable of being character builders, patient, loving, strong, and true, whose homes will be an uplifting power in the race. This is one of the greatest needs of the hour. No race can afford to neglect the enlightenment of its mothers. If you would have a clergy without virtue or morality, a manhood without honor, and a woman-hood frivolous, mocking, and ignorant, neglect the education of your daughters. But if, on the other hand, you would have strong men, virtu-ous women, and good homes, then enlighten your women, so that they may be able to bless their homes by the purity of their lives, the tender-ness of their hearts, and the strength of their intellects. From schools and colleges your children may come well versed in ancient lore and modern learning, but it is for us to learn and teach, within the shadow of our own homes, the highest and best of all sciences, the science of a true life. When the last lay of the minstrel shall die upon his ashy lips, and the sweetest numbers of the poet cease to charm his death-dulled ear; when the eye of the astronomer shall be too dim to mark the path of worlds that roll in light and power on high; and when all our earthly knowledge has performed for us its mission, and we are ready to lay aside our en-vironments as garments we have outworn and outgrown: if we have learned the science of a true life, we may rest assured that this acquirement will go with us through the valley and shadow of death, only to grow lighter and brighter through the eternities.

Fiction

◆

"Shalmanezer, Prince of Cosman" (1886)

"Shalmanezer, Prince of Cosman" was added to the 1886 edition of *Sketches of Southern Life*. Again, Harper presents a morality story, a narrative of critical decisions and the importance of righteous living. Shalmanezer learns that Desire and his companions, Pleasure, Wealth, and Fame, cannot offer the satisfaction that Peace can, but Peace and Self-Denial are inseparable companions: One cannot have peace without self-denial. As in "The Fatal Pledge," a woman entices the young man to drink and thus begins his moral descent. In fact, "Shalmanezer" includes four female figures who are negative influences upon the young prince. However, there is a gender balance of sorts. Desire is male and the three femmes fatales, Pleasure, Wealth, and Fame, are his subordinates. But Peace winning as she does at the end with the help of her male companion, Self-Denial, is more than the equal of Desire and his cohorts.

"Shalmanezer, Prince of Cosman" is based loosely upon the story of the Assyrian ruler Shalmanezer from the Bible. While it certainly echoes "Moses: A Story of the Nile," in setting, historicity, and theme, this is a far more exotic work. Its lush descriptions of the palace of Pleasure and Wealth's elegant residences are the most sensuous in all Harper's writings. The grim images of oppressed factory workers who service Wealth and of Fame's cold halls retreat before the brilliant, even voluptuous descriptions of "The vernal freshness of Spring," the comparisons of Wealth to "golden harvests, and ripe autumnal fruits," and Shalmanezer leaving "the faded woman," Pleasure, in his "Boudoir" and entering Wealth's wait-ing carriage. Though *Iola Leroy* retreats into a more pristine and intellec-tual view of romance, the overall effect of "Shalmanezer" may well be the sort of Oriental luxuriance and tropical fervor that, in her "Note" to her novel, Harper suggests African-American writers will one day bring to American literature.

Iola Leroy; Or, Shadows Uplifted (1892)

Iola Leroy was published in 1892, four years after "Shalmanezer." In its endnote, Harper says that she wove her novel "from threads of fact and fiction." Combining elements of the historical, the political, and the sen-timental novel and contrasting the experiences of blacks during slavery with those afterward, Harper wrote to document the progress during Recon-struction, to inspire African-Americans to continue to develop themselves economically, politically, and culturally, and to persuade all Americans that the general welfare of the nation required "a stronger sense of justice and a more Christlike humanity." The novel unites the threads of Har-per's concerns and themes during the previous half century. In addition to racial justice and Christian humanity, it advocates temperance, eco-nomic freedom, educational advancement, and women's rights.

Like the slave narratives, *Iola Leroy* follows the progression from bondage to freedom, from south to north, and from alienation to community. Har-per incorporates portions of her own essays and poems into what is also an example of the local color story and thereby expands the novel form beyond entertainment into a moral guide. In many ways Harper's novel follows the conventions established by William Wells Brown's *Clotel* (1853) and Frank Webb's *The Garies and Their Friends* (1857). The women are beautiful, refined, educated, and sensitive mulattoes. They are products of loving but doomed relationships between white men and black wom-en. Slavery and racism destroy these amours and deny their children the freedom to achieve and to contribute to society in the manner appropri-ate to their intelligence and conscience. Harper extends this tragic mulatto convention by developing more complex characterizations, by giving more serious consideration to characters of "pure African" blood, by incorporat-ing techniques of "women's fiction," and by exploring the literary possi-bilities of African-American folk characters.

The excerpts chosen for this collection, chapters 17, 18, and 24, demon-strate the ways in which Harper wove examples from real life into her novel. In these chapters, she focuses upon the ambitions and abilities of the newly freed slaves to become educated and productive citizens and upon the sexist and racist attitudes that hinder such development. "Flames in the School-Room" (chapter 17) begins at the conclusion of the war. Iola Leroy, a beautiful, talented, and educated former slave who served with great distinction as a nurse during the Civil War, has volunteered to teach in one of the newly established schools for ex-slaves. In this way she is able to combine her need to support herself with her desire to contribute to society. After the Civil War, countless numbers of young women did this. They braved the suspicion of freed slaves and the hostility of former slaveholders. "Searching for Lost Ones" (chapter 18) documents the progress of former slaves through education, hard work, and common sense. It continues the theme of Reconstruction through its emphasis upon the reunion of families and friends. Aunt Chloe and Uncle Jacob, first introduced in *Sketches of Southern Life*, reappear here as Aunt Linda and Uncle Daniel. "Northern Experience" (chapter 24) combines Harper's ideas that women must be educated, self-reliant, and contributing members of society with demonstrations of the kinds of sexism and racism that make this difficult. As usual in this novel, Iola's perseverance and the courageous humanitarianism of some Northern whites result in her success.

◆

Shalmanezer,
Prince of Cosman

Shalmanezer, Prince of Cosman, stood on the threshold of manly life, having just received a rich inheritance which had been left him by his father.

He was a magnificent-looking creature—the very incarnation of manly strength and beauty. The splendid poise of his limbs, the vigor and litheness of his motions, the glorious light that flashed from his splendid dark eyes, the bright joyous smiles that occasionally wreathed his fresh young lips, and the finely-erect carriage of his head, were enough to impress the beholder with the thought, "Here is an athlete armed for a glorious strife!"

While Shalmanezer was thinking upon his rich inheritance and how he should use it, he suddenly lifted his eyes and saw two strange-looking personages standing near him. They both advanced towards Shalmanezer when they saw their presence had attracted his attention.

The first one that approached the young man and addressed him, was named Desire. He was a pleasant-looking youth, with a flushed face, and

---

Shalmanezer, Prince of Cosman: Sketches of Southern Life (1886), 33–46.

eager restless eyes. He looked as if he had been pursuing a journey, or had been grasping at an object he had failed to obtain. There was something in his manner that betrayed a want of rest—a look in his eyes which seemed to say, "I am not satisfied." But when he approached, he smiled in the most seductive manner, and, reaching out his hand to Shalmanezer said,

"I have come to welcome thee to man's estate, and for thy enjoyment, I have brought thee three friends who will lead thee into the brightest paths, and press to thy lips the sweetest elixirs."

Gladly the young man received the greeting of Desire, who immediately introduced his three companions, whose names were, Pleasure, Wealth, and Fame—Pleasure was a most beautiful creature. Her lovely dark eyes flashed out a laughing light; upon her finely-carved lips hovered the brightest and sweetest smiles, which seemed ever ready to break into merry ripples of laughter; her robe was magnificently beautiful, as if it had imprisoned in its warp and woof the beauty of the rainbow and the glory of the setting sun; in her hand she held a richly wrought chalice in which sparkled and effervesced a ruby-colored liquid which was as beautiful to the eye as it was pleasant to the taste. When Pleasure was presented to Shalmanezer, she held out to him her cup and said in the sweetest tones:

> "Come, drink of my cup, it is sparkling and bright
> As rubies distilled in the morning light;
> A truce to sorrow and adieu to pain—
> Here's the cup to strengthen, soothe and sustain."

Just as Shalmanezer was about to grasp the cup, the other personage approached him. Her name was Peace, and she was attended by a mild, earnest-looking young man called Self-Denial. In the calm depths of her dark-blue eyes was a tender, loving light, and on her brow a majestic serenity which seemed to say, "The cares of earth are at my feet; in vain its tempests sweep around my path." There was also a look of calm, grand patience on the brow of her attendant, which gave him the aspect of one who had passed through suffering unto Peace. Shalmanezer was gazing eagerly on the fair young face of Pleasure, and about to quaff the sparkling nectar, when Peace suddenly arrested his hand and exclaimed:

> "Beware of this cup! 'Neath its ruddy glow,
> Is an undercurrent of shame and woe;
> 'Neath its sparkling sheen so fair and bright,
> Are serpents that hiss, and adders that bite."

The young man paused a moment, looked on the plain garb of Peace and then on the enchanting loveliness of Pleasure, and, pushing aside the hand of Peace with a scornful gesture, he said proudly and defiantly: "I will follow Pleasure!"

Peace, thus repulsed, turned sadly away; and Self-Denial, wounded by Shalmanezer's rude rejection bowed his head in silent sorrow and disappeared from the scene.

As Peace departed, Shalmanezer eagerly grasped the cup of Pleasure and pressed it to his lips, while she clasped her hand in his and said in a most charming manner, "Follow me;" and then he went willingly to the place where she dwelt.

As Shalmanezer approached the palace of Pleasure he heard the sweetest music rising on the air in magnificent swells or sinking in ravishing cadences; at his feet were springing the brightest and fairest flowers; the sweetest perfumes were bathing the air with the most exquisite fragrance; beautiful girls moved like visions of loveliness through the mazy dance; rare old wines sparkled on the festal board; the richest viands and most luscious fruits tempted the taste; and laughter, dance and song filled the air with varied delights. For a while Shalmanezer was enraptured with the palace of Pleasure. But soon he became weary of its gay confusion. The merry ripples of laughter lost their glad freshness; the once delightful music seemed to faint into strange monotones—whether the defect was in his ear or in the music he could not tell, but somehow it had ceased to gratify him; the constant flow of merry talk grew strangely distasteful to him; the pleasant viands began to pall upon his taste; at times he thought he detected a bitterness in the rare old wines which Pleasure ever and anon presented to his lips, and he turned wearily away from everything that had pleased his taste or had charmed and entranced his senses.

Shalmanezer sat moodily wishing that Desire would return and bring with him another attendant to whom he had been introduced when he had first clasped hands with Pleasure, and whose name was Wealth. While he was musing, he lifted up his eyes and saw Wealth and Desire standing at the door of his Boudoir, and near them he saw the sweet loving face of Peace, who was attended by Self-Denial. Peace was about to approach him, but he repulsed her with an impatient frown, and turning to Desire he said:

"I have grown weary of Pleasure, and I wish to be introduced to the halls of Wealth."

Taller, graver and less fair was Wealth, than her younger sister, Pleasure. If the beauty of Pleasure could be compared to the vernal freshness of Spring—that of Wealth suggested the maturity of golden harvests, and ripe autumnal fruits. Like Pleasure, she was very richly attired; a magnificent velvet robe fell in graceful folds around her well-proportioned form;

like prisms of captured light, the most beautiful jewels gleamed and flashed in her hair; a girdle of the finest and most exquisitely wrought gold was clasped around her waist; her necklace and bracelets were formed of the purest jewels and finest diamonds.—But there was something in her face which betokened a want which all her wealth could not supply. There was a mournful restlessness in her eye that at times seemed to border on the deepest sadness; and yet, there was something so alluring in her manner, so dazzling in her attire, and fascinating in her surroundings, that men would often sacrifice time, talent, energy, and even conscience and manhood, to secure her smiles and bask in her favor.

"Shalmanezer," said Desire to Wealth, "has grown weary of thy sister, Pleasure, and would fain dwell in thy stately halls, Is there aught to hinder him from being one of thy favored guests?"

"Nothing at all," said Wealth, smiling. "The rich inheritance left him by his father has been increasing in value, and I am glad that he was too wise to throw in Pleasure's cup life's richest gifts away."

With these words she reached out her jewelled hand to Shalmanezer and said, "Follow me!"

Weary of the halls of Pleasure, Shalmanezer gladly rose to follow Wealth. As he was leaving, he paused a moment to bid adieu to Pleasure. But she was so changed, that he did not recognize in the faded woman with the weary, listless manner, dull eyes and hollow cheeks, the enchanting girl, who, a few years before, had led him to her halls a welcome and delighted guest. All was so changed. It seemed more like a dream than a reality, that he had dwelt for years in what now seemed like a disenchanted palace. The banquet table was strewn with broken and tasteless fragments; the flowers had lost their fragrance and beauty, and lay in piles of scentless leaves; the soft sweet music had fainted into low breathed sighs, and silence reigned in the deserted halls where dance and revelry and song had wreathed with careless mirth the bright and fleeting hours.

"Come," said Wealth, "my Chariot waits thee at the door."

Without one pang of regret, Shalmanezer turned from the halls of Pleasure, to ride with Wealth in her magnificent chariot.

As they drove along, Wealth showed Shalmanezer the smoke rising from a thousand factories. Pausing a moment, she said:—"I superintend these works and here are my subjects."

Shalmanezer gazed on the colossal piles of brick and mortar, as those castles of industry met his eye. Just then the bell rang, and he saw issuing from amid the smoke and whir of machinery a sight that filled his soul with deep compassion.

There were pale, sad-looking women wending their way home to snatch some moment's rest, and an humble meal before returning to their tasks. There were weary-looking men, who seemed to be degenerating in mental strength and physical vigor. There were young children who looked as if the warm fresh currents of life in their veins had been touched with premature decay. And saddest of all—he saw young girls who looked as if they were rapidly changing from unsophisticated girlhood into over-ripe womanhood.

"Are these thy servants?" said Shalmanezer, sadly.

"These," said Wealth, "are my servants, but not my favorites. In dark mines—close factories—beneath low roofed huts—they dig the glittering jewels, and weave the webs of splendor and beauty with which I adorn my favorites. But I see that the sight pains thee. Let us pass on to fairer scenes."

Bending down to her finely-liveried coachman, she whispered in his ear, and in a few minutes the factories, with their smoke and din, were left behind. Beautiful lawns, lovely parks, and elegant residences rose before the pleased eyes of Shalmanezer; beautiful children sported on the lawns; lovely girls roamed in the parks; and the whole scene was a bright contrast to those he had left behind.

At length they rode up an avenue of stately trees, and stopped at the home of Wealth. "Here is my dwelling," she said, "enter and be my welcome guest."

Shalmanezer accepted the invitation, and entering, gazed with delighted wonder on the splendor and beauty of the place. On the walls hung most beautiful pictures surrounded by the richest frames—rare creations of the grand old masters; lovely statues suggested the idea of life strangely imprisoned in marble; velvet carpets sank pleasantly beneath his tread; elegant book cases, inlaid with ivory and pearl, held on the shelves the grand and noble productions of the monarchs of mind who still rule from their graves in the wide realms of thought and imagination. In her halls were sumptuous halls for feasting; delightful alcoves for thought and meditation; lovely little boudoirs for cozy chats with cherished friends. Even religion found costly bibles and splendidly embossed prayer books in the chambers of repose, where beneath the softened light of golden lamps, the children of Wealth sank to rest on beds of down.

"Surely," said Shalmanezer, "he must be a strangely restless creature, who cannot be satisfied in this home of beauty, grace and affluence." And yet, while he spake, he was conscious of a sense of unrest. He tried to shake it off, but still it would return. He would find himself sighing amid the fairest scenes—oppressed with a sense of longing for something he could not define. His eye was not satisfied with seeing, nor his ear with hearing. It seemed as if life had been presented to him as a luscious fruit, and he had eagerly extracted its richest juices, and was ready to throw away the bitter rind in hopeless disgust.

While he sat gloomily surveying the past, and feeling within his soul a hunger which neither Wealth nor Pleasure could appease, he lifted his eyes towards a distant mountain whose summit was crowned with perpetual snows, although a thousand sunbeams warmed and cheered the vale below. As he gazed, he saw a youth with a proud gait, buoyant step and flashing eye, climbing the mount. In his hand he held a beautifully embossed card, on which was written an invitation from Fame to climb her almost inaccessible heights and hear the sweetest music that ever ravished mortal ear. As the youth ascended the mount, Shalmanezer heard the shouts of applause which were wafted to the ears of the young man, who continued to climb with unabated ardor.

"Here," said Shalmanezer, "is a task worthy of my powers. I have wasted much of my time in the halls of Pleasure; I have grown weary of the stately palaces of Wealth; I will go forth and climb the heights of Fame, and find a welcome in the suncrowned palaces of Renown. O, the sight of that young man inspires my soul, and gives new tone and vigor to my life. I will not pause another moment to listen to the blandishments of Wealth. Instead of treading on these soft carpets, I will brace my soul to climb the rugged heights to gaze upon the fair face of Fame."

Just as he was making this resolve, he saw Peace and her attendant gazing anxiously and silently upon him. His face flushed with sudden anger; a wrathful light flashed from his eyes; and turning his face coldly from Peace, he said: "I do wish Peace would come without her unwelcome companion—Self-Denial I do utterly and bitterly hate." Peace again repulsed, turned sadly away, followed by Self-Denial. With eager haste Shalmanezer rose up and left the bowers of Ease and halls of Pride, to tread the rugged heights of Fame, with patient, ready feet. As he passed upward, new vigor braced his nerves. He felt an exhilaration of spirits he had never enjoyed in the halls of Wealth or bowers of Pleasure. Onward and upward he proudly moved, as the multitude, who stood at the base, cheered him with rapturous applause, and no music was ever so sweet to his ear as the plaudits of the crowd; but, as he ascended higher and higher, the voices of the multitude grew fainter and fainter; some voices that cheered him at the beginning of his journey had melted into the stillness of death; others had harshened into the rough tones of disapprobation; others were vociferously applauding a new aspirant who had since started to climb the summit of Renown; but, with his eye upon the palace of Fame, he still climbed on, while the air grew rarer, and the atmosphere colder. The old elasticity departed from his limbs, and the buoyancy from his spirits, and it seemed as if the chills of death were slowly creeping around his heart. But still, with fainter step he kept climbing upward, until almost exhausted, he sank down at the palace-gate of Fame, exclaiming, "Is this all?"

Very stately and grand was the cloud-capped palace of Fame. The pillars of her lofty abode were engraven with the names of successful generals, mighty conquerors, great leaders, grand poets, illustrious men and celebrated women. There were statues on which the tooth of Time was slowly gnawing; the statues of men whose brows had once been surrounded by a halo of glory, but were now darkened by the shadow of their crimes. Those heights which had seemed so enchanting at a distance, now seemed more like barren mounds, around which the chills of Death were ever sweeping.

Fame heard the voice of her votary, and came out to place upon his brow her greenest bays and brightest laurels, and bid him welcome to her palace; but when she saw the deathly whiteness of his face, she shrank back in pity and fear. The light was fading from his eye; his limbs had lost their manly strength; and Fame feared that the torpor of Death would overtake him before she could crown him as her honored guest. She bent down her ear to the sufferer, and heard him whisper slowly, "Peace! Peace!"

Then said Fame to her servants, "Descend to the vale, bring the best medical skill ye can find, and search for Peace, and entreat her to come; tell her that one of my votaries lies near to death, and longs for her presence." The servants descended to the vale, and soon returned, bringing with them a celebrated physician.—Peace had heard the cry of Shalmanezer, and had entered the room with her companion before the doctor had come. When the physician saw Shalmanezer, he gazed anxiously upon him, felt the fluttering pulse, and chafed the pale cold hands to restore the warmth and circulation.

In the meantime, Pleasure and Wealth having heard the story of Shalmanezer's illness, entered the room. "There is but one thing," said the physician, "can save Shalmanezer's life: some one must take the warm healthy blood from his veins and inject it into Shalmanezer's veins before he can be restored to health."

Pleasure and Wealth looked aghast when they heard the doctor's prescription. Pleasure suddenly remembered that she had a pressing engagement; Wealth said, "I am no longer young, nor even well, and am sure I have not one drop of blood to spare;" Fame pitied her faithful votary, but amid the cold blasts that swept around her home, was sure it would be very imprudent for her to attempt to part with so much blood.

Just as Pleasure, Wealth and Fame had refused to give the needed aid, Desire entered the room, but when he heard the conditions for the restoration of Shalmanezer, shrank back in selfish dismay, and refused also.

As Shalmanezer lay gasping for breath, and looking wistfully at his old companions, Peace, attended by Self-Denial, drew near the sick man's couch. Shalmanezer opened his eyes languidly, and closed them wearily; when life was like a joyous dream, he had repulsed Peace and utterly hated Self-Denial, and what could he dare hope from either in his hour of dire extremity. While he lay with his eyes half-closed, Self-Denial approached the bedside, and baring his arm, said to the doctor:

"Here is thy needed remedy. Take the blood from these veins, and with it restore Shalmanezer to health and strength."

The doctor struck his lancet into Self-Denial's arm, and drawing from it the needed quantity of blood, injected it into Shalmanezer's veins. The remedy was effectual. Health flushed the cheeks of Shalmanezer, and braced each nerve with new vigor, and he soon recovered from his fearful exhaustion. Then his heart did cleave unto Self-Denial. He had won his heart by his lofty sacrifice. He had bought his love by the blood from his own veins. Clasping hands with Self-Denial, he trod with him the paths of Peace, and in so doing, received an amount of true happiness which neither Pleasure, Wealth nor Fame could give.

Flames in the School-room

"Good morning," said Dr. Gresham, approaching Robert and Iola. "How are you both? You have mended rapidly," turning to Robert, "but then it was only a flesh wound. Your general health being good, and your blood in excellent condition, it was not hard for you to rally."

"Where have you been, Doctor? I have a faint recollection of having seen you on the morning I was brought in from the field, but not since."

"I have been on a furlough. I was running down through exhaustion and overwork, and I was compelled to go home for a few weeks' rest. But now, as they are about to close the hospital, I shall be permanently relieved. I am glad that this cruel strife is over. It seemed as if I had lived through ages during these last few years. In the early part of the war I lost my arm by a stray shot, and my armless sleeve is one of the mementos of battle I shall carry with me through life. Miss Leroy," he continued, turning respectfully to Iola, "would you permit me to ask you, as I would have some one ask my sister under the same circumstances, if you have matured any plans for the future, or if I can be of the least service to you?

Flames in the School-room: Iola Leroy, 2d ed. (1893), chapter 17, 144–47.

If so, I would be pleased to render you any service in my power."

"My purpose," replied Iola, "is to hunt for my mother, and to find her if she is alive. I am willing to go anywhere and do anything to find her. But I will need a standpoint from whence I can send out lines of inquiry. It must take time, in the disordered state of affairs, even to get a clue by which I may discover her whereabouts."

"How would you like to teach?" asked the Doctor. "Schools are being opened all around us. Numbers of excellent and superior women are coming from the North to engage as teachers of the freed people. Would you be willing to take a school among these people? I think it will be uphill work. I believe it will take generations to get over the duncery of slavery. Some of these poor fellows who came into our camp did not know their right hands from their left, nor their ages, nor even the days of the month. It took me some time, in a number of cases, to understand their language. It saddened my heart to see such ignorance. One day I asked one a question, and he answered, "I no shum'. ""

"What did he mean?" asked Iola.

"That he did not see it," replied the doctor. "Of course, this does not apply to all of them. Some of them are wide-awake and sharp as steel traps. I think some of that class may be used in helping others."

"I should be very glad to have an opportunity to teach," said Iola. "I used to be a great favorite among the colored children on my father's plantation."

In a few days after this conversation the hospital was closed. The sick and convalescent were removed, and Iola obtained a position as a teacher. Very soon Iola realized that while she was heartily appreciated by the freedmen, she was an object of suspicion and dislike to their former owners. The North had conquered by the supremacy of the sword, and the South had bowed to the inevitable. But here was a new army that had come with an invasion of ideas, that had come to supplant ignorance with knowledge, and it was natural that its members should be unwelcome to those who had made it a crime to teach their slaves to read the name of the ever blessed Christ. But Iola had found her work, and the freedmen their friend.

When Iola opened her school she took pains to get acquainted with the parents of the children, and she gained their confidence and cooperation. Her face was a passport to their hearts. Ignorant of books, human faces were the scrolls from which they had been reading for ages. They had been the sunshine and shadow of their lives.

Iola had found a school-room in the basement of a colored church, where the doors were willingly opened to her. Her pupils came from miles around, ready and anxious to get some "book larnin'." Some of the old folks were eager to learn, and it was touching to see the eyes which had grown dim under the shadows of slavery, donning spectacles and trying to make out the words. As Iola had nearly all of her life been accustomed to colored children she had no physical repulsions to overcome, no prejudices to conquer in dealing with parents and children. In their simple childish fashion they would bring her fruits and flowers, and gladden her lonely heart with little tokens of affection.

One day a gentleman came to the school and wished to address the children. Iola suspended the regular order of the school, and the gentleman essayed to talk to them on the achievements of the white race, such as building steamboats and carrying on business. Finally, he asked how they did it?

"They've got money," chorused the children.

"But how did they get it?"

"They took it from us," chimed the youngsters. Iola smiled, and the gentleman was nonplussed; but he could not deny that one of the powers of knowledge is the power of the strong to oppress the weak.

The school was soon overcrowded with applicants, and Iola was forced to refuse numbers, because their quarters were too cramped. The school was beginning to lift up the home, for Iola was not satisfied to teach her children only the rudiments of knowledge. She had tried to lay the foundation of good character. But the elements of evil burst upon her loved and cherished work. One night the heavens were lighted with lurid flames, and Iola beheld the school, the pride and joy of her pupils and their parents, a smouldering ruin. Iola gazed with sorrowful dismay on what seemed the cruel work of an incendiary's torch. While she sat, mournfully contemplating the work of destruction, her children formed a procession, and, passing by the wreck of their school, sang:—

"Oh, do not be discouraged,
For Jesus is your friend."

As they sang, the tears sprang to Iola's eyes, and she said to herself, "I am not despondent of the future of my people; there is too much elasticity in their spirits, too much hope in their hearts, to be crushed out by unreasoning malice."

Searching for Lost Ones

To bind anew the ties which slavery had broken and gather together the

---

Searching for Lost Ones: Iola Leroy 2d ed. (1893), chapter 18, 148–63.

remnants of his scattered family became the earnest purpose of Robert's life. Iola, hopeful that in Robert she had found her mother's brother, was glad to know she was not alone in *her* search. Having sent out lines of inquiry in different directions, she was led to hope, from some of the replies she had received, that her mother was living somewhere in Georgia.

Hearing that a Methodist conference was to convene in that State, and being acquainted with the bishop of that district, she made arrangements to accompany him thither. She hoped to gather some tidings of her mother through the ministers gathered from different parts of that State.

From her brother she had heard nothing since her father's death. On his way to the conference, the bishop had an engagement to dedicate a church, near the city of C——, in North Carolina. Iola was quite willing to stop there a few days, hoping to hear something of Robert Johnson's mother. Soon after she had seated herself in the cars she was approached by a gentleman, who reached out his hand to her, and greeted her with great cordiality. Iola looked up, and recognized him immediately as one of her last patients at the hospital. It was none other than Robert Johnson.

"I am so glad to meet you," he said. "I am on my way to C—— in search of my mother. I want to see the person who sold her last, and, if possible, get some clew to the direction in which she went."

"And I," said Iola, "am in search of *my* mother. I am convinced that when we find those for whom we are searching they will prove to be very nearly related. Mamma said, before we were parted, that her brother had a red spot on his temple. If I could see that spot I should rest assured that my mother is your sister."

"Then," said Robert, "I can give you that assurance," and smilingly he lifted his hair from his temple, on which was a large, red spot.

"I am satisfied," exclaimed Iola, fixing her eyes, beaming with hope and confidence, on Robert. "Oh, I am so glad that I can, without the least hesitation, accept your services to join with me in the further search. What are your plans?"

"To stop for awhile in C——," said Robert, "and gather all the information possible from those who sold and bought my mother. I intend to leave no stone unturned in searching for her."

"Oh, I *do* hope that you will succeed. I expect to stop over there a few days, and I shall be *so* glad if, before I leave, I hear your search has been crowned with success, or, a least, that you have been put on the right track. Although I was born and raised in the midst of slavery, I had not the least idea of its barbarous selfishness till I was forced to pass through it. But we lived so much alone I had no opportunity to study it, except on our own plantation. My father and mother were very kind to their slaves. But it was slavery, all the same, and I hate it, root and branch."

Just then the conductor called out the station.

"We stop here," said Robert. " I am going to see Mrs. Johnson, and hunt up some of my old acquaintances. Where do you stop?"

"I don't know," replied Iola. "I expect that friends will be here to meet us. Bishop B——, permit me to introduce you to Mr. Robert Johnson, whom I have every reason to believe is my mother's brother. Like myself, he is engaged in hunting up his lost relatives."

"And I," said Robert, "am very much pleased to know that we are not without favorable clues."

"Bishop," said Iola, " Mr. Johnson wishes to know where I am to stop. He is going on an exploring expedition, and wishes to let me know the result."

"We stop at Mrs. Allston's, 313 New Street," said the bishop. "If I can be of any use to you, I am at your service."

"Thank you," said Robert, lifting his hat, as he left them to pursue his inquiries about his long-lost mother.

Quickly he trod the old familiar streets which led to his former home. He found Mrs. Johnson, but she had aged very fast since the war. She was no longer the lithe, active woman, with her proud manner and resolute bearing. Her eye had lost its brightness, her step its elasticity, and her whole appearance indicated that she was slowly sinking beneath a weight of sorrow which was heavier far than her weight of years. When she heard that Robert had called to see her she was going to receive him in the hall, as she would have done any of her former slaves, but her mind immediately changed when she saw him. He was not the light-hearted, careless, mischief-loving Robby of former days, but a handsome man, with heavy moustache, dark, earnest eyes, and proud military bearing. He smiled, and reached out his hand to her. She hardly knew how to address him. To her colored people were either boys and girls, or "aunties and uncles." She had never in her life addressed a colored person as "Mr. or Mrs." To do so now was to violate the social customs of the place. It would be like learning a new language in her old age. Robert immediately set her at ease by addressing her under the old familiar name of "Miss Nancy." This immediately relieved her of all embarrassment. She invited him into the sitting-room, and gave him a warm welcome.

"Well, Robby," she said, "I once thought that you would have been the last one to leave me. You know I never ill-treated you, and I gave you everything you needed. People said that I was spoiling you. I thought you were as happy as the days were long. When I heard of other people's servants leaving them I used to say to myself, 'I can trust my Bobby; he will stick to me to the last.' But I fooled myself that time. Soon as the Yankee soldiers got in sight you left me without saying a word. That morning I came down into the kitchen and asked Linda, 'Where's Robert? Why hasn't he set the table?' She said 'she hadn't seen you since the night before.' I thought maybe you were sick, and I went to see, but you were not in your room. I couldn't believe at first that you were gone. Wasn't I always good to you?"

"Oh, Miss Nancy," replied Robert; "you were good, but freedom was better."

"Yes," she said, musingly, "I suppose I would have done the same. But, Robby, it did go hard with me at first. However, I soon found out that my neighbors had been going through the same thing. But its all over now. Let by-gones be by-gones. What are you doing now, and where are you living?"

"I am living in the city of P——. I have opened a hardware store there. But just now I am in search of my mother and sister."

"I hope that you may find them."

"How long," asked Robert, "do you think it has been since they left here?"

"Let me see; it must have been nearly thirty years. You got my letter?"

"Yes, ma'am; thank you."

"There have been great changes since you left here," Mrs. Johnson said. "Gundover died, and a number of colored men have banded together, bought his plantation, and divided it among themselves. And I hear they have a very nice settlement out there. I hope, since the Government has set them free, that they will succeed."

After Robert's interview with Mrs. Johnson he thought he would visit the settlement and hunt up his old friends. He easily found the place. It was on a clearing in Gundover's woods, where Robert and Uncle Daniel had held their last prayer-meeting. Now the gloomy silence of those woods was broken by the hum of industry, the murmur of cheerful voices, and the merry laughter of happy children. Where they had trodden with fear and misgiving, freedmen walked with light and bounding hearts. The school-house had taken the place of the slave-pen and auction-block.

"How is yer, ole boy?" asked one laborer of another.

"Everything is lobly," replied the other. The blue sky arching overhead and the beauty of the scenery justified the expression.

Gundover had died soon after the surrender. Frank Anderson had grown reckless and drank himself to death. His brother Tom had been killed in battle. Their mother, who was Gundover's daughter, had died

insane. Their father had also passed away. The defeat of the Confeder-
ates, the loss of his sons, and the emancipation of his slaves, were blows
from which he never recovered. As Robert passed leisurely along, delighted
with the evidences of thrift and industry which constantly met his eye,
he stopped to admire a garden filled with beautiful flowers, clambering
vines, and rustic adornments.

On the porch sat an elderly woman, darning stockings, the very em-
bodiment of content and good humor. Robert looked inquiringly at her.
On seeing him, she almost immediately exclaimed, "Shore as I'se born,
dat's Robert! Look yere, honey, whar did yer come from? I'll gib my head
fer a choppin' block ef dat ain't Miss Nancy's Bob. Ain't yer our Bobby?
Shore yer is."

"Of course I am," responded Robert. "It isn't anybody else. How did
you know me?"

"How did I know yer? By dem mischeebous eyes, ob course. I'd a
knowed yer if I had seed yer in Europe."

"In Europe, Aunt Linda? Where's that?"

"I don't know. I specs its some big city, somewhar. But yer looks jis'
splendid. Yer looks good 'nuff ter kiss."

"Oh, Aunt Linda, don't say that. You make me blush."

"Oh you go 'long wid yer. I specs yer's got a nice little wife up dar
whar yer comes from, dat kisses yer ebery day, an' Sunday, too."

"Is that the way your old man does you?"

"Oh, no, not a bit. He isn't one ob de kissin' kine. But sit down," she
said, handing Robert a chair. "Won't yer hab a glass ob milk? Boy, I'se
a libin' in clover. Neber 'spected ter see sich good times in all my born days."

"Well, Aunt Linda," said Robert, seating himself near her, and drink-
ing the glass of milk which she had handed him, "how goes the battle?
How have you been getting on since freedom?"

"Oh, fust rate, fust rate! Wen freedom com'd I jist lit out ob Miss John-
son's kitchen soon as I could. I wanted ter re'lize I war free, an' I couldn't,
tell I got out er de sight and soun' ob ole Miss. When de war war ober
an' de sogers war still stopping' yere, I made pies an' cakes, sole em to
de sogers, an' jist made money han' ober fist. An' I kep' on workin' an'
a savin' till my ole man got back from de war wid his wages and his bounty
money. I felt right set up an' mighty big wen we counted all dat money.
We had neber seen so much money in our lives befo', let alone hab it
fer ourselbs. An' I sez, 'John, you take dis money an' git a nice place wid
it.' An' he sez, 'Dere's no use tryin', kase dey don't want ter sell us any
lan'.'" Ole Gundover said, 'fore he died, dat he would let de lan' grow
up in trees 'fore he'd sell it to us. An' dere war Mr. Brayton; he buyed

some lan' and sole it to some cullud folks, an' his ole frien's got so mad wid him dat dey wouldn't speak ter him, an' he war borned down yere. I tole ole Miss Anderson's daughter dat we wanted ter git some homes ob our ownselbs. She sez, 'Den you won't want ter work for us?' Jis' de same as ef we could eat an' drink our houses. I tell yer, Robby, dese white folks don't know eberything."

"That's a fact, Aunt Linda."

"Den I sez ter John, 'wen one door shuts anoder opens.' An' shore 'nough, ole Gundover died, an' his place war all in debt, an' had to be sole. Some Jews bought it, but dey didn't want to farm it, so dey gib us a chance to buy it. Dem Jews hez been right helpful to cullud people wen dey hab lan' to sell. I reckon dey don't keer who buys it so long as dey gits de money. Well, John didn't gib in at fust; didn't want to let on his wife knowed more dan he did, an' dat he war ruled ober by a woman. Yer know he is an' ole Firginian, an' some ob dem ole Firginans do so lub to rule a woman. But I kep' naggin at him, till I specs he got tired of my tongue, an' he went and buyed dis piece ob lan'. Dis house war on it, an' war all gwine to wrack. It used to belong to John's ole marster. His wife died right in dis house, an' arter dat her husband went right to de dorgs; an' now he's in de pore-house. My! but ain't dem tables turned. When we knowed it war our own, warn't my ole man proud! I seed it in him, but he wouldn't let on. Ain't you men powerful 'ceitful?"

"Oh, Aunt Linda, don't put me in with the rest!"

"I don't know 'bout dat. Put you all in de bag for 'ceitfulness, an' I don't know which would git out fust."

"Well, Aunt Linda, I suppose by this time you know how to read and write?"

"No, chile, sence freedom's com'd I'se bin scratchin' too hard to get a libin' to put my head down to de book."

"But, Aunt Linda, it would be such company when your husband is away, to take a book. Do you never get lonesome?"

"Chile, I ain't got no time ter get lonesome. Ef you had eber so many chickens to feed, an' pigs squealin' fer somethin' ter eat, an' yore ducks an' geese squakin' 'roun' yer, yer wouldn't hab time ter git lonesome."

"But, Aunt Linda, you might be sick for months and think what a comfort it would be if you could read your Bible."

"Oh, I could hab prayin' and singin'. Dese people is mighty good 'bout prayin' by de sick. Why, Robby, I think it would gib me de hysterics ef I war to try to git book larnin' froo my pore ole head. How long is yer gwine to stay? An' whar is yer stoppin?"

"I got here to-day," said Robert, "but I expect to stay several days."

"Well, I wants yer to meet my ole man, an' talk 'bout ole times. Couldn't yer come an' stop wid me, or isn't my house sniptious 'nuff?"

"Yes, thank you; but there is a young lady in town whom I think is my niece, my sister's daughter, and I want to be with her all I can."

"Your niece! Whar did you git any niece from?"

"Don't you remember," asked Robert, "that my mother had a little daughter, when Mrs. Johnson sold her? Well, I believe this young lady is that daughter's child."

"Laws a marcy!" exclaimed Aunt Linda, "yer don't tell me so! Whar did yer ketch up wid her?"

"I met her first," said Robert, "at the hospital here, when our poor Tom was dying; and when I was wounded at Five Forks she attended me in the field hospital there. She was just as good as gold."

"Well, did I eber! You jis' fotch dat chile to see me, ef she ain't too fine. I'se pore, but I'se clean, an' I ain't forgot how ter git up good dinners. Now, I wants ter hab a good talk 'bout our feller-sarvants."

"Yes, and I," said Robert, "want to hear all about Uncle Daniel, and Jennie, and Uncle Ben Tunnel."

"Well, I'se got lots an' gobs ter tell yer. I'se kep' track ob dem all. Aunt Katie died an' went ter hebben in a blaze ob glory. Uncle Dan'el stayed on de place till Marse Robert com'd back. When de war war ober he war smashed all ter pieces. I did pity him from de bottom ob my heart. When he went ter de war he looked brave an' han'some; an' wen he com'd back he looked so orful. 'Fore he went he gib Uncle Dan'el a bag full ob money ter take kere ob. 'An wen he com'd back Uncle Dan'el gibed him ebery cent ob it. It warn't ebery white pusson he could hab trusted wid it. 'Cause yer know, Bobby, money's a mighty temptin' thing. Dey tells me dat Marster Robert los' a heap ob property by de war; but Marse Robert war always mighty good ter Uncle Dan'el and Aunt Katie. He war wid her wen she war dyin' an' she got holt his han' an' made him promise dat he would meet her in glory. I neber seed anybody so happy in my life. She singed an' prayed ter de last. I tell you dis ole time religion is good 'nuff fer me. Mr. Robert didn't stay yere long arter her, but I beliebs he went all right. But 'fore he went he looked out fer Uncle Dan'el. Did you see dat nice little cabin down dere wid de green shutters an' nice little garden in front? Well, 'fore Marse Robert died he gib Uncle Dan'el dat place, an' Miss Mary and de chillen looks arter him yet; an' he libs jis' as snug as a bug in a rug. I'se gwine ter axe him ter take supper wid you. He'll be powerful glad ter see you."

"Do you ever go to see old Miss?" asked Robert.

"Oh, yes; I goes ebery now and den. But she's jis' fell froo. Ole Johnson jis' drunk hisself to death. He war de biggest guzzler I eber seed in my life. Why, dat man he drunk up ebery thing he could lay his han' on. Sometimes he would go 'roun' tryin' to borrer money from pore cullud folks. 'Twas rale drefful de way dat pore feller did frow hisself away. But drink did it all. I tell you, Bobby, dat drink's a drefful thing wen it gits de upper han' ob you. You'd better steer clar ob it."

"That's so," assented Robert.

"I know'd Miss Nancy's fadder and mudder. Dey war mighty rich. Some ob de real big bugs. Marse Jim used to know dem, an' come ober ter de plantation, an' eat an' drink wen he got ready, an' stay as long as he choose. Ole Cousins used to have wine at dere table ebery day, an' Marse Jim war mighty fon' ob dat wine, an' sometimes he would drink till he got quite boozy. Ole Cousins liked him bery well, till he foun' out he wanted his darter, an' den he didn't want him fer rags nor patches. But Miss Nancy war mighty headstrong, an' allers liked to hab her own way; an' dis time she got it. But didn't she step her foot inter it? Ole Johnson war mighty han'some, but when dat war said all war said. She run'd off an' got married, but wen she got down she war too spunkey to axe her pa for anything. Wen you war wid her, yer know she only took big bugs. But wen de war com'd 'roun' it tore her all ter pieces, an' now she's as pore as Job's turkey. I feel's right sorry fer her. Well, Robby, things is turned 'roun' mighty quare. Ole Mistus war up den, an' I war down; now, she's down, an' I'se up. But I pities her, 'cause she warn't so bad arter all. De wuss thing she eber did war to sell your mudder, an' she wouldn't hab done dat but she snatched de whip out ob her han' an' gib her a lickin.' Now I belieb in my heart she war 'fraid ob your mudder arter dat. But we women had ter keep 'em from whippin' us, er dey'd all de time been libin' on our bones. She had no man ter whip us 'cept dat ole drunken husband ob hern, an' he war allers too drunk ter whip hisself. He jis' wandered off, an' I reckon he died in somebody's pore-house. He warn't no 'count nohow you fix it. Weneber I goes to town I carries her some garden sass, er a little milk an' butter. An' she's mighty glad ter git it. I ain't got nothin' agin her. She neber struck me a lick in her life, an' I belieb in praising de bridge dat carries me ober. Dem Yankees set me free, an' I thinks a powerful heap ob dem. But it does rile me ter see dese mean white men comin' down yere an' settin' up dere grog-shops, tryin' to fedder dere nests sellin' licker to pore culled people. Deys de bery kine ob men dat used ter keep dorgs to ketch de runaways. I'd be chokin' fer a drink 'fore I'd eber spen' a cent wid dem, a spreadin' dere traps to git de black folks' money. You jis' go down town 'fore sun up to-morrer mornin' an' you see ef dey don't hab dem bars open to sell dere drams to dem hard workin' culled people 'fore dey goes ter work. I thinks some niggers is mighty big fools."

"Oh, Aunt Linda, don't run down your race. Leave that for the white people."

"I ain't runnin' down my people. But a fool's a fool, wether he's white or black. An' I think de nigger who will spen' his hard-earned money in dese yere new grog-shops is de biggest kine ob a fool, an' I sticks ter dat. You know we didn't hab all dese low places in slave times. An' what is dey fer, but to get the people's money. An' its a shame how dey do sling de licker 'bout 'lection times."

"But don't the temperance people want the colored people to vote the temperance ticket?"

"Yes, but some ob de culled people gits mighty skittish ef dey tries to git em to vote dare ticket 'lection time, an' keeps dem at a proper distance wen de 'lection's ober. Some ob dem say dere's a trick behine it, an' don't want to tech it. Dese white folks could do a heap wid de culled folks ef dey'd only treat em right."

"When our people say there is a trick behind it," said Robert, "I only wish they could see the trick before it—the trick of worse than wasting their money, and of keeping themselves and families poorer and more ignorant than there is any need for them to be."

"Well, Bobby, I beliebs we might be a people ef it warn't for dat mizzable drink. An' Robby, I jis' tells yer what I wants; I wants some libe man to come down yere an' splain things ter dese people. I don't mean a politic man, but a man who'll larn dese people how to bring up dere chillen, to keep our gals straight, an' our boys from runnin' in de saloons an' gamblin' dens."

"Don't your preachers do that?" asked Robert.

"Well, some ob dem does, an' some ob dem doesn't. An' wen dey preaches, I want dem to practice wat dey preach. Some ob dem says dey's called, but I jis' thinks laziness called some ob dem. An' I thinks since freedom come deres some mighty pore sticks set up for preachers. Now dere's John Anderson, Tom's brudder; you 'member Tom."

"Yes; as brave a fellow and as honest as ever stepped in shoe leather."

"Well, his brudder war mighty diff'rent. He war down in de lower kentry wen de war war ober. He war mighty smart, an' had a good head-piece, an' a orful glib tongue. He set up store an' sole whisky, an' made a lot ob money. Den he wanted ter go to de legislatur. Now what should he do but make out he'd got 'ligion, an' war called to preach. He had no more 'ligion dan my ole dorg. But he had money an' built a meetin' house, whar he could hole meeting, an' hab funerals; an' you know cullud folks is mighty great on funerals. Well dat jis' tuck wid de people, an' he got 'lected to de legislatur. Den he got a fine house, an' his ole wife warn't good 'nuff for him. Den dere war a young school-teacher, an' he begun cuttin' his eyes at her. But she war as deep in de mud as he war in de mire, an' he jis' gib up his ole wife and married her, a fusty thing. He war a mean ole hypocrit, an' I wouldn't sen' fer him to bury my cat. Robby, I'se down on dese kine ob preachers like a thousand bricks."

"Well, Aunt Linda, all the preachers are not like him."

"No; I knows dat; not by a jug full. We's got some mighty good men down yere, an' we's glad when dey comes, an' orful sorry when dey goes 'way. De las preacher we had war a mighty good man. He didn't like too much hollerin'. "

"Perhaps," said Robert, "he thought it were best for only one to speak at a time."

"I specs so. His wife war de nicest and sweetest lady dat eber I did see. None ob yer airish, stuck up folks, like a tarrapin carryin' eberything on its back. She used ter hab meetins fer de mudders, an' larn us how to raise our chillen, an' talk so putty to de chillen. I sartinly did lub dat woman."

"Where is she now?" asked Robert.

"De Conference moved dem 'bout thirty miles from yere. Deys gwine to hab a big meetin' ober dere next Sunday. Don't you 'member dem meetins we used to hab in de woods? We don't hab to hide like we did den. But it don't seem as ef de people had de same good 'ligion we had den. 'Pears like folks is took up wid makin' money an' politics."

"Well, Aunt Linda, don't you wish those good old days would come back?"

"No, chile; neber! neber! Wat fer you take me? I'd ruther lib in a corncrib. Freedom needn't keep me outer heben; an' ef I'se sich a fool as ter lose my 'ligion cause I'se free, I oughn'ter git dere."

"But, Aunt Linda, if old Miss were able to take care of you, wouldn't you just as leave be back again?"

There was a faint quiver of indignation in Aunt Linda's voice, as she replied:—

"Don't yer want yer freedom? Well I wants ter pat my free foot. Halleluyah! But, Robby, I wants yer ter go ter dat big meetin' de wuss kine."

"How will I get there?" asked Robert.

"Oh, dat's all right. My ole man's got two ob de nicest mules you eber set yer eyes on. It'll jis' do yer good ter look at dem. I'spect you'll see some ob yer ole frens dere. Dere's a nice settlemen' of cullud folks ober dere, an' I wants yer to come an' bring dat young lady. I wants dem folks to see wat nice folks I kin bring to de meetin'. I hope's yer didn't lose all your 'ligion in de army."

"Oh, I hope not," replied Robert.

"Oh, chile, yer mus' be shore 'bout dat. I don't want yer to ride hope's hoss down to torment. Now be shore an' come to-morrer an' bring dat young lady, an' take supper wid me. I'se all on nettles to see dat chile."

Northern Experience

"Uncle Robert," said Iola, after she had been North several weeks, "I have a theory that every woman ought to know how to earn her own living. I believe that a great amount of sin and misery springs from the weakness and inefficiency of women."

"Perhaps that's so, but what are you going to do about it?"

"I am going to join the great rank of bread-winners. Mr. Waterman has advertised for a number of saleswomen, and I intend to make application."

"When he advertises for help he means white women," said Robert.

"He said nothing about color," responded Iola.

"I don't suppose he did. He doesn't expect any colored girl to apply."

"Well, I think I could fill the place. At least I should like to try. And I do not think when I apply that I am in duty bound to tell him my great-grandmother was a negro."

"Well, child, there is no necessity for you to go out to work. You are perfectly welcome here, and I hope that you feel so."

"Oh, I certainly do. But still I would rather earn my own living."

That morning Iola applied for the situation, and, being prepossessing in her appearance, she obtained it.

For awhile everything went as pleasantly as a marriage bell. But one day a young colored lady, well-dressed and well-bred in her manner, entered the store. It was an acquaintance which Iola had formed in the colored church which she attended. Iola gave her a few words of cordial greeting, and spent a few moments chatting with her. The attention of the girls who sold at the same counter was attracted, and their suspicion awakened. Iola was a stranger in that city. Who was she, and who were her people? At last it was decided that one of the girls should act as a spy, and bring what information she could concerning Iola.

The spy was successful. She found out that Iola was living in a good neighborhood, but that none of the neighbors knew her. The man of the house was very fair, but there was an old woman whom Iola called "Grandma," and she was unmistakably colored. The story was sufficient.

Northern Experience: Iola Leroy, 2d ed. (1893), chapter 24, 205–12.

If that were true, Iola must be colored, and she should be treated accordingly.

Without knowing the cause, Iola noticed a chill in the social atmosphere of the store, which communicated itself to the cash-boys, and they treated her so insolently that her situation became very uncomfortable. She saw the proprietor, resigned her position, and asked for and obtained a letter of recommendation to another merchant who had advertised for a saleswoman.

In applying for the place, she took the precaution to inform her employer that she was colored. It made no difference to him; but he said:—

"Don't say anything about it to the girls. They might not be willing to work with you."

Iola smiled, did not promise, and accepted the situation. She entered upon her duties, and proved quite acceptable as a saleswoman.

One day, during an interval in business, the girls began to talk of their respective churches, and the question was put to Iola:—

"Where do you go to church?"

"I go," she replied, "to Rev. River's church, corner of Eighth and L Streets."

"Oh, no; you must be mistaken. There is no church there except a colored one."

"That is where I go."

"Why do you go there?"

"Because I liked it when I came here, and joined it."

"A member of a colored church? What under heaven possessed you to do such a thing?"

"Because I wished to be with my own people."

Here the interrogator stopped, and looked surprised and pained, and almost instinctively moved a little farther from her. After the store was closed, the girls had an animated discussion, which resulted in the information being sent to Mr. Cohen that Iola was a colored girl, and that they protested against her being continued in his employ. Mr. Cohen yielded to the pressure, and informed Iola that her services were no longer needed.

When Robert came home in the evening, he found that Iola had lost her situation, and was looking somewhat discouraged.

"Well, uncle," she said, "I feel out of heart. It seems as if the prejudice pursues us through every avenue of life, and assigns us the lowest places."

"That is so," replied Robert, thoughtfully.

"And yet I am determined," said Iola, "to win for myself a place in the fields of labor. I have heard of a place in New England, and I mean to try for it, even if I only stay a few months."

"Well, if you *will* go, say nothing about your color."

"Uncle Robert, I see no necessity for proclaiming that fact on the house-top. Yet I am resolved that nothing shall tempt me to deny it. The best blood in my veins is African blood, and I am not ashamed of it."

"Hurrah for you!" exclaimed Robert, laughing heartily.

As Iola wished to try the world for herself, and so be prepared for any emergency, her uncle and grandmother were content to have her go to New England. The town to which she journeyed was only a few hours' ride from the city of P——, and Robert, knowing that there is no teacher like experience, was willing that Iola should have the benefit of her teaching.

Iola, on arriving in H——, sought the firm, and was informed that her services were needed. She found it a pleasant and lucrative position. There was only one drawback—her boarding place was too far from her work. There was an institution conducted by professed Christian women, which was for the special use of respectable young working girls. This was in such a desirable location that she called at the house to engage board.

The matron conducted her over the house, and grew so friendly in the interview that she put her arm around her, and seemed to look upon Iola as a desirable accession to the home. But, just as Iola was leaving, she said to the matron: "I must be honest with you; I am a colored woman."

Swift as light a change passed over the face of the matron. She withdrew her arm from Iola, and said: "I must see the board of managers about it."

When the board met, Iola's case was put before them, but they decided not to receive her. And these women, professors of a religion which taught, "If ye have respect to persons ye commit sin," virtually shut the door in her face because of the outcast blood in her veins.

Considerable feeling was aroused by the action of these women, who, to say the least, had not put their religion in the most favorable light.

Iola continued to work for the firm until she received letters from her mother and uncle, which informed her that her mother, having arranged her affairs in the South, was ready to come North. She then resolved to return to the city of P——, to be ready to welcome her mother on her arrival.

Iola arrived in time to see that everything was in order for her mother's reception. Her room was furnished neatly, but with those touches of beauty that womanly hands are such adepts in giving. A few charming pictures adorned the walls, and an easy chair stood waiting to receive the travel-worn mother. Robert and Iola met her at the depot; and grandma was on her feet at the first sound of the bell, opened the door, clasped Marie to her heart, and nearly fainted for joy.

"Can it be possible dat dis is my little Marie?" she exclaimed.

It did seem almost almost impossible to realize that this faded woman, with pale cheeks and prematurely whitened hair, was the rosy-cheeked child from whom she had been parted more than thirty years.

"Well," said Robert, after the first joyous greeting was over, "love is a very good thing, but Marie has had a long journey and needs something that will stick by the ribs. How about dinner, mother?"

"It's all ready," said Mrs. Johnson.

After Marie had gone to her room and changed her dress, she came down and partook of the delicious repast which her mother and Iola had prepared for her.

In a few days Marie was settled in the home, and was well pleased with the change. The only drawback to her happiness was the absence of her son, and she expected him to come North after the closing of his school.

"Uncle Robert," said Iola, after her mother had been with them several weeks, "I am tired of being idle."

"What's the matter now?" asked Robert. "You are surely not going East again, and leave your mother?"

"Oh, I hope not," said Marie, anxiously. "I have been so long without you."

"No, mamma, I am not going East. I can get suitable employment here in the city of P——."

"But, Iola," said Robert, "you have tried, and been defeated. Why subject yourself to the same experience again?"

"Uncle Robert, I think that every woman should have some skill or art which would insure her at least a comfortable support. I believe there would be less unhappy marriages if labor were more honored among women."

"Well, Iola," said her mother, "what is your skill?"

"Nursing. I was very young when I went into the hospital, but I succeeded so well that the doctor said I must have been a born nurse. Now, I see by the papers, that a gentleman who has an invalid daughter wants some one who can be a nurse and companion for her, and I mean to apply for the situation. I do not think, if I do my part well in that position, that the blood in my veins will be any bar to my success."

A troubled look stole over Marie's face. She sighed faintly, but made no remonstrance. And so it was decided that Iola should apply for the situation.

Iola made application, and was readily accepted. Her patient was a frail girl of fifteen summers, who was ill with a low fever. Iola nursed her carefully, and soon had the satisfaction of seeing her restored to health. During her stay, Mr. Cloten, the father of the invalid, had learned some of the particulars of Iola's Northern experience as a bread-winner, and he resolved to give her employment in his store when her services were no longer needed in the house. As soon as a vacancy occurred he gave Iola a place in his store.

The morning she entered on her work he called his employés together, and told them that Miss Iola had colored blood in her veins, but that he was going to employ her and give her a desk. If any one objected to working with her, he or she could step to the cashier's desk and receive what was due. Not a man remonstrated, not a woman demurred; and Iola at last found a place in the great army of bread-winners, which the traditions of her blood could not affect.

"How did you succeed?" asked Mrs. Cloten of her husband, when he returned to dinner.

"Admirably! 'Everything is lovely and the goose hangs high.' I gave my employés understand that they could leave if they did not wish to work with Miss Leroy. Not one of them left, or showed any disposition to rebel."

"I am very glad," said Mrs Cloten. "I am ashamed of the way she has been treated in our city, when seeking to do her share in the world's work. I am glad that you were brave enough to face this cruel prejudice, and give her a situation."

"Well, my dear, do not make me a hero for a single act. I am grateful for the care Miss Leroy gave our Daisy. Money can buy services, but it cannot purchase tender, loving sympathy. I was also determined to let my employés know that I, not they, commanded my business. So, do not crown me a hero until I have won a niche in the temple of fame. In dealing with Southern prejudice against the negro, we Northerners could do it with better grace if we divested ourselves of our own. We irritate the South by our criticisms, and, while I confess that there is much that is reprehensible in their treatment of colored people, yet if our Northern civilization is higher than theirs we should 'criticise by creation.' We should stamp ourselves on the South, and not let the South stamp itself on us. When we have learned to treat men according to the complexion of their souls, and not the color of their skins, we will have given our best contribution towards the solution of the negro problem."

"I feel, my dear," said Mrs. Cloten, "that what you have done is a right step in the right direction, and I hope that other merchants will do the same. We have numbers of business men, rich enough to afford themselves the luxury of a good conscience."

Part Four
1893–1911

◆

There is light beyond the darkness,
 Joy beyond the present pain;
There is hope in God's great justice
 And the negro's rising brain.
Though the morning seems to linger
 O'er the hill-tops far away,
Yet the shadows bear the promise
 Of a brighter coming day.

from Iola Leroy

Letters

◆

The three letters included in this section were written to Francis Grimké, pastor of the Fifteenth Avenue Presbyterian Church in Washington, D.C. His wife was Charlotte Forten, like Harper a poet, essayist, and Reconstruction activist. The correspondence demonstrates the network that existed among African-American writers and activists and Harper's continued belief in the efficacy of literature as an agent of social change.

◆

"There Is Sunshine Still"

Philadelphia
1006 Bainbridge Street
March 20, 1903

Rev. Mr. Grimké

Respected friend, permit me to thank you for the strong, brave words you have spoken, in your pamphlet of sermons and to ask you if you can furnish me with one or two of those [pamphlets] and at what price can they be obtained? I like your idea of suggesting a day of praying. What sight would be more impressive than a race upon its knees appealing from the injustice of man to the everlasting justice of God. Well although the shadows of the past are still projected into the life of the race, there is

---

There Is Sunshine Still: Francis Grimké Papers, Moorland-Spingarn Research Center, Howard University.

sunshine still mingled with the shadows when you and others are able to present our cause as you can at the present times. May God bless you and strengthen you to do valiant work for those whose feebleness should be their best defence, their weakness an ensign of protection

Remember me to Mrs. Grimké,

Yours respectfully,
Frances E. W. Harper

"Count on Me as a Subscriber"

[Spring 1903(?)]

Dear Sir:

I received your sermons on lynching for which accept my thanks for your remembrance of me. And also permit me to emphasize my gratitude to you especially for your manly refusal to accept the verdict of the mob, in the cases of lynching. I hold that as long as there are such things as mental imbecility, mistaken identity, as long as Potiphar's wife stands in the world's pillory of shame that no man however guilty should be deprived of life, or liberty without due process of law. I saw some time since in the *Voice of Missions* what seemed was a fatal admission of the criminality of a victim of lynching by a very prominent man of our race. I suppose he meant Hale. I do not believe that Hale was guilty of all alleged against him, and we do not know who murdered that woman in Kentucky.

We do not know whether she fell by the hand of the colored man, or by some one who had sufficient reason to hide his own crime by imputing it to another, and so I sincerely thank you for the stand you have taken on this subject. Do these sermons have a circulation outside of our people? Could there not be some contrivance planned by which your sermons would reach larger audiences than they do now? Could not the council plan for their circulation, and the women's clubs be induced to scatter them among the white people in different localities?

I would so like to be able to have an opportunity to give at least one to Rev. Joseph May, whose wife informs me as though he has this subject under consideration, if I understood her aright.

Perhaps after New Year's day I will get a few from you to distribute. The first Thursday in next month I expect to read a paper on personal

---

Count on Me . . . : Francis Grimké Papers. This letter to Francis Grimké bears no date, but its content suggests it was written in the spring of 1903.

religion. Please if you are selling them send me the price. Please remember me to Mrs. Grimké. And if you have one more that you can spare send it to me. If at any time there is any movement to circulate these sermons, although my means are limited, count on me as a subscriber. Oh my friend, when we have among us such men as you, who can handle our cause as you can, we have reached the place where we can "Thank God and take courage." And instead of only looking "Gloomily to the past," we should learn to look more hopefully to the future. Oh there is a field before us which well might fill an angels hand, and thrill an angels heart. Is there not an amount of unused power among us? A lack of Christly consecration to the attainment of life's highest excellence and beauty? Oh that God may ever help you to help others, and teach you to teach others. I am an old woman, whose span of life may soon, very soon be done. I belong to a generation whose ranks are thinner and whose graves are thicker, but upon you my younger brother has not God himself laid a burden of loving service? Oh thanks, many thanks to you for sending the sermons, and pardon my delay in acknowledging them.

Well in life perhaps you will sometimes meet with coldness where you might hope for cooperation, and true sympathy in your work, but if your life is in harmony with God and Christly sympathy for man, take it for granted that for such a life there is no such word as fail.

F. E. W. Harper

"These Lines . . . the Expiring Flicker of a Lamp"

[Philadelphia, Pennsylvania
June 27, 1903]

My dear friend and brother:

You do not know how grateful and pleased I am to receive your welcome and timely sermons. Oh if they could only be scattered broadcast through the whole country, to open the eyes of this generation to the duties and dangers of the hour, and create within them an earnest desire to create and develop within the race the most precious thing that a man or woman can possess, and that is good character. "And who will harm us if we follow that which is good." I do not think there has been an hour since the surrender that there has been more need of the wisest counsels,

---

These Lines . . .: Francis Grimké Papers. At the conclusion of this letter, Harper appended the text of "Lines to Charles Sumner," but without the title. She preceded the poem with the following words: "Respectfully dedicated to Rev. Francis J. Grimké."

the warmest hearts, the holiest influences, and the most Christ-like endeavors. When the race produces many men like you, so able to understand, and so ready to bestow such instruction as is contained in your sermons, we may thank God and take courage, and look beyond the present pain with hope for a better and brighter future, in which love shall conquer hate, and both branches of the human family in this country realize that their interests and duties all lie in one direction, and that we cannot violate the one without dissevering the other. Please accept these lines which I send you as the expiring flicker of a lamp whose earthly light is well nigh spent, whose span of life may very soon be done. May God bless you and your wife, and keep you both as the apple of His eye and beneath the hollow of His hand.

Yours gratefully,
Frances E. W. Harper

Poetry

◆

Frances Harper's last years were extremely busy ones for the aging artist. Between 1893 and 1900, she published numerous reprints and revisions of her earlier works and several substantially new volumes of poetry. The addition of the five biblical poems to the 1893 edition of *Moses: A Story of the Nile* significantly changed that book. Three other collections, *Light Beyond Darkness* (c. 1892), *The Sparrow's Fall* (c. 1894), and *Martyr of Alabama* (c. 1895), were apparently published during this period, though the publication dates of all three are unclear. In 1895, *Atlanta Offerings: Poems* combined new and recently published poems with the contents of *The Sparrow's Fall* and *Martyr of Alabama*. Her 1900 publication, *Poems*, was a reprinting of poems from recent collections plus four previously uncollected works. The uncollected poems from 1893 to 1900 were usually on religious subjects, stressing the need for action fortified by hopeful patience.

Light Beyond Darkness (c. 1892)

Theodora Daniels, Maryemma Graham, and others indicate that "A Fairer Hope, a Brighter Morn" comes from a small, undated publication called *Light Beyond Darkness* published in Chicago by Donohue and Hennesberry. Daniels indicates that *Light* has eight pages. The title suggests that the poem that concludes *Iola Leroy* may have been in that work.

Moses: A Story of the Nile (1893)

In 1893, Frances Harper added another five poems to the volume titled *Moses: A Story of the Nile*. Each of these poems was biblically inspired. Three, "Christ's Entry into Jerusalem," "The Resurrection of Jesus," and "Simon's Countrymen," are about the crucifixion and resurrection. One, "Simon's Feast," retells the story of the woman who bathes Christ's feet, the same subject Harper treated twenty-two years earlier in "Mary at the Feet of Christ." And in the fifth, "Deliverance," which bears the same title as an earlier poem, Harper returns to one of her favorite topics, the liberation of Israel from Egyptian bondage. This time, however, the emphasis is not upon the heroic leadership of Moses. The 1893 "Deliverance" urges the people themselves to "Rise up!" This time, there is no mistaking the identification of African-Americans as a new Israel.

The Sparrow's Fall and Other Poems (c. 1894)

The Sparrow's Fall and Other Poems bears no publication date. However, one of its poems, "Our Hero," is based upon an incident that happened in 1888 and is a revised version of a poem that first appeared in 1892. Another work, "The Present Age," was published in *The African Methodist Episcopal Church Review* in 1895. And the first twenty-two pages of *Atlanta Offerings: Poems*, which was published in 1895, are the same as those in *The Sparrow's Fall*. If one assumes that Harper was following her usual pattern of appending new poems to existing works, it seems most likely that *The Sparrow's Fall* was published late in 1894 or early in 1895.

In *The Sparrow's Fall*, Harper revised an earlier poem by adding one more stanza, making several mechanical alterations, changing the title, and deleting a footnote. The mechanical changes are not particularly interesting, but the others are intriguing. The deleted footnote identified the poem as being based upon an incident that occurred in Louisiana in 1888 in which a black fireman became a "willing martyr to save his fellow man." The additional stanza says that all hopes for survival depended upon the success of this hero. This serves to emphasize the importance of this individual's action. Most remarkable, however, is that Harper changed the title from "The Black Hero" to the broader "Our Hero."

Though she published a revised version of *Moses* shortly after "The Black Hero" had been published, Harper chose not to include the poem in that collection. Instead she inserted it into *The Sparrow's Fall* along with several other poems that show heroic sacrifices by ordinary people. This suggests that Harper's thematic intent took precedence over simply compiling uncollected poems and keeping her volumes in print.

Atlanta Offering: Poems (1895)

Atlanta Offering: Poems is the most structurally unusual of all Harper's volumes of poetry. Its first ten poems were published as *The Sparrow's Fall and Other Poems*. To these she appended nine previously uncollected poems. Then, Harper broke with her tradition of presenting reprinted poems in the order in which they originally appeared. After the new poems, she added two, "Truth" and "Death of the Old Sea King," from the 1871 edition of *Poems*. Following these are "Save the Boys" and "Nothing and Something" from the 1893 version of *Sketches of Southern Life*. They are followed by two more from the 1871 *Poems*, "Vashti" and "Thank God for Little Children." The volume ends with nine poems that are also included in *Martyr of Alabama*.

Martyr of Alabama and Other Poems (c. 1895)

The *Martyr of Alabama and Other Poems* does not have a publication date. Since nine of its twelve poems appear in *Atlanta Offerings: Poems* published in 1895 and a note to the title poem identifies its inspiration as an incident that occurred in December 1894, it seems likely that *Martyr* was published in 1895.

Poems (1895–1900)

In 1895, a volume titled *Poems* was published that included all the *Atlanta Offering* poems plus two others: "Let the Light Enter," the only poem in the 1895 book that was also included in *Poems* of 1871, and "An Appeal to My Country Women." Apparently this volume was reprinted twice in 1896 and two or three times in 1898. The edition of *Poems* published in 1900 bears an 1895 copyright. But included in the 1900 volume are seven additional poems, which are not listed in its table of contents. "Then and Now" and "Maceo" had appeared in *Martyr of Alabama*. "Fishers of Men" and "Signing the Pledge" are in the 1887 edition of *Sketches*. Three of the poems, "The Lost Bells," "Do Not Cheer," and "The Burdens of All," are apparently collected here for the first time.

◆

A Fairer Hope, A Brighter Morn

From the peaceful heights of a higher life
I heard your maddening cry of strife;

A Fairer Hope . . . : Graham, 199–202. Sources such as Theodora Daniels and Maryemma Graham say this poem appeared in *Light Beyond the Darkness*.

It quivered with anguish, wrath and pain,
Like a demon struggling with his chain.

A chain of evil, heavy and strong,
Rusted with ages of fearful wrong,
Encrusted with blood and burning tears,
The chain I had worn and dragged for years.

It clasped my limbs, but it bound your heart,
And formed of your life a fearful part;
You sowed the wind, but could not control
The tempest wild of a guilty soul.

You saw me stand with my broken chain
Forged in the furnace of fiery pain,
You saw my children around me stand
Lovingly clasping my unbound hand.

But you remembered my blood and tears
'Mid the weary wasting flight of years,
You thought of the rice swamps, lone and dank,
When my heart in hopeless anguish sank.

You thought of your fields with harvest white,
Where I toiled in pain from morn till night;
You thought of the days you bought and sold
The children I loved, for paltry gold.

You thought of our shrieks that rent the air—
Our mourns of anguish and deep despair;
With chattering teeth and paling face,
You thought of your nation's deep disgrace.

You wove from your fears a fearful fate
To spring from your seeds of scorn and hate;
You imagined the saddest, wildest thing,
That time, with revenges fierce, could bring.

The cry you thought from a Voodo breast
Was the echo of your soul's unrest;
When thoughts too sad for fruitless tears
Loomed like the ghosts of avenging years.

Oh prophet of evil, could not your voice
In our new hopes and freedom rejoice?
'Mid the light which streams around our way
Was there naught to see but an evil day?

Nothing but vengeance, wrath and hate,
And the serpent coils of an evil fate—
A fate that shall crush and drag you down;
A doom that shall press like an iron crown?

A fate that shall crisp and curl your hair
And darken your faces now as fair,
And send through your veins like a poisoned flood
The hated stream of the Negro's blood?

A fate to madden the heart and brain
You've peopled with phantoms of dread and pain,
And fancies wild of your daughter's shriek
With Congo kisses upon her cheek?

Beyond the mist of your gloomy fears,
I see the promise of brighter years,
Through the dark I see their golden hem
And my heart gives out its glad amen.

The banner of Christ was your sacred trust,
But you trailed that banner in the dust,
And mockingly told us amid our pain
The hand of your God had forged our chain.

We stumbled and groped through the dreary night
Till our fingers touched God's robe of light;
And we knew he heard, from his lofty throne,
Our saddest cries and faintest moan.

The cross you have covered with sin and shame
We'll bear aloft in Christ's holy name.
Oh, never again may its folds be furled
While sorrow and sin enshroud our world!

God, to whose fingers thrills each heart beat,
Has not sent us to walk with aimless feet,
To cower and couch with bated breath
From margins of life to shores of death.

Higher and better than hate for hate,
Like the scorpion fangs that desolate,
Is the hope of a brighter, fairer morn
And a peace and love that shall yet be born;

When the Negro shall hold an honored place,
The friend and helper of every race;

His mission to build and not destroy,
And gladden the world with love and joy.

Christ's Entry into Jerusalem

He had plunged into our sorrows,
   And our sin had pierced his heart,
As before him loomed death's shadow,
   And he knew he must depart.

But they hailed him as a victor
   As he into Salem came,
And the very children shouted
   Loud hosannas to his name.

But he knew behind that triumph,
   Rising gladly to the sky,
Soon would come the cries of malice:
   Crucify him! Crucify!

Onward rode the blessed Saviour,
   Conscious of the coming strife
Soon to break in storms of hatred
   Round his dear, devoted life.

Ghastly in its fearful anguish
   Rose the cross before his eyes,
But he saw the joy beyond it,
   And did all the shame despise.

Joy to see the cry of scorning
   Through the ages ever bright,
And the cross of shame transfigured
   To a throne of love and light.

Joy to know his soul's deep travail
   Should not be a thing in vain,
And that joy and peace should blossom
   From his agonizing pain.

Christ's Entry into Jerusalem: This and the four poems that follow (pages 330–338) are reprinted from *Moses: A Story of the Nile* (1893) in the order in which they appear in that volume.

The Resurrection of Jesus

It was done, the deed of horror;
  Christ had died upon the cross,
And within an upper chamber
  The disciples mourned their loss.

Peter's eyes were full of anguish,
  Thinking sadly of the trial
When his boasted self-reliance
  Ended in his Lord's denial.

Disappointment, deep and heavy,
  Shrouded every heart with gloom,
As the hopes so fondly cherished
  Died around the garden tomb.

And they thought with shame and sorrow
  How they fled in that dark hour,
When they saw their Lord and Master
  In the clutch of Roman power.

We had hoped, they sadly uttered,
  He would over Israel reign,
But to-day he lies sepulchred,
  And our cherished hopes are vain.

In the humble home of Mary
  Slowly waned the hours away,
Till she rose to seek the garden
  And the place where Jesus lay.

Not the cross with all its anguish
  Could her loving heart restrain,
But the tomb she sought was empty,
  And her heart o'erflowed with pain.

To embalm my Lord and Master
  To this garden I have strayed,
But, behold, I miss his body,
  And I know not where he's laid.

Then a wave of strange emotion
  Swept her soul, as angels said,
"Wherefore do ye seek the living
  'Mid the chambers of the dead?"

Unperceived, her Lord stood by her,

Silent witness of her grief,
Bearing on his lips the tidings
  Sure to bring a glad relief.

But her tear-dimmed eyes were holden
  When she heard the Master speak;
Thought she, only 'tis the gardener
  Asking whom her soul did seek.

Then a sudden flush of gladness
  O'er her grief-worn features spread;
When she knew the voice of Jesus
  All her bitter anguish fled.

Forth she reached hands in rapture.
  Touch me not, the Saviour said;
Take the message to my brethren,
  I have risen from the dead.

Take them words of joy and comfort,
  Which will all their mourning end;
To their Father and my Father,
  Tell them that I will ascend.

"Brethren, I have seen the Master:
  He is risen from the dead."
But like words of idle meaning
  Seemed the glorious words she said.

Soon they saw the revelation
  Which would bid their mourning cease:
Christ, the risen, stood before them
  Breathing words of love and peace.

Timid men were changed to heroes,
  Weakness turned to wondrous might,
And the cross became their standard,
  Luminous with love and light.

From that lonely upper chamber,
  Holding up the rugged cross,
With a glad and bold surrender
  They encountered shame and loss.

In these days of doubt and error,
  In the conflict for the right,

May our hearts be ever strengthened
  By the resurrection's might.

Simon's Countrymen

They took away his seamless robe,
  With thorns they crowned his head,
As harshly, fiercely cried his foes:
  "Barabbas in his stead."

The friends he loved unto the end,
  Who shared his daily bread,
Before the storms of wrath and hate
  Forsook their Lord and fled.

To rescue men from death and sin
  He knew the awful cost,
As wearily he bent beneath
  The burden of the cross.

When Pilate had decreed his fate,
  And Jews withheld their aid,
Then Simon, the Cyrenean, came:
  On him the cross was laid.

Not his to smite with cruel scorn,
  Nor mock the dying one,
That helpful man came from the land
  Kissed by the ardent sun—

The land within whose sheltering arms
  The infant Jesus lay
When Herold vainly bared his sword
  And sought the child to slay.

Amid the calendar of saints
  We Simon's name may trace,
On history's page thro' every age
  He bears an honored place.

He little knew that cross would change
  Unto a throne of light;
The crown of thorns upon Christ's brow
  Would be forever bright.

Beneath the shadow of that cross

Brave men with outstretched hands
Have told the wondrous tale of love
    In distant heathen lands.

And yet within our favored land,
    Where Christian churches rise,
The dark-browed sons of Africa
    Are hated and despised.

Can they who speak of Christ as King,
    And glory in his name,
Forget that Simon's countrymen
    Still bear a cross of shame?

Can they forget the cruel scorn
    Men shower on a race
Who treat the hues their Father gives
    As emblems of disgrace?

Will they erect to God their fanes
    And Christ with honor crown,
And then with cruel weights of pain
    The African press down?

Oh, Christians, when we faint and bleed
    In this our native land,
Reach out to us when peeled, opprest,
    A kindly helping hand,

And bear aloft that sacred cross,
    Bright from the distant years,
And say for Christ's and Simon's sake,
    We'll wipe away your tears.

For years of sorrow, toil and pain
    We'll bring you love and light,
And in the name of Christ our Lord
    We'll make your pathway bright.

That seamless robe shall yet enfold
    The children of the sun,
Till rich and poor and bond and free
    In Christ shall all be one.

And for his sake from pride and scorn
    Our spirits shall be free,
Till through our souls shall sound the words
    He did it unto me.

Deliverance

Rise up! rise up! Oh Israel,
  Let a spotless lamb be slain;
The angel of death will o'er you bend
  And rend your galling chain.

Sprinkle its blood upon the posts
  And lintels of your door;
When the angel sees the crimson spots
  Unharmed he will pass you o'er.

Gather your flocks and herds to-night,
  Your children by your side;
A leader from Arabia comes
  To be your friend and guide.

With girded loins and sandled feet
  Await the hour of dread,
When Mizraim shall wildly mourn
  Her first-born and her dead.

The sons of Abraham no more
  Shall crouch 'neath Pharoah's hand,
Trembling with agony and dread,
  He'll thrust you from the land.

And ye shall hold in unborn years
  A feast to mark this day,
When joyfully the fathers rose
  And cast their chains away.

When crimson tints of morning flush
  The golden gates of day,
Or gorgeous hue of even melt
  In sombre shades away,

Then ye shall to your children teach
  The meaning of this feast,
How from the proud oppressor's hand
  Their fathers were released,

And ye shall hold through distant years
  This feast with glad accord,
And children's children yet shall learn
  To love and trust the Lord.

Ages have passed since Israel trod

In triumph through the sea,
And yet they hold in memory's urn
   Their first great jubilee.

When Moses led the ransomed hosts,
   And Miriam's song arose,
While ruin closed around the path
   Of their pursuing foes.

Shall Israel thro' long varied years
   These memories cherish yet,
And we who lately stood redeemed
   Our broken chains forget?

Should we forget the wondrous change
   That to our people came,
When justice rose and sternly plead
   Our cause with sword and flame?

And led us through the storms of war
   To freedom's fairer shore,
When slavery sank beneath a flood
   Whose waves were human gore.

Oh, youth and maidens of the land,
   Rise up with one accord,
And in the name of Christ go forth
   To battle for the Lord.

Go forth, but not in crimson fields,
   With fratricidal strife,
But in the name of Christ go forth
   For freedom, love and life.

Go forth to follow in his steps,
   Who came not to destroy,
Till wastes shall blossom as the rose,
   And deserts sing for joy.

Simon's Feast

He is coming, she said, to Simon's feast,
   The prophet of Galilee,
Though multitudes around him throng
   In longing his face to see.

He enters the home as Simon's guest,
   But he gives no welcome kiss;
He brings no water to bathe his feet—
   Why is Simon so remiss?

The prophet's face is bright with love,
   And mercy beams from his eye;
He pities the poor, the lame and blind,
   An outcast, I will draw nigh.

If a prophet, he will surely know
   The guilt of my darkened years;
With broken heart I'll seek his face,
   And bathe his feet with my tears.

No holy rabbi lays his hand
   In blessing on my head;
No loving voice floats o'er the path,
   The downward path I tread.

Unto the Master's side she pressed,
   A penitent, frail and fair,
Rained on his feet a flood of tears,
   And then wiped them with her hair.

Over the face of Simon swept
   An air of puzzled surprise;
Can my guest a holy prophet be,
   And not this woman despise?

Christ saw the thoughts that Simon's heart
   Had written upon his face,
Kindly turned to the sinful one
   In her sorrow and disgrace.

Where Simon only saw the stains,
   Where sin and shame were rife,
Christ looked beneath and saw the germs
   Of a fair, outflowering life.

Like one who breaks a galling chain,
   And sets a prisoner free,
He rent her fetters with the words,
   "Thy sins are forgiven thee."

God be praised for the gracious words
   Which came through that woman's touch

That souls redeemed thro' God's dear Son
  May learn to love him so much;

That souls once red with guilt and crime
  May their crimson stains outgrow;
The scarlet spots upon their lives
  Become whiter than driven snow.

My Mother's Kiss

My mother's kiss, my mother's kiss,
  I feel its impress now;
As in the bright and happy days
  She pressed it on my brow.

You say it is a fancied thing
  Within my memory fraught;
To me it has a sacred place—
  The treasure house of thought.

Again, I feel her fingers glide
  Amid my clustering hair;
I see the love-light in her eyes,
  When all my life was fair.

Again, I hear her gentle voice
  In warning or in love.
How precious was the faith that taught
  My soul of things above.

The music of her voice is stilled,
  Her lips are paled in death.
As precious pearls I'll clasp her words
  Until my latest breath.

The world has scattered round my path
  Honor and wealth and fame;
But naught so precious as the thoughts
  That gather round her name.

And friends have placed upon my brow
  The laurels of renown;

My Mother's Kiss: This and the nine poems that follow (pages 339–351) are the complete text of *The Sparrow's Fall and Other Poems* and the first ten poems of *Atlanta Offering: Poems* (1895). They are reprinted here from *The Sparrow's Fall*.

But she first taught me how to wear
  My manhood as a crown.

My hair is silvered o'er with age,
  I'm longing to depart;
To clasp again my mother's hand,
  And be a child at heart.

To roam with her the glory-land
  Where saints and angels greet;
To cast our crowns with songs of love
  At our Redeemer's feet.

A Grain of Sand

Do you see this grain of sand
Lying loosely in my hand?
Do you know to me it brought
Just a simple loving thought?
When one gazes night by night
On the glorious stars of light,
Oh how little seems the span
Measured round the life of man.

Oh! how fleeting are his years
With their smiles and their tears;
Can it be that God does care
For such atoms as we are?
Then outspake this grain of sand
"I was fashioned by His hand
In the star lit realms of space
I was made to have a place.

"Should the ocean flood the world,
Were its mountains 'gainst me hurled,
All the force they could employ
Wouldn't a single grain destroy;
And if I, a thing so light,
Have a place within His sight;
You are linked unto his throne
Cannot live nor die alone.

In the everlasting arms
Mid life's dangers and alarms
Let calm trust your spirit fill;

Know He's God, and then be still."
Trustingly I raised my head
Hearing what the atom said;
Knowing man is greater far
Than the brightest sun or star.

The Crocuses

They heard the South wind sighing
  A murmur of the rain;
And they knew that Earth was longing
  To see them all again.

While the snow-drops still were sleeping
  Beneath the silent sod;
They felt their new life pulsing
  Within the dark, cold clod.

Not a daffodil nor daisy
  Had dared to raise its head;
Not a fairhaired dandelion
  Peeped timid from its bed;

Though a tremor of the winter
  Did shivering through them run;
Yet they lifted up their foreheads
  To greet the vernal sun.

And the sunbeams gave them welcome,
  As did the morning air—
And scattered o'er their simple robes
  Rich tints of beauty rare.

Soon a host of lovely flowers
  From vales and woodland burst;
But in that fair procession
  The crocuses were first.

First to weave for Earth a chaplet
  To crown her dear old head;
And to beautify the pathway
  Where winter still did tread.

And their loved and white haired mother
  Smiled sweetly 'neath the touch,

When she knew her faithful children
  Were loving her so much.

The Present Age

Say not the age is hard and cold—
  I think it brave and grand;
When men of diverse sects and creeds
  Are clasping hand in hand.

The Parsee from his sacred fires
  Beside the Christian kneels;
And clearer light to Islam's eyes
  The word of Christ reveals.

The Brahmin from his distant home
  Brings thoughts of ancient lore;
The Bhuddist breaking bonds of caste
  Divides mankind no more.

The meek-eyed sons of far Cathay
  Are welcome round the board;
Not greed, nor malice drives away
  These children of our Lord.

And Judah from whose trusted hands
  Came oracles divine;
Now sits with those around whose hearts
  The light of God doth shine.

Japan unbars her long sealed gates
  From islands far away;
Her sons are lifting up their eyes
  To greet the coming day.

The Indian child from forests wild
  Has learned to read and pray;
The tomahawk and scalping knife
  From him have passed away.

From centuries of servile toil
  The Negro finds release,

The Present Age: Also appeared in the *African Methodist Episcopal Church Review* in 1895; the last two stanzas were dropped.

And builds the fanes of prayer and praise
　Unto the God of Peace.

England and Russia face to face
　With Central Asia meet;
And on the far Pacific coast,
　Chinese and natives greet.

Crusaders once with sword and shield
　The Holy Land to save;
From Moslem hands did strive to clutch
　The dear Redeemer's grave.

A battle greater, grander far
　Is for the present age;
A crusade for the rights of man
　To brighten history's page.

Where labor faints and bows her head,
　And want consorts with crime;
Or men grown faithless sadly say
　That evil is the time.

There is the field, the vantage ground
　For every earnest heart;
To side with justice, truth and right
　And act a noble part.

To save from ignorance and vice
　The poorest, humblest child;
To make our age the fairest one
　On which the sun has smiled;

To plant the roots of coming years
　In mercy, love and truth;
And bid our weary, saddened earth
　Again renew her youth.

Oh! earnest hearts! toil on in hope,
　'Till darkness shrinks from light;
To fill the earth with peace and joy,
　Let youth and age unite;

To stay the floods of sin and shame
　That sweep from shore to shore;
And furl the banners stained with blood,
　'Till war shall be no more.

Blame not the age, nor think it full
   Of evil and unrest;
But say of every other age,
   "This one shall be the best."

The age to brighten every path
   By sin and sorrow trod;
For loving hearts to usher in
   The commonwealth of God.

Dedication Poem

Dedication Poem on the reception of the annex to the
home for aged colored people, from the bequest of Mr.
Edward T. Parker

Outcast from her home in Syria
   In the lonely, dreary wild;
Heavy hearted, sorrow stricken,
   Sat a mother and her child.

There was not a voice to cheer her
   Not a soul to share her fate;
She was weary, he was fainting,—
   And life seemed so desolate.

Far away in sunny Egypt
   Was lone Hagar's native land;
Where the Nile in kingly bounty
   Scatters bread throughout the land.

In the tents of princely Abram
   She for years had found a home;
Till the stern decree of Sarah
   Sent her forth the wild to roam.

Hour by hour she journeyed onward
   From the shelter of their tent,
Till her footsteps slowly faltered
   And the water all was spent;

Then she veiled her face in sorrow,
   Feared her child would die of thirst;
Till her eyes with tears so holden
   Saw a sparkling fountain burst.

Oh! how happy was that mother,
  What a soothing of her pain;
When she saw her child reviving,
  Life rejoicing through each vein

Does not life repeat this story,
  Tell it over day by day?
Of the fountains of refreshment
  Ever springing by our way.

Here is one by which we gather,
  On this bright and happy day,
Just to bask beside a fountain
  Making gladder life's highway.

Bringing unto hearts now aged
  Who have borne life's burdens long,
Such a gift of love and mercy
  As deserves our sweetest song.

Such a gift that even heaven
  May rejoice with us below,
If the pure and holy angels
  Join us in our joy and woe.

May the memory of the giver
  In this home where age may rest,
Float like fragrance through the ages,
  Ever blessing, ever blest.

When the gates of pearl are opened
  May we there this friend behold,
Drink with him from living fountains,
  Walk with him the streets of gold.

When life's shattered cords of music
  Shall again be sweetly sung;
Then our hearts with life immortal,
  Shall be young, forever young.

A Double Standard

Do you blame me that I loved him?
  If when standing all alone
I cried for bread a careless world
  Pressed to my lips a stone.

Do you blame me that I loved him,
   That my heart beat glad and free,
When he told me in the sweetest tones
   He loved but only me?

Can you blame me that I did not see
   Beneath his burning kiss
The serpent's wiles, nor even hear
   The deadly adder hiss?

Can you blame me that my heart grew cold
   That the tempted, tempter turned;
When he was feted and caressed
   And I was coldly spurned?

Would you blame him, when you draw from me
   Your dainty robes aside,
If he with gilded baits should claim
   Your fairest as his bride?

Would you blame the world if it should press
   On him a civic crown;
And see me struggling in the depth
   Then harshly press me down?

Crime has no sex and yet to-day
   I wear the brand of shame;
Whilst he amid the gay and proud
   Still bears an honored name.

Can you blame me if I've learned to think
   Your hate of vice a sham,
When you so coldly crushed me down
   And then excused the man?

Would you blame me if to-morrow
   The coroner should say,
A wretched girl, outcast, forlorn,
   Has thrown her life away?

Yes, blame me for my downward course,
   But oh! remember well,
Within your homes you press the hand
   That led me down to hell.

I'm glad God's ways are not our ways,
   He does not see as man;

Within His love I know there's room
  For those whom others ban.

I think before His great white throne,
  His throne of spotless light,
That whited sepulchres shall wear
  The hue of endless night.

That I who fell, and he who sinned,
  Shall reap as we have sown;
That each the burden of his loss
  Must bear and bear alone.

No golden weights can turn the scale
  Of justice in His sight;
And what is wrong in woman's life
  In man's cannot be right.

Our Hero

Onward to her destination,
  O'er the stream the Hannah sped,
When a cry of consternation
  Smote and chilled our hearts with dread.

Wildly leaping, madly sweeping,
  All relentless in their sway,
Like a band of cruel demons
  Flames were closing 'round our way

Oh! the horror of those moments;
  Flames above and waves below—

Our Hero: Published as "The Black Hero" in the *African Methodist Episcopal Church Review* 9 (1892):178–9. That version included the following footnote:

In 1888 the steamer "John H. Hannah," heavily laden with cotton and having on board a large number of passengers, took fire near Baton Rouge, La. Suddenly the flames, leaping from cotton bale to cotton bale, enveloped the ill-fated boat. The pilot remained at his post until death stared him in the face and then forsook the wheel. The burning vessel swept into the swift current of the deep rolling tide and all seemed lost. Suddenly the fireman, a black man, rushed up to the pilot-house, seized the wheel and headed the boat for the bank. In due time it struck the mud-bank and most of the passengers were saved. The black man stood and held the wheel till literally burned to death—dying a willing martyr to save his fellow-men. The citizens of New Orleans, recognizing his glorious heroism, bought a home and paid for it, and gave it to his wife and children, and added a handsome sum of money.

The 1892 version does not contain stanza 9.

Oh! the agony of ages
  Crowded in one hour of woe.

Fainter grew our hearts with anguish
  In that hour with peril rife,
When we saw the pilot flying,
  Terror-stricken, for his life.

Then a man uprose before us—
  We had once despised his race—
But we saw a lofty purpose
  Lighting up his darkened face.

While the flames were madly roaring,
  With a courage grand and high,
Forth he rushed unto our rescue,
  Strong to suffer, brave to die.

Helplessly the boat was drifting,
  Death was staring in each face,
When he grasped the fallen rudder,
  Took the pilot's vacant place.

Could he save us? Would he save us?
  All his hope of life give o'er?
Could he hold that fated vessel
  'Till she reached the nearer shore?

All our hopes and fears were centered
  'Round his strong, unfaltering hand;
If he failed us we must perish,
  Perish just in sight of land.

Breathlessly we watched and waited
  While the flames were raging fast;
When our anguish changed to rapture—
  We were saved, yes, saved at last.

Never strains of sweetest music
  Brought to us more welcome sound
Than the grating of that steamer
  When her keel had touched the ground.

But our faithful martyr hero
  Through a fiery pathway trod,
Till he laid his valiant spirit
  On the bosom of his God.

Fame has never crowned a hero
  On the crimson fields of strife,
Grander, nobler, than that pilot
  Yielding up for us his life.

The Dying Bondman

Life was trembling, faintly trembling
  On the bondman's latest breath,
And he felt the chilling pressure
  Of the cold, hard hand of Death.

He had been an Afric chieftain,
  Worn his manhood as a crown;
But upon the field of battle
  Had been fiercely stricken down.

He had longed to gain his freedom,
  Waited, watched and hoped in vain,
Till his life was slowly ebbing—
  Almost broken was his chain.

By his bedside stood the master,
  Gazing on the dying one,
Knowing by the dull grey shadows
  That life's sands were almost run.

"Master," said the dying bondman,
  "Home and friends I soon shall see;
But before I reach my country,
  Master write that I am free;

"For the spirits of my fathers
  Would shrink back from me in pride,
If I told them at our greeting
  I a slave had lived and died;—

"Give to me the precious token,
  That my kindred dead may see—
Master! write it, write it quickly!
  Master! write that I am free!"

The Dying Bondman: Also appeared in *African Methodist Episcopal Church Review* 1
(1884):45; and the Cleveland *Gazette*, August 30, 1884.

At his earnest plea the master
  Wrote for him the glad release,
O'er his wan and wasted features
  Flitted one sweet smile of peace.

Eagerly he grasped the writing;
  "I am free!" at last he said.
Backward fell upon the pillow,
  He was free among the dead.

"A Little Child Shall Lead Them"

Only a little scrap of blue
  Preserved with loving care,
But earth has not a brilliant hue
  To me more bright and fair.

Strong drink, like a raging demon,
  Laid on my heart his hand,
When my darling joined with others
  The Loyal Legion* band.

But mystic angels called away
  My loved and precious child,
And o'er life's dark and stormy way
  Swept waves of anguish wild.

This badge of the Loyal Legion
  We placed upon her breast,
As she lay in her little coffin
  Taking her last sweet rest.

To wear that badge as a token
  She earnestly did crave,
So we laid it on her bosom
  To wear it in the grave.

Where sorrow would never reach her
  Nor harsh words smite her ear;
Nor her eyes in death dimmed slumber
  Would ever shed a tear.

"What means this badge?" said her father,
  Whom we had tried to save;

---

*The Temperance Band.

Who said, when we told her story,
　"Don't put it in the grave."

We took the badge from her bosom
　And laid it on a chair;
And men by drink deluded
　Knelt by that badge in prayer.

And vowed in that hour of sorrow
　From drink they would abstain;
And this little badge became the wedge
　Which broke their galling chain.

And lifted the gloomy shadows
　That overspread my life,
And flooding my home with gladness,
　Made me a happy wife.

And this is why this scrap of blue
　Is precious in my sight;
It changed my sad and gloomy home
　From darkness into light.

The Sparrow's Fall

Too frail to soar—a feeble thing—
　It fell to earth with fluttering wing;
But God, who watches over all,
　Beheld that little sparrow's fall.

'Twas not a bird with plumage gay,
　Filling the air with its morning lay;
'Twas not an eagle bold and strong,
　Borne on the tempest's wing along.

Only a brown and weesome thing,
　With drooping head and listless wing;
It could not drift beyond His sight
　Who marshals the splendid stars of night.

Its dying chirp fell on His ears,
　Who tunes the music of the spheres,
Who hears the hungry lion's call,
　And spreads a table for us all.

Its mission of song at last is done,
No more will it greet the rising sun;
That tiny bird has found a rest
More calm than its mother's downy breast.

Oh, restless heart, learn thou to trust
In God, so tender, strong and just;
In whose love and mercy everywhere
His humblest children have a share.

If in love He numbers ev'ry hair,
Whether the strands be dark or fair,
Shall we not learn to calmly rest,
Like children, on our Father's breast?

God Bless Our Native Land

God bless our native land,
Land of the newly free,
Oh may she ever stand
For truth and liberty.

God bless our native land,
Where sleep our kindred dead,
Let peace at thy command
Above their graves be shed.

God help our native land,
Bring surcease to her strife,
And shower from thy hand
A more abundant life.

God bless our native land,
Her homes and children bless,
Oh may she ever stand
For truth and righteousness.

Dandelions

Welcome children of the Spring,
In your garbs of green and gold,

God Bless Our Native Land: This and the seventeen poems that follow (pages 351–371) are from *Atlanta Offering: Poems* (1895).

Lifting up your sun-crowned heads
  On the verdant plain and wold.

As a bright and joyous troop
  From the breast of earth ye came
Fair and lovely are your cheeks,
  With sun-kisses all aflame.

In the dusty streets and lanes,
  Where the lowly children play,
There as gentle friends ye smile,
  Making brighter life's highway.

Dewdrops and the morning sun,
  Weave your garments fair and bright,
And we welcome you to-day
  As the children of the light.

Children of the earth and sun,
  We are slow to understand
All the richness of the gifts
  Flowing from our Father's hand.

Were our vision clearer far,
  In this sin-dimmed world of ours,
Would we not more thankful be
  For the love that sends us flowers?

Welcome, early visitants,
  With your sun-crowned golden hair
With your message to our hearts
  Of our Father's loving care.

The Building

"Build me a house," said the Master,
  "But not on the shifting sand,
Mid the wreck and roar of tempests,
  A house that will firmly stand.

"I will bring thee windows of agates,
  And gates of carbuncles bright,
And thy fairest courts and portals
  Shall be filled with love and light.

"Thou shalt build with fadeless rubies,
  All fashioned around the throne,

A house that shall last forever,
  With Christ as the cornerstone.

"It shall be a royal mansion,
  A fair and beautiful thing,
It will be the presence-chamber
  Of thy Saviour, Lord and King.

"Thy house shall be bound with pinions
  To mansions of rest above,
But grace shall forge all the fetters
  With the links and cords of love.

"Thou shalt be free in this mansion
  From sorrow and pain of heart,
For the peace of God shall enter,
  And never again depart."

Home, Sweet Home

Sharers of a common country,
  They had met in deadly strife;
Men who should have been as brothers
  Madly sought each other's life.

In the silence of the even,
  When the cannon's lips were dumb,
Thoughts of home and all its loved ones
  To the soldier's heart would come.

On the margin of a river,
  'Mid the evening's dews and damps,
Could be heard the sounds of music
  Rising from two hostile camps.

One was singing of its section
  Down in Dixie, Dixie's land,
And the other of the banner
  Waved so long from strand to strand.

In the land where Dixie's ensign
  Floated o'er the hopeful slave,
Rose the song that freedom's banner,
  Starry-lighted, long might wave.

From the fields of strife and carnage,
  Gentle thoughts began to roam,

And a tender strain of music
  Rose with words of "Home, Sweet Home."

Then the hearts of strong men melted,
  For amid our grief and sin
Still remains that "touch of nature,"
  Telling us we all are kin.

In one grand but gentle chorus,
  Floating to the starry dome,
Came the words that brought them nearer,
  Words that told of "Home, Sweet Home."

For awhile, all strife forgotten,
  They were only brothers then,
Joining in the sweet old chorus,
  Not as soldiers, but as men.

Men whose hearts would flow together,
  Though apart their feet might roam,
Found a tie they could not sever,
  In the mem'ry of each home.

Never may the steps of carnage
  Shake our land from shore to shore,
But may mother, home and Heaven,
  Be our watchwords evermore.

The Pure in Heart Shall See God

They shall see Him in the crimson flush
  Of morning's early light,
In the drapery of sunset,
  Around the couch of night.

When the clouds drop down their fatness,
  In late and early rain,
They shall see His glorious footprints
  On valley, hill and plain.

They shall see Him when the cyclone
  Breathes terror through the land;
They shall see Him 'mid the murmurs
  Of zephyrs soft and bland.

They shall see Him when the lips of health,
  Breath vigor through each nerve,
When pestilence clasps hands with death,
  His purposes to serve.

They shall see Him when the trembling eart[h]
  Is rocking to and fro;
They shall see Him in the order
  The seasons come and go.

They shall see Him when the storms of war
  Sweep wildly through the land;
When peace descends like gentle dew
  They still shall see His hand.

They shall see Him in the city
  Of gems and pearls of light,
They shall see Him in his beauty,
  And walk with Him in white.

To living founts their feet shall tend,
  And Christ shall be their guide,
Beloved of God, their rest shall be
  In safety by His side.

He "Had Not Where to Lay His Head"

The conies had their hiding-place,
  The wily fox with stealthy tread
A covert found, but Christ, the Lord,
  Had not a place to lay his head.

The eagle had an eyrie home,
  The blithesome bird its quiet rest,
But not the humblest spot on earth
  Was by the Son of God possessed.

Princes and kings had palaces,
  With grandeur could adorn each tomb,
For Him who came with love and life,
  They had no home, they gave no room.

The hands whose touch sent thrills of joy
  Through nerves unstrung and palsied frame,
The feet that travelled for our need,
  Were nailed unto the cross of shame.

How dare I murmur at my lot,
  Or talk of sorrow, pain and loss,
When Christ was in manger laid,
  And died in anguish on the cross.

That homeless one beheld beyond
  His lonely agonizing pain,
A love outflowing from His heart,
  That all the wandering world would gain.

Go Work in My Vineyard

Go work in my vineyard, said the Lord,
  And gather the bruised grain;
But the reapers had left the stubble bare,
  And I trod the soil in pain.

The fields of my Lord are wide and broad,
  He has pastures fair and green,
And vineyards that drink the golden light
  Which flows from the sun's bright sheen.

I heard the joy of the reapers' song,
  As they gathered golden grain;
Then wearily turned unto my task,
  With a lonely sense of pain.

Sadly I turned from the sun's fierce glare,
  And sought the quiet shade,
And over my dim and weary eyes
  Sleep's peaceful fingers strayed.

I dreamed I joined with a restless throng,
  Eager for pleasure and gain;
But ever and anon a stumbler fell,
  And uttered a cry of pain.

But the eager crowd still hurried on,
  Too busy to pause or heed,
When a voice rang sadly through my soul,
  You must staunch these wounds that bleed.

My hands were weak, but I reached them out
  To feebler ones than mine,
And over the shadows of my life
  Stole the light of a peace divine.

Oh! then my task was a sacred thing,
  How precious it grew in my eyes!
'Twas mine to gather the bruised grain
  For the "Lord of Paradise."

And when the reapers shall lay their grain
  On the floors of golden light,
I feel that mine with its broken sheaves
  Shall be precious in His sight.

Though thorns may often pierce my feet,
  And the shadows still abide,
The mists will vanish before His smile,
  There will be light at eventide.

Renewal of Strength

The prison-house in which I live
  Is falling to decay,
But God renews my spirit's strength,
  Within these walls of clay.

For me a dimness slowly creeps
  Around earth's fairest light,
But heaven grows clearer to my view,
  And fairer to my sight.

It may be earth's sweet harmonies
  Are duller to my ear,
But music from my Father's house
  Begins to float more near.

Then let the pillars of my home
  Crumble and fall away;
Lo, God's dear love within my soul
  Renews it day by day.

Jamie's Puzzle

There was grief within our household
  Because of a vacant chair.
Our mother, so loved and precious,
  No longer was sitting there.

Our hearts grew heavy with sorrow,
  Our eyes with tears were blind,
And little Jamie was wondering,
  Why we were left behind.

We had told our little darling,
  Of the land of love and light,
Of the saints all crowned with glory,
  And enrobed in spotless white.

We said that our precious mother,
  Had gone to that land so fair,
To dwell with beautiful angels,
  And to be forever there.

But the child was sorely puzzled,
  Why dear grandmamma should go
To dwell in a stranger city,
  When her children loved her so.

But again the mystic angel
  Came with swift and silent tread,
And our sister, Jamie's mother,
  Was enrolled among the dead.

To us the mystery deepened,
  To Jamie it seemed more clear;
Grandma, he said, must be lonesome,
  And mamma has gone to her.

But the question lies unanswered
  In our little Jamie's mind,
Why she should go to our mother,
  And leave her children behind;

To dwell in that lovely city,
  From all that was dear to part,
From children who loved to nestle
  So closely around her heart.

Dear child, like you, we are puzzled,
  With problems that still remain;
But think in the great hereafter
  Their meaning will all be plain.

The Martyr of Alabama

[The following news item appeared in the newspapers
throughout the country, issue of December 27th, 1894:
  "Tim Thompson, a little negro boy, was asked to
dance for the amusement of some white toughs. He re-
fused, saying he was a church member. One of the men
knocked him down with a club and then danced upon
his prostrate form. He then shot the boy in the hip.
The boy is dead; his murderer is still at large."]

He lifted up his pleading eyes,
  And scanned each cruel face,
Where cold and brutal cowardice
  Had left its evil trace.

It was when tender memories
  Round Beth'lem's manger lay,
And mothers told their little ones
  Of Jesu's natal day.

And of the Magi from the East
  Who came their gifts to bring,
And bow in rev'rence at the feet
  Of Salem's new-born King.

And how the herald angels sang
  The choral song of peace,
That war should close his wrathful lips,
  And strife and carnage cease.

At such an hour men well may hush
  Their discord and their strife,
And o'er that manger clasp their hands
  With gifts to brighten life.

Alas! that in our favored land,
  That cruelty and crime
Should cast their shadows o'er a day,
  The fairest pearl of time.

  The Martyr of Alabama: The bracketed text following the title was included in the
original publication.

A dark-browed boy had drawn anear
  A band of savage men,
Just as a hapless lamb might stray
  Into a tiger's den.

Cruel and dull, they saw in him
  For sport an evil chance,
And then demanded of the child
  To give to them a dance.

"Come dance for us," the rough men said;
  "I can't," the child replied,
"I cannot for the dear Lord's sake,
  Who for my sins once died."

Tho' they were strong and he was weak,
  He wouldn't his Lord deny.
His life lay in their cruel hands,
  But he for Christ could die.

Heard they aright? Did that brave child
  Their mandates dare resist?
Did he against their stern commands
  Have courage to resist?

Then recklessly a man (?) arose,
  And dealt a fearful blow.
He crushed the portals of that life,
  And laid the brave child low.

And trampled on his prostrate form,
  As on a broken toy;
Then danced with careless, brutal feet,
  Upon the murdered boy.

Christians! behold that martyred child!
  His blood cries from the ground;
Before the sleepless eye of God,
  He shows each gaping wound.

Oh! Church of Christ arise! arise!
  Lest crimson stain thy hand,
When God shall inquisition make
  For blood shed in the land.

Take sackcloth of the darkest hue,
  And shroud the pulpits round;

Servants of him who cannot lie
  Sit mourning on the ground.

Let holy horror blanch each brow,
  Pale every cheek with fears,
And rocks and stones, if ye could speak,
  Ye well might melt to tears.

Through every fane send forth a cry,
  Of sorrow and regret,
Nor in an hour of careless ease
  Thy brother's wrongs forget.

Veil not thine eyes, nor close thy lips,
  Nor speak with bated breath;
This evil shall not always last,—
  The end of it is death.

Avert the doom that crime must bring
  Upon a guilty land;
Strong in the strength that God supplies,
  For truth and justice stand.

For Christless men, with reckless hands,
  Are sowing round thy path
The tempests wild that yet shall break
  In whirlwinds of God's wrath.

The Night of Death

'Twas a night of dreadful horror,—
  Death was sweeping through the land;
And the wings of dark destruction
  Were outstretched from strand to strand

Strong men's hearts grew faint with terror,
  As the tempest and the waves
Wrecked their homes and swept them downward
  Suddenly to yawning graves.

'Mid the wastes of ruined households,
  And the tempest's wild alarms,
Stood a terror-stricken mother
  With a child within her arms.

Other children huddled 'round her,
  Each one nestling in her heart;

Swift in thought and swift in action,
  She at least from one must part.

Then she said unto her daughter,
  "Strive to save one child from death.
"Which one?" said the anxious daughter,
  As she stood with bated breath.

Oh! the anguish of that mother;
  What despair was in her eye!
All her little ones were precious;
  Which one should she leave to die?

Then outspake the brother Bennie:
  "I will take the little one."
"No," exclaimed the anxious mother;
  "No, my child, it can't be done."

"See! my boy, the waves are rising,
  Save yourself and leave the child!"
"I will trust in Christ," he answered;
  Grasped the little one and smiled.

Through the roar of wind and waters
  Ever and anon she cried;
But throughout the night of terror
  Never Bennie's voice replied.

But above the waves' wild surging
  He had found a safe retreat,
As if God had sent an angel,
  Just to guide his wandering feet.

When the storm had spent its fury,
  And the sea gave up its dead,
She was mourning for her loved ones,
  Lost amid that night of dread.

While her head was bowed in anguish,
  On her ear there fell a voice,
Bringing surcease to her sorrow,
  Bidding all her heart rejoice.

"Didn't I tell you true?" said Bennie,
  And his eyes were full of light,
"When I told you God would help me
  Through the dark and dreadful night?"

And he placed the little darling
   Safe within his mother's arms,
Feeling Christ had been his guardian,
   'Mid the dangers and alarms.

Oh! for faith so firm and precious,
   In the darkest, saddest night,
Till life's gloom-encircled shadows
   Fade in everlasting light.

And upon the mount of vision
   We our loved and lost shall greet,
With earth's wildest storms behind us,
   And its cares beneath our feet.

Mother's Treasures

Two little children sit by my side,
   I call them Lily and Daffodil;
I gaze on them with a mother's pride,
   One is Edna, the other is Will.

Both have eyes of starry light,
   And laughing lips o'er teeth of pearl.
I would not change for a diadem
   My noble boy and darling girl.

To-night my heart o'erflows with joy;
   I hold them as a sacred trust;
I fain would hide them in my heart,
   Safe from tarnish of moth and rust.

What should I ask for my dear boy?
   The richest gifts of wealth or fame?
What for my girl? A loving heart
   And a fair and a spotless name?

What for my boy? That he should stand
   A pillar of strength to the state?
What for my girl? That she should be
   The friend of the poor and desolate?

I do not ask they shall never tread
   With weary feet the paths of pain.
I ask that in the darkest hour
   They may faithful and true remain.

I only ask their lives may be
   Pure as gems in the gates of pearl,
Lives to brighten and bless the world—
   This I ask for my boy and girl.

I ask to clasp their hands again
   'Mid the holy host of heaven,
Enraptured say: "I am here, oh! God,
   "And the children Thou hast given."

The Refiner's Gold

He stood before my heart's closed door,
   And asked to enter in;
But I had barred the passage o'er
   By unbelief and sin.

He came with nail-prints in his hands,
   To set my spirit free;
With wounded feet he trod a path
   To come and sup with me.

He found me poor and brought me gold,
   The fire of love had tried,
And garments whitened by his blood,
   My wretchedness to hide.

The glare of life had dimmed my eyes,
   Its glamour was too bright.
He came with ointment in his hands
   To heal my darkened sight.

He knew my heart was tempest-tossed,
   By care and pain oppressed;
He whispered to my burdened heart,
   Come unto me and rest.

He found me weary, faint and worn,
   On barren mountains cold;
With love's constraint he drew me on,
   To shelter in his fold.

Oh! foolish heart, how slow wert thou
   To welcome thy dear guest,
To change thy weariness and care
   For comfort, peace and rest.

Close to his side, oh! may I stay,
  Just to behold his face,
Till I shall wear within my soul
  The image of his grace.

The grace that changes hearts of stone
  To tenderness and love,
And bids us run with willing feet
  Unto his courts above.

A Story of the Rebellion

The treacherous sands had caught our boat,
  And held it with a strong embrace
And death at our imprisoned crew
  Was sternly looking face to face.

With anxious hearts, but failing strength,
  We strove to push the boat from shore;
But all in vain, for there we lay
  With bated breath and useless oar.

Around us in a fearful storm
  The fiery hail fell thick and fast;
And we engirded by the sand,
  Could not return the dreadful blast.

When one arose upon whose brow
  The ardent sun had left his trace;
A noble purpose strong and high
  Uplighting all his dusky face.

Perchance within that fateful hour
  The wrongs of ages thronged apace;
But with it came the glorious hope
  Of swift deliverance to his race.

Of galling chains asunder rent,
  Of severed hearts again made one,
Of freedom crowning all the land
  Through battles gained and victories won.

"Some one," our hero firmly said,
  "Must die to get us out of this;"

A Story of the Rebellion: Originally published as "Our Hero—A Story of the Rebel-
lion" in the New York *Freeman*, March 7, 1885.

Then leaped upon the strand and bared
  His bosom to the bullets' hiss.

"But ye are soldiers, and can fight,
  May win in battles yet unfought;
I have no offering but my life,
  And if they kill me it is nought."

With steady hands he grasped the boat,
  And boldly pushed it from the shore;
Then fell by rebel bullets pierced,
  His life work grandly, nobly o'er.

Our boat was rescued from the sands
  And launched in safety on the tide;
But he our comrade good and grand,
  In our defence had bravely died.

Burial of Sarah

He stood before the sons of Heth,
  And bowed his sorrowing head;
"I've come," he said, "to buy a place
  Where I may lay my dead.

"I am a stranger in your land,
  My home has lost its light;
Grant me a place where I may lay
  My dead away from sight."

Then tenderly the sons of Heth
  Gazed on the mourner's face,
And said, "Oh, Prince, amid our dead,
  Choose thou her resting-place.

"The sepulchres of those we love,
  We place at thy command;
Against the plea thy grief hath made
  We close not heart nor hand."

The patriarch rose and bowed his head,
  And said, "One place I crave;
'Tis at the end of Ephron's field,
  And called Machpelah's cave.

Burial of Sarah: Based on Genesis 23:7–20.

"Entreat him that he sell to me
  For her last sleep that cave;
I do not ask for her I loved
  The freedom of a grave."

The son of Zohar answered him,
  "Hearken, my lord, to me;
Before our sons, the field and cave
  I freely give to thee."

"I will not take it as a gift,"
  The grand old man then said;
"I pray thee let me buy the place
  Where I may lay my dead."

And with the promise in his heart,
  His seed should own that land,
He gave the shekels for the field
  He took from Ephron's hand.

And saw afar the glorious day
  His chosen seed should tread,
The soil where he in sorrow lay
  His loved and cherished dead.

Going East

She came from the East a fair, young bride,
  With a light and a bounding heart,
To find in the distant West a home
  With her husband to make a start.

He builded his cabin far away,
  Where the prairie flower bloomed wild;
Her love made lighter all his toil,
  And joy and hope around him smiled.

She plied her hands to life's homely tasks,
  And helped to build his fortunes up;
While joy and grief, like bitter and sweet,
  Were mingled and mixed in her cup.

He sowed in his fields of golden grain,
  All the strength of his manly prime;
Nor music of birds, nor brooks, nor bees,
  Was as sweet as the dollar's chime.

She toiled and waited through weary years
    For the fortune that came at length;
But toil and care and hope deferred,
    Had stolen and wasted her strength.

The cabin changed to a stately home,
    Rich carpets were hushing her tread;
But light was fading from her eye,
    And the bloom from her cheek had fled.

Her husband was adding field to field,
    And new wealth to his golden store;
And little thought the shadow of death
    Was entering in at his door.

Slower and heavier grew her step,
    While his gold and his gains increased;
But his proud domain had not the charm
    Of her humble home in the East.

He had no line to sound the depths
    Of her tears repressed and unshed;
Nor dreamed 'mid plenty a human heart
    Could be starving, but not for bread.

Within her eye was a restless light,
    And a yearning that never ceased,
A longing to see the dear old home
    She had left in the distant East.

A longing to clasp her mother's hand,
    And nestle close to her heart,
And to feel the heavy cares of life
    Like the sun-kissed shadows depart.

The hungry heart was stilled at last;
    Its restless, baffled yearning ceased.
A lonely man sat by the bier
    Of a corpse that was going East.

The Hermit's Sacrifice

From Rome's palaces and villas
    Gaily issued forth a throng;
From her humbler habitations
    Moved a human tide along.

Haughty dames and blooming maidens,
  Men who knew not mercy's sway,
Thronged into the Coliseum
  On that Roman holiday.

From the lonely wilds of Asia,
  From her jungles far away,
From the distant torrid regions,
  Rome had gathered beasts of prey.

Lions restless, roaring, rampant,
  Tigers with their stealthy tread,
Leopards bright, and fierce, and fiery,
  Met in conflict wild and dread.

Fierce and fearful was the carnage
  Of the maddened beasts of prey,
As they fought and rent each other
  Urged by men more fierce than they.

Till like muffled thunders breaking
  On a vast and distant shore,
Fainter grew the yells of tigers,
  And the lions' dreadful roar.

On the crimson-stained arena
  Lay the victims of the fight;
Eyes which once had glared with anguish,
  Lost in death their baleful light.

Then uprose the gladiators
  Armed for conflict unto death,
Waiting for the prefect's signal,
  Cold and stern with bated breath.

"Ave Caesar, morituri,
  Te, salutant," rose the cry
From the lips of men ill-fated,
  Doomed to suffer and to die.

Then began the dreadful contest,
  Lives like chaff were thrown away,
Rome with all her pride and power
  Butchered for a holiday.

Eagerly the crowd were waiting,
  Loud the clashing sabres rang,

When between the gladiators
  All unarmed a hermit sprang.

"Cease your bloodshed," cried the hermit,
  "On this carnage place your ban;"
But with flashing swords they answered,
  "Back unto your place, old man."

From their path the gladiators
  Thrust the strange intruder back,
Who between their hosts advancing
  Calmly parried their attack.

All undaunted by their weapons,
  Stood the old heroic man;
While a maddened cry of anger
  Through the vast assembly ran.

"Down with him," cried out the people,
  As with thumbs unbent they glared,
Till the prefect gave the signal
  That his life should not be spared.

Men grew wild with wrathful passion,
  When his fearless words were said
Cruelly they fiercely showered
  Stones on his devoted head.

Bruised and bleeding fell the hermit,
  Victor in that hour of strife;
Gaining in his death a triumph
  That he could not win in life.

Had he uttered on the forum
  Struggling thoughts within him born,
Men had jeered his words as madness,
  But his deed they could not scorn.

Not in vain had been his courage,
  Nor for naught his daring deed;
From his grave his mangled body
  Did for wretched captives plead.

From that hour Rome, grown more thoughtful,
  Ceased her sport in human gore;
And into her Coliseum
  Gladiators came no more.

Songs for the People

Let me make the songs for the people,
  Songs for the old and young;
Songs to stir like a battle-cry
  Wherever they are sung.

Not for the clashing of sabres,
  For carnage nor for strife;
But songs to thrill the hearts of men
  With more abundant life.

Let me make the songs for the weary,
  Amid life's fever and fret,
Till hearts shall relax their tension,
  And careworn brows forget.

Let me sing for little children,
  Before their footsteps stray,
Sweet anthems of love and duty,
  To float o'er life's highway.

I would sing for the poor and aged,
  When shadows dim their sight;
Of the bright and restful mansions,
  Where there shall be no night.

Our world, so worn and weary,
  Needs music, pure and strong,
To hush the jangle and discords
  Of sorrow, pain, and wrong.

Music to soothe all its sorrow,
  Till war and crime shall cease;
And the hearts of men grown tender
  Girdle the world with peace.

Then and Now

"Build me a nation," said the Lord.
The distant nations heard the word,
Build me a nation true and strong,
Bar out the old world's hate and wrong;

Then and Now: This and the next two poems are the final poems in *The Martyr of Alabama and Other Poems* (c. 1895).

For men had traced with blood and tears
The trail of weary wasting years,
And torn and bleeding martyrs trod
Through fire and torture up to God.

While in the hollow of his hand
God hid the secret of our land,
Men warred against their fiercest foes,
And kingdoms fell and empires rose,
Till, weary of the old world strife,
Men sought for broader, freer life,
And plunged into the ocean's foam
To find another, better home.

And, like a vision fair and bright,
The new world broke upon their sight.
Men grasped the prize, grew proud and strong,
And cursed the land with crime and wrong.
The Indian stood despoiled of lands,
The Negro bound with servile bands,
Oppressed through weary years of toil,
His blood and tears bedewed the soil.

Then God arose in dreadful wrath,
And judgment streamed around his path;
His hand the captive's fetters broke,
His lightnings shattered every yoke.
As Israel through the Red sea trod,
Led by the mighty hand of God,
They passed to freedom through a flood,
Whose every wave and surge was blood.

And slavery, with its crime and shame,
Went down in wrath and blood and flame.
The land was billowed o'er with graves
Where men had lived and died as slaves.
Four and thirty years—what change since then!
Beings once chattles now are men;
Over the gloom of slavery's night,
Has flashed the dawn of freedom's light.

To-day no mother with anguish wild
Kneels and implores that her darling child
Shall not be torn from her bleeding heart,
With its quivering tendrils rent apart.

The father may soothe his child to sleep,
And watch his slumbers calm and deep.
No tyrant's tread will disturb his rest
Where freedom dwells as a welcome guest.

His walls may be bare of pictured grace,
His fireside the lowliest place;
But the wife and children sheltered there
Are his to defend and guard with care.
Where haughty tyrants once bore rule
Are ballot-box and public school.
The old slave-pen of former days
Gives place to fanes of prayer and praise.

To-night we would bring our meed of praise
To noble friends of darker days;
The men and women crowned with light,
The true, and tried in our gloomy night.
To Lundy, whose heart was early stirred
To speak for freedom an earnest word;
To Garrison, valiant, true and strong,
Whose face was as flint against our wrong.

And Phillips, the peerless, grand and brave,
A tower of strength to the outcast slave.
Earth has no marble too pure and white
To enrol his name in golden light.
Our Douglass, too, with his massive brain,
Who plead our cause with his broken chain,
And helped to hurl from his bloody seat
The curse that writhed and died at his feet.

And Governor Andrew, who, looking back,
Saw none he despised, though poor and black;
And Harriet Beecher, whose glowing pen
Corroded the chains of fettered men.
To-night with greenest laurels we'll crown
North Elba's grave where sleeps John Brown,
Who made the gallows an altar high,
And showed how a brave old man could die.

And Lincoln, our martyred President,
Who returned to his God with chains he had rent.
And Sumner, amid death's icy chill,
Leaving to Hoar his Civil Rights Bill.

And let us remember old underground,
With all her passengers northward bound,
The train that ran till it ceased to pay,
With all her dividends given away.

Nor let it be said that we have forgot
The women who stood with Lucretia Mott;
Nor her who to the world was known
By the simple name of Lucy Stone.
A tribute unto a host of others
Who knew that men though black were brothers,
Who battled against our nation's sin,
Whose graves are thick whose ranks are thin.

Oh, people chastened in the fire,
To nobler, grander things aspire;
In the new era of your life,
Bring love for hate, and peace for strife;
Upon your hearts this vow record
That ye will build unto the Lord
A nobler future, true and grand,
To strengthen, crown and bless the land.

A higher freedom ye may gain
Than that which comes from a riven chain;
Freedom your native land to bless,
With peace, and love and righteousness,
As dreams that are past, a tale all told,
Are the days when men were bought and sold;
Now God be praised from sea to sea,
Our flag floats o'er a country free.

Maceo

Maceo dead! a thrill of sorrow
   Through our hearts in sadness ran
When we felt in one sad hour
   That the world had lost a man.

He had clasped unto his bosom
   The sad fortunes of his land—
Held the cause for which he perished
   With a firm, unfaltering hand.

On his lips the name of freedom
  Fainted with his latest breath.
Cuba Libre was his watchword
  Passing through the gates of death.

With the light of God around us,
  Why this agony and strife?
With the cross of Christ before us,
  Why this fearful waste of life?

Must the pathway unto freedom
  Ever mark a crimson line,
And the eyes of wayward mortals
  Always close to light divine?

Must the hearts of fearless valor
  Fail 'mid crime and cruel wrong,
When the world has read of heroes
  Brave and earnest, true and strong?

Men to stay the floods of sorrow
  Sweeping round each war-crushed heart;
Men to say to strife and carnage—
  From our world henceforth depart.

God of peace and God of nations,
  Haste! oh, haste the glorious day
When the reign of our Redeemer
  O'er the world shall have its sway.

When the swords now blood encrusted,
  Spears that reap the battle field,
Shall be changed to higher service,
  Helping earth rich harvests yield.

Where the widow weeps in anguish,
  And the orphan bows his head,
Grant that peace and joy and gladness
  May like holy angels tread.

Pity, oh, our God the sorrow
  Of thy world from thee astray,
Lead us from the paths of madness
  Unto Christ the living way.

Year by year the world grows weary
  'Neath its weight of sin and strife,

Though the hands once pierced and bleeding
  Offer more abundant life.

May the choral song of angels
  Heard upon Judea's plain
Sound throughout the earth the tidings
  Of that old and sweet refrain.

Till our world, so sad and weary,
  Finds the balmy rest of peace—
Peace to silence all her discords—
  Peace till war and crime shall cease.

Peace to fall like gentle showers,
  Or on parchéd flowers dew,
Till our hearts proclaim with gladness:
  Lo, He maketh all things new.

Only a Word

Only a word—a little word,
  Tender and kind and true,
A fainting heart may drink it in
  As flowers absorb the dew.

Only a word—a faithful word,
  Feet that had gone astray
May be turned from a downward trend
  To Christ, the living way.

Only a word—a loving word,
  Sown 'mid prayers and tears,
May bloom in time, and fruitage bear
  Throughout the eternal years.

Let There Be Light

"Let there be light," a joyous thrill
  Ran through the dark, chaotic earth;
Throughout the vast, wide universe
  Each star and planet leaped to build.

  Only a Word: As it appeared in Harper's essay "True and False Politeness," *African Methodist Episcopal Church Review* 14 (April 1898):343.

  Let There Be Light: *Christian Recorder*, October 7, 1897.

Let there be light, and darkness fled
  Into the silent cave of gloom
And o'er his path fair flowers sprang
  Fragrant and lovely in their bloom.

The fair, young earth from chaos rose,
  Without a shadow or alloy,
While angels gazed with glad surprise,
  And hailed the new born earth with joy.

Then glit'ring dews and sunshine wove
  Her garments with resplendent dyes,
Within whose meshes lay the light
  Of lovely dawn and sunset skies.

And Earth so beautiful and bright
  Was flushed and filled with joyous life,
The soft air breathing all around
  Had not one tone of care or strife.

And man, the eldest born of time,
  Stood monarch of the world so fair,
And peace and joy reigned thro the earth
  And love and light were everywhere.

But 'mid her fair, enchanting scenes
  An awful presence entered in
And shuddering angels bowed their heads
  And called the dreadful presence "Sin."

And o'er the earth he cast a trial
  That mingled all its light with gloom,
It deepened as he onward trod—
  It was the shadow of a tomb.

A shade that spread o'er all the earth,
  With which she had no power to cope,
Until a white-winged angel laid
  Upon her breast the balm of hope.

Another came with tender love,
  A sun-crowned, pure and lovely wrath,
He cheered the fainting heart of earth
  And calmly whispered, "I am faith."

And one transcending all the rest
  With eyes of light and heart of flame,

Bent o'er the sorrow-stricken earth
   And "Love," the angels called her name.

Our earth would be a wilderness,
   And life a weary, wasting wild,
If 'mid our sorrow and our gloom
   The love of God had never smiled.

If hope and faith had never made
   Upon earth a dwelling place,
And God upon our longing eyes
   Had never yet unveiled his face.

Where streams the restless sea of sin
   With care and pain and anguish rife,
Shall flow the ocean of God's love,
   In waves of everlasting life.

Till grace shall triumph over sin
   And man shall cease to fail and fall;
When Christ shall in His Kingdom reign,
   And God himself be all in all.

Give My Love to the World

Dying Words of John G. Whittier

The world was fading from his view,
   The world so fair and bright,
The shadows of the mystic vale
   Were fading from his sight.

The chill of death was on his brow,
   Its pallor on his cheek,
And tenderly we bent to hear
   The dying poet speak.

We saw upon his death paled lips
   A gentle tremor stir,
And paused with loving eagerness
   His latest words to hear.

In evil days when men could boast
   That Cotton was their king,

Give My Love to the World: Christian Recorder, January 13, 1898.

His word, against the nation's crime,
　Had no uncertain ring.

To men who plead for outcast slaves,
　He brought the gift of song,
And lived to see in blood and tears,
　Go down the nation's wrong.

He lived to hear the joyous songs
　Of men made newly free,
And join with them to celebrate
　The nation's jubilee.

Upon the lips that breathed sweet songs
　Or strong invectives hurled,
Painted the precious dying words
　"My love to all the world."

Oh faithful friend, thy gracious words,
　"Of sweetness and of light,"
Shall teach us 'mid life's darksome hours
　To make the world more bright.

Down through the corridors of time
　And on the scrolls of fame
Shall float the music of thy songs
　The lustre of thy name.

Oh may thy last and gracious words
　Our hearts inspire and nerve
To make the motto of our lives
　'Tis ours to love and serve.

Proclaim a Fast

Proclaim a fast, a solemn fast,
　From snow clad hills to sunny lands,
Till Ethiopia shall arise
　And stretch to God her bleeding hands.

Though days be dark and courage faint,
　And justice lies distraught, o'erthrown,
Remember in the darkest hour,
　That God is still upon his throne.

Proclaim a Fast: The Richmond *Planet*, December 17, 1898.

Our prostrate race in darksome days,
    Groped through oppression's gloomy night,
Until their feeble hands grew strong
    To grasp God's robe of love and light.

And He who led his ancient flock
    In triumph through the parted sea,
Shattered and rent their galling chains
    And set his captive people free.

Say not that hope and faith are myths
    And prayer is but a useless breath,
Though evil seems to thrive and grow,
    Its end is sorrow, shame and death.

Ye men who strode up San Juan's hill,
    And tramped our streets with martial tread.
Go veil your arms with heavy crepe
    And mourn above our murdered dead.

Boast not of victories proudly won,
    In distant climes, and far off shores,
When law lies trampled in your midst,
    And men are murdered at your doors.

Shall veterans of a former strife
    Who counted not their lives too dear
Be harried, hunted from their homes
    And crouched in agony and fear?

Shall they who helped in former days
    To check and turn the battle tide
Be cast aside as worthless chaff,
    And trampled down by scorn and pride?

Shall suffering Cuba find relief
    From tender hearts and outstretched hands,
While hapless men and women slain,
    With blood bedew our fairest lands?

Trust not in rulers to avenge
    Your wrongs when victims bite the dust
But ease your burden on the Lord
    And in his love and mercy trust.

O injured race stand in thy lot
    United, faithful, true and strong,

Assured that in the darkest hour
  Our God can never side with wrong.

The man who sides with God and truth
  Can never, never stand alone,
His cause is linked by God's own hand
  To chords that vibrate round His throne.

Help us, oh God, to look within,
  Our sins and follies to deplore,
And from the pride and hate of man,
  Hide us oh Lord! forevermore.

The Vision of the Czar of Russia

To the Czar of all the Russia's
  Came a vision bright and fair,
The joy of unburdened millions,
  Floating gladly on the air.

The laughter and songs of children,
  Of maidens, so gay and bright,
Of mothers who never would tremble,
  Where warfare and carnage blight.

Instead of the tramp of armies,
  Was patter of little feet;
The blare of bugles and trumpets,
  Had melted in music sweet.

The harvests had ceased to ripen,
  On fields that were drenched with blood;
The seas no more were ensanguined
  With an awful crimson flood.

The peaceful pavements no longer
  Re-echoed the martial tread;
And over the ransomed nations
  The banner of love was spread.

The streams tripped lightly seaward,
  Unfreighted with human gore;
The valleys and hills were brightened,
  And shuddered with strife no more.

The Vision of the Czar of Russia: African Methodist Episcopal Church Review 16 (1899):140–1.

There were homes where peace and plenty
  Around happy hearths did smile;
And the touch of baby fingers,
  Could sorrow and care beguile.

The cannon had ceased its bristling,
  Its mission of death was o'er;
And the world so weary of carnage,
  Learned the art of war was no more.

And Earth, once so sorrow laden,
  Grew daily more fair and bright;
Till peace our globe had enfolded,
  And millions walked in its light.

'Twas a bright and beautiful vision,
  Of nations disarmed and free;
As to heaven arose the chorus
  Of the world's first jubilee.

How long shall the vision tarry?
  How long shall the hours delay,
Till war shrinks our saddened Earth,
  As the darkness shrinks from day?

Till barracks shall change to churches,
  The prison become a school;
And over the hearts and homes of men,
  The peace of our God shall rule?

And Earth, like a barque, storm riven,
  The sport of tempest and tide;
Shall find rest and a haven,
  The heart of the Crucified.

"How Are the Mighty Fallen?"

"I'll be a lady forever,"
  Said Babylon in her pride;
But God held the scales of justice,
  And against her he did decide.

"I will rule," said Xerxes, "the mighty,"
  The Hellespont at his feet;

"How Are the Mighty Fallen?": Christian Recorder, February 21, 1899.

But the storm arose in its fury
  And scattered and rent his fleet.

Bright and beautiful and sparkling,
  Stood Greece 'mid her own fair lands;
But the Roman snatched the sceptre
  From her pale and trembling hands

Israel, to whom was given
  The law as a sacred trust,
Forgetting her holy mission,
  Captive, has mourned in the dust.

Jerusalem, gray-haired and smitten,
  A wanderer to a[n]d fro ,
Has drained with her quivering lips
  The bitter chalice of woe.

Rome in the pride of her power,
  Ruled o'er nations, small and great;
Till her sins had gained momentum,
  And dragged her down with their weight.

"I will bind you with heavy fetters,"
  Said the New World to the slave;
But justice rose and slavery sleeps
  In a dark, dishonored grave.

The shores of Time are strewed with wrecks,
  Where armies in might o[n]ce trod:
Till their shields and swords were broken
  By the armament of God.

O'er the tombs of fallen nations,
  Of kingdoms made desolate,
Is written, in light, the sentence;
  Only God himself is great.

The Lake City Tragedy

The shadow of an awful crime
  On Carolina rests,
That well might whiten mothers' cheeks
  With babes upon their breasts.

The Lake City Tragedy: Peacemaker and Court of Arbitration 18 (1899):199.

And draw from eyes, unused to weep,
  Hot tears of burning shame;
For reckless men with cruel hands,
  With blood have blurred her name.

They came, but not as brave men come,
  To meet an equal foe;
But veiled in darkness, struck the weak,
  Who bore, as Christ, the blow.

The fiery breath of kindled flames,
  Around a dwelling rose;
And suddenly a father faced
  A band of cruel foes.

The trembling mother clasped in vain
  Her babe, whose innocence
And weakness, should have been a shield;
  Its feebleness, defense.

Affrighted girls in terror rose
  And fled, in wild dismay;
While o'er their path a fiery hail,
  With blood drops marked their way.

Behind them were the crackling flames,
  Before them rifled men
Who harried them, as savages
  Might raid a tigers' den.

That home, where laughing children played,
  Was made a dreary wild;
Within its smouldering ruins lay
  The father and his child.

Ah! had that father pitched his tent
  Where deadly serpents lay,
Would not a rattle or a hiss,
  Have warned his feet away?

But when he dwelt where churches rose,
  And women knelt to pray,
Justice had fainted in the streets,
  And mercy turned away.

Oh mournful mother on whose heart,
  Rough, brutal feet have trod;

Reach out thy wounded bleeding hand
   And gather strength from God.

Oh! Carolina, disavow
   This blot upon thy name;
 And brand this brutal cowardice,
   With everlasting shame.

And teach thy sons, who ne'er should trail
   Their manhood in the dust;
'Tis gracious to be merciful,
   And noble to be just.

Though judgment seems to slumber long
   And evil thrive and grow,
The hands that sow the seeds of crime
   Must reap the crops of woe.

An Appeal to My Countrywomen

You can sigh o'er the sad-eyed Armenian
   Who weeps in her desolate home.
You can mourn o'er the exile of Russia
   From kindred and friends doomed to roam.

You can pity the men who have woven
   From passion and appetite chains
To coil with a terrible tension
   Around their heartstrings and brains.

You can sorrow o'er little children
   Disinherited from their birth,
The wee waifs and toddlers neglected,
   Robbed of sunshine, music and mirth.

For beasts you have gentle compassion;
   Your mercy and pity they share.
For the wretched, outcast and fallen
   You have tenderness, love and care.

But hark! from our Southland are floating
   Sobs of anguish, murmurs of pain,

An Appeal to My Countrywomen: This and the next three poems (pages 385–390) are reprinted from Poems (1900).

And women heart-stricken are weeping
   Over their tortured and their slain.

On their brows the sun has left traces;
   Shrink not from their sorrow in scorn.
When they entered the threshold of being
   The children of a King were born.

Each comes as a guest to the table
   The hand of our God has outspread,
To fountains that ever leap upward,
   To share in the soil we all tread.

When ye plead for the wrecked and fallen,
   The exile from far-distant shores,
Remember that men are still wasting
   Life's crimson around your own doors.

Have ye not, oh, my favored sisters,
   Just a plea, a prayer or a tear,
For mothers who dwell 'neath the shadows
   Of agony, hatred and fear?

Men may tread down the poor and lowly,
   May crush them in anger and hate,
But surely the mills of God's justice
   Will grind out the grist of their fate.

Oh, people sin-laden and guilty,
   So lusty and proud in your prime,
The sharp sickles of God's retribution
   Will gather your harvest of crime.

Weep not, oh my well-sheltered sisters,
   Weep not for the Negro alone,
But weep for your sons who must gather
   The crops which their fathers have sown.

Go read on the tombstones of nations
   Of chieftains who masterful trod,
The sentence which time has engraven,
   That they had forgotten their God.

'Tis the judgment of God that men reap
   The tares which in madness they sow,
Sorrow follows the footsteps of crime,
   And Sin is the consort of Woe.

The Lost Bells

Year after year the artist wrought
  With earnest, loving care,
The music flooding all his soul
  To pour upon the air.

For this no metal was too rare,
  He counted not the cost;
Nor deemed the years in which he toiled
  As labor vainly lost.

When morning flushed with crimson light
  The golden gates of day,
He longed to fill the air with chimes
  Sweet as a matin's lay.

And when the sun was sinking low
  Within the distant West,
He gladly heard the bells he wrought
  Herald the hour of rest.

The music of a thousand harps
  Could never be so dear
As when those solemn chants and thrills
  Fell on his list'ning ear.

He poured his soul into their chimes,
  And felt his toil repaid;
He called them children of his soul,
  His home a'near them made.

But evil days came on apace,
  War spread his banner wide,
And from his village snatched away
  The artist's love and pride.

At dewy morn and stilly eve
  The chimes no more he heard;
With dull and restless agony
  His spirit's depths was stirred.

A weary longing filled his soul,
  It bound him like a spell;
He left his home to seek the chimes—
  The chimes he loved so well.

Where lofty fanes in grandeur rose,
  Upon his ear there fell
No music like the long lost chimes
  Of his beloved bell.

And thus he wandered year by year,
  Touched by the hand of time,
Seeking to hear with anxious heart
  Each well remembered chime.

And to that worn and weary heart
  There came a glad surcease:
He heard again the dear old chimes,
  And smiled and uttered peace.

"The chimes! the chimes!" the old man cried,
  "I hear their tones at last;"
A sudden rapture filled his heart,
  And all his cares were past.

Yes, peace had come with death's sweet calm,
  His journeying was o'er,
The weary, restless wanderer
  Had reached the restful shore.

It may be that he met again,
  Enfolded in the air,
The dear old chimes beside the gates
  Where all is bright and fair;

That he who crossed and bowed his head
  When Angelus was sung
In clearer light touched golden harps
  By angel fingers strung.

"Do Not Cheer, Men Are Dying," Said Capt. Phillips, in the Spanish-American War

Do not cheer, for men are dying
  From their distant homes in pain;
And the restless sea is darkened
  By a flood of crimson rain.

Do Not Cheer, Men Are Dying . . . : Also appeared in the Richmond *Planet*, December 3, 1898. A notation indicates that it was reprinted from the *Christian Recorder*.

Do not cheer, for anxious mothers
  Wait and watch in lonely dread;
Vainly waiting for the footsteps
  Never more their paths to tread.

Do not cheer, while little children
  Gather round the widowed wife,
Wondering why an unknown people
  Sought their own dear father's life.

Do not cheer, for aged fathers
  Bend above their staves and weep,
While the ocean sings the requiem
  Where their fallen children sleep.

Do not cheer, for lips are paling
  On which lay the mother's kiss;
'Mid the dreadful roar of battle
  How that mother's hand they miss!

Do not cheer: once joyous maidens,
  Who the mazy dance did tread,
Bow their heads in bitter anguish,
  Mourning o'er their cherished dead.

Do not cheer while maid and matron
  In this strife must bear a part;
While the blow that strikes a soldier
  Reaches to some woman's heart.

Do not cheer till arbitration
  O'er the nations holds its sway,
And the century now closing
  Ushers in a brighter day.

Do not cheer until the nation
  Shall more wise and thoughtful grow
Than to staunch a stream of sorrow
  By an avalanche of woe.

Do not cheer until each nation
  Sheathes the sword and blunts the spear,
And we sing aloud for gladness:
  Lo, the reign of Christ is here,

And the banners of destruction
  From the battlefield are furled,

And the peace of God descending
  Rests upon a restless world.

The Burdens of All

We may sigh o'er the heavy burdens
  Of the black, the brown and white;
But if we all clasped hands together
  The burdens would be more light.
How to solve life's saddest problems,
  Its weariness, want and woe,
Was answered by One who suffered
  In Palestine long ago.

He gave from his heart this precept,
  To ease the burdens of men,
"As ye would that others do to you
  Do ye even so to them."
Life's heavy, wearisome burdens
  Will change to a gracious trust
When men shall learn in the light of God
  To be merciful and just.

Where war has sharpened his weapons,
  And slavery masterful had,
Let white and black and brown unite
  To build the kingdom of God.
And never attempt in madness
  To build a kingdom or state,
Through greed of gold or lust of power,
  On the crumbling stones of hate.

The burdens will always be heavy,
  The sunshine fade into night,
Till mercy and justice shall cement
  The black, the brown and the white.
And earth shall answer with gladness,
  The herald angel's refrain,
When "Peace on earth, good will to men"
  Was the burden of their strain.

Behold the Lilies!

Behold the lilies of the field

Behold the Lilies!: African Methodist Episcopal Church Review 16 (1900):468.

How beautiful and fair;
Their fragrance as a breath of heaven
  Refreshes all the air.

No sordid labors bow them down,
  Nor dull depressing care;
They only tell of God's great love,
  And that is everywhere.

The wings of morning are too slow
  To bear us from His sight;
The midnight has no shadows deep
  To hide from us His light.

If not a sparrow falls to earth
  Unnoticed by His eye,
Will He, our Father and our Friend
  Unheeded pass us by?

Shall we not learn from fading flowers—
  Frail children of the dust—
To lay our cares before His throne,
  And in His mercy trust?

There's not a care that weights us down,
  No blinding tears that fall,
Nor sorrow piercing to the heart
  But he beholds them all;

And offers us with tender love,
  Mid dangers and alarms,
A refuge for our souls within
  His everlasting arms.

Words for the Hour

Others shall sing the song,
Others shall right the wrong;
Finish what I begin
All that I fail of win,
What matters it I or they,
Mine or another's day
So the right word be said
And life be sweeter made.

Words for the Hour: Christian Recorder, September 18, 1902. A footnote reads as follows: "Respectfully dedicated to the Association for Colored Youth, Atlantic City."

Ring bells, unreared steepless
The joy of unborn peoples
To trumpets far off blown
Your triumphs are my own.

These are the words of John G.
Whittier, our bard of freedom, who
in passing from us left to the world
his legacy of love:

"MY LOVE TO THE WORLD"

He heard the chant of unseen lips
  All vocalized with praise,
As 'round him flowed the joyous light
  Of better, brighter days

The time when men should requiem sing
  O'er slavery, war and crime,
The days whose light was streaming round
  The slopes of coming time.

What matters if his death paled lips
  Should never join the song
Of fresh young hearts triumphant o'er
  The overthrow of wrong.

He felt that other hands would reap
  The harvests he had sown;
The laurels that he could not grasp
  He knew would be his own.

In darker days when he beheld
  His country's shame and wrong,
He on the nation's altar laid
  The glorious gift of song. ·

So freedom true he lived to see
  The strife of battle cease,
As o'er the gloomy storm rent sky
  Was arched the bow of peace[.]

Oh, men with freedom newly dowerd,
  How precious is the trust
That came to your unfettered hands
  When slavery bit the dust.

While others strive for wealth and fame,

For broad dominions plan,
Be yours to teach all the world
  The brotherhood of man.

As shadows flee before the dawn,
  As days succeed to night
Bid ignorance and crime give place
  To freedom, love and light.

Till peace shall build anew the wastes
  By war made desolate,
And brighter days shall gladden earth
  And love shall conquer hate[.]

Oh, youth and maidens of the land
  Rise up with one accord
And in the name of Christ go forth
  To battle for the Lord.

'Tis yours to guard with faithful care
  The citadel of Truth,
And on your country's altar lay
  The heritage of youth.

This is no time for careless ease,
  No time for idle sleep.
O'er freedom's high and sacred trust
  Eternal vigils keep.

Go forth, but not to crimson fields
  With fratricidal strife,
But in the name of Christ go forth
  For justice, peace and life.

Go forth to follow in His steps
  Who came not to destroy,
'Till masses shall blossom as the rose
  And deserts sing for joy.

The grandest men who've trodden earth
  'Mid sorrow, pain and wrong,
By lofty faith have taught us how
  To suffer and be strong.

Armored by hope, by faith and love,
  Oh, strive with glad accord
Until earth's kingdoms shall become

The kingdoms of our Lord.

Respectfully Dedicated to Dr. Alexander Crummell on the Fiftieth Anniversary of His Pastorate

The man who puts his armor on
  May feel a strange delight,
But not like him who puts it off
  A victor from the fight;

Around whose path a thousand foes
  For triumph did contend,
While he his banner held aloft
  Courageous to the end.

In five decades thy field was wide
  To scatter love and light;
To war with error, sin, and crime
  And make the world more bright.

What matter if around thy way
  Were dangers dark and rife,
Before thee was the promised rest
  And everlasting life.

Around thee were the stumbling feet
  Of men so wont to stray,
'Twas thine to show the wanderers
  The new and living way.

Impetuous youth from thee did need
  Restraining words of love,
And lonely age a guiding hand
  To fairer worlds above.

It may be oft thy heart grew faint
  When unexpected foes—
Strangers unto thy soul's intent—
  Thy pathway did oppose.

Respectfully Dedicated . . .: December 1894. Frances E. Watkins Harper Collection, Miscellaneous American Letters and Papers, Schomburg Center for Research in Black Culture, the New York Public Library, Astor, Lenox and Tilden Foundations.

If thoughtless lips and careless deeds
  Have made thy spirit grieve,
How precious are the gracious words
  "He chastens to receive."

May God our Father lead thee on
  Through sunshine and through shade
Unto the land of crystal founts
  Whose flowers never fade.

Among that pure and holy throng
  Who never shed a tear
May many greet thee with the words
  " 'Tis He who led us here."

And more than all may He whose eyes
  Are like a fiery flame,
Pronounce thy welcome in his courts
  And give thee a new name.

May all thy future days be blessed
  Till life itself shall cease,
And angels welcome thee above
  To never ending peace.

Essay

◆

From the age of sixty-eight until the end of her life, Frances Harper's public appearances were less frequent, but she remained active in the kinds of causes that characterize her life. In 1896, she was one of the founders of the National Association of Colored Women, and as late as 1899, she addressed that assembly on the subject of "Racial Literature." Harper's essays regularly appeared in the *African Methodist Episcopal Church Review*. Though she continued to speak with authority on political and moral issues, in "True and False Politeness" Harper takes on more subtle but divisive subjects of class snobbery and hypocrisy.

"True and False Politeness" is one of the last pieces Harper published. In this essay, Harper continues to instruct her readers through examples from biblical and contemporary times of the difference between the appearance of good and good itself. Here, more so than in other works, she emphasizes the spiritual needs and the ability of every person to speak and to comfort. As in her very earliest writings, Harper reminds her readers that material comforts and intellectual achievements do not assuage "Our Greatest Want."

◆

True and False Politeness

There is a vast and vital difference between true and false politeness. One is the child of the cultured heart, the other is the offspring of the devis-

True and False Politeness: African Methodist Episcopal Church Review 14 (1898):339–45.

ing brain. One springs from the kindly impulses of the heart, the other from the devices of the intellect. True politeness is to social life what oil is to machinery, a thing to oil the ruts and grooves of existence. False politeness can shine without warming and glitter without vivifying. It may conform to all the ceremonies and forms of etiquette without inspiring a lofty purpose, kindling an earnest aspiration, or cheering a fainting heart. It has been used to cover the barest purposes, and subserve the most unworthy ends. With words of courtesy upon her lips, and offer of kindness in her hand, Jael invites Sisera into her tent, pretends protection to her retreating guest, and then, false to the claims of hospitality, dooms her unsuspecting victim to death by driving a nail into his head. Ehud, professing to bring a message from God to Eglon, takes advantage of his confidence, and cruelly deprives him of life. With words of peace upon his lips and treachery in his heart, Joab salutes Abner, and then smites him under the fifth rib; and yet there may have been no lack of oriental courtesy in these breaches of hospitality, no harsh nor bitter words to awaken fear, or arouse suspicion. The courtesy which takes advantage of the unsuspecting may plead the exigencies of war, but it richly deserves to be ranked under the head of false politeness. A politeness which finds its counterpart in the words of Ward McAllister when he said, "The highest cultivation of social manners enables a man to conceal from the world his real feelings. He can go through any annoyance as if it were a pleasure, go to a rival's house as to a dear friend's, smile and smile, and murder while he smiles,"—could any social club or fashionable circle adopt such sentiments without weakening its mental fibre or dimming its moral perception?

From these dark pages we will turn to fairer ones in the annals of time. Very charming is the picture of true politeness as shown in the story of the settlement of a land question between Abraham and Lot, in which the uncle, instead of pressing pre-emption of claim, or priority of years, gives his nephew the right of choice, by saying, "Let there be no strife between me and thee, between my herdmen and thine, for we be breth[r]en. . . . Separate thyself I pray thee from me. If thou wilt take the right, I will go to the left." Was ever compromise more manly, concession more gracious, or politeness more generous? The grand old man who bowed before the sons of Heth, but would not accept from them the freedom of a grave, nor take anything from the King of Sodom, from a thread to a shoe latchet, could blunt the edge of a refusal, as well as entertain heaven-sent messengers.

Writers may elaborate their finest systems of manners and behavior, but we do not need to go any further than the New Testament for the purest code of morals, and the best rules of true politeness. Honor all men, be pitiful, be courteous. "Whatsoever ye would that men should do to you, do ye even so to them," and God has shown me that I should call no man unclean. These injunctions received into the life of our modern civilization and fully permeating its character, would change the moral aspect of the present age. If all the wealthy and influential honored all men as the Bible teaches, would they ever throw their lives between God's sunshine and the shivering poor, and fence in leagues of land by bonds and claims and title deeds; when land and water, air and light are God's own gifts and heritage to man? Should they not remember that the humblest and poorest human being who enters the threshold of life, comes as the child of a King, and should be treated as the child of a King, and at the feast of life be received as the guest of the living God? Would not the vision of Christians grow clearer to see, beneath the darkened skin and shaded countenance, poverty of condition, or the dust and grime of labor, the human soul all written over with the handmarks of Divinity, and the common claims of humanity?

While false politeness may see no necessity to wear her blandest smiles or display her most charming manners outside of her own little coterie or social set, true politeness has a mission everywhere; whether it be where labor faints beneath her burden, or moral cripples tread on velvet carpets. The best test of true politeness is not seen in the deference men pay to their superiors, or to the social amenities they bestow upon their equals, but in the Christian courtesy they dispense to their supposed inferiors. Horace Mann gave us an exquisite idea of true politeness when he said, "I will not boast of my superior eyesight before the blind. I will moderate my steps before the lame." Worthy to be written in letters of gold, are the words of Governor Andrew, who knew not what record of sin would await him in the eternities, but it would not be that he had ever despised a man because he was poor or black.

The truly polite woman has no snub in her voice nor scorn upon her lips for those who occupy a lower social grade than herself. Nor will she thoughtlessly and carelessly shut the door of opportunity in the face of any one who is striving to rise in the scale of character, and build, over a sad past, more stately temples of thought and action. True politeness is consistent with perfect sincerity. If we are true to ourselves, we cannot be false to others. "I will tell this story," said a person in the presence of General Grant, "as there are no ladies present." "But," replied the general, "there are gentlemen here." The man who could crush down defeat and organize victories had the manly politeness to guard the ears of others from being assaulted by unbecoming words.

True politeness is the social currency of every day life. False politeness is a counterfeit coin with its brassy ring on the counters of existence. One improves the heart; the other enervates the soul. There is one place among, if not above, all others where true politeness has a mission, and a ministry of love. It is in the church of God. If men and women have a religion of divine assurance, should not a welcome beam in their eyes and quiver on their lips for every stranger who comes to join them in their worship of God, and the adoration of a divine Saviour? The worship of a Christian church should not be regarded as an exclusive luxury for the pew-holder and a tardy charity for the new-comer. God knows all the sunshine and shadows which rest on the hearts of those who enter the different churches in our land. Some may come harassed by doubts and distracted by fears, and seeking rest and finding none. A stricken heart may be aching beneath magnificent attire. A human heart may be starving, not for bread, but for heart support and Christly sympathy. A warm pressure of the hand, a word fitly spoken, may seem to the giver a little thing, but to the receiver it may be as a well, springing up in the desert dust.

> "Only a word—a little word,
>   Tender and kind and true,
> A fainting heart may drink it in
>   As flowers absorb the dew.
>
> Only a word—a faithful word,
>   Feet that had gone astray
> May be turned from a downward trend
>   To Christ, the living way.
>
> Only a word—a loving word,
>   Sown 'mid prayers and tears,
> May bloom in time, and fruitage bear,
>   Throughout the eternal years."

Persons too ignorant to read a single sentence may be learned enough in heart-love to translate the language of an eye that beams with sympathy, or a countenance that glows with compassion. After the outbreak of the rebellion, when the school was taking the place of the slave-pen, a number of my acquaintances went South as teachers. Among them was a plain looking woman with a limited education, and a young woman from the culture of a New England school. One seemed to possess the warmer heart, the other the riper intellect. Both from their standpoints may have done the best they knew. I have heard of some of those people to whom they ministered saying of the younger woman who attempted to advise them: "God knows she ain't white, but she puts on mighty white airs." But of the other teacher: "She is low down, but she feels for we."

False politeness can cast a glamour over fashionable follies and popular vices and shrink from uttering unpalatable truths, when truth is needed more than flattery. True politeness, tender as love and faithful as truth, values intrinsic worth more than artificial surroundings. It will stem the current of the world's disfavor, rather than float ignobly on the tide of popular favor, with the implied disrespect to our common human nature, that it is a flaccid thing to be won by sophistry, and satisfied with shams.

False politeness is an outgrowth from the surface of life. True politeness is the fair outflowing of a kind and thoughtful life, the sweet ripe fruit of a religion which gives to life its best expression and to humanity its crowning glory. True politeness is broadly inclusive; false politeness narrowly exclusive. It was with a clarified vision the apostle uttered the words: "And God has shown me that I shall call no man common or unclean." True politeness has no scornful epithets for classes or races, who, if not organically inferior, have been born under, or environed by inferior conditions. Humanity is God's child, and to fail in true kindness and respect to the least of His "little ones" is to fail in allegiance to Him. Contemptuous injustice to man is treason to God, and one of the worst forms of infidelity is to praise Christ with our lips and trample on the least of His brethren with our feet,—to talk sweetly of His love, and embitter the lives of others by cold contempt, and cruel scorn. Beyond the narrow limitations of social lines are humanity's broader interests, which true politeness may subserve with tender love and gentle graciousness. If to-day you believe that your faith is simple and vision clearer than that of other forms of belief, should not the clasp of your hand be warmer, the earnestness of your soul greater, and the throbbings of your heart quicker to clasp the world in your arms and bring it nearer to the great heart of God and His Son, Our Lord Jesus Christ?

Appendix
Contents of Frances E. W. Harper's Books

◆

This directory includes the earliest extant editions of Harper's published books, as well as editions whose contents have been significantly revised by the addition, deletion, or rearrangement of material. See section 3 of the Introduction and headnotes to individual volumes for discussion of Harper's complex publishing history.

◆

Poems on Miscellaneous Subjects

(Boston: J. B. Yerrinton & Son, 1854)

Poems

The Syrophenician Woman
The Slave Mother
Bible Defence of Slavery
Eliza Harris
Ethiopia
The Drunkard's Child
The Slave Auction
The Revel
That Blessed Hope
The Dying Christian
Report
Advice to the Girls
Saved by Faith

Died of Starvation
A Mother's Heroism
The Fugitive's Wife
The Contrast
The Prodigal's Return
Eva's Farewell

Prose

Christianity
The Bible
The Colored People of America

Poems on Miscellaneous Subjects

(Philadelphia: Merrihew & Thompson, Printers, 1857)

Poems

The Syrophencian Woman
The Slave Mother
Bible Defence of Slavery
Eliza Harris
Ethiopia
The Drunkard's Child
The Slave Auction
The Revel
That Blessed Hope
The Dying Christian
Report
Advice to the Girls
Saved by Faith
Died of Starvation
A Mother's Heroism
The Fugitive's Wife
The Contrast
The Prodigal's Return
Eva's Farewell
The Tennessee Hero
Free Labor
Lines
The Dismissal of Tyng
The Slave Mother (A Tale of the Ohio)
Rizpah, the Daughter of Ai
Ruth and Naomi

Prose

Christianity
The Colored People of America
Breathing the Air of Freedom

Moses: A Story of the Nile, 2d ed.

(Philadelphia: Merrihew & Son, Printers, 1869)

Poem

Moses: A Story of the Nile

Prose

The Mission of the Flowers

Poems

(Philadelphia: Merrihew & Thompson, Printers, 1857)

Poems

Lines to Hon. Thaddeus Stevens
An Appeal to the American People
Truth
Death of the Old Sea King
"Let the Light Enter!"
Youth in Heaven
Death of Zombi, the Chief of a Negro Kingdom in South America
Lines to Charles Sumner
"Sir, We Would See Jesus"
The Bride of Death
Thank God for Little Children
The Dying Fugitive
Bury Me in a Free Land
The Freedom Bell
Mary at the Feet of Christ
The Mother's Blessing
Vashti
The Change
The Dying Mother
Words for the Hour
President Lincoln's Proclamation of Freedom
To a Babe Smiling in Her Sleep
The Artist

Jesus
Fifteenth Amendment
Retribution
The Sin of Achar
Lines to Miles O'Reiley
The Little Builders
The Dying Child to Her Blind Father
Light in Darkness

Sketches of Southern Life

(Philadelphia: Merrihew & Son, Printers, 1872)

Poems

Our English Friends
Aunt Chloe
  The Deliverance
  Aunt Chloe's Politics
  Learning to Read
  Church Building
  The Reunion
"I Thirst"
The Dying Queen

Sketches of Southern Life

(Philadelphia: Ferguson Bros. & Co., Printers, 1886)

Poems

Aunt Chloe
  The Deliverance
  Aunt Chloe's Politics
  Learning to Read
  Church Building
  The Reunion
"I Thirst"
The Dying Queen
The Jewish Grandfather's Story

Prose

Shalmanezer, Prince of Cosman

Poems

Out in the Cold

Save the Boys
Nothing and Something
Wanderer's Return
"Fishers of Men"
Signing the Pledge

Moses: A Story of the Nile

(Philadelphia: The Author, 1889)

Poems

Moses: A Story of the Nile
The Ragged Stocking
The Fatal Pledge

Prose

The Mission of the Flowers

Iola Leroy; Or, Shadows Uplifted

(Philadelphia: Garrigues Bros., 1892) [Novel]

Moses: A Story of the Nile

(Philadelphia: The Author, 1893; contents identical to those of *Idylls of the Bible* [Philadelphia: 1006 Bainbridge Street, 1901])

Poems

Moses: A Story of the Nile

Poems

The Ragged Stocking
The Fatal Pledge
Christ's Entry into Jerusalem
The Resurrection of Jesus
Simon's Countrymen
Deliverance
Simon's Feast

Prose

The Mission of the Flowers

The Sparrow's Fall and Other Poems

(n.p., n.d.; c. 1894)

Poems

My Mother's Kiss
A Grain of Sand
The Crocuses
The Present Age
Dedication Poem
A Double Standard
Our Hero
The Dying Bondman
"A Little Child Shall Lead Them"
The Sparrow's Fall

Atlanta Offering: Poems

(Philadelphia: George S. Ferguson Co., 1895)

Poems

My Mother's Kiss
A Grain of Sand
The Crocuses
The Present Age
Dedication Poem
A Double Standard
Our Hero
The Dying Bondman
"A Little Child Shall Lead Them"
The Sparrow's Fall
God Bless Our Native Land
Dandelions
The Building
Home, Sweet Home
The Pure in Heart Shall See God
He "Had Not Where to Lay His Head"
Go Work in My Vineyard
Renewal of Strength
Jamie's Puzzle
Truth
Death of the Old Sea King
Save the Boys
Nothing and Something
Vashti
Thank God for Little Children
The Martyr of Alabama

Appendix   ♦   407

The Night of Death
Mother's Treasures
The Refiner's Gold
A Story of the Rebellion
Burial of Sarah
Going East
The Hermit's Sacrifice
Songs for the People

Martyr of Alabama and Other Poems

(n.p., n.d.; c. 1895)

Poems

The Martyr of Alabama
The Night of Death
Mother's Treasures
The Refiner's Gold
A Story of the Rebellion
Burial of Sarah
Going East
The Hermit's Sacrifice
Songs for the People
Then and Now
Maceo
Only a Word

Poems

(Philadelphia: The Author, 1895; Philadelphia: 1006 Bainbridge Street, 1900)

Poems

My Mother's Kiss
A Grain of Sand
The Crocuses
The Present Age
Dedication Poem
A Double Standard
Our Hero
The Dying Bondman
"A Little Child Shall Lead Them"
The Sparrow's Fall
God Bless Our Native Land

Dandelions
The Building
Home, Sweet Home
The Pure in Heart Shall See God
He "Had Not Where to Lay His Head"
Go Work in My Vineyard
Renewal of Strength
Jamie's Puzzle
Truth
Death of the Old Sea King
Save the Boys
Nothing and Something
Vashti
Thank God for the Children
The Martyr of Alabama
The Night of Death
Mother's Treasures
The Refiner's Gold
A Story of the Rebellion
Burial of Sarah
Going East
The Hermit's Sacrifice
Songs for the People
"Let the Light Enter!"
An Appeal to My Countrywomen
Then and Now*
Maceo*
"Fishers of Men"*
The Lost Bells*
"Do Not Cheer, Men Are Dying," Said Capt. Phillips, in the
    Spanish-American War*
The Burdens of All*

---

*Not included in 1895 edition.

Selected Bibliography

◆

Ammons, Elizabeth. "Frances Ellen Watkins Harper." *Legacy* 2 (1985): 61–66.

Arnett, Benjamin. *Centennial Thanksgiving Sermon at St. Paul A.M.E. Church.* Urbana, Ohio: n.p., 1876.

Bentley, Mrs. Fannie C. L. "The Women of Our Race Worthy of Imitation." *African Methodist Episcopal Church Review* 6 (1890): 473–77.

Brawley, Benjamin. "Three Negro Poets: Horton, Mrs. Harper, and Whitman." *Journal of Negro History* 2 (1917): 384–92.

Brown, Hallie Quinn. "Frances Ellen Watkins Harper." *Homespun Heroines and Other Women of Distinction.* 1926. Reprint. Freeport, N.Y.: Books for Libraries Press, 1971.

Brown, William Wells. *The Black Man, His Antecedents, His Genius, and His Achievements.* 1863. Reprint. New York: Johnson Reprint Corporation, 1968.

———. *Clotel, or, The President's Daughter.* 1853. Reprint. New York: Arno, 1969.

———. *The Rising Son; or, the Antecedents and Advancement of the Colored Race.* 1873. Reprint. Miami, Fla.: Mnemosyne Publishers, 1969.

Carby, Hazel V. *Reconstructing Womanhood: The Emergence of the Afro-American Woman Novelist.* New York: Oxford University Press, 1987.

Child, Lydia Maria. *The Freedman's Book.* 1865. Reprint. New York: Arno, 1968.

Christian, Barbara. *Black Women Novelists: The Development of a Tradition, 1892–1976.* Westport, Conn.: Greenwood, 1980.

Daniel, Theodora Williams. "The Poems of Frances E. W. Harper, Edited with a Biographical and Critical Introduction, and Bibliography." Master's thesis, Howard University, 1937.

Dannett, Sylvia G. L. "Freedom Lecturers." In *Profiles of Negro Womanhood.* Vol. 1. New York: M. W. Lads, 1964.

[DuBois, W. E. B.]. "Writers." *The Crisis* 1 (April 1911): 20–21.

Filler, Louis. "Frances Ellen Watkins Harper." *Notable American Women, 1607–1950: A Biographical Dictionary.* Vol. 2. Cambridge, Mass.: Harvard University Press, 1971.

Garrison, William Lloyd. "Introduction." In *Poems on Miscellaneous Subjects,* by Frances Ellen Watkins. Boston: J. B. Yerrinton Sons, 1854.

Gilbert, Sandra M. and Susan Gubar. *Madwoman in the Attic.* New Haven, Conn.: Yale University Press, 1979.

Graham, Maryemma. "Frances Ellen Watkins Harper." *Afro-American Writers Before the Harlem Renaissance,* edited by Trudier Harris and Thadious M. Davis. Detroit: Gale, 1986.

———. "The Threefold Cord: Blackness, Womanness and Art: A Study of the Life and Works of Frances Ellen Watkins Harper." Master's thesis, Cornell University, 1973.

———, ed. *The Complete Poems of Frances E. W. Harper.* New York: Oxford University Press, 1988.

Greer, Beatrice Tatum. "A Study of the Life and Works of Mrs. Frances Ellen Watkins Harper." Master's thesis, Hampton Institute, 1952.

Hanaford, Phebe A. *Daughters of America.* Augusta, Maine: True and Co., 1882.

Hart, James D. *The Popular Book: A History of America's Literary Taste.* Berkeley, Calif.: University of California Press, 1963.

Hill, Patricia Liggins. "Frances Watkins Harper's *Moses: A Story of the Nile:* Apologue of the Emancipation Struggle." *The A.M.E. Zion Quarterly Review* 95 (1984):11–19.

Jelinek, Estelle C. *The Tradition of Women's Autobiography: From Antiquity to the Present.* Boston: Twayne, 1986.

Johnson, Edward A. *A School History of the Negro Race in America from 1619–1860.* 1911. Reprint. New York: A. M. S. Press, 1969.

Johnson, James H. A., D.D. "Rev. William H. Watkins." *African Methodist Episcopal Church Review* 3 (1886):11–12.

Kletzing, H. F., and W. H. Crogman. *Progress of a Race, or, The Remarkable Advancement of the Afro-American.* 1897. Reprint. New York: Negro Universities Press, 1969.

Lowenberg, Bert James, and Bogin, Ruth. *Black Women in Nineteenth-Century American Life.* University Park, Pa.: The Pennsylvania State University Press, 1976.

Majors, Monroe. *Noted Negro Women: Their Triumphs and Activities.* Chicago: Donohue and Henneberry, Printers, 1893.

Montgomery, Janey Weinhold. *A Comparative Analysis of the Rhetoric of Two Negro Women Orators: Sojourner Truth and Frances E. Watkins Harper.* Hays, Kans.: Fort Hays Kansas: Fort Hays Kansas State College, 1968.

Morris, Rev. William H., A. M. "William Watkins." *African Methodist Episcopal Church Review* 3 (1886):5–11.

Nell, William C. *The Colored Patriots of the American Revolution.* Boston: R. F. Wallcut, 1855.

———. "Letter from William Nell." *Liberator,* September 17, 1858.

O'Connor, Lillian. *Pioneer Women Orators: Rhetoric in the Ante-Bellum Reform Movement.* New York: Columbia University Press, 1954.

Payne, Daniel. *History of the African Methodist Episcopal Church.* 1891. Reprint. New York: Arno, 1969.

Pearce, Roy Harvey. *The Continuity of American Poetry.* Princeton, N.J.: Princeton University Press, 1961.

Penn, I. Garland. *The Afro-American Press and Its Editors.* 1891. Reprint. New York: Arno, 1969.

Quarles, Benjamin. *Black Abolitionists.* New York: Oxford, 1969.

Redding, J. Saunders. *To Make a Poet Black.* 1939. Reprint. College Park, Md.: McGrath, 1968.

Redpath, James. *Echoes of Harper's Ferry.* Boston: Thayer and Eldridge, 1860.

Rossetti, William A. "Introduction." In *The Poetical Works of Mrs. Felicia Hemans.* New York: A. L. Burt, n.d.

Scruggs, Lawson Andrew. *Women of Distinction: Remarkable in Works and Invincible in Character.* Raleigh, N.C.: L. A. Scruggs, 1893.

Still, William. *The Underground Rail Road.* Philadelphia: Porters and Coates, 1872.

Stowe, Harriet Beecher. *Uncle Tom's Cabin.* Boston: John P. Jewett and Co., 1852.

Walden, Daniel. "Frances Ellen Watkins Harper." In *Dictionary of American Negro Biography.* Edited by Rayford Whittingham Logan. New York: W.W. Norton, 1982.

Wagner, Jean. *Black Poets of the United States: From Paul Laurence Dunbar to Langston Hughes.* Translated by Kenneth Douglas. Urbana, Ill.: University of Illinois Press, 1973.

Washington, Mary Helen. *Invented Lives: Narratives of Black Women, 1860–1960.* New York: Anchor-Doubleday, 1987.

Webb, Frank J. *The Garies and Their Families.* London: G. Routledge, 1857.

White, Charles Fred. *Who's Who in Philadelphia.* Philadelphia: A. M. E. Book Concern, 1912.

Whittier, John Greenleaf. *The Complete Poetical Works of John Greenleaf Whittier.* Cambridge Edition. Boston, 1894.

Index of First
Lines of Poetry

◆